Edge of Reason

Twenty minutes later, when the image of the front page of the third paper appeared, the breath was taken from Mohamed Rahman's body. He sat frozen, his fingers clenched around the computer's mouse, his mouth hanging loosely, a dribble of unnoticed saliva slithering from its corner. A bombshell had exploded in Mo's head destroying all logical thought, the words in front of him engulfing the whole of his consciousness.

IDENTITY OF MAN FOUND IN DITCH REVEALED.
The identity of the man found in a water-filled ditch in a remote Norfolk lane on the outskirts of Reepham on Wednesday last was revealed by the police today. The dead man is believed to be Atif Dasti. At the moment the police are unable to reveal further details other than that Dasti is a British citizen of Pakistani descent. The police are treating his death as suspicious.

Mo stared at the report, his eyes drifting from the familiar name to the last sentence: *the police are treating his death as suspicious.* Finally, tearing his eyes away from the screen, he looked again at the note lying alongside the laptop, knowing now what it really meant.

Number 2 soon.
Guess who's Number 3?

Other Works From The Pen Of
A.W. LAMBERT

A Lethal Quest. Released July 2009.

The slaying of a foreign diplomat and a London cabby bequeathed £250,000 by a mother he hasn't associated with for years would seem to be unconnected incidents, but when Frank Barnes asks where and how his mother died he is drawn into a world where nothing is as it seems.

Payback. Released November 2009.

Racial attacks in the back streets of Norwich and the kidnap of a London gangster. Theo Stern is dragged in to both cases; one conjuring a nightmare from the past, the other becoming too close for comfort.

Best Served Cold. Released January 2011.

Anonymous, threatening telephone calls prompt Theo Stern to ask the question: genuine or just a crank? The answer becomes clear when Annie, Stern's wife, is abducted and the terrifying demands begin.

Sleeping Dogs. Released October 2011.

A piece of an aircraft that's lain hidden since the Second World War is found in a Norfolk wood. Its find sparks a search; two families, each desperate to discover the fate of relatives believed to have been aboard an aircraft that mysteriously disappeared in 1940. But is this find part of that aircraft? Theo Stern is asked to investigate and finds himself embroiled in a web deceit and half-truths where someone is prepared to mete out savage violence, even commit murder, to hide the truth.

Wings

EDGE OF REASON

A. W. Lambert

Wings ePress, Inc.

Suspense/Thriller Novel

Wings ePress, Inc.

Edited by: Jeanne Smith
Copy Edited by: Joan C. Powell
Senior Editor: Jeanne Smith
Executive Editor: Marilyn Kapp
Cover Artist: Pat Evans
Photo by Pete Lambert

Wings ePress Books
http://www.wings-press.com

Copyright © A. W. Lambert 2014
ISBN 978-1-61309-816-5

Published In the United States Of America

April 2014

Wings ePress Inc.
403 Wallace Court
Richmond, KY 40475

Dedication

To Pete for never failing to surprise and, as always, to Val for
her endless dedicated support.

Prologue

The sharp chime announcing the arrival of an email invaded the tense silence of the room. It made the man, closeted alone in his home-study sitting hunched at the desk, jump. An indication, he angrily thought, of his present state of mind. He gave an aggravated shake of his head and dragged his eyes away from the mountain of paperwork in front of him. There had been no time to clear it during the previous working week and he was irritated that it was now consuming hours of his precious weekend. But he had little option—his new, much younger, arrogant prick of a boss had already hinted, not very subtly either, that maybe he was finding things a little difficult, not hacking it quite as he used to.

After all, he wasn't as young as he was. Of course there was no consideration that, due to the first round of redundancies, his work load had almost doubled over the past year. Or any mention of the twenty-two loyal years of service already given. No, just the constant drip, drip reminder, or should he say threat, of the second round of redundancies due to be announced sometime in the next few months.

So right now, the last thing he needed was some probably pointless email breaking his concentration and eating into even more of his time. But frequent emails at any time, day or night, was another aggravating trait of his twenty-four-seven whizz kid manager, so reaching across, he drew the laptop toward him. Clicking on the mail icon, he opened the offending email. The good news was, it was not from the boy-wonder, but as he read, an increasing shadow of concern drifted across his already tired, troubled eyes.

SimonWright@gmail.co.uk
To: Dad

Hi Dad.

Just thought I'd let you know about a piece of extracurricular excitement I've got myself involved in. Last week a guy I've got to know invited me to a party. His name's Martin Baldwin and he's graduating this year. The party was a sort of early graduation do, and I spent the evening drinking with Martin and three of his friends. There were two Muslim guys, Mo Rahman and Atif Dasti, both doing Pharmacy, and a guy called Ralph Armitage; never did find out what he was doing. I got on well with them all except Dasti. Didn't like him much; he was too full of himself and I got the impression, me being a year behind the others, he saw me as a lesser mortal.

Anyway, it was getting late and we'd all had a few, including Dasti who, unlike Rahman, didn't seem troubled by any religious vetoes regarding alcohol. He was waxing lyrical about how earlier he'd outswam a whole bunch of guys in the local pool. The way he kept on about it you'd have thought he'd won gold at the Olympics. Anyway, he began to get on my nerves, so I said I didn't think swimming in a pool was much of a challenge.

At this Dasti got really angry, started throwing challenges, saying he'd take me on anytime, anywhere. It had just been a throw away remark and I hadn't expected him to react so violently, so I tried to play it down, tried to back off, saying I wasn't looking to take anyone on anywhere. He must have seen this as me getting cold feet because he starts name calling, egging the others to do the same. Well, that was like a red rag to a bull and from somewhere it came to me: the annual John Hurley Mersey swim. You remember we've been there, haven't we? Anyway, I said if he was really serious, how about Albert Dock to Monks Ferry.

It stopped him in his tracks, but only for a minute. I'd realised earlier that Dasti was the alpha male of the group and now I could see he wasn't about to lose kudos in front of the others. He thought about it for a bit, then upped the ante by saying we should do it at night. Okay, I know you might think me stupid. And maybe I should have backed off, or at least told them about me, what I'd done. But, hey, not one of them bothered to ask, so what the hell. I just kept a straight face and agreed to the challenge. Well, there was no way I was going to back down, was there? The man's a braggart and needs taking down a peg or two.

Anyway, since then I've checked him out. Others have warned me; seems he can be a real nasty piece of work. Those that know him say he'll do anything to win and I'm now told he's also got the other guys in the group involved, too. Looks like he's got a plan. I'm not surprised; his type always needs the support of others. Not worried, though; whatever he tries he'll have to catch me first. Can't see that happening, can you?

I'll let you know how it goes. By the way, don't tell Mum; you know how she worries.

Lots of Love, Simon.

After reading the last few words, the man was very still for a long moment, the computer cursor hovering tentatively over the reply icon. Finally he gave a small shake of his head. His son had long since left the fold and was more than capable of looking after himself, especially in the sort of situation he'd outlined. Besides, when dealing with one's offspring, especially beyond a certain age, there was a fine line between advice and interference. It was a father's job to know where to draw that line. As for his wife and worry; if she had the slightest inkling of how precarious her husband's position was at work, she really would have something to worry about. He hesitated for a moment longer then, the decision made, he exited Windows Live Mail and slid the mouse to one side. With a heavy, resigned sigh, he dragged his attention reluctantly back to the paperwork.

One

Spring 2013
Sheringham, the county of Norfolk, UK

Bloated black clouds rested on rooftops and rain thrashed horizontally in from the North Sea, great goblets smacking against the window, the deserted Sheringham High Street below little more than a distorted, slithering image through the streaming glass pane.

The dismal scene was a perfect reflection of Theo Stern's mood. "Bloody weather," he grumbled, turning from the window and moving lethargically across the office to his desk. Slumping down, he rocked back and hoiked his heels onto the desk, the usual groan of complaint from the ancient chair sounding more mournful than ever. He took a breath and ran his fingers through his unruly greying thatch. It desperately needed a cut, but right now he didn't care, just couldn't be bothered. There were dark days, he thought, and there were dark days. And boy, this was one heck of a dark day.

It was a day, after a fretful night, that had turned into one of those self-assessment days he was plagued with recently. When from the moment he woke he was into self-criticism mode: life passing him by, so many wasted years, nothing achieved, and most of all, nothing left to look forward to. And it had nothing to do with the rain, though this morning it hadn't helped; out of nowhere it had kicked off as he'd walked along the promenade to work. By the time he'd gotten here, he was soaked.

But even so, his dark mood was nothing to do with the weather. No, this was about Annie. Okay, she wasn't *his* Annie anymore, hadn't been since the divorce was finalised. But since then, neither had she been anyone else's. So however slender, hope had still sprung eternal. His or not, she'd always been there, in the flesh, to talk to, give a hug and occasionally even more. Now, though, she was gone. He glanced down at his watch, the date. Yes, there it was; the real reason for his depressed state. It was exactly a month to the day since the love of his life had climbed aboard the Asiana Airways 747 and headed off to Australia. Yup, and he'd counted every single day since.

There'd been the occasional email and once, at her request, they'd even chatted face to face on Skype. But that had only made things worse because she'd looked so good—tanned, healthy and, worst of all, happy. Bugger it. So that's what this is all about, isn't it Stern, you miserable toe-rag? You've lost Annie.

'Course it didn't help that for the first time in an age, Stern Investigations was going through a lull. Well, if he were honest, more than a lull. Truth was, right now he didn't have a single client. When the hell did that last happen?

Cherry had taken the day off, too. He wasn't sure and she hadn't thrown out any hints, but he had a feeling wedding bells were in the air. Stern smiled, for a moment the morning's misery lifting just a tad. Thinking of Cherry could do that for him. Did he say nothing achieved? Well, in Cherry's case, that certainly wasn't so. What was it now…sixteen, seventeen years? He couldn't remember exactly, but the incident stood out as clearly now as it ever did.

The East End of London and the call reporting violent exchanges had taken Detective Inspector Theo Stern to the Bethnal Green flat. They'd found the teenage drug addicted prostitute alone and beaten to a pulp, a damaged artery slowly pumping her life's blood into the filthy mattress she lay huddled on. Only his swift action and the dedicated expertise of a fast response medical unit had saved her life.

For some reason, among the many violent scenes Stern had witnessed during his thirty year career with Metropolitan Police Force, the mental picture of this pathetic young woman had refused to leave him. He'd visited her in hospital, forged a friendship, and on her release cajoled her into therapy, soon realising beneath the fragile exterior lay a strong determined character. A character until then severely suppressed by a vicious father who, seeing his daughter's young body as a source of income, had sold her to a pimp for a measly cut in the profits. It was the drug trafficking pimp who, when Cherry objected to certain requirements of a customer, had carried out the beating. On her recovery, Stern had persuaded a hesitant Cherry to act as a witness against the pimp and the drug ring he controlled, arranging a safe house away from London and personally financing evening classes to help the young Cherry pave her way to a new future.

Eight years later, after being forced into unimaginable retirement from the job he idolised, Stern had left London and was living in Norfolk. But retirement was Stern's worst nightmare and he'd become a depressed, lost soul searching for a way forward. He wasn't to know fate was about to take a hand in the form of the new Cherry Hooker hitting town. She, too, was searching; searching for the man who back then had changed her life, had given her the opportunity to become the woman she now was. Cherry was about to pay back a huge debt of gratitude.

On that fateful day, Stern had been standing on the Sheringham promenade staring out over the North Sea. The germ of an idea was very tentatively beginning to form in the back of his mind.

"Don't know why I bothered to come here," she'd said, tapping him on the shoulder. "Still, I suppose it's as good a place as any." She'd laughed, glorying in his amazed, utter disbelief as he spun round to face her. "Don't have a job by any chance, do you, boss?"

Well yes, as it happened, he might well have.

Another eight years had passed since that day, the day Stern Investigations had been born and they'd worked side by side ever since. So yes, even when she wasn't here, even on a day like today, just the thought of his ever faithful assistant could raise a smile.

He dropped his feet from the desk and heaved himself out of the chair. Heading into the outer office, he crossed to the makings in the corner of Cherry's domain. He'd make coffee and hit the biscuit tin. Then, if nothing happened by midday, he'd give it best and leave the office to the answer machine. In his present mood, lunch and a jar at the local, maybe chew the fat for an hour with a couple of the regulars, sounded inviting.

It was five to twelve and he was halfway out the door when the phone rang.

Two

"Dad?"

For a second, Stern baulked. To receive a call from his son at the office was unusual. Normally it was at weekends and to Stern's home phone at the flat. "Andrew?"

"Yeah, how are you, Dad?"

"I'm okay, son. Something wrong?"

"No, nothing, I'm fine." A short pause. "Have you spoken to Mum recently?"

Now aged twenty-seven and Assistant Technical Director of a company based in Liverpool, Andrew, unlike Stern, had long since accepted the breakdown of his parents' marriage. So when Annie decided to move to Australia and become a partner in her brother's retail business, he'd been delighted. He saw his mother's move as a great opportunity, and not only for her. Holiday prospects in the sun loomed large in Andrew's mind. But with Stern at an all-time low, he'd chosen the perfect time to call and ask about Annie. Or not. Nevertheless, the question sparked concern in Stern. "Not for a while, no. She's okay, isn't she?"

"Yes, I spoke to her yesterday and she was really upbeat. Just wondered if you'd been in touch, that's all."

Stern relaxed. "We exchange the occasional e-mail from time to time, but that's about it. Your mum's a busy woman now, Andrew. She has more on her mind than keeping in touch with me."

"That's not true, Dad. Every time we speak she asks after you. You know she wants you to go over and see her, don't you?"

Stern felt an all too familiar sinking feeling in his stomach. It was true; Annie had asked him to visit. More than once. But Stern figured if there had been the slightest chance of them getting back together, Annie would never have moved away as she had. So to go all that way, have all the old feelings rekindled, maybe hopes raised, was not an option. He didn't want Annie as a friend, someone to visit from time to time. Having her back as his wife was all he could accept. That was never going to happen so better to accept it was over, push through the shitty days, like today, and move on. "Yeah, well, maybe sometime," he said. He wanted out of this conversation. It was too painful. "So, I'm sure you didn't phone me at the office to talk about your mum, did you?"

"No, you're right," Andrew said hesitantly. "I was hoping you might be able to help a friend of mine."

"Oh?"

"We were at Uni together. I must have mentioned him; Martin Baldwin, remember?"

Stern thought back to Andrew's days at Liverpool University, the excited conversations they'd had in the early days. "The guy studying engineering?"

"That's him. Martin graduated a year ahead of me. He was good, too. Got a first."

"So what's his problem?"

"I'm not sure. If you remember, I graduated in two thousand and seven, Martin in two thousand six. We were good friends at the university and though we've only met a few times since, we have kept in touch. Mostly by e-mail, sometimes by phone and on the odd occasion Skype. Thing is, Dad, three years ago he moved to Norfolk to take up a position with a company called Cain Engineering."

"Doing what?"

"He never said exactly. From what he told me, Cain is a small outfit, but very high tech, specialises in micro engineering. It would be right up Martin's street."

"Where's this company based?"

"It's based on the industrial estate, just to the south of the Norwich airport."

"I know it. All sorts of setups there."

"Yeah, well Martin was well made up when he got the job and since he's been there he's had a ball. Every time we speak, he goes on about how interesting the work is. Reckons he loves every minute of it."

"But he's never told you exactly what he does?"

"No. I did push him once, but he said because the work had something to do with government, it was classified. Said he wasn't allowed to talk about it."

"Okay, so what's his problem?"

"Well a few weeks ago, we made contact on Skype.

When he came on screen, he looked a bit dark eyed, as if he hadn't been sleeping well. I didn't think too much of it because, depending on the transmission, Skype can make you look pretty awful sometimes, can't it? Anyway, at first he seemed okay and we chatted for a while. No different from other times. Then out of the blue he tells me he thinks he's being stalked."

"Stalked? A woman?"

"No, a man. He said time and again, wherever he was, he'd look round and see this guy standing watching him. Said it had been going on for best part of a month."

"Has he tried approaching the man?"

"A couple of times, but each time he made a move, the guy just melted away."

"He does know that stalking is now a crime in this country, doesn't he? He could report it to the police."

"Yes, I told him that."

"And?"

"That's when I thought of you, Dad. You see, when I mentioned the police, Martin got really agitated. He said whatever happened the police mustn't get involved. Said if they did, it would all fall apart."

"What? What would fall apart?"

"That's just it, I don't know. I asked him, but he wouldn't say. Told me to forget it, said he shouldn't have said anything in the first place. Thing is, Dad, since we had that conversation I've tried to contact him umpteen times. He never seems to be on line, so Skype's out and his mobile is always switched off."

Stretching, Stern scrunched back in the old chair, the

telephone wedged between shoulder and ear. "Three weeks, you say?"

"That's right."

"Could he be on holiday?"

"No, he would have said. Anyway, even if he was, his mobile would still be on, wouldn't it?"

"Mmmm, 's'pose so. And not making contact for three weeks is unusual, is it?"

"Yes it is. When we left Uni, we agreed to do our best to meet up once or twice a year and talk at least every couple of weeks, which we always have."

"So what d'you want me to do, son?"

"I thought you might make a few enquiries. I mean, you're not the police, but you're the next best thing. I'd just like to know if he's okay."

Stern took the phone from his shoulder, leaned forward, elbows propped on the desk. "Could be a legitimate reason, you know. Maybe he was asked to work away and didn't think of letting you know."

He heard the heavy sigh on the other end of the line. "Maybe, but... Well it was just the way he looked when we spoke on Skype. It wasn't until afterwards, when I thought about it..."

"What?"

"Well, as I said, he did look tired, but there was something else. I think he looked scared. Particularly when I mentioned the police. Dad, I think Martin was frightened of something."

"I see. When you spoke to him last, did you talk about contacting me, asking me to look into it?"

"Hell no, I wasn't worried then. It was only later, when I couldn't contact him, when I thought back to how scared he looked on Skype."

Stern thought for a beat. "Martin Baldwin, you say?"

"That's right."

"Okay. I can't promise anything, son, but I'll make a few enquiries."

~ * ~

It was almost one when Stern locked up and made his way down the short stairway to the bakery below. The heavy smell of baking bread and cakes filled his nostrils as he passed the warm ovens at the rear and made his way through the shop. He gave Dave, the owner of the shop, and his landlord, his usual farewell wave and let himself out onto Sheringham High Street. The rain had stopped and the heavy clouds had drifted away. Saturated pavements steamed under unusually warm early spring sunshine and people were again drifting between shops. Stern made his way down the high street to the sea front promenade and his local, a large square, Norfolk flint building looking out across the North Sea. Inside he crossed to the bar, returning the usual nod of greeting, the cheery hello, from regulars he'd got to know over the years. Bubbly Eileen behind the bar welcomed him warmly and took his order of Shepherd's pie, the day's special, and a pint of best.

Settled at a table, Stern savoured the bitter sweetness of the local ale, his mind revisiting the conversation he'd had with his son. He still thought there was probably a perfectly innocent explanation for Martin Baldwin's silence. People, once close, drifted apart as time went by—frequent contacts and calls becoming less, eventually stopping altogether. It was life, the way things went. Andrew had insisted this was not the case, so maybe there was another explanation. Maybe Baldwin was working away. If that were the case and he was working on something government sensitive, maybe his whereabouts was deliberately being withheld. Stern picked up a beer mat, swivelling it absently between his fingers. That wouldn't account for the stalker, of course, or for Baldwin appearing to be frightened, particularly when the police were mentioned. Stern thought about that side of his son's story, remembering how from a very early age Andrew had been capable of exaggerating, sometimes to the extreme. He recalled how, in the early days, he and Annie would laugh at some of the stories their son conjured up. Maybe this was the case now. Then again, maybe not. Anyway, one way or the other, it mattered not. Stern had promised his son he would at least make a few enquiries. He would do that.

But that would be tomorrow. Right now Eileen was approaching the table, a plate with a steaming mound of Shepherd's pie in one hand and his customary second pint in the other. That would be enough to occupy his mind, for the moment anyway.

Three

Stern had a good breakfast and enjoyed a forty minute beach run before showering and heading out. He called Cherry, informing her he wouldn't be in until later, batting off the expected question, assuring her he would explain when he returned.

Leaving Sheringham, he took the Holt road, the B1149, into Norwich, the Hyundai humming happily to the haunting notes of Sidney Bechet's soprano sax and 'Nobody knows how I feel 'dis morning' wafting gently from the CD player. Stern enjoyed this road, loved its variations, the twists and turns, ups and downs that made it a driver's road. The road also featured heavily in his past, conjuring both good and bad memories. Good because it led directly to his very favourite restaurant, The Marsham Arms Coaching Inn, where he had spent some of his most pleasant evenings since living in Norfolk. Particularly those when he and Annie, even though divorced, had come together as close as ever. Then bad because it was where he had been shot at by a crazy Irish assassin sent to kill him and even before that where he had been deliberately driven off the road and almost killed. He'd survived, but the same couldn't be said for his previous beloved; the ancient Volkswagen Scirocco he'd nurtured lovingly for many years. It had been tantamount to a bereavement, the grave loss only lessened by his subsequent acquisition of the Hyundai coupé which he'd now grown to love equally as much.

He arrived at the Norwich airport traffic lights just after half ten. Waiting for the change, he checked the piece of blue paper tacked to the dash...Martin Baldwin's address dictated to him by Andrew yesterday. He'd scribbled directions alongside the address and now, released by the lights, headed toward the junction with Mile Cross Lane where he swung a left. He followed Mile Cross into Chartwell Road then left again into St Clements Hill. From there he wound his way through Magdelen Road, Churchill Street and Spencer Street, finally taking a right into Beaconsfield Road, his destination.

Her name was Saunders, but she insisted, 'call me Marge, dear.' Doing his best to look beyond the trowelled on makeup, Stern guessed she was somewhere in her mid to late forties. Her hair was short and dark with spikes and highlights. Bulbous arms protruded from a t-shirt, a size or more too small, on the verge of losing its battle to contain the huge, wayward breasts. Lower down, the black tights under a short skirt were involved in a similar engagement with the fleshy thighs. Marge was friendly, though, maybe a little too friendly, and didn't hesitate to invite him in.

The living room was comfortable. Patterned wallpaper, wide deep armchairs, huge widescreen TV and, Stern couldn't help noticing, the glass fronted sideboard well stocked with the hard stuff. He was pretty sure the clear liquid in the tumbler on the coffee table alongside the armchair into which Marge lowered herself wouldn't be water. Possibly the reason for the permanent smile and the rosy cheeks. She waved him to the chair opposite.

"So, dear, what can I do for you?" she asked, raising the thin pencil-lined eyebrows questioningly.

"I'm looking for Martin Baldwin. I understand he's staying here."

"Ah, Martin." Her voice took on a wistful tone. "Such a lovely lad. Good looking and chunky with it." Those eyebrows did their thing again. This time, Stern thought, more suggestively than anything else. "Loved having him around. Gave him the run of the place, en-suit and all mod cons, whatever he wanted. Y'know what I mean, dear?"

Stern dared not think. "He's not with you anymore then?"

Her eyes drifted to the corner of the room. "Difficult for a woman on her own, you know. Feel vulnerable sometimes. Always nice to have a man about the place."

Stern played along. "Oh, I'm sorry. I didn't realise you lived alone."

She gave a snort, her eyes glancing toward the tumbler, her fingers intertwining agitatedly in her lap. "I didn't until my husband had a midlife crisis. Decided he preferred a secretary half his age. Stupid old fool." She sniffed angrily. "It wasn't as if we didn't... I mean I always felt he was satisfied with... Well, you know. But no, the stupid idiot decided he could do better with her.

He soon found out, didn't he?" The tirade petered out and she looked across at Stern. "Sorry, I didn't mean to..."

"Don't be sorry, I didn't realise."

She pulled a deep breath, calming herself. "That's alright, dear. You weren't to know, were you?"

He pushed on quickly. "So Martin's not here any longer?"

"No, dear, mores the pity. We got on so well. Tried to encourage him to stay. Even offered to reduce the rent. Made no difference."

"Did he say why he was leaving?"

"Not exactly." The eyebrows headed south this time, a thoughtful frown. "He said he'd like to stay, but things were becoming very awkward." The frown persisted. "Awkward. I couldn't understand that. I asked what he meant, was it anything to do with me or his accommodation? He assured me it wasn't, said I'd given him more than he could have wished for." She turned sad eyed to Stern. "He wouldn't elaborate any further, though, just insisted he had to go."

"I don't suppose he left a forwarding address?"

She shook her head, averting her eyes just a fraction. "No. He just got up one morning, packed his bag and left."

Stern watched those eyes closely. "When was this?"

She took her time, gave the question some consideration. Maybe a little too long, too deliberate, Stern thought. "Something like three weeks back," she said finally.

"And you've heard nothing from him since?"

Another shake of the head. "No, nothing."

She tried to get Stern to stay, offering tea, coffee, maybe even something a little stronger, but Stern headed for the door, thanking her for the information.

"You're welcome, dear," she called after him. "Like I said to the other man…if you find him, tell him from me he'll always be welcome back here."

Stern stopped and turned. "Other man? You've had someone else looking for Martin?"

"Oh yes. A big man, he was, red faced, seemed very agitated. Expect it was because I couldn't tell him any more than I've told you. Still you can't help it if you don't know, can you, dear?"

~ * ~

Fifteen minutes later, Stern pulled into the airport industrial estate, Marge's words still rattling round his head. A big, red faced man. Agitated. Stern had questioned her further about the visitor; did he give a name, say where he was from?

"He didn't say who he was or where he was from, dear," she'd answered with a shrug. "All I can say is he came back a second time and was just as bolshie then. Not at all nice like you."

Cain Engineering was housed in a small industrial unit sandwiched between a company offering plumbing supplies and service, and a printing outfit boasting no print to be too small or too large for them to handle. Stern nosed the Hyundai into one of the parking spaces allocated to Cain and climbed out.

Automatic glass doors emblazoned with the company name and logo slid to one side, allowing him into a surprisingly spacious reception area. The walls were clad from floor to ceiling in light coloured wood with large hanging photographs showing various engineering achievements, a dramatic shot of a space shuttle liftoff holding centre stage. The floor, highly buffed, was tiled a light beige. Stern thought, with any amount of foot fall, someone had to work pretty hard to keep it looking as it did. To one side, a long low table with strategically placed magazines and newspapers was flanked by two leather sofas. To the other, a number of screens holding more photographs of people in white coats standing over benches and at machines. Directly in front of him, a woman sat behind a reception desk. As he approached, Stern judged her age to be around fifty. She wore her hair short, pulled forward to frame a pleasant face. She was dressed in an immaculate white blouse, a tiny gold heart hanging on a fine chain around her neck. Her tag identified her as Melanie. She smiled warmly as Stern approached.

"Good morning, sir. Can I help you?"

Stern wasn't quite sure how he was going to play this, but initially anyway it might be a good idea to see if Martin Baldwin was available. "Yes, my name is Stern and I was hoping I might have a quick word with one of your employees. A few moments are all I need."

The smile stayed in place. "Can you give me a name, Mr Stern?"

"Martin Baldwin."

There was a change, the smile faltering. Only a tad and only for a millisecond, but there it was. "I really don't know if Mr Baldwin is on site today," she said, reaching for the telephone in front of her. "But I'll see if I can raise our HR manager. I'm sure he'll be able to help you."

Stern turned his back and took a pace away from the desk, giving the woman space. After a few words, she replaced the phone and said, "Our Mr Chapman will be with you shortly, Mr Stern." She indicated toward the sofas. "Would you like to take a seat?"

Stern shook his head. "No, I'm fine...thanks. A dedicated Human Resources Manager. I'm surprised for such a small firm."

The smile was back now, genuine, her head tilted questioningly. "Not dedicated, Mr Stern. Mr Chapman is also responsible for finance and marketing."

"Ah, I see. How many are employed here?"

"A total of twenty eight. That includes Research and Development, Design and our small production unit. Then there are the office and support staff." The smile broadened a little. "Like me."

"And where does Mr Baldwin fit into the structure?"

Her eyes narrowed, a suspicious little frown. "I'm a receptionist, Mr Stern. The last person you should be asking a question like that."

Stern accepted the rebuke with his own best smile. "Of course, I'm sorry. Didn't mean to..." He stopped, noting her eyes swivel toward the door at the end of the area.

He was tall, very tall, standing a good six inches above Stern. He carried his weight well. Not narrow like many of his height and not heavy, but well-proportioned and fit looking. He was tanned with a square, determined jaw and dark, searching eyes. He moved across the room with a casual athletic fluidity that indicated physical confidence. He was dressed in a perfectly fitting dark suit over a light blue shirt and a tie sporting the company logo. His expression remained impassive as he offered his hand. "Robert Chapman. What can I do for you?"

Stern slipped his card from his pocket and handed it across. "I was hoping I could have a short word with one of your employees; Martin Baldwin."

Chapman scrutinised the card for long seconds before dropping it onto Melanie's desk and looking back at Stern. "Come this way, will you?" He turned on his heel and headed back toward the door.

Stern glanced toward Melanie and raised his eyebrows before falling obediently into step behind the big man.

On the other side of the door, a flight of stairs led to the upper floor where Chapman ushered Stern into a small but plush office. Moving behind the desk and lowering himself into the high backed chair, he motioned toward the visitor's chair opposite. "So we have a real life private investigator in our midst." The sneer wasn't apparent, but the inference was in the tone.

Stern didn't bite, just sat and smiled sweetly.

If Chapman were expecting a response, he was disappointed. He dropped his eyes and lifted a pen from the desk, rolling it between his fingers. "Why are you looking for Baldwin?"

No need for lies. "I have a client who is a close friend and hasn't heard from Mr Baldwin for some time. The lack of contact is unusual and completely out of character. He asked if I would look into it for him."

"Why?"

Stern felt the adrenalin kick up just a notch, but held back. "As I just said, lack of contact is unusual. My client is concerned for his friend's welfare. He simply wants to be sure he is well."

"And your client?"

Stern shook his head, but said nothing.

Chapman sniffed disdainfully. "Okay, so why wasn't your client able to look into this for himself? Why find it necessary to hire the likes of you?"

The cynical emphasis on the words 'likes of you' didn't go unnoticed. Strange how after only knowing someone for just a few moments, you could recognise them for what they were. The words arrogant and moron sprung to mind, but Stern still hung onto the smile. "Well now, for a reason that has absolutely nothing to do with you, my client is unable to. Were that not the case, he wouldn't have hired the likes of me now, would he?"

Chapman took the hit, but not graciously. He was a force in this office, not expecting or used to being challenged. His face dropped like a stone. He carefully placed the pen back on the desk. Thinking time. "And you think you can wander in here and expect me to give out information about one of our employees just like that? Have you not heard of the Data Protection Act?"

Shaking his head, Stern gave a sigh and pushed himself out of the chair. Experience had taught him that at a point very early on in any confrontation, the die would be cast. He had long since learned to recognise that point. "I came here and asked very politely if it were possible to have a word with one of your employees," he said softly, his face a stone mask. "I didn't ask for information of any kind and if I had, I wouldn't have expected you to give it to me. A minute or two was all that was required. It would have been a simple process for someone of your standing, with no responsibility on your part except to allow one of your people away from his place of work for a very short time. But for some reason, you chose not to do that. Instead you have dragged me into your own little domain, I suspect a place where you feel all powerful, and tried to interrogate me. Now why would you feel it necessary to do that?"

Chapman's face tightened, colour slowly spreading from neck to cheek. "I have a duty of care to my employees which I believe gives me the right to question anyone asking about them. I have to say your attitude does nothing to help your cause. Indeed, I suggest if you want to contact Mr Baldwin, you try another channel. Under the circumstances I feel I am unable to release him from his duties at this time." He stood and stared defiantly across the desk. "I think this conversation is over."

Stern crossed to the door then turned. "If we're talking attitude here, maybe a little self-assessment on your part wouldn't go amiss. As for my cause, as you put it, I think that was lost the moment you showed your face." He pulled open the door. "Question is, why? Now that's a question I shall be seeking to answer."

Descending the stairs, Stern crossed the reception area to the door. As he passed he gave Melanie a nod. "Thanks for your help. Pity others can't be as helpful."

She gave him a tight lipped, seemingly apologetic smile, but said nothing.

Four

Cherry placed the steaming mug on the desk in front of Stern before curling herself into the chair opposite. It was usual discussion mode at Stern Investigations. Coffee all round with Stern at his desk, rocked back in his ancient leather chair and Cherry opposite, legs curled beneath her, cradling the mug to her chest. Stern had arrived back in the office twenty minutes before. He'd given Cherry a brief outline on what had happened, but as usual she kept digging for detail.

"So this guy, Martin Baldwin, is a friend of Andrew's, right?" she prompted.

"That's right, they were at university together. I met him once... I think," Stern said hesitantly. "Can't be sure, though, so I've asked Andrew to email us a photo." He picked up the mug, wrinkling his nose over the coffee fumes before taking a sip. "Suppose if I'm going to try and find him, I guess I should know what he looks like."

Cherry grinned. "Would never have thought of that," she chided. "Still I suppose that's why you're the top gun and I make the coffee."

Stern returned the grin. "Not bad coffee, though. You're improving."

"Gee thanks, boss. So, are you going to try and find him?"

Stern gave a shrug and drank some more coffee. "We've nothing else on the books right now, have we? And I get the feeling all is not as it should be at Cain Engineering."

"You sure it's not just because the boss man pulled your chain?"

Stern shook his head. "You do have a way with words, Hooker."

"I know…it's a result of my sophisticated education. He did wind you up, though, didn't he?"

"Yeah, he did that," Stern admitted. "But I've fronted too many arrogant prats in my time to let it worry me. No, the thing that struck me most was I could see from the start he wasn't prepared to give me any information about Baldwin."

"But he did take you to his office."

"Yes, but that was so he could pump *me* for information, not the other way round. As soon as he saw I wasn't a pushover, he kicked me out." He leaned forward and put the mug down on the desk, resting his chin on a clenched fist. "Then there was the receptionist."

Cherry frowned. "You never mentioned a receptionist."

"No, I didn't, did I?" He paused, remembering. "Anyway it was the receptionist who first made me think. At first she was all smiles, anything she could do to help, but as soon as I mentioned Baldwin's name, her expression changed."

"In what way?"

"Well unless I've lost my touch, I reckon she looked worried. She certainly clammed up pretty quick anyway. That's when she called for Chapman."

"Mmmm, so we have a receptionist who looks worried when you mention Baldwin's name and a manager who won't tell you anything about him."

"Or let me talk to him."

"Must admit it does sound a bit iffy."

"And don't forget, Baldwin's done a runner from his lodgings and there are others looking for him."

Cherry nodded. "True, but surely, boss, it can't be that difficult to get hold of this guy. I mean, once we know what he looks like, we could wait outside the company until he shows himself."

"Yup, we could do that."

Cherry watched him closely, a tiny frown appearing. For eight years she had worked side by side with this man, the man who pulled her from a life of drugs and prostitution, literally saving her life in the process. She had come to idolise him, see him as the father figure she'd never known. That closeness had led her to knowing his every mood, every mannerism. Like right now. "Except there's a 'but' in there somewhere, right?"

Stern rubbed his chin thoughtfully. "The other guy, the one that went to Baldwin's lodgings, don't you think he'd have already done that?"

"'Spose, unless he don't know where he works."

"Yup, that's a possibility. Or, then again, maybe he knows Baldwin doesn't work at Cain Engineering anymore."

"What? You don't think..."

"If I'm honest, I don't know what to think," Stern broke in. "But it did occur to me the reason our convivial friend, Chapman, wouldn't let me speak to Baldwin wasn't because he didn't want to, but because he couldn't."

"You mean because he wasn't there?"

Stern shrugged. "It's a thought, don't you think?"

Cherry chewed the possibility over for a moment. "Okay, so why didn't he just say so?"

Draining the last of the coffee, Stern rolled the empty mug between his hands. "D'you know, that's exactly the question I've been asking myself."

They sat quietly for some moments, each with their own thoughts. It was Cherry who broke the silence. "Okay, let's suppose what you're saying is true and Baldwin isn't at his flat or at work. That would mean he was missing, right? I mean really missing, a missing person."

"Yes, I suppose. So what's your point?"

"If you remember, this all started because Baldwin told Andrew he was being stalked."

"Uh-huh."

"Well, in the past, stalkers have sometimes abducted the person they've been stalking, haven't they? I mean, if Baldwin is genuinely missing, maybe..."

Stern raised a hand. "Whoa, slow down, girl. You could be heading into crime fiction here. Don't forget he left his lodgings of his own free will...he didn't just mysteriously disappear without trace."

"Not exactly, no," Cherry was adamant. "But from what his landlady told you, she'd given him everything on a plate while he was there and he didn't exactly explain why he was off, did he? What was it he told her; things were getting out of hand?"

"Things were getting too awkward," Stern corrected.

"Okay, awkward, but that doesn't sound to me as if he wanted to leave. Sounds more like he had to."

Cherry was on a roll and Stern knew better than to hold her back. She had a quick brain and over the eight years they'd worked together, she'd learned well, blossoming from little more than a coffee making helper to a genuine assistant, sometimes taking on cases of her own. So yes, he listened to her as much as she did to him. It was two-way traffic at Stern Investigations, and it worked. "Okay, so you're suggesting he had to move because of this person or persons stalking him?"

"I'm saying it's possible. It could also be why he left his job, couldn't it?" She waved a hand quickly. "I know, I know, we don't know he has left his job yet, not for sure anyway. But following on from your theory that he might have, it would stack up, wouldn't it?"

Stern gave a half-hearted, not really conclusive nod. "Maybe, except for one thing; if he had just disappeared, just not turned up for work one day, and hadn't been seen since, Cain Engineering would have no reason to hide the fact, would they? They'd want to know where he was as much as anyone."

"You mean this Chapman character would have said so from the off?"

"I would have thought so, but he didn't, did he? Quite the opposite, in fact. Seemed to me the last thing he wanted me to know was that Baldwin wasn't there."

"Which is why you think there's something amiss?"

"Yup."

"Like maybe the company, or someone at the company has something to do with his disappearance?"

"Maybe, but I think we're getting ahead of ourselves here. One thing at a time. Let's find out if he is actually missing from his workplace as well as his lodgings before going any further."

"And how are you going to do that?"

"It's an outside chance, but there might be one way." He checked his watch. Four-thirty, still time. "Grab the telephone directory for me, will you?"

A few minutes later, the Cain Engineering number scribbled on his pad, Stern punched the buttons on the phone. He recognised the voice that answered. "Melanie?"

"Yes."

"It's Theo Stern. We met earlier."

"Oh..." Instant caution.

"Melanie, I know I'm out of order here and I don't want to cause you any trouble, but d'you think I could ask you just one question?"

"Mr Stern, you must realise I'm not allowed to discuss company business with anyone." Yup, Chapman had already got to her.

"I do accept that and I'm not about to ask you anything about the company."

"Well..."

"Melanie, would you think me forward if I asked you to have dinner with me?"

Five

Stern gave himself the once over in the mirror. Broad, heavy browed features and firm, determined jaw. Hair a shining well groomed thick iron grey mass. Eyes deep grey and, he kidded himself, still sharply intelligent. Yeah, he was no George Clooney, but he scrubbed up pretty good when he made the effort. For a fifty-nine year-old, anyway. He still stood a good solid six feet, well almost, and thanks in the main to the regular morning beach runs and the rowing machine tucked in the corner of the bedroom, he hadn't fluctuated more than a smidgen either side of fourteen stone for years. Earlier he'd dragged a suit he hadn't worn in an age out of the wardrobe and was glad to see it still looked half decent and, more importantly, still fit. Now, he considered, the image looking back at him from the mirror was the best he could manage.

As he turned from the mirror, he felt the fluttering in his stomach erupt again and took a long deep breath. He hadn't felt like this since he couldn't remember when. Okay, he had an ulterior motive here...he'd asked the woman out so he could pump her for information about Martin Baldwin, but regardless of that, for some reason he felt nervous. Asking a woman to have dinner with you, however you looked at it, was a date, wasn't it? If it wasn't, why had he showered longer than usual and ponced himself up like this? He shook himself—*pull yourself together, Stern, you're a fifty-nine year-old detective, a professional about to question a woman about a case. You've done it a million times before, there's nothing different here, right?*

Well yeah but, he had to admit, when first approaching her in the Cain Engineering reception area, he'd been taken by the smile she'd flashed at him. Not practiced like so many in her position, but a genuine natural lighting up of her face. Close up he'd realised she'd worn makeup to a minimum and as far as he was concerned looked better for it. He remembered thinking fifty maybe, but certainly not, as the old London saying went, 'mutton done up like lamb.' It wasn't only the smile, either. As she'd picked up the phone to call Chapman, the ringless left hand hadn't gone unnoticed either.

On leaving the Cain Engineering reception and heading back to his car, a man moving some packages on a stacker truck had nodded a greeting. On impulse, taking advantage of the eye contact, Stern had waved him down and asked the question. The man had been happy to oblige...her name was Melanie Campbell and she'd joined the company something like a year back. At that time, the idea of asking her out, seeing if away from the company she might be more forthcoming about Baldwin, had seemed a good idea. Right now, though, he was beginning to wonder.

He checked his watch. Seven fifteen, just about right. They'd agreed seven-thirty and it was less than a ten minute drive to the little pub on the coast road just outside Sheringham. He moved across and checked the security lock on the glass door leading to the tiny balcony overlooking the Sheringham sea front. There was a time when he wouldn't have bothered, the second floor flat being pretty inaccessible from the outside—he'd thought. That was until a freak from his past, hell bent on destroying him, had proved the opposite. Since that time, the toughened glass and specially fitted security lock had been the order of the day. He headed for the front door, looking around as he went, reminding himself it was about time he had a clear up. How many times had he told himself that in the last few weeks?

Nine years earlier, buying the flat had been a knee jerk reaction, a panic buy. They'd split the year before and Annie was already here in Norfolk. She'd fought the good fight for fifteen years before, like so many other frustrated policemen's wives, giving it best to an unbeatable rival: the London Metropolitan Police Force. She had moved back to her birth place here in Norfolk. Stern, ever the dedicated copper, incapable of comprehending his wife's unreasonable behaviour, had still been unable to tear himself away from the job.

Then came the temporary secondment to Manchester and the drug bust. The crazed addict had come out of nowhere and the long serrated knife he was wielding had come within a millimetre of taking Stern's life. He'd survived, but the powers to be had decided, at fast approaching fifty, his time was up. An enforced retirement on medical grounds had seen the end of the only job he had ever known, the job that had been his world for over thirty years. Recovery had been slow, giving him time to take stock, time to realise, because of his complete intransigence, he'd lost the only woman he'd ever loved. And for what? Released from hospital, he'd found himself meandering in a wilderness. He was living in one of the largest cities in the world, among sixty million souls, yet feeling totally alone? He missed her so much; he had to do something. He'd searched the ads and found the Sheringham flat. On the upper floor of a two story block, it was small...only one bedroom, bathroom, kitchen and living room, but the tiny balcony overlooking the sea front was a bonus. The next day he'd bought it and hadn't regretted the impulsive move for a moment. Even now, with Annie again out of reach, he couldn't imagine living anywhere else.

He left the flat and made his way round to the back of the building to his lockup and the Hyundai coupé. Seven minutes later, he pulled into the car park alongside the pub.

She was already there, sitting at a table tucked away in the far corner. A little more makeup this time, she was wearing dark slacks, the same gold heart glinting against the dark blue of a close fitting high necked jumper showing a trim figure. As he approached, there was that same smile.

He glanced down at his watch. "Am I late?"

She shook her head, her hair bobbing softly around her ears. "No, not at all." The smile broadened just a tad. "I've never believed in keeping a man waiting. Especially if he's buying."

The butterflies were easing already. "What can I get you?"

"A small lager and lime would be nice."

A few minutes later he returned with the drinks. She indicated toward the pint glass in front of him. "A real ale man?"

"'Fraid so. It's my only weakness."

She held his eyes, cocking her head to one side. "A man with only one weakness?"

He smiled. "The only one I'll admit to, anyway."

They laughed together and he realised the butterflies were no more. "I've booked a table in the restaurant. Said about half an hour. That okay?"

Half an hour later, formal introductions over, a second drink in front of them, they were seated at a table in the restaurant at the rear of the building. The waiter approached with the menu. Stern had eaten there before and held up his hand. "No need," he smiled. "Is the steak and ale pie on?"

"It is, sir."

"Then for me, say no more." He turned to Melanie and raised his eyebrows questioningly.

She looked to the waiter. "Couldn't ask for a better recommendation. I'll have the same."

Stern felt a lift. He'd been badgered for years by the two women in his life. Both Annie and Cherry, constantly banging on about how he should eat more responsibly, lower his cholesterol, live longer. He'd expected no less from this slender lady; maybe a salad or something light, healthy. Not so and he liked that, liked it a lot.

While waiting for the food, Stern apologised, admitted to the real reason for his approach; the search for information about Martin Baldwin.

She shook her head. "No need for apologies. I knew why you asked me out. In fact you only just beat me to it."

"Oh?"

"Yes, given another fifteen minutes and I'd have called you. You see, Martin was a nice lad. He'd only been with the company for about a year when I arrived. He was the first to say hello and introduce himself. He said he knew how it felt to be new at a job and asked if I wanted to join him for lunch. After that it became routine and most days we had lunch together in the canteen. He told me all about university, his degree and how he was pleased to have got the job at Cain's. He loved his work and from what I heard from others, he was good at it. Everyone seemed to like him, too. Funny thing was, though, when he disappeared I seemed to be the only one concerned. Nobody else wanted to talk about it. Until you came along."

"Disappeared...?" Stern stopped as the waiter approached with their food, waiting until they were again alone. "So Martin *has* disappeared?"

She frowned. "Yes, but wasn't that what you came about?"

Stern picked up his knife and fork. A thoughtful frown

puckering his forehead. "In a way, I suppose it was." As they ate he explained how Andrew's call had led to his visit to Beaconsfield Road and to Cain Engineering. "Didn't think much of it when the landlady told me Martin had left," he admitted with a smile. "I could imagine she would have been a bit of a handful. Thought she may have come on too strong and he'd felt better out of it. But now you've put a different light on it."

They finished the meal and refused sweet, opting for just coffee. Stern stirred in the two spoonsful of sugar slowly. "Have you any idea why they clammed up at Cain's?"

Melanie leaned her elbows on the table, resting her chin on clasped hands. "I can't be sure, but I think it had something to do with the meeting."

"Meeting?"

"Uh-huh. About a week ago the management called a meeting. Everyone went except me. They said someone had to watch the fort and anyway whatever they were talking about didn't affect me." She smiled. "I've learned, as a receptionist, you're only part of things as long as they want you to be. Anyway, nothing was said, but after the meeting it seemed Martin was off limits. It was like he was never there." She gave a tiny shrug of her shoulders. "I couldn't understand it. I felt I needed to talk to someone, find out what had happened, but it was like everyone had been gagged. I mentioned it to a couple of others and the result was a visit from Chapman. He was nice enough, but went on about company confidentiality and made it clear he would prefer me to drop the subject. I have to admit I felt frustrated so when you came asking questions it was a relief, at last someone to talk to. After you left, Chapman had a few words, reminded me again of company confidentiality, so I knew I couldn't say anything over the phone or at the company. I still had your card, though, and was just plucking up enough courage to call you when you rang."

Stern thought for a moment, then said, "When did you last see Martin?"

"The day before he disappeared. I used to meet him in the canteen, but that day, just before lunch, he turned up in reception. He said he had some shopping to do so he wouldn't be eating in. There was nothing strange about that. There were times when one or the other of us didn't use the canteen for some reason or other."

"You didn't see him after that?"

"No, that was the last time..." She paused, the coffee cup hovering just below her lips.

"What?"

"Well, from where I sit at my desk I've got a pretty good view of the car park. Through the glass doors, I mean. I knew Martin drove a Ford Focus which he habitually parked in the same place. When he left that day, I watched him walk across the car park, but not toward his own car." She took a sip of coffee before replacing the cup gently back on the saucer. "Farther along there was a man standing leaning against the boot of another car. Martin made his way across to him. They stood talking for a while, then Martin went to his own car and drove off."

"And the other man?"

"He stood watching until Martin left, then got in his car and drove out."

"The conversation, was it friendly, were they smiling, or did they seem to be arguing, maybe aggressive?"

She thought for a moment. "Neither, they just talked."

"And this other guy, what do you remember about him, about his car?"

"The car's easy; it was a silver Jaguar. Not a new one, I can only recognise the older models. The guy was probably in his thirties and quite tall. He was well built, with wide shoulders and I remember he was wearing a grey suit with a collar and tie. He looked... I don't know, probably Indian, or Pakistani maybe. From that part of the world anyway."

Six

Albert Parkinson loved Banjo. Only a couple of years old, he was a rescue and certainly not a pedigree. Truth be told, Banjo was the result of an adventurous Boxer taking a shine to the kennel club registered Labrador living next door and not letting a heavily paneled, six foot fence dampen his ardour. The daring escapade and frantic tryst that followed produced Banjo and four other sturdy offspring who were sold off quickly and very cheaply so as not to tarnish the beloved pedigree's reputation. A combination of Boxer and Labrador meant size and weight and Banjo didn't disappoint. He weighed in at a brawny four stone plus and true to his Boxer genes, had a mind of his own. His first owner, initially falling for the cheap cuddly bundle but then unable to cope with the power of the full grown cross breed, had eventually and tearfully given in and let him go.

Of course Albert Parkinson knew nothing of Banjo's background and even if he had, it would have made little difference. Albert was big and very strong and unlike the previous owner was equal to anything Banjo had to throw at him. Within just a few months of their first meeting at the Blue Cross rescue kennels, Banjo had come to realise who was master and a perfect relationship had been forged. And neither man nor dog was happier than during their hour long early morning romp through the remote Norfolk lanes bordering Albert's old cottage on the outskirts of Reepham, a few miles to the north of Norwich.

This morning's walk was long since over and it was in the kitchen of the cottage that Albert sat facing his latest visitor across the battered old pine kitchen table. Detective Inspector David O'Connor was here as a result of Albert's earlier call.

"It was Banjo," Albert said, nodding toward the animal sitting, drooling, in a large wicker basket in the corner, his eyes fixed suspiciously on O'Connor. "It was unusual for him. He's always a bit of a handful, but normally he comes when I call him."

"But not this time," O'Connor prompted, following Albert's gaze toward the corner of the room. The inspector didn't like dogs, especially big ones and in particular big ones that slobbered.

"No, not this time. He had his nose down in that ditch and he wasn't about to come out. Not for no one. Had to go in after him, I did."

"What time was this?"

"Some time before six. Always out at the crack, we are. Have to be, I start at eight."

"What do you do, Mr Parkinson?"

"Work on the farm. Man and boy. Ain't nothing I can't do on the land. You name it, I'll do it. Take old Banjo with me now, I do. Good as gold he is. Mind you, he never used to be. When I first got him..."

"Yes, I understand," O'Connor was swift to cut off what he could see was about to be a potted history of the ugly brute eyeing him from the corner of the room. "You live here alone?"

"Ay, me and Banjo." Albert looked crestfallen. The story of how he mastered the dog's early unruliness was a favourite.

"And you take this walk every morning?"

"Yes."

"Same route every day?"

"Pretty much. Make a change some mornings."

"How about yesterday?"

Albert gave the question some thought before replying. "Yesterday, we went the same way as usual."

"And you didn't notice anything then?"

"Well, truth is, wasn't me what noticed it this morning, was it? It was Banjo..."

O'Connor sighed. "Okay, Banjo didn't notice anything yesterday?"

Albert gave a positive shake of the head. "Nope. Good as gold then, he was. Never went near the ditch. S'morning was different, though. Couldn't understand why Banjo wouldn't come out of that ditch. Just stood there, he did. Up to his belly almost. It'd rained heavy in the night and everything was soaking wet and muddy. Must've been four or five inches in that ditch. Anyway I climbed down after him and that's when I saw it. Pulling him off it took some doing, I can tell you. Strong old boy is Banjo." He looked toward the corner, eyes shining proudly. "At first I thought it was an old piece of canvas. But when I looked closer I could see what it was." He paused and gave a heavy sniff. "I came straight back here and called you people."

"Did you see anything else at the time? Anyone else around, maybe something else in the ditch?"

Albert shook his head. "Just the body."

O'Connor hoped uniform had sealed the area, and Scene of Crime Officers had taken control. "You were sure the man was dead?"

Albert gave a snort. "He was face down in six inches of water. Seemed pretty obvious to me."

"And you didn't touch the body?"

"Not likely."

O'Connor gave a nod of approval. "Excellent." He stood and offered Albert his hand. "Thanks for your swift action, Mr Parkinson. We'll probably want to talk to you again, so if you decide to leave the area for any reason you will let us know, won't you?"

Albert took the inspector's hand in his meaty, calloused paw. "Me and Banjo got no plans to go anywhere soon."

O'Connor sidled out of the room, giving the watchful Banjo a wide birth.

~ * ~

It had been a long day and at one time O'Connor thought he wasn't going to be able to manage his usual get-together with Theo Stern. Fortunately however, at the last minute things cleared and he was able to get out before anything else cropped up. He was glad because the regular chats away from the station, even though they often involved work, were a welcome break. He and Stern had first met years before when Stern, having just inaugurated Stern Investigations had become involved in a case overseen by O'Connor, then a newly promoted inspector.

Over time, an initial tense, suspicious relationship between policeman and private eye had developed into something more trusting; Stern pleased to occasionally be involved in real policing again and O'Connor grateful for any help Stern's immense experience could offer. Since that time, their professional paths had crossed many times and a close, genuine friendship had developed. These regular evenings, alternating between Stern's local in Sheringham and O'Connor's in Norwich, had become valued by both men; each using the other as a sounding post for their various problems as well as enjoying a social evening.

Fortunately for O'Connor, they'd arranged tonight at his local in Norwich, just minutes from the station. Nevertheless he was late and Stern was already into his first pint, at the same time munching on a cheese and pickle sandwich.

"You made it then? Thought you were going to stand me up."

O'Connor took off his coat and threw it across the back of the chair. "Up to my ears in crap all day. Thought I was never going to get out of the bloody place. I'm gasping." He pointed at Stern's glass. "D'you want a top up?"

"Might as well."

O'Connor made his way to the bar and minutes later returned with two fresh pints. He slid into the chair opposite Stern with a heavy sigh and reached for the glass, taking a long pull.

Stern took a bite at the sandwich, chewed for a bit then washed it down with beer. "Okay so what's kept you so busy?" he asked, easing himself back in the chair. "Give me all the gory details."

O'Connor grimaced. "It's not gory, well not all of it, anyway. Main problem is we're so bloody short of staff. Everything on a shoestring and now half of my lot have gone down with the bloody lurgy. It's driving me mad."

Stern smiled, the memories flooding back. "I can't remember it being any different, mate. Tell you what, I'll put out the word, tell the villains to behave 'emselves 'til you've caught up, okay."

"Thanks, Theo. Always knew I could count on you."

"So tell me."

O'Connor took another drink and eased himself toward the table. He was aware that he was out of order sharing information with Stern, but confidentiality on both sides had long since been a given. However, in a crowded pub like tonight, care had to be taken not to be overheard. He dropped his voice. "Long before sparrow chirp this morning, a guy's out walking his dog. Bloody great ugly brute, it is. He calls it Banjo. Can you believe that?"

Stern grinned. He knew of his friend's fear of dogs. "What is it, a Chihuahua?"

O'Connor grinned sheepishly. "No, it bloody well isn't. I swear it's a cross between a bear and a buffalo. All teeth and slobber." He waved away Stern's continued grin. "Anyway, suddenly the dog dives into a ditch and however much the bloke calls it, refuses to come out. Eventually he has to go in and physically pull the hound out. Thing is, when he gets in the ditch he realises the dog's found a body."

Stern instinctively pushed the remains of the sandwich to one side and leaned closer. "Male? Female?"

"It was a man and that's about all I know right now. We've yet to identify cause of death."

"Identification?

"No, nothing yet

"Age?"

O'Connor wrinkled his nose. "Difficult to tell. But at a guess I'd say late twenties, maybe early thirties. A big guy, strong. My guess a bit of a weight pumper, heavy stuff."

"Anything else found at the scene?" Stern had been out of the force for ten years and yet still easily slipped into question mode.

You can take the policeman out of the force...

O'Connor was used to his friend's inquisition, expected it, and frequently welcomed it even. So many times in the past, Stern's digging had led to a fruitful follow up line of an enquiry. "Nothing. The area is sealed and they'll continue with a fingertip first thing tomorrow. Hopefully we'll get something back from the pathologist then."

Stern couldn't help feeling a little deflated. "Nothing else then?"

O'Connor shook his head. "Only thing we can be sure of was the guy was Asian, possibly Indian or maybe even of Pakistani descent."

Seven

Ralph Armitage lived in a semi-detached house a stone's throw from Eastfield Park in the Kingsley Park area of Northampton. He was twenty-eight years old, had a wife, an eighteen-month old son, a soppy Labrador bitch called Mabel and a daughter on the way. He also had a hefty, twenty-five year mortgage. But that was okay because Ralph was a highly qualified, well paid Chartered Accountant and was well able to afford the repayments.

Ralph enjoyed his work and was a morning person, meaning rising early and preparing for work was never a chore. His wife, particularly in her present condition, was definitely not a morning person and was happy to leave her husband to his own resources first thing. This gave Ralph a period of quiet time to relax over his breakfast before leaving home and facing the ever increasing rush hour traffic into town.

Fortunately the road in which Ralph lived was the first destination for the postman on his morning round, giving Ralph the added bonus of having first peek at whatever dropped through the letter box before he left for work. He seldom opened any mail, usually recognising it as mostly junk or bills which he was happy to leave for his wife to deal with later. Just occasionally, however, there would be something not instantly recognisable and peaked his interest.

Like this morning.

The envelope was plain white bearing his name and address and a single first class stamp. There was no indication on the rear as to who it was from and Ralph wondered why it was not addressed to Mr and Mrs, but featured a bold *F.A.O.* in front of *Mr R Armitage*. Sipping his coffee and chewing on his last piece of honeyed toast, he opened the envelope.

It was a single sheet of paper and when he first read the few words printed on it, a frown creased his forehead and his nose wrinkled in confusion. But then Ralph read it again and slowly a past time returned, worming its way back into his head, bringing with it a long since forgotten memory. A frightening memory. Then, as full understanding dawned, Ralph's face dropped and the remains of the toast slipped from his fingers.

Murderers all four
A killer every one
One by one you have to pay
Justice will be done

~ * ~

Theo Stern sat behind his desk also chewing. In his case, however, there was no sign of honeyed toast. Stern's

46

attention was focussed on a single, already battered thumbnail. For some reason, when deep in thought, particularly troubled thought, this same sorry nail suffered the treatment. Today was no exception, the reason being the man found by the dog in the ditch. The instant O'Connor had mentioned it last night, Stern's mind had flashed to the description Melanie Campbell had given of the man met by Martin Baldwin in the Cain Engineering car park. He'd questioned O'Connor about the man's clothing, and, yes, O'Connor had confirmed, he had been dressed in a grey suit, though after lying for however long in a muddy ditch it didn't look very grey anymore. The man was also wearing a collar and tie. Coincidence? Stern wasn't a great believer in coincidence. If things looked like they tied together, they probably did.

Stern had told O'Connor about Andrew's call and his own subsequent visits to Baldwin's address and work place, including the receptionist's account of the meeting of the two men in the car park. David agreed there could be a connection, but there was little more he could do until they knew more about the man found in the ditch. Which meant waiting until the man's belongings had been examined and for the results of the post mortem. The clincher would have been if they'd found an abandoned Jaguar somewhere nearby, but they hadn't. Not yet anyway.

O'Connor promised to keep Stern informed and, impatient as ever, Stern was hoping he would get a call this morning. So far there had been nothing and the sorry thumbnail was under attack.

Cherry poked her head round the door, watched him for

a moment. "Down to the knuckle yet?"

Dragged from his thoughts, Stern looked up. "Sorry?"

Cherry came across the room and pointed at his hand, still hovering in front of his mouth. "The knuckle, have you reached it yet?"

Stern wiped the soggy digit on his trousers. "Thinking about the bloke in the ditch."

Cherry curled herself into the chair opposite. "D'you think it's the same guy?"

"Yeah, I think so. It's a good bet anyway. I'm just waiting for David to call, give me some more info. It'd be a bonus if they pulled a Jag close to the scene."

"You do realise it's only half nine, I suppose?"

He looked at his watch. "Seemed later."

"Patience is a virtue, have it if you can. Always in a woman, never in a man," Cherry quoted with a grin. "Certainly not in my man, anyway."

"Shut up, Hooker." He leaned forward and pulled the phone from its cradle. "Andrew should be at work by now. I've got a couple of questions I'd like to ask him, too." He punched in a number and waited. "I'd like to speak to Andrew Stern," he said finally.

Another wait and Andrew was on the line.

"Andrew, it's Dad. Can you talk?"

"Hi Dad. Sure, got something for me?"

"Not much. So far all I've established is that your friend has disappeared from both his lodgings and his place of work."

"Christ. Anyone know where he's gone?"

"If they do, they're not telling me. But there's something

I'd like to ask you. Do you know if Martin has any friends of Indian or maybe Pakistani origin?"

The line was silent for a while, Andrew thinking. "Not that I know of. But then he's been down in your neck of the woods for three years or more. I'm not familiar with all the friends he may have made since moving there. Can't say I know of anyone in particular, though."

"Okay, how about the person Martin thought was stalking him. Did he happen to describe him to you?"

"No, just said it was a bloke. Why d'you ask?"

Stern had already decided not to mention anything about the man in the ditch or the treatment he'd received at Cain Engineering. At this point it would achieve nothing. "Just before he disappeared, Martin was seen talking to a man thought to be of Indian or Pakistani extraction. It's the last sighting we have of him."

"Oh I see. Don't think I can help, Dad. Since we left university, we've kept in touch, even met up from time to time when for some reason or other we've been in the same vicinity. But that's about it. Whenever we met it was just the two of us."

"Okay, son, just thought I'd ask. D'you know it looks as if your friend could have voluntarily gone to ground for some reason. Maybe right now he just doesn't want to be found. Maybe it would be better for me to back off. Given time, he might eventually make contact."

Stern heard the sigh from the other end. "Maybe you're right. Anyway I don't want to put on you, Dad. You've probably got enough on your plate as it is."

Stern stayed silent. He had nothing at all on his plate at

the moment, but unless O'Connor and his pathologist came up with something on the man in the ditch that could be linked to Martin Baldwin, he couldn't see a way forward anyway. "Might be best to let it lie for the time being, son. I will keep my ear to the ground, though. If I hear anything interesting, I'll look into it and let you know."

"Okay, Dad. Thanks for that. By the way, I was thinking. Why don't we both take a few weeks off sometime later this year and pay Mum a visit? She's loving it out there, but she misses you. I can tell by the way she talks. Always asks me if you ever mention going out."

Here we go again. Stern felt a knot clench in his stomach. He wished his son could let it lie. "Yeah, well I'm pretty busy right now, but it sounds like an idea," he lied. "Don't think I can manage this year, though. Maybe next." There was an awkward pause, as usual the mention of Annie bringing an instant tension to the conversation, Stern knowing full well his son wouldn't be fooled by the prevarication. "I'll call you if I hear any more about your friend."

"Okay, Dad. But try, will you? You might not be married anymore, but you're still my mum and dad. It'd be nice to think we all stayed in touch, even met up some times. If you could find some time, going out there together might be fun."

The knot tightened at his son's plea, but it fell on stony ground; it had to. A trip to Australia wouldn't happen. He was having a hard enough time getting over losing Annie without travelling all those miles just to rekindle the flame. While she was here there was always a chance, but Annie had made her choice: her brother and Australia over him. He understood why and bore no grudge. How could he, it was due to his own years of intransigence the marriage had failed in the first place. Now she was gone and the only way he could cope was to accept it and get on with his life. Stern couldn't bring himself to voice the truth. "All right, son, I'll think on it, promise."

"Thanks, Dad."

Stern wanted the conversation to end. "Bye, son."

"Bye, Dad. Keep in touch, eh?"

"Yeah, will do."

Even hearing only one side of the call, Cherry knew what the latter part of the conversation had been about. She knew Andrew had been distressed by his parents' separation and subsequent divorce and ever since had attempted to keep them as close together as he could. He regularly badgered his father to keep in touch with Annie. But what Andrew didn't understand was, for his father, friendship would never be enough. As far as Stern was concerned, Annie had closed that door. He wasn't about to try and open it again. It was his way of handling it. The only way he knew how. Nevertheless, he was finding it hard and Andrew's constant pushing didn't help. Cherry, on the other hand, knew when to keep her mouth shut.

"No luck?"

"No. But, as he said, Baldwin's been living here for three years or more. In that time he could have made any number of friends that Andrew wasn't aware of."

"So what now?"

"Nothing. We let it lie. Unless David comes up with something, of course."

Eight

It had been an unusually quiet day for PC's Daly and Morton. Normally they could guarantee at least a couple of stops for speeding, and spotting one or two vehicles with defects was also part of a standard day. But not today. A seized, seriously defective vehicle earlier that morning and a suspect drunk driver who after a breathalyser test turned out not to be, had been it. So with several hours still to run before their shift was due to end, they weren't unduly disappointed when the call came through for them to attend a disturbance. Sitting in a lay-by on the A47 watching cars go by was okay for a while, but Daly and Morton were young. They needed action and sitting around was not to their liking. Morton spun the Ford Mondeo on a quick three pointer and gunned the engine.

It was in a cul-de-sac, a domestic that had got out of hand, spreading to the neighbours alongside the offending property. Now the action was taking place in the front garden with two men squaring up to each other. Even before Morton pulled on the hand brake and switched off the engine they could see neither man's heart was in the confrontation. Daly was out of the car first. He strode through the gate and up to the two men who instantly, and he could see gratefully, pulled away from each other.

Daly was a big man with a square, thick-jawed face. His heavy brows and dark, intimidating eyes were usually enough to quieten most situations. This was no exception. He stood before the two men, arms casually folded across his barrel chest for several seconds and said nothing. Holding back, Morton smiled. His partner may be young, but he certainly had a way of dealing with a situation.

"So?" Daly said finally. "You about to tell me why me and my partner have been dragged away from an important assignment just to deal with a couple of wasters who decide to have a punch up in the front garden? What, you trying to show the street how macho you both are?"

The first man squared his shoulders defiantly. "I'm pissed off with hearing him knocking his missus about. You people should do something about him. He's nothing but a bully."

Second man: "It's stuff all to do with you. You just keep your snotty nose out of my business."

Daly had seen it all before and assessed the situation in a second. Morton joined the fray, moving the first man to one side. "Okay, sir, you just go back home and leave this to us."

"I'm telling you," the man protested. "You people better..."

Morton took him gently but firmly by the elbow. "No, you're not telling us anything, sir." Whatever the situation, the 'sir' was important. "You're just going to be very quiet and go home, okay?"

The man felt the strong fingers tighten on his arm and recognised the tone behind the quietly spoken words. Mumbling to himself, he headed out of the garden.

It was half an hour later, having interviewed man and wife and been assured by the good lady that all was well—her husband just got a little boisterous sometimes— the pair headed back to the car. They'd informed the wife there was help out there if she ever felt she needed it, and reminded the man, without accusing him, the penalty for assault could be up to five years inside. Not quite the whole truth, but enough, they hoped, to make him think next time he felt like getting 'a little boisterous'. Without a formal complaint from the wife, even if the man was beating her, there was little else they could do.

They were back in the car and almost ready to pull away when a little old lady tapped on the window.

Daly buzzed the window down. "Yes, my love, what can we do for you?"

"Are you going to do anything about the car?"

"The car?"

"Yes, I phoned and the nice lady said she would send you round as soon as you were free."

"Ah, okay, so what car would this be?"

She turned and pointed a bony finger toward the end of the cul-de-sac where several cars were parked. "The silver one. It's been here for a while now and I know for a fact it don't belong to anyone living here."

Daly screwed his head round and looked to where she was pointing. "You mean the big one, the Jaguar?

~ * ~

Ralph Armitage arrived at his desk with little memory of the drive to work. He'd grabbed a coffee on his way through and now sat staring at the piece of paper on his desk. Just plain white, eighteen words, and no indication as to who had sent it. But the threat was implicit and aimed directly at him.

An only child, Ralph was a pretty placid individual. He had been an extremely well behaved and happy youngster, if a little spoiled by doting parents, and had been a dedicated pupil from his very first day at school. Throughout his young life, he had shunned the extremes, keeping well away from the outrageous antics of some of his more daring friends. He had never smoked a cigarette, would never venture within a mile of drugs, even the lesser recreational substances often tried openly by others, and an occasional beer or two when with friends was his only encounter with alcohol. In short, Ralph had led a pretty blameless young life that had revolved around his studies and good clean sporting activities. So why would he be sent such a threat? Truth be told, the answer to that question was simple and Ralph knew it.

When you lead a life such as Ralph, days, months, even years roll predictably and unremarkably from one to the other with nothing much happening that isn't planned. So should there be an event that breaks the trend, an occasion that, heaven forbid, becomes out of your control, it stays with you forever. And if that event had resulted in terrifying consequences, even though you believe those consequences had long since been buried, there is always a lurking fear that one day, because of that one stupid event, your world would explode around you.

So, Ralph Armitage may have had no idea who had sent that single sheet of paper with the eighteen scribbled words, but he had no doubt why it had been sent. He also felt the time had come when his comfortable, controlled world was indeed about to explode around him. He fumbled in his pocket, dragged out his keys and unlocked his desk. Pulling open a drawer, he hunted among a pile of documents, finally finding what he was looking for hidden away at the bottom. He flicked through the pages of the old address book he'd often thought should have been disposed of long ago. It was unlikely after so long, but if just one of the telephone numbers in the book were still current...

Nine

It was Monday morning and Stern felt better. He'd had a relaxed weekend working on the Hyundai until it sparkled, enjoying a few pints with the locals and just generally chilling out. He was particularly pleased with himself for not once switching on the dreaded box. Instead he'd devoured two complete novels by his favourite crime writer. Now the sun was shining from a crystal sky and the gloom of the previous week had evaporated. Even the tide was working in his favour; 7:00 a.m. and it was as far out as it could go.

Breathing steadily, the early, brine-saturated air pleasantly sharp in his lungs, he padded comfortably along the beach. Mornings like this never failed to lift his spirits. He could banish dark thoughts, put his brain into neutral and enjoy the moment; the soft, yielding sand beneath his feet, the warm, spring sunshine on his back. He'd lived in Norfolk for nine years and still blessed the day he had made the move. Two minutes after leaving his flat he was here, the miles of soft white sand stretching before him, the only sound the gentle roll of the surf caressing the sand, not another human being in sight. He smiled broadly. Try and find that in central London.

He'd run for an hour; half an hour out and half an hour back, the middle twenty minutes broken into five minute spurts, pushing himself hard, his breathing coming in short gasps, lungs stinging with the effort, calves burning. Then the last ten minutes warming down, plodding at little more than a slow jog, leaving the beach, onto the promenade and up the steep steps to the flat.

Sweating profusely, he dumped his running gear and climbed under the shower, first running it hot then, for the last few minutes, cold. Drying himself vigorously, he dressed and spent twenty minutes on the tiny balcony, enjoying coffee, cornflakes and a banana, watching the sun climb slowly higher over a sparkling North Sea. The perfect start to the day. At a minute or two after eight-thirty, he was climbing the short flight of stairs at the back of the bakery leading up to the glass panelled door signed *Stern Investigations.*

Cherry was already there. As he came through the door, she had her back to him, standing at the table in the corner that held the makings, the kettle hissing its way to the boil. She swung round. "Morning, boss."

She was wearing a plain, light blue dress sitting just above the knee and those impossible, God knows how many inch high heeled shoes she always wore. A simple gold chain supporting the letter 'C' hung at her neck. As always she wore little makeup, her face naturally pale, and a smile that knocked his socks off.

Stern did a quick calculation. Cherry was around thirty-four years old now and it never ceased to amaze him how little she had changed since the day she'd buttonholed him on the Sheringham seafront eight years ago. She stood no more than five eight—that included the heels—and was a slim 50 kilos at most. She'd never grace the cover of a fashion magazine; even without Botox, her lips were too full and her jaw a mite too aggressive. But there was something almost unfathomable about her looks, something that caught and held the eye. Maybe it was the clear, intelligent eyes; Annie always said Cherry had eyes that reflected her heart. Then again, maybe it could be the way the soft, natural fair hair framed her pale features or just the confident, very female way she held herself. Whatever it was, she was a sight for sore eyes every morning and he couldn't imagine the place without her. He paused for a second. Was he imagining it, or was there an extra gleam in those sparkling eyes this morning?

"Morning, kid. How's things? Anything new?"

Cherry shook her head. "Nothing. Never known things to be so quiet. Everybody's behaving themselves and that's not good."

Stern crossed the room to his own office, his inner sanctum. "How d'you stand up in those things?" he threw over his shoulder.

He heard her chuckle. "It's a secret," she called after him. "Being an oldie you wouldn't understand."

Grinning, he dropped into the old chair. "Might be old, but I can still drink coffee," he called. "What's keeping you?"

They were each cradling their coffee, Stern his heels

hoiked onto the desk, Cherry in the chair opposite, when the phone rang. Stern dropped his feet to the floor and pulled it from the cradle. "Stern."

"Theo, it's David. D'you want the good news or the bad?"

"Start with the good."

"That's twofold. First we have the results of the autopsy, and second we've found an abandoned silver Jaguar."

Stern's mind again flicked instantly to Melanie Campbell and her account of the meeting between Martin Baldwin and the man with the silver Jaguar in the Cain Engineering car park. "Okay, that's the good. What about the bad?"

"The guy had been completely cleaned out, not a thing on him."

"Nothing at all?"

"Nothing. Every pocket as empty as my bank account."

"Wow, that's empty. So how did he die?"

"He drowned."

"In the ditch?"

"Looks that way, the water in his lungs matched that in the ditch. But here's the interesting bit; at some time, the guy had been tied up."

"At some time? What does that mean?"

"Well according to the doc, there were abrasions around the wrists and ankles showing the guy had previously been bound hand and foot."

"But he wasn't when they found him?"

"No, and there's something else. He had a lump on the back of his head the size of a chicken's egg."

"So I'm guessing the doc doesn't think this was an accident?"

"Good guess, Sherlock. Now I know why you were a top cop in your day."

"What d'you mean, *were*?" Stern chided. "Do we know who this character is?"

"No idea yet."

"Okay, we have an unknown male who at some time has been given a bash on the head, bound hand and foot and dumped in a ditch to drown. That sound about right?"

"That about sums it up," O'Connor agreed. "And don't forget he's completely clean, nothing on him at all."

Stern gave that some thought. "Does the doc think the head damage happened before or after the guy went into the ditch?"

"A good point and we specifically asked him that. He didn't think it happened when the guy nosedived into the ditch. It happened before. For a start, it's on the back of the head and it was caused by a round blunt instrument. Doc thinks probably a hammer, or something like it."

"Okay, so how d'you see it, David?"

"Well we've more work to do, of course, but from where I sit right now, it looks like the guy was knocked unconscious, probably somewhere else, then tied up and taken to the ditch where he was dumped face down in the water."

"And at some time during the process was stripped of all he owned."

"That's right. Then, for some reason, after he'd drowned, the bonds were removed from his wrists and ankles."

They were both silent for a moment, each considering the situation. Then Stern said, "What about the guy who found him? Could he have had a quick shufti through the man's pockets before he called your lot?"

"Anything's possible, Theo," O'Connor admitted. "But I don't think so. He's old school. Straight as a die, I'd lay money on it. Anyway, even if it was him, he might have swiped a few notes from a wallet, but everything? No, that wouldn't make sense."

"So we're definitely talking murder here?"

"Looks that way. The SOCOs have finished now, combed every inch, so what we have is what we have, I'm afraid."

"What about the car?

"The same. One of our patrols found it abandoned in a housing estate on the outskirts of Norwich. We've got it in the garage now, forensics going over it. They still might find something, I guess, but I'm not holding my breath. Whoever did this was thorough, Theo; he would have used gloves for sure. Still, you never know."

Stern reminded O'Connor of Melanie Campbell's account of the meeting in the car park at Cain Engineering. "It does look like there could be a link between this and the guy I'm looking for, doesn't it? I mean the ethnic identity, the clothes and the car. Nothing concrete, I know, but too much of a coincidence, don't you think?"

"I do, and that brings me to the other reason I phoned."

"Go on."

"You remember I was whinging the other night about how we're under the hammer?"

"I do, but it was ever thus, David. As far back as I can remember we never seemed to have enough staff to cover everything."

"Yeah, it's true, but right now it's worse than that. Fact is, I can't remember it ever being as bad. Even the Super's pulling his hair out. The government cuts are damaging enough, but right now we have this sickness problem as well. Some bloody virus going through the place like a dose of salts. This little lot couldn't have come at a worse time. Thing is, Theo, I've had a word with the Super and he's happy to okay it..."

"Okay what?"

"Seems we have limited funding to cover the temporary employment of civilian staff, particularly if they're ex-policemen, better still ex-detective inspectors."

"Whoa, hang on there..."

"Oh come on, Theo, your reputation goes before you and we're bloody desperate. When I mentioned your name, the Super latched onto it right away."

"Look, David, I left the force a long time ago. You know I'm glad to help out whenever I can, but join up again? I don't think so."

"I'm talking short term here, Theo," O'Connor persisted. "Not really joining up. Just this particular case. You'd be reporting directly in to me, which means you'd be your own boss. Think about it...if we can prove it's connected with Andrew's missing friend, you're already working on the case anyway."

Apart from the fact he'd told Andrew he was standing down, for the moment anyway, Stern couldn't argue with that.

Besides, Stern Investigations wasn't exactly brimming with work, was it? "And I'd have a free hand," he said cautiously.

"Well, sort of."

"Sort of?"

"Normally civilians wouldn't be employed on front line duty. They'd be doing administrative work and other back up duties. Well, on paper so would you. But working for me would enable us to bend the rules a little."

"And you say just this case?"

"Right, as much of it as I can give you without committing career suicide."

Stern thought for a moment then shook his head. "No, I'm sorry, David, I'm too used to my freedom these days. I couldn't tie myself down to a nick again, I'd go stir crazy."

"Look, Theo, we've already got the Chief Constable breathing down our necks because we haven't immediately come good on another couple of cases. You know the score, mate; keep nailing the baddies and your flavour of the month, otherwise stand by for blasting. I don't give a toss where you work from as long as you stick to the reporting procedure. You'd have to come in for briefings sometimes, just to show good faith, but I'll keep that to a minimum, and I'll allocate tasks, but other than that, I'll give you a free hand. How's that?"

A few minutes later, the conversation terminated, Stern dropped back in the chair and ran his fingers through his hair. "Well, I'll be damned."

Cherry leaned forward in the chair. "What?"

"Would you believe I'm back in the bloody police force?"

Ten

Robert Chapman was under the hammer. It wasn't often he felt threatened, particularly in his own office, but if anyone could do it, that person was sitting in front of him right now. Frank Runcie was a bull of a man. He had a natural dominating presence, his huge frame able to dominate space, almost literally suck air out of a room. It was said when Runcie came in the sun went out.

Runcie was the ultimate rough diamond, the self-made man, the chancer who had left school without a single qualification to his name, but with the unshakable belief that one day he would be a millionaire. His chance had come when his best friend, and naturally gifted engineer, the demure Rupert Cain, had created a simple but brilliant piece of engineering design. Cain, totally uninterested in anything but the engineering design side of life, had deferred to Runcie, allowing him to take care of all else. With his innate ability to spot a good thing when he saw it, Runcie went to work. With empty pockets but an incredibly persuasive gift of the gab to back his huge intimidating frame, he'd persuaded a private financier to back the initiation of Cain Engineering. That was fifteen years ago. The financier had long since been repaid with considerable interest and both Cain and Runcie, as he'd predicted, had passed the million mark.

It is true fortunes can be made on a single successful idea. But Runcie had foreseen that to maintain the credibility of what had become internationally known as a specialist in cutting edge engineering technology, Cain Engineering could not be allowed to stand still. Small they may be, but over the years the demands on the company had been ever increasing. Though his friend and business partner was as dedicated and brilliant as ever, for him to continually carry the burden of worldwide expectations alone was unreasonable and unsustainable. Runcie had therefore determined some years before to recruit a small team of design engineers whose expertise or potential was at least the equal of Rupert Cain. Only the most outstanding candidates had been considered and only the absolute top of the crop were welcomed into the Cain family. For that chosen few, the expectations were as high as the rewards they received.

Runcie did not suffer fools gladly and at this particular time he considered the man in front of him to be an utter fool. "Is that all you can say…you don't understand? You're supposed to be the HR Manager here, aren't you? You're bloody well supposed to understand," he growled.

Chapman visibly shrunk in the large leather chair he valued so much. "It's the truth," he stuttered. "There was absolutely no indication he was unhappy or discontent in any way. Only a week before, he'd had his annual evaluation interview. Mr Cain himself had given him a glowing report, recommending him for an upgrade in status and authorising a substantial salary increase. He gave no sign of being dissatisfied nor did he have any reason to be so." He pointed to a folder on the desk in front of him. "See here...Mr Cain's last comment." He leaned forward and read:

This man is the design engineer of the future. We must do all in our power to retain his services.

Runcie snorted derisively. "And yet a week later the treacherous bastard walks off with one of the best designs Cain has developed in years."

"It was his design," Chapman said, then instantly realised the comment was a big mistake.

"It was a fucking Cain design," Runcie thundered. "Every one of them knows everything designed within these walls is the property of Cain Engineering. And I mean everything. It's in their contract. They know it from the first day they walk through those doors." He glared across the desk. "Jesus, you of all people should know that."

"Of course... I do... I was only saying... er, Baldwin was the engineer who..." Under the excruciating gaze the words dried on his lips.

Runcie gave a huge exasperated sigh and ran a banana-fingered hand across a stubbled dome. He turned to the third person sitting quietly to one side. "What have we got, Rupert? Is there anything left? Anything we can build on?" His tone had softened considerably. This was the man who had made their fortunes. Sure it had taken Runcie's daring and drive to make things happen, but he knew full well that without the man sitting so demurely to his right there would never have been anything to make happen. However he dominated, even bullied others, during their long association, Frank Runcie had never once raised his voice to the man he so admired.

Cain gave a sad shake of the head. "I've checked it out with our IT man. Seems Baldwin downloaded everything onto a remote hard drive, then erased it from the main frame."

"Hard copies, drawings?" Runcie said hopefully.

Cain gave another shake of the head. "All we have is the original protocol. Baldwin put that together at the very start."

"Couldn't you pick it up and run with it?"

Cain gave a sad smile. "Frank, I have to admit I fouled up on this one. During the time he'd been with us, I'd come to trust him implicitly." He raised both hands submissively. "I had no reason not to. Robert's right; Baldwin was totally dedicated and never put a foot out of place. He worked all hours, sometimes so engrossed in his work he just didn't want to go home. He seemed so happy with what he was doing I saw him as a long term company man. When he first came to me with that protocol, I could see if he made it work, it was a show stopper. But it was complicated, and to pull it off I could see he needed all the space he could get. I decided to give him a free hand, told him I was there if he needed me, but otherwise to keep me informed. You know what our work load is like. I was so wrapped up in my own stuff I never looked at it in any detail after that."

Chapman, buoyed by Cain's support, chanced his arm again. "It seems it was on one of the evenings he stayed behind that Baldwin took the opportunity to steal the data. We don't know exactly when that was, but on the day he disappeared he came in during the morning, worked until lunchtime then just walked away."

"He walked away from his bloody lodgings, too," Runcie growled angrily. "I've been there; talked to his landlady. Bit of a tart and as thick as a brick. She knew nothing." He looked again to Chapman. "So what about this so-called private investigator? What did he want?"

"He said he was working on behalf of a client, a friend of Baldwin, who was concerned because he hadn't been able to make contact for some time. Seems he was just checking that Baldwin was okay."

"D'you believe him?"

"I had no reason not to, but because of what had happened I brought him to the office and asked him what it was about."

"And?"

"He became aggressive and told me it was none of my business. Before I knew it he'd stormed out."

"What was his name?"

"Stern. He gave me his card, calls himself Stern Investigations."

"Still got the card?"

Chapman thought quickly. He remembered throwing the card down on the reception desk and hoped like hell Melanie had hung onto it. "It's in the reception files," he said, his fingers crossed under the desk.

Runcie pushed himself up out of the chair. "Get hold of it and give it to my secretary. I'll have a word with the guy. If he knows anything, we need to get it out of him. Sounds like he just needs a bit of persuading."

Chapman recalled his little session with the private investigator. *Sooner you than me*, he thought.

Eleven

Mo Rahman stood on the pavement and studied the two redressed windows. He nodded his satisfaction. The displays looked sharp and inviting and that was only part of it. Mo had spent the whole weekend on the shop's reorganisation. He moved back inside and let his eyes roam around the interior. Not only was the new layout aesthetically more attractive, now every inch of available space was being used to the full. Mo's efforts had also achieved his other objective: customers would now have to weave their way past almost every display shelf to get to the counter set at the rear of the shop. It was the technique used by supermarkets to remind customers of the items not on their list, items they may not even need but might as well have seeing as they were invitingly there within arm's length. Mo was pleased with that. More importantly, when his father visited, as he did every week, he would also be pleased, Mo was sure of it. Keeping his father happy was important. Mo had to remember, he may be the pharmacist, but the shop was owned by his father, whose standards were very high.

He heard the door open behind him and looked at his watch. It was a few minutes before nine and without looking round he knew it would be his assistant, Sally Buckingham.

"Morning, Mo."

He turned and waited, smiling as he saw her stop in her racks.

"Wow, what have you done?"

He was pleased with her response. "You like it?"

Sally spun on her heel. "I do. It looks fantastic. Must have taken ages."

"Finished after midnight last night. Had the cops in once, thought I was a burglar. I ended up making them tea, would you believe?"

Sally laughed and wandered through the shop, pulling off her coat and looking all around as she went. "Your dad'll be mighty chuffed."

"Hope so." He followed her to the rear of the shop and as they pulled on fresh, immaculate white coats, they heard the first customer enter the shop. The start of another busy day.

An hour and a half later, just after ten thirty, the postman arrived with the usual fist full of mail. Sally brought it through to the dispensary where Mo was busy filling prescriptions.

"Mostly rubbish," she said dumping it on the side.

"Thanks, I'll check it out over lunch."

~ * ~

Sally returned from her lunch break at a little before one thirty. She was always prompt because, though he never left the shop, Mo took his break between one thirty and two, settling himself in the store room at the back of the shop with his sandwiches and thermos flask. The room, though remote from the shop, contained a CCTV monitor linked to a security camera scanning the shop area out front and, as a further failsafe, a buzzer that sounded when the shop door was opened. Other than the stock stacked in one corner, the room held only a small table, where Mo sat with his lunch, and a large, old fashioned Belfast sink fed by a single cold water tap; this no doubt a legacy left from one of the shop's previous lives. Three doors led from the room. The first, leading to a yard at the back of the premises, was alarmed and heavily bolted top and bottom. The second led to a cloakroom housing a toilet and washbasin, and the third, the door leading back into the shop area. Though open during the day, this door was also locked and alarmed at all times when the shop was closed.

Without a window and only a single hanging lamp in the middle of the ceiling, it was a pretty dark and drab little room and more than once, Sally had suggested Mo take a proper lunch break; take an hour, leave the shop, maybe visit a café or restaurant. But he never had. His father, he'd told her, had taught him the work ethic as a child; if a business is yours, it's yours twenty four seven…delegating responsibility to anyone other than family was asking for trouble. Besides, a half hour lunch break was sufficient for anyone.

Mo was serving a customer and Sally quickly changed and joined him behind the counter. She waited for him to finish serving, then, as she always did, moved into his place allowing him to leave.

It was busy and the time passed quickly. Sally didn't notice until there was a lull that there had been no sign of Mo. She checked the clock on the wall, two-thirty. She glanced through the hatch into the dispensary; it was empty. Sally had worked with Mo in the little chemist shop for almost two years and in all that time had never known him not to stick rigidly to his routine. It was another fifteen minutes before she found herself alone in the shop and was able to trip quickly down the short corridor to the little room at the rear.

Mo Rahman was sitting where he always sat. The sandwich pack on the little table in front of him was opened but untouched and the top of the flask was still firmly screwed in place. He was staring at a piece of paper in his hand and even when Sally spoke his name, it was a long moment before he looked up.

Twelve

"No ulterior motive this time, just a bloke asking a lady to have dinner with him." Stern felt butterflies of anticipation as he spoke into the phone.

He'd left the office wondering why the hell he'd given in and agreed to O'Connor's suggestion of signing up. It was true he'd insisted it be short term, a maximum of three months, less if they wrapped up the case before then. Also, unless it was absolutely crucial, he would stay well away from the station.

He thought David had to really be in the mire to agree to that one. Nevertheless, whatever assurances his friend had given, Stern knew he would inevitably be drawn into the usual bone-aching petty bureaucracy he'd rebelled so much against during his time with the Met. If Stern Investigations had been up to its elbows in work, as it so frequently was, he wouldn't have given David's suggestion the slightest consideration. As it was, he just hoped the phone didn't ring too much. Not for three months anyway.

Back at the flat, he didn't feel like being alone. He'd

been right about the gleam in Cherry's eye, but with everything else going on, he hadn't noticed the engagement ring until she'd literally flashed it under his nose. He couldn't be more pleased for her. Rob, the young, gentle, giant, Norfolk-born boat builder had become the rock she'd so needed. He worshipped the ground she walked on and during the two years they'd been together had restored her faith in the male gender. And after the treatment Cherry had received from men as a young girl, that had taken some doing.

They were perfect for each other and Stern was delighted to hear her news. But, inexplicably, there was also a feeling of disappointment. Strange, but maybe understandable. From the time he'd rescued her from that filthy, East End of London flat until now, he'd been the one. Not as Rob had become, but as a revered, totally trusted father figure. It was in her eyes when they bantered, and again when he was troubled and she was concerned for him. *Eyes that reflected her heart.* Maybe Annie had been right. Annie…there she was again, barging into his thoughts. Was that why he felt like he did? He'd not only lost Annie, now, in a way, he'd also lost Cherry. Well maybe not lost, but certainly taken a step down in her pecking order.

So he didn't feel like being alone right now. Neither did the usual company at his local appeal. On impulse he'd called Melanie Campbell and asked if she fancied having dinner with him again. Now listening to the hesitant silence on the other end of the line, he was wondering how sensible that had been.

"I was going to take a bath and wash my hair," she said. "Does that sound awfully old fashioned?"

He felt disappointed, but not completely surprised. "A simple no would have done the trick," he said.

"No never crossed my mind," she said quickly. Then after another pause. "It's only six-thirty, do I have time?"

His spirits rose. "Of course, take all the time you need. Shall I choose somewhere and book a table?"

"That would be nice."

She'd given him her address, a tiny rented cottage on the outskirts of Aylsham, halfway between Sheringham and Norwich on the A140. Its location pretty well decided for him where they should eat, but then he'd hesitated. From the cottage he could be at the Marsham Arms in fifteen minutes, but was it a good choice? The Marsham Arms was Annie's very favourite restaurant. She'd loved going there, insisting it served the best food in the whole of Norfolk. As a result, they'd spent many happy evenings together there. So should he take another woman? Would it feel like treachery? He shook the stupid thought from him. It was a restaurant, for crying out loud, the ambience was pleasant and it served some of the best food around. Treachery, the past, didn't come into it.

He picked her up just before eight. She looked good, a light, unbuttoned top coat hanging open over dark trousers, a simple top and a silk scarf knocked loosely about her neck. She smelled good too, a perfume he remembered from somewhere, but he couldn't remember where. He wasn't wearing the suit this time, but was glad he'd taken the trouble to shower, shave and put on a decent pair of slacks, a clean open-necked shirt and the only sports jacket he possessed.

It took him little more than fifteen minutes to drive to the Marsham Arms and as he always did when he drove onto the gravelled car park, he recalled the time when an Irish assassin had nearly taken his life on this very spot. It seemed a lifetime ago now, but the incident was still clear in his mind. He nosed the car into a space and as he climbed out, his eyes involuntarily drifting to the place on the brick face of the building still scarred by the bullets that on that day had missed him by a fraction.

Inside, as they were guided to a table, Stern ordered drinks. As he'd thought it would, it seemed bizarre for him to be sitting in this particular place looking across at anyone but Annie. He concentrated on the menu on the table in front of him, again, this time angrily, pushing the thought from his mind.

"You've been here before?" He looked up and she was smiling.

"It shows, eh?"

"Well the fact everyone calls you by your Christian name gave me a hint. Then when you ordered drinks, the girl asked if you wanted the usual. Sort of says something, don't you think?"

He smiled sheepishly. Might as well get it out of the way up front. "Used to come here with my wife quite a lot."

"Used to?"

"Yeah, she's no longer..."

"Oh...I'm so sorry."

He waved a hand. "No I didn't mean she's no longer with us. I meant we're not together."

"I'm still sorry."

"Don't be, it was my own fault and she's now in Australia." *Hell why was he finding this so difficult? Just tell her you're divorced, for Christ's sake.*

"Divorced?"

There you go. Typical woman; straight to the heart of it. "'Fraid so. A policeman's lot, like so many before me."

"Ex-policeman then?"

"Uh-huh, over thirty years in the Met. How about you?"

"No, never managed the Met," she said, giving him an impish little smile.

They laughed together, whatever tension there might have been instantly drifting away. "No," she went on. "I can't match the excitement of the London Metropolitan Police, I'm afraid. For years, because of my husband's work, we travelled a lot, both in the UK and abroad. In fact for a time, if I were to do a count, I'd probably find we spent more time abroad than we did here at home. But unfortunately he died back in two thousand and seven."

Tight lipped, Stern said, "Oh. My turn to say I'm sorry."

She smiled, a sad soft movement of her lips. "Thank you, but it's been six years now." She sighed. "Like they say; you never get over it, you just learn to live with it."

Stern was grateful to see the young waitress appear at his shoulder carrying a tray with their drinks. She smiled down at Stern. "Are you ready to order, Theo?"

Forty minutes later, the food finished, they sat facing each other in comfortable leather armchairs, fresh coffee just served on the table between them. During the meal, talk had been light and spasmodic. Now Stern was keen to know more about Melanie Campbell. "Where were you based when you were in England?"

She laughed, a soft pleasant sound. "Whew, how long have you got? You name it, we were probably there at some time. Abroad too. My husband's job, always on the move."

"So how did you end up here in Norfolk?"

"We'd holidayed here a number of times and my husband, Joe, adored the place. He said it topped anywhere we'd ever been, reckoned it had a rustic charm that got into his bones. He even hinted on retiring here. I think, had he lived, he would have, too. For some time after he died I was at a total loss. Then I remembered the good times we'd had here." She gave a little shrug of her shoulders. "I don't know, coming here seemed right somehow. Seemed the thing to do. I took the cottage on a short term lease just to see how I got on. Thought if it turned out how I hoped, I would eventually buy something. Fact is I've settled so well at the cottage I haven't bothered to even look to buy yet." She smiled. "If I stay, I'll get round to it sometime."

Stern thought about how, after all these years, he still loved living where he was. "I think I know what you mean. Norfolk does that to some of us." He cocked a questioning eye. "You said *if* you stay? Does that mean you might move on?" He suddenly realised he was really hoping she would say no.

She took a sip of coffee and there was thought in her eyes. "Well, I've been here for over a year now and I have to admit there is something about the place. But I do have things I need to do, places I must visit." She looked across at him and there was that smile again. "In the long term, though, yes, I think I would like to settle here." The smile faded a little. "But I guess it's like everything else in this life; we just have to wait and see how things turn out."

Thirteen

Martin Baldwin let himself into the bungalow. He closed and locked the door and threw the keys on the side table in the passageway. He moved through to the sitting room and slumped down in an armchair with a tired sigh. His eyes scanned the small room with its couple of armchairs, a settee and the TV in the corner. The place was nothing to write home about but with two bedrooms, a decent sized combined kitchen dining room and a large bathroom with a double shower, it was perfect for his needs. It was also tucked out of the way in a quiet side road just a short walk from the high street and shops. It was owned by the man who lived in another larger bungalow sitting directly behind who was happy to rent it out on a short term lease. Baldwin had signed up for twelve months. He was sure it would be more than enough. He hoped, if he played his cards right, he'd be out of there long before then.

He heaved himself wearily out of the chair and slouched into the bedroom. Studying himself in the mirror, he smiled. He hadn't been able to change his identity...he wouldn't have known how, and anyway he'd had no option but to retain his true identity, it was essential. He wouldn't have got this far if he hadn't. But he had been able to change his appearance. The dyed hair and short, neatly cropped beard had certainly done that. He looked older, a completely different person and he was sure it would do the trick. Why was he so sure? Because he knew very well that Cain Engineering, or to be more precise, Frank Runcie, would never formally report the situation. He wouldn't dare. To do so would mean word of the new design would get out before it could be locked up tightly in Cain's patents and any other legal safeguard they could manage. Runcie, the ultimate control freak, would never allow that to happen.

So his face, his real face, couldn't be plastered all over the nationals, which meant he only had to worry about being accidentally recognised. The chances of that here were almost nil, but stranger things had happened, so just to be sure, he felt his new image would cover it.

And the uniform? He chuckled. He was an engineering wizard, wasn't he? Hadn't Rupert Cain said so himself? And hadn't he proved it by designing probably the most ingenious, most complex electro-mechanical switching system in the world today? Its uses were endless. Small enough to be used in any number of medical applications, robust enough for engineering machinery and, most promising of all, fast enough to be used in the most sophisticated of weapon systems.

Oh yes, he was a genius alright. So why at this moment was he hiding away in a rented bungalow in the middle of Mordialloc, a suburb of Melbourne, Australia? And why was he dressed in the overalls of a lowly maintenance man employed by a small, discreet hotel in Melbourne? Baldwin smiled to himself as he started to pull off his working clothes. "There are a few who would like to know the answer to that one," he muttered to himself.

~ * ~

"He's big and he's ugly," Cherry whispered, nodding toward the outer office. "Reckons it's imperative he talks to you now."

Stern's lips turned down and he frowned. "Does this big ugly person have a name?"

"Runcie. Frank Runcie."

Stern shrugged, the name meaning nothing. "Better bring him in then."

Cherry headed toward the door, turning halfway and mouthing silently, "You won't like him."

"Ah, Stern." The big man pushed past Cherry before she could announce him and paced purposefully across the office. He was dressed in a dark, expensive suit, the material of which Stern estimated could have made a couple for him. Including waistcoats. He was clean shaven, a broad, florid face with a heavy forehead and thick eyebrows overhanging dark eyes. The smile he gave as he offered Stern a huge hand was false and a struggle to maintain. The handshake was little more than a brief touch before he thumped heavily down in the chair opposite Stern and waved a banana finger across the desk.

"Now you and I have to talk, Stern." It wasn't a request but a demand, the words sounding like the rough edge of a very coarse file.

Stern glanced quickly toward Cherry, slowly closing the

door. She was grinning broadly. "Told you so," she mouthed through the diminishing gap.

He turned his attention back to the mountain squatting in front of him. "About what?"

Another wave of the podgy digit. "Oh come on, I think you know, Stern. It's about this Baldwin malarkey."

Stern was a great believer in first impressions. This was a man who had supreme confidence in himself. A man who had probably bullied his way through life, using his physical size to supplement an overpowering, demanding character. This was also a man who always got his own way, and, what got up Stern's nose more than anything, insisted on calling people by their surname in a degrading attempt to dominate.

He eased back in the old chair, his face a straight, noncommittal mask. "Like to explain?"

The big man harrumphed. "Come on, Stern, don't shilly-shally with me. You know very well what I'm talking about. You came to my place demanding information about one of my people and I want to know what it was all about."

Stern gave a slow, tight lipped nod of the head and eased forward, resting his elbows on the desk. "Tell you what," he said, his voice a flat calm. "Just so we all know where we stand, why don't you start by telling me who the hell you are and where you come from?"

Runcie's mouth fell open, the heavy brows coming together, forming a thick black caterpillar along his forehead. But the surprise lasted but a second before he again collected himself. "Ah, yes, should have said. Name's Runcie. I'm Chief Executive, Cain Engineering. So

I'm sure you can see I have a right to know..."

"With regard to my private investigations?" Stern butted in.

"What?"

"You're implying you have a right to details of my private investigations. Which, of course, you don't."

"Damn it man," Runcie thundered. "You barge your way onto my premises and demand information about one of my employees, then have the audacity to say I have no rights. Of course I have rights and I insist you tell me what you're up to."

Stern remained poker faced, kept his voice soft, controlled. Even if he did feel like giving the big oaf a slap. "Well to start with, Runcie, I never *barge,* never found it necessary. But what I did do was visit your reception area, which I assume is where you would expect a visitor to be received on your premises. There I was met by a very polite woman who I respectfully asked if I could have a few very brief moments with one of your people. She referred me to a Mr Chapman, who I now have to assume learned his manners from you." He noted with some satisfaction the trembling lips and the colour darkening even further. He quickly held up a hand, halting the impending outburst. "Now, my reason for coming to your company and making a very simple, respectful request is confidential to the client I'm representing. As for your belligerent, ill-mannered response, I can only guess both you and your equally ignorant minion have your own reasons for that." He pushed himself up from the chair. "Now I think we're done here."

It was the big man's turn to hold up a hand. "Now hold

on," he said, his voice just a tad less harsh. "Okay, I may have come on a bit strong there. It's just the way I am, something you'll just have to accept." He tried a smile but failed miserably, it faltering almost immediately. "Can't change who you are, Stern."

Stern was having none of it. "Have to accept? No, I don't think so. You're a big man, Runcie, and from what I've witnessed, a bully. But you're on my turf now, and here I decide who or what I accept. Here I don't accept bullying from you or anyone else. So, like I said, I think we're done." He pointed to the door. "My assistant will show you out."

It took some long moments, and if steam could literally have come out of someone's ears it would be pumping from Runcie's with some force right then. Finally he took a huge deep breath and this time held up both hands. "Okay, okay I apologise if I was a little brusque. It was not my intention to be disrespectful."

Not bloody much, Stern thought, but he said nothing, just stood looking down at Runcie, maintaining the high ground. If he was waiting for an acceptance of the puny apology, he would wait a long time.

Runcie dropped his hands into his lap. "Can we start again, talk this through?"

Stern wanted nothing more than to kick the arrogant lump's arse out of the office, but something about the way the big man had backed away from outright confrontation made him hesitate. Maybe there was something he could learn from this. Before he could respond, Runcie spoke again, just a little of the sharpness back in his tone.

"I accept your reprimand, Stern, and I apologise unreservedly, but I don't beg."

Stern lowered himself slowly back into the chair. "Don't expect you to beg," he said, his face still an angry mask. "Just general respect and civility would suffice."

Runcie gave a heavy growling sigh. "Okay, okay, I've said I apologise, so can we start over?" He held Stern's harsh gaze for a tense moment before following up with, "Please."

Stern relaxed back in the chair and gave a brief nod. "Go on."

"Good. Now first I would like to discuss the situation surrounding Martin Baldwin, one of my employees. Then, if you feel my case to be appropriate, I would like to employ your services."

This time it was Stern's mouth that dropped open. "*What?*"

His knuckles were white as Runcie clenched his hands together in front of him. He was finding this *asking* business bloody difficult, but he needed help and formal channels were out of the question. He'd read up on Stern before coming here today. He had the reputation and the background. This confrontation had proved he was also a hard case. Just what Runcie needed right now. So, if diplomacy were needed, then so be it. He took a breath. "Regarding Baldwin, I have a feeling you and I may be running on parallel but different paths," he said, his tone the complete opposite to when he had arrived. "With your agreement, I would like to discuss that and, as I said, if we both feel it appropriate, I would like to employ your services."

Fourteen

"But he's such an obnoxious piece of work."

Stern grinned. "I know, but most of it's just a front."

"*A front?* He's got a front alright, the fat pig."

Stern gave a shake of the head. "It's what I love about you, kid. You don't take prisoners."

Eyes sparking, Cherry gave a derisive snort. "Not when they're as horrible as him. He treated me like dirt, boss. Demanding to see you like that and not a please or thank you anywhere." There were few times when Cherry didn't sit when discussing things in Stern's office, but this was one of those times. She hopped angrily from one high heeled foot to another. "Did you see, he actually pushed me out of the way when he came in here?"

"Must admit there was a time when I wanted to give him a slap."

"So why on earth didn't you? I can't believe you agreed to work for him."

Stern waved a hand at the chair opposite. "Cherry, for Christ's sake, calm down and get your backside on that chair, will you? Those flippin' shoes make me nervous."

Cherry stopped the hopping and reluctantly sat. "Well, he's a..."

"Yeah, I know, you've already told me what he is, but if you'll just get off your high horse for a minute, I'll explain." He waited until she'd stopped her agitated wriggling. "Right, it's no excuse for his behaviour, but once I'd nailed him down he did apologise." He paused for a beat, a half smile forming. "Well sort of, anyway.

"It was the best a guy like him could manage. He did try to explain, too. There's no doubt Rupert Cain, the man the company's named after and a brilliant engineer, is the brains behind the outfit. But he's a boffin; his nose is forever buried in his work and he has no idea about running a company. Runcie's the complete opposite. He admitted he left school with nothing but a huge frame and an ego to match. But it was he who recognised the potential in Cain's design ability and as a result persuaded Cain to form a company. He let Cain get on with all the technical stuff and set about making the company what it is today. He did it by using the only attributes he had...his size and his total self-belief, call it arrogance if you like. Whatever, it became his trademark and now, after so many years, he couldn't change if he tried. He even admitted his bully-boy tactic sometimes worked as much against him as it did for him."

Cherry was unmoved by the story. "I'm not surprised and it makes no difference anyway," she said stiffly. "Pig ignorance is pig ignorance, however you look at it."

Cherry's history with men had been catastrophic and at times like this it showed. Stern knew when to back off.

"You're right, but it's not because of the man I took the job. It's because of the situation."

"The situation?"

"Yup. You see, Runcie might be a bully, but right now he's so deep in the mire it's lapping at his bottom lip. You remember we surmised the reception I received at Cain Engineering may not have been because they didn't want me to talk to Baldwin, but because they didn't know where he was?"

"Yes."

"Well, we were right. But that's not all. It seems Baldwin's didn't only abscond. According to Runcie, he simply left a note of resignation and walked off with the full design details of Cain's latest piece of high tech equipment. And in a time of financial hardship, like now, that ain't good. A small company like Cain only survives on continuous innovation and for the last couple of years that hasn't been happening. Runcie admitted Cain engineering had made both him and his partner wealthy men, but lately things had been going downhill. The last thing they wanted was to lose control of the company, get involved with outside investment like some large corporation or venture capitalist. They'd done that to start the company, but that was in the past. Now it was theirs and they didn't want to lose control. So to keep the ship afloat, they've both had to reinvest some of their own personal cash back into the business. They believed this latest piece of brilliance, designed by Baldwin himself, by the way, was to be their salvation. According to Runcie, it had huge potential and would have enabled them to recoup their personal losses together with sealing the company's future for a number of years."

The agitation had eased and Cherry leaned forward with renewed interest. "And at the very time they lose their main man and his magic design, Theo Stern turns up looking for that very same man. Jeez, boss, it's no wonder they were all beside themselves and wanted to know what you were up to."

"You got it."

The gleam in Cherry's eye showed the fat pig, if not forgotten, had for the moment anyway been pushed to one side. "But that doesn't sound like it has anything to do with Baldwin's call to Andrew about a stalker, does it?"

Stern smiled. "It just so happens it does. See, not only is Runcie an obnoxious piece of work, as you rightly put it, he's also one very shrewd cookie; remember it was him who got the company going in the first place. He told me, though no one else at Cain's seemed to notice, he'd had suspicions for a while that Baldwin had not been a happy bunny."

"Why am I not surprised at that?" Cherry snorted. "With someone like him as my boss, neither would I be."

Stern ignored the renewed rancour. "Thing is, they all knew Baldwin was knee deep in something that could turn the fortunes of the company around. But only Runcie sensed that Baldwin was dissatisfied with his lot. Runcie was also concerned that Baldwin was keeping the new design close to his chest. Not even Rupert Cain knew the details of this revolutionary thingamajig. But he had complete faith in Baldwin and was happy to leave it to him until it was finished. Runcie didn't like that at all, but there was little he could do about it because if there was one person he never argued or disagreed with, it was Cain. So being the devious character he is, he decided, unknown to the others, to quietly keep an eye on Baldwin."

Cherry's eyes lit up. "You mean it was his man who was following Baldwin?"

"Got it in one."

"But who...? I mean who did he use?"

"He paid an old mate who just happened to be between jobs at the time."

"Just like that?"

"Just like that."

"You're kidding me."

"No. The guy had to follow Baldwin from the moment he left home to when he arrived at work in the morning and the reverse in the evening. Weekends, too. Paid him a hundred notes a day."

"Runcie told you this?"

"I didn't make it up, Cherry."

"So what did they find out?"

"Absolutely nothing."

Cherry gave a happy little chuckle. "So the fat pig wasted his money. Good, I'm glad."

"That you might be, but as it happens, Runcie's intuition was spot on, because before he could turn round, Baldwin had skipped. And he'd taken the super design with him."

"So now Runcie comes to the professionals."

"That's right. One bonus is, by telling me about having

Baldwin followed Runcie's solved one of our problems; I can at least now tell Andrew what that was all about."

"But that doesn't solve Runcie's problem, does it? He's still lost his man and the design that could be the salvation of Cain Engineering."

Stern grinned. "I'll make a gumshoe out of you yet, Hooker."

"You should have told him to stuff his job, boss. Let him fry in his own fat juice."

"Maybe, but remember, we're already on the job, aren't we? And it's not as if we're overrun with work. I thought we might as well get paid for doing what we were already doing for nothing."

Cherry stood up and headed for the door. "Yeah, okay, I guess that warrants a cup of tea."

Stern eased himself back in the chair, a broad grin spreading. "Yup, so do I. Oh, and by the way, just for your info, when the big fat pig asked how much I charged, I doubled our fee."

She stopped short and swung round. "D'you know, boss, you really don't know how good that makes me feel."

"Good enough for a chocolate hobnob with my tea?"

She wrinkled her nose and gave a sniff. "That's pushing it, but I'll see what I can do."

As Cherry left the room, the telephone came to life. "I'll get it," Stern called, dropping forward and picking up the receiver. "Stern."

"Theo, it's David. Got some news…we've identified the dead man."

Stern picked up a pen and pulled his desk pad toward him. "Fire away."

"His name is Atif Dasti." O'Connor spelled out the name. "He was twenty-eight years old and of Pakistani descent. Born in the UK to parents who came here in the early nineties. His father's a doctor and the family home is in Nottingham."

"Twenty-eight," Stern mused. "And still living at home?"

"No. He was a pharmacist, worked at a private clinic in Kings Lynn. Lived in that area somewhere, but we've yet to establish where. Our people in Nottingham are giving his parents the bad news now. They'll establish his address in Lynn and check it out. Should get something from them tomorrow, maybe sooner."

Stern reminded himself he was now part of O'Connor's team. "Anything you want me to do?"

"Not right now, Theo, but considering the possible link with your lad's pal, it might be as well if I get clearance for you to have a nose around Nottingham and Lynn, talk to the parents and visit Dasti's place. I'll clear it with our lads over there, tell them you're working on a possible link with one of our own cases."

"You mean Baldwin?"

"Yeah. I just have this feeling."

Stern knew all about policeman's 'feelings.' "You think Baldwin might be at risk?"

"Well yes, I suppose that could be the case, but I was thinking more of the reverse."

"You mean maybe Baldwin was involved in the killing?"

"Can't rule it out, can we?"

"I suppose not." If he were honest, that side of the coin hadn't crossed Stern's mind, probably because Baldwin was a friend of Andrew's and again because Melanie Campbell had painted him as such a nice character. He must be losing his old suspicious touch.

O'Connor broke into his thoughts. "I know up till now Baldwin's not officially been on my books and I only have what you've told me about him. But it looks like he was the last person to be seen with Dasti and now he's disappeared, so I have to consider his involvement as a likely suspect or, as you say, maybe even a potential victim. Also, if I'm considering that side of things, I have to remember how he thought he was being stalked."

Stern came in quickly. "Hold on, David, that may not be the case." He outlined his discussion with Runcie and the big man's admission to having Baldwin followed. "I still think there's a link there somewhere, but knowing it was Runcie's man doing the following at least clears that point." Stern refrained from mentioning he had also agreed to work for Runcie, justifying not doing so by telling himself it was client confidential. Besides he had already figured by approaching the thing from both sides might just give him an advantage. Only time would tell, but for now anyway he felt it best to keep O'Connor in the dark about his double whammy.

"Okay, at least that side of it is now clear," O'Connor said. "And this Runcie character has no idea where Baldwin might have hotfooted to."

"None at all. I can assure you, if he did, he'd have had

Baldwin by the throat by now."

"Okay, so back to where we were then. When I get Dasti's address, I'd like you to give it the once over. Have a word with his parents too. That'll kick things off. Then you can take the reins, okay? Just keep me informed."

"Sure, just let me know when you want me to move."

"Will do. Oh, and you might have a little surprise coming your way."

Stern hesitated, and frowned. "I'm not a lover of surprises, David."

"Too bad, you'll have to put up with this one. See ya." There was a click, then the dialing tone.

Fifteen

O'Connor had called Stern at home and given him three addresses; Dasti's parents', his place of work and the flat he'd been renting in Kings Lynn.

"I've also okayed it with our people in Nottingham and Lynn for you to visit," O'Connor said. "I've given them your name and confirmed you're on the payroll, my representative. Just let them know you're in the area and give them a rough itinerary, where you'll be and when. They won't interfere as long as they know you're there."

"Got contacts for me?"

O'Connor read out contact names for both areas. "When will you go?"

"Well, Lynn's on the way to Nottingham, isn't it, so I reckon I'll be able to crack the two in one day if I get a move on. Could make an early start tomorrow."

"That would be good. By the way, I'm having a warrant card prepared for you. Won't have it for tomorrow, but that shouldn't be a problem. If you're challenged by our lot, just produce a driver's licence or anything that confirms you are who you say. Anyone else, get them to ring me."

Having made the calls to the relevant contacts, telling them his plans, Stern was on the road by six-thirty. He'd decided to hit Nottingham and Dasti's parents first and get the most traumatic part of the visit over with. He would then call in at Kings Lynn on the return journey, first visiting Dasti's flat, then the private clinic where the murdered man had worked. The flat, O'Connor had told him, occupied the upper floor of a detached house. The owner of the house lived on the ground floor. He'd been briefed and would allow Stern access.

At such an early hour, Stern had sailed through Fakenham and skirted Kings Lynn without delay. He'd arrived at the outskirts of Nottingham, crossing the Trent just before nine-thirty then spent another thirty minutes locating the Dasti residence, a large detached house just off the Carlton road, close to the King Edwards Park. Pulling onto the driveway, he cut the engine and eased himself stiffly out of the car. The Hyundai was a comfortable car to drive, but despite that, these days he still stiffened up after a long journey. He lifted his arms above his head and stretched backward, feeling the joints in his spine crackle ominously. Dropping his arms, he turned and headed along the drive to the front door of the house. It was pulled open before he reached it and a tall, immaculately dressed man stepped out. He was, Stern guessed, somewhere in his fifties and was wearing a dark suit over a matching waistcoat and a blue satin tie positioned perfectly at the neck of a pure white shirt. The greying sideburns of his otherwise black hair combed straight back, emphasized his glowing dark features and accentuated an already distinguished stature. His expression solemn, he extended his hand as Stern approached.

"Mr Stern, I presume?"

Stern took the hand, a dry powerful grip. "Yes and can I say how sorry I am to have to bother you under such traumatic circumstances, Mr Dasti." Up close, Stern realised he was a good two or three inches shorter than the other man. He also became aware of the unusual, penetrating light grey eyes probing out at him from the dark features. Without another word, Dasti stood back and beckoned him inside.

In the hallway, a door immediately to his right stood open and Dasti ushered Stern toward it. As he turned, Stern looked to the far end of the hall and another door, again open. A woman stood looking toward him. She was dressed traditionally, if Stern remembered correctly, in what was called an *abaya* or *jilbab*. Only the woman's face was visible, but even from where he stood, Stern could see the red rimmed swollen eyes staring out from etched, grief-ridden features. Involuntarily he paused and smiled at the woman. Seeing this, Dasti swung round, looking toward the woman, his face darkening. The woman immediately lowered her eyes and turned away. Dasti took Stern by the arm and steered him into the room, closing the door quietly behind them.

It was a large room with a wide window looking out to the front of the house. Bookcases stood tall against two walls, their shelves packed with various sizes of books, folders and magazines. A coffee table with an armchair on either side stood against the third wall which was covered with a variety of pictures, some photographic, others actual paintings or prints. A large desk stood before the window, its highly polished surface almost completely clear but for a few papers, an ornate pen and pencil rack and several more framed pictures. Dasti motioned Stern to one of the armchairs and slid himself carefully into the other. He steepled his fingers below his chin and fixed Stern with a piercing gaze.

"So, Mr Stern, I'm informed that you represent the Norfolk constabulary." His voice was authoritative, the words precise and perfectly pronounced.

"Yes, I do."

"So in your case, what does *represent* mean exactly? I was given no indication of rank or position, so are you not actually a policeman?"

"A fair question," Stern admitted with a smile. "At this time, the Norfolk police force has been hit with an unprecedented bout of sickness and other problems. As a result, their numbers are at an all-time low. I am a retired London Metropolitan Police Detective Inspector with over thirty years' experience. I've accepted temporary recruitment to help fill the current gap in their resources."

"Ah," Dasti nodded his understanding. "That explains it. So, how can I help you?"

Stern was well aware that he had just been vetted and, it seemed, accepted. But Dasti's business-like approach and lack of emotion intrigued him. They were about to discuss the man's son who had recently been murdered, but Dasti's demeanour showed no signs of stress or anxiety at all. Either the man was able to hold his feelings in check, maybe his doctor's training coming to the fore, or there was more to it. Time to find out.

"As I said, I apologize for my intrusion at such a delicate time, Mr Dasti. But it is important we find out as much about your son and his recent movements and activities as soon as we can. It can make a huge difference to our investigation. Atif's family home was here and he worked in Kings Lynn, so we have to ask what was he doing in a remote area of North Norfolk? Was he there to meet someone or visit some place? If we knew that, we could be a step closer to piecing together his last movements. Such information could be vitally important in our search for your son's killer."

Dasti gave a tight-lipped nod. "I understand what you're saying, Mr Stern, but I'm afraid there is little I can do to help. You see, my son has been estranged from the family for over five years. For the greater proportion of that time, we've had no idea where he was or what he was doing."

"Oh, I didn't realise."

"No, of course you didn't. Why should you? You see, my son lost his way the moment he left the protection of the family home. That was early two thousand and three when he went to study at university. We are devout Muslims, you see. We have a strict code of conduct and, contrary to the image given by the radicals, we are peace loving and devoted to our principles. My son drifted away from our faith almost the moment he left home." He shook his head, the first sign of sadness touching his eyes.

"We tried, my wife in particular, but it was no good. I warned him of the consequences a number of times, but he took no heed. The end became inevitable and my decision was final." The last words were said with grim faced determination.

Stern knew what had happened here. He'd seen it before; youngsters born to devout Muslim families, but desperate for the freedom of the western way of life. The result could range from what appeared to have happened here...the family simply disowning the offspring, to violent reprisals, sometimes even death. "So may I ask what your son did that was so bad?"

Dasti took a deep breath, his lips tightening as if just to say the word was a profanity. "Alcohol, Mr Stern," he said bitterly through his teeth. "The abomination of man, the devil's route to all things evil. My son took to drink and cared not who knew about it."

"He became an alcoholic?"

Dasti shook his head. "Initially no, I wouldn't say alcoholic." He gave a resigned shrug. "Later, of course, maybe, I wouldn't know. But it was the drink that set him on the path that took him away from us. At college he mixed with those who had no boundaries, no code or principles to bind them, to show them the way."

"You're saying he was led astray by others?"

Dasti smiled for the first time and Stern could have sworn, just for a fleeting second, he saw a touch of pride glint in those penetrating grey eyes. But it was there and gone so quickly he couldn't be sure. "Oh no, Mr Stern. My son was never led by anyone. He was his own man, if anything a leader of men. A trait that in his youth made us so proud. But sadly, that very same forceful attribute came to the fore when, the last time we met, he told me he was an Englishman first and foremost, and wasn't about to be tied down by any mumbo jumbo that in a progressive world could only make his life a misery." Dasti looked across at Stern, his eyes filled only with sadness. "His exact words, Mr Stern, verbatim. They will remain burned into my soul for the rest of my life. It was the day I ordered him out of my house. I have neither seen nor heard from him since."

"That was a sad day, Mr Dasti. To lose a son..." It was all Stern could think of saying.

Dasti pushed himself out of the chair and stood looking down at Stern. "Yes I agree, Mr Stern, it was a sad day. But the tragedy is not mine, it is Atif's. You see he not only lost a most devout, sacred way of life, he also lost his family." Straightening his shoulders, he looked down at his watch. "And there I'm afraid we must leave it. To facilitate seeing you this morning, I engaged a locum to cover my early surgery. I have to be back at the practice soon so you'll have to forgive me." He raised a hand and motioned toward the door.

Back in the hall, Stern hesitated. "Just one last question if I may, Mr Dasti. Does the name Martin Baldwin mean anything to you?"

"No, not at all. Should it?"

"No, maybe not," Stern said, making to move toward the front door then stopping and turning again. As he did so, he caught the movement from the corner of his eye, the woman again watching him from the open door at the far end of the hall. Eye contact was made and this time the woman stayed put, ignoring Dasti's annoyed glare. Stern paused again. "Mr Dasti, I'm sincerely sorry for the tragedies you've had to face, both with your son's straying from the straight and narrow and now your sad loss, but despite this it is still important we find your son's killer. It's our job and regardless of all else, justice has to be done. It would therefore help us greatly if we had a photograph of Atif, a recent one if possible, but if not...? Do you think maybe your wife...? Sometimes a mother..." He left the question unfinished, fearing that the last thing he would find in this house was a photograph, particularly a recent one, of the outcast son.

"Mr Stern." The words were snapped out. "My wife knows no more than I do. She also holds exactly the same opinion as I. It is a sad and regretful fact, but our grieving has long since taken its course. We lost our son a very long time ago, Mr Stern. Our paths through life are preordained and if it was written he should end this way, then so be it. I will, of course, take care of the funeral arrangements. Despite Atif's estrangement, it will be expected of me, but that will be the end of the matter. Now I must insist..."

"Badar!"

Both Stern and Dasti turned toward the woman, Dasti frozen, his hand holding Stern's arm, on the point of steering him out of the house.

The woman moved toward them, rattling angry words Stern didn't understand as she came. She stopped in front of the two men, ignoring her open-mouthed husband, her eyes softening as she looked at Stern. "My boy may have strayed, Mr Stern, may have chosen a path alien to our beliefs, but he was still my boy, still my blood." From beneath her gown she produced a photograph, maybe six by four inches. "It is all I have, so I would be grateful for its return. All I ask is that you find whoever did this abominable thing. Find him and make him pay. Please do that for me, Mr Stern." She looked toward her husband, no more than a disdainful, reprimanding glance, before turning and walking slowly back down the hallway.

Sixteen

The interview with Atif Dasti's father had taken exactly half an hour and Stern found himself climbing back into the Hyundai at ten thirty. He backed off the drive and headed toward the A52 and the return drive to Kings Lynn. As he drove he reviewed the thirty minutes he'd spent at the house. It could be said to have been a waste of time and as far as getting any closer to why Dasti was killed or who may have killed him, maybe that was true. But he'd learned much about the murdered man himself and a good deal about his father, too.

Of course the situation outlined by Dasti was nothing new to Stern. He again recalled how often, during his time with the Met, he'd seen it in all its forms. Young, born in Briton, Muslim girls rebelling against the most suffocating restrictions including forced marriages, their dissent sometimes reaping the severest of penalties. Men also facing problems of their own, desperate to share the social freedom of their non-Muslim peers. The pressure for them to retain the family beliefs was intense, but then so was the draw of a society with no boundaries. Sometimes the family won and held onto the offspring. Sometimes, like it seemed with Atif Dasti, they lost. This could bring the fiercest of reprisals.

Here, Stern's thoughts stalled, another scenario looming large. In this case just how fierce had the father's reaction been to his son's transgressions? Had it really ended in just the ejection from the family home, the father's disinheritance of his son? Or could it have gone further, much further? Family honour killings were nothing new and Dasti's head-of-the-family intransigent stance reflected just how deeply his belief ran. Could family shame have forced him into more than just disowning his son? And did the tragic figure at the end of the hallway, peering out through grief ravaged eyes, suspect that? Her desperate plea for her son's killer to be found and brought to justice indicated maybe she didn't, but she wanted justice and that final look she had given her husband may have said differently.

In Stern's experience, fathers were the most intractable. It was the inbuilt male pride, the necessity to be the dominant one, the alpha male. A decision made, particularly one as serious as involving religion, there must be no renunciation. The mother, on the other hand, normally had no such hang-ups. It was her offspring, the tiny being that had grown inside her, caused the birth pain that had made her scream, and the joy when she held it close for the first time, that had made her cry. With such a bond, nothing could ever come between a mother and her child.

The male may dominate, force feelings to be held in check, the truth to be hidden. But in the mother, those feelings, that truth, would still be there deep below the surface. If Stern hadn't seen abject devastation staring out at him from the eyes of the woman he could only assume to be Mrs Dasti, then all his years of training, studying human behaviour, had gone to waste. So were those sad swollen eyes trying to tell him something, something that only the loyalty to her husband was holding back? Right then he didn't know, but Stern was convinced she could be the chink in Dasti's inflexible armour. If all else failed, if he couldn't make progress in any other way, somehow he would have to get to Atif Dasti's mother.

Stern had pushed his card into Dasti's hand as he left, requesting should anything happen that could help the police with their enquiries it would be his duty to call. He'd also thrown in the reminder that it was a criminal offence to obstruct the police in their enquiries. He knew in Dasti's case he'd been wasting his breath, but the card, his number, for the moment anyway, was in the Dasti household. So was a woman wracked with grief, who he was sure had something to say. You could never tell.

The drive back to Kings Lynn took a couple of hours and before even attempting to locate Atif Dasti's flat, Stern needed food. Leaving the A17, he joined the A47 and crossed the bridge over the river Great Ouse. From there he kept on the lookout for anywhere he could eat. It came up sooner than he expected, the chalk board outside the pub boasting the finest ales and top pub grub. That would do nicely.

An hour later, he was back on the road. He couldn't be sure that a thin, watery, microwaved fish pie could be classified as top pub grub; it certainly wouldn't be at his local in Sheringham, but the beer was acceptable and at least he had food inside him.

It took a further twenty minutes to find the large detached house in which Atif Dasti had lived and this time there was nobody at the front door to greet him. Instead, it took several prolonged shoves at the bell push followed by a number of knuckle raps on the door before he heard any movement inside and finally the door was pulled open.

The man was lean with an ageing stoop. He was wearing an immaculate pair of light fawn trousers with creases so sharp they looked like they could draw blood. The grey, military-style shirt and red waistcoat with matching cravat tied at the neck were as sharp and flawless as the trousers. At odds with the whole ensemble were the broke-backed carpet slippers on his feet. They had seen better days, but Stern thought, that was probably a very long time ago. Probably well into his eighties, he stood for some moments, sleepy eyes taking a while to focus, the brain slow to assess.

"My apologies for the delay in my response, dear boy. I am rarely called upon during siesta, you understand." The voice, totally at odds with the appearance, was a deep baritone, the diction precise.

Stern also figured the heavy smell of whiskey that wafted toward him as the man spoke helped considerably at siesta time. He was about to introduce himself, but got only as far as opening his mouth to speak.

"Now let me see, you must be the chappie they told me

about, the one destined to give young Atif's bed space the once over. Am I right?"

Stern held out his hand. "You are. Name's Stern, Theo Stern. Nice to meet you Mr...?" At the last second he realised he hadn't been given the man's name."

But he need not have worried; his hesitation seemed not to register. But a frown had puckered the old man's forehead. "Stern, eh?" After a moment his face cleared and his eyes widened, sparkling. "I say, old chap, you're not one of the Aintree Sterns, are you? Good lord, that would be a shot in the arm. Served with two of them back in..." The frown was back. "When was that?" He shook his head and gave a shrug of his narrow shoulders. "Damned if I can remember now, there were so many."

Stern wondered if he was ever getting past the door step. "No, I'm not one of the Aintree Sterns," he confirmed. "No military in my family background, I'm afraid." He guessed that's what this was about.

"Mmmm, pity that. Damned good fellows, the Sterns. Never did know what happened to them. Still, onwards and upwards, as they say." He shuffled backward and motioned Stern inside. "Now, don't stand on ceremony, old chap. Welcome to headquarters."

It looked, as far as Stern could see, as if the military theme spread throughout the lower floor, with photographs of uniformed individuals and groups adorning the hallway walls and trophies, obviously from a host of different countries, sitting in every corner. The old man ushered Stern into a living room again cluttered with military memorabilia, even a complete dress uniform hanging resplendent on a tailor's dummy in one corner. He gave a casual wave toward a chair and moved across to a drinks cabinet. Lifting a half filled cut glass decanter from its stand, he held it up for Stern to see, the question needing no words.

Stern smiled and shook his head. "A little early for me, Mr...?"

This time it registered. "Just Collins, old chap. Out of uniform now, no need for rank. Surnames only. Standing orders, don't y'know." He poured himself a generous measure of whiskey and slumped into a chair opposite Stern. "'Course, if you want to be precise, it's Brigadier, or was. Still use it occasionally, of course." He gave an impish wink. "If I think it'll do me any good."

Stern smiled. "And why not?"

Collins took a slurp at the whiskey and smacked his lips. "Now what's this about young Atif? They tell me the silly bugger's got himself killed."

"Yes, I'm afraid he has."

The old man gave a harrumph. "Damned inconvenient, that," he grumbled. "Good payer was Atif. On the button every month. Mind you, I didn't overcharge the lad. Just enough to keep me and my friend here together." He lifted the glass and took another swallow.

There spoke an old soldier, Stern thought. Had probably seen death in all its guises and had long since come to terms with the inevitability of it. His first thought a military one; what affect did it have on those remaining, the job in hand. "So what can you tell me about him, Brigadier?"

The old man smiled, pleased to hear his old rank thrown at him. "Clever lad and strong with it. Impressive build, hit the old weights several times a week. Knew what he wanted and went for it. If he'd been with us back then, he would have made excellent officer material, that's for sure. I liked him, you know. Liked him a lot. Once in a while he'd come down and join me for a snifter or two. Or three. Even brought me the occasional bottle; always the best malt, too. Damned good company he was."

"He was a Muslim," Stern said. "Did you know that?"

The old man's face darkened. "Of course I knew it. But dammit, man, what difference does that make? I served with the Gurkhars back in..." There was the frown again, then an agitated shake of the head. "Well, whenever, but they were a damned good bunch. Nothing wrong with the Gurkhars, I can tell you. Did as they were told and did it bloody well. It's not what they are, not the nationality or religion, it's the man inside that counts, old chap. You should remember that."

"Yes, I'm sure," Stern said. "But what I meant was, Muslims don't touch alcohol."

"Ah, yes, I see what you mean." The slow nod of understanding turned to a vigorous shake of the head. "Young Atif was having none of that. Said it was a load of old tosh. Told me from square one he had just one life to live and he was going to enjoy it while he could. He told me how his father had kicked him out and he was miserable about that. But it made no difference. Atif was his own man and cared not who knew it." The brigadier drained the whiskey tumbler and laid it on the floor beside his chair. "Mind you, he was no lush. Oh no, far from it. He enjoyed a drink, of course, but only the odd one or two. I never saw him over the top. No, not ever."

Stern chewed things over for a moment then asked, "Did he ever mention the name Martin Baldwin to you at any time?"

"Baldwin." The old man shook his head. "Not that I recall."

"And last week, did he seem troubled at all?"

"No, not the slightest." His face screwed into thought, then he said, "Tuesday it was. He popped in and told me he would be away, maybe a couple of nights. Said he was going to see an old school chum." His old face creased into a grin. "I remember asking if this friend was male or female. He told me to mind my own bloody business." He shook his head and chuckled. "That was Dasti for you."

"Okay." Stern eased himself to the edge of the chair. "So d'you think I could see his apartment now?"

The flat, covering the whole of the top floor of the house, was completely self-contained. Stern took only a cursory glance at the bathroom, and the bedroom held nothing of any significance other than a pair of frilly panties tucked away in the bottom drawer of the bedside cabinet. Stern smiled; Dasti was obviously a souvenir keeper. The kitchen and small dining room were functional but again contained nothing of interest. It seemed to Stern that if he were to find anything worth finding, anything that hadn't already been removed by the local police, it would be in the living room.

He stood and scanned the room, taking in the wide

screen television, various easy chairs and a desk tucked away in one corner. The cabinet on which the TV sat had a single drawer below, and a set of three drawers made up one side of the desk. As far as he could see, these were the only unexposed areas. Pulling open the drawer below the TV, he found it contained only a television instruction manual and a pile of CDs and DVDs.

Moving across to the desk, he cast an eye over its surface. A leather edged blotter lay in the centre with various scribbles on its surface and several pens and pencils scattered across it. The only other item was a book entitled *The British National Formulary EDITION: 62 (September 2011 – March 2012)*. Leaning down, he pulled open the top drawer.

The brigadier had followed him from room to room, standing silently watching as Stern carefully searched. "What exactly is it you're looking for, old chap?" he asked. "I mean, the local bobbies have already been over the place once."

"I know, Brigadier, and to be honest, I don't really know what I'm looking for."

The brigadier nodded his understanding. "I'm with you, old son. One of those times when you know it if you see it, eh?"

"That's about the size of it," Stern admitted, raking through the drawer and finding only a stapler, a calculator, a couple of blank writing pads and a roll of Sellotape. The second drawer held a couple of pharmacy ref books and the third was empty. Disappointed, he straightened and smiled at the old man, raising his hands in a defeated gesture. "And if there's nothing to find, there's nothing to know."

"Bad luck, old boy. Bit of a wasted journey, what?"

Stern eased his rump onto the edge of the desk and took one last look around the room. He was thinking though he hadn't found anything of interest here, the trip had certainly not been a waste of time. Between them, Dasti's father and the brigadier had told him a lot about the murdered man. For that alone, it had been worth coming. But still he had to be sure he wasn't missing something. He glanced down at the desk and the book lying there, it reminding him of Dasti's profession and that he still had a clinic to visit before heading home. He reached down and picked up the book. "Atif worked at a clinic here in Lynn, didn't he?"

The brigadier gave a shrug. "Wouldn't know, old boy. Never spoke about his work."

"He never told you what he did, where he worked?"

"Well, of course, when he first came he told me he was a pharmacist. Said he'd be working in the area and needed somewhere to live. He seemed a jolly sort and said he liked this place. I equally liked the look of the lad and that was it. He came and went as he pleased and paid his rent on the dot. I ignored the young fillies he had stay over and we got on splendidly."

"I see." Stern noticed the piece of paper used as a page marker protruding from the pages of the book and casually flicked it open at the spot. He read a couple of lines, frowning at words alien to him, gleaning only it was something to do with the digestive system. About to close the book, he noticed something scribbled on the page marker. He read the words, his brow wrinkling thoughtfully. He paused for a further second before slipping the piece of paper surreptitiously into his pocket and dropping the book back on the desk. "All double Dutch to me," he said, hoiking himself off the desk and offering the Brigadier his hand. "I think that about wraps it up, Brigadier. Thanks very much for your time."

"No problem at all, old chap. Now how about that little snifter, eh?"

Seventeen

It had been a frustrating day for Ralph Armitage. He'd been snowed under with work, but somehow had found time to call a couple of the relevant numbers in his little book. Each one without success. He told himself he shouldn't have been too surprised; the entries had been made more than seven years before, people moved on. But if the note meant what he thought, he just had to make contact somehow. Eventually he gave up, partly because of the work load and again because of the suspicious looks he was getting from his boss. Use of the company phone for private reasons was restricted and to be seen with a mobile clamped to your ear when you were supposed to be concentrating on your work was not tolerated. He would have to somehow hide himself away this evening and try again.

As usual the drive home was slow, the traffic seemingly getting worse by the day. No point in getting frustrated, though, it was all part of modern life. He turned on the radio and tried to relax. As he braked for the umpteenth time, pulling up behind the car in front, his mobile warbled into life. Spotting the police car in the oncoming traffic, he was glad the Audi had Bluetooth hands free.

He hit the button on the steering wheel. "Armitage."

"Did you get a note?"

For that moment the unexpected, amplified question, harsh in the confines of the car, stopped his world. "What? I...er." Disorientated, he scrabbled with the gear lever, releasing the clutch too sharply as he realised the car in front had again moved forward. The police car was now right alongside and a hard-eyed lawman scowled suspicious disapproval at the Audi's sudden uncontrolled jerk forward. Armitage, his mouth dry, kept his eyes to the front. "Who is this?"

"Did you get a note?" The words more insistent this time.

Heart thumping, Armitage tried to collect his thoughts, to recognise the deep muffled voice, but it was indistinct like nothing he'd heard before. He realised he was shaking and cursed softly as once again the car in front ground to a halt. He stopped well short and applied the hand brake, pulling the car out of gear, grateful to be able to relax his trembling legs. "Yes I did, but who is this?"

It was as though the person on the other end hadn't heard his replies. "We should talk."

Slowly it dawned that, though he'd failed to make contact with the others, one of them had managed to find him. He gave a heavy relieved sigh, forcing himself to calm down. Whoever it was had also received the note and they were as anxious as he was. As a result they were being cautious, refusing to say too much over the telephone. He could understand that; phone calls could be traced, conversations recorded. As his grandfather, an old military man, used to say, no names, no pack drill. And, anyway, it didn't matter which one of them it was. He didn't care as long as he wasn't alone, wasn't the only one. Now he had someone to talk to, to discuss the situation with.

"I agree," he said, eager to talk. "It's come back to haunt us, hasn't it?"

"Yes. Everyone hoped it wouldn't, didn't they? But it was inevitable."

"I didn't think... After all this time, but I suppose..."

"So we have to talk," the muffled voice interrupted again. "But not now, not over the phone. We must meet."

Armitage nodded enthusiastically. "I agree, but where are you?"

"I'm here."

"In Northampton?"

"Yes."

Another grateful sigh. "So where, then? When?"

"It has to be tonight. I came here specially, I can't stay longer."

Still Armitage tried to identify the voice and still it eluded him. Deep, but muffled, indistinguishable. Never mind. "Where then?"

"Do you know the park?"

"Eastfield?"

"Yes."

"I know it." He very nearly revealed how close he lived

to the park, but bit his lip, holding back.

"Good. Tonight then. Nine o'clock, by the lake, south side."

"Okay, I'll be there."

~ * ~

At around the time Ralph Armitage ended the call and breathed a deep sigh of relief, Stern was approaching the clinic where Atif Dasti had worked. It looked like an old mansion house, maybe Edwardian or Victorian, Stern had never learned how to tell the difference, situated in walled, gated grounds just off the A148 and a stone's throw from the golf course. Stern pulled through the gates and followed the visitor's 'car park' sign along a gravelled driveway down the side and to the rear of the house. He parked the car and wandered slowly back to the front, scanning the impressive surroundings as he went. A rough guess would be some ten acres and, from the portion he could see, every inch was perfectly maintained. Lawned areas either side of the drive were meticulously manicured and the flower beds landscaped within them trimmed to perfection. The broad six feet plus walls surrounding the place were old and various fruit trees sculptured esplanade fashion along their face provided a perfect backdrop to the colourful shrubs and flowered areas within. This was a labour of love for someone who was an expert, probably an expensive expert, in their field. Stern guessed, if the gardens reflected the quality of the rest of the place, we were talking high class care here. He climbed the steps and pushed his way through the heavy, ornate oak front doors.

Inside he faced an extensive reception area, the floor covered in perfectly smooth, immaculately laid black and white checkerboard stone tiled flooring. A number of heavy, dark wood doors led off the area. They'd probably, Stern thought, been hanging there since day one. They were all closed. Large paintings, some rural settings, others portraits of individuals long gone and, Stern guessed, mostly forgotten, adorned the walls. Bulbous reproduction armchairs and sofas were strategically placed around the area. Looking around, Stern imagined in its original incarnation this was where visitors were met, probably by a butler, and chaperoned to the drawing room or maybe the library, whichever room his Lordship chose to receive them.

A young woman in an immaculate white nurse's uniform sat directly opposite behind a large reception desk. Oak, he guessed again and, even to his untrained eye, undoubtedly original. Probably worth as much as the Hyundai, if not more. As he approached, his footsteps ringing clearly on the beautifully buffed stone floor, she looked up, an automatic, well-practised smile lighting her face. Stern's mind went immediately to the similar situation at Cain Engineering. There the smile was just as radiant, but somehow more natural, more genuine. He wondered why, out of the blue, Melanie Campbell had invaded his thoughts. It wasn't the first time either.

"Good afternoon, sir. Can I help you?"

Stern searched his pockets, finding the piece of paper he'd used to copy the name given him by the local contact at the Lynn nick, the individual he needed to talk to. He checked the name. "Yes, my name is Stern and I'd like to speak to Doctor Peter Lancaster if that's possible."

Her eyes flicked to the PC monitor in front of her, dwarfed on the wide expanse of the desk, its cheap plastic grey totally out of place against the beautiful patina of the dark, age old wood. For a moment long slender fingers with perfectly manicured pale orange nails danced across a keyboard. Finally she looked up, the smile still in place, but now a little unsure. "Is the doctor expecting you, Mr Stern? I'm sorry to have to ask, but I don't seem to have you on his schedule this afternoon."

"No, I don't expect you do, not at this particular time anyway," he admitted. "But the doctor is expecting me to call in at some time. I was in the area and hoped now would be convenient."

"I see. Just one moment and I'll check." She picked up the phone, fingered a button and spoke softly into the receiver. Nodding, she carefully returned the receiver into its cradle. "Doctor Lancaster is in conference right now, Mr Stern, but his secretary says he should be free in fifteen minutes or so." She indicated toward the deep cushioned sofa opposite. "You're very welcome to wait and I'd be happy to get you some tea or coffee, whichever you prefer."

He said, yes, he would wait and coffee would be appreciated. He settled himself on one of the sofas, immediately deciding, though large and impressive, comfort was not one of its main attributes.

No more than fifteen minutes later, as he was taking the last sip of an excellent cup of coffee, a short rotund man with a round scarlet face bundled through a door on the far side of the area. He was dressed in a dark three piece suit over a glowing blue shirt and psychedelic bow tie and bustled busily toward Stern, his hand outstretched. "Mr Stern, sorry to keep you waiting. I hope Janine looked after you." He didn't wait for an answer. "If you'd like to come this way."

Just a few feet from where Stern was sitting, one of the heavy doors led into another room. Here a number of soft chairs were positioned around a central coffee table. Closing the door quietly, the doctor motioned Stern toward a chair and positioned himself opposite. Stern noticed how the closing of the door had a deadening effect on the room. He guessed this to be a consulting room where both good and bad news was conveyed to friends and relatives, it being soundproofed for a good reason.

"Now," Lancaster began. "I'm told you are here about our Mr Dasti." His moonlike face drooped into a well-practiced sadness. "Such a sad case and a severe shock to us all, of course."

"I'm sure," Stern said. "And I hope you understand how vitally important it is for us to find out as much about him, and in particularly his movements immediately prior to his death, as quickly as possible."

"Yes of course." Lancaster puffed out his cheeks and exhaled slowly. "But unfortunately that could prove a little difficult. You see, though Mr Dasti was an extremely competent and highly respected member of the team here, he kept his private life to himself."

"So you wouldn't have any idea why he was in Norfolk at that particular time?"

"None whatsoever."

"I understand he worked for you?"

The doctor gave a nod. "Yes he did. He was assigned to my team from the day he joined us."

"So, regardless of his private life, what can you tell me about his character, how he performed, his relationship with other members of your team?"

Lancaster looked down and gave a sharp cough, maybe a prelude, Stern thought, to an admission. Good or bad? "Well, character wise he was certainly self-opinionated." He raised his eyes and held up a cautionary hand. "Not in a bad way, you understand. He just had his views, his way of doing things and expected others to... Well..."

Stern took advantage of what he saw as an embarrassing pause to alleviate the doctor's plight. "Doctor, I was told by another source that Mr Dasti was a particularly dominant character. Is that what you're trying to tell me?"

Lancaster took a breath and sighed. "It's not in my nature to speak ill of the dead, Mr Stern."

"No, I'm sure it isn't, but in this case, if we are to find who carried out the killing, it's important we know things as they really were. Nothing you say can harm Dasti now, Doctor. Regardless of what he was like, he deserves justice and we can only give him that by finding his killer. What you tell me here will go no further, I can assure you of that, and may well be of significant importance to our investigation. So...?" Stern cocked his head questioningly and waited.

Lancaster leaned back in his chair and eyeballed Stern

Edge of Reason
A. W. Lambert

for some moments, his lips a tight line. "Dasti was an excellent pharmacist," he began finally. "And I mean excellent. He achieved a first at university and his knowledge in his field was exceptional, particularly when you realise how relatively young he was. We were all truly delighted when he accepted our offer to come here."

"Somehow I feel a *but* coming on," Stern interrupted softly.

Lancaster shook his head sadly. "No point in beating about the bush. Dasti hadn't been with us but a short while when his true character came to the fore. In short, Mr Stern, he was the most arrogant, demanding and most obnoxious individual I've ever met in my entire life."

"Ah."

"Once he got his feet under the table, everything had to be done his way. Everyone had to bend to his whim. If for any reason things didn't turn out as expected, it was never his fault. As I've already said, he was very good, exceptional even, but he wasn't perfect; he made mistakes. Nothing dangerous, you understand, just minor, irritating lapses of concentration. Mainly because of his casual approach to the job.

"He was so laid back it didn't seem to worry him in the least. If things went pear-shaped, even if he was to blame, Dasti wasn't beyond pointing the finger elsewhere and washing his hands of the situation. If anyone dared to criticise or, heaven forbid, challenge him, he would fly into a rage, fiercely protesting his innocence and demanding an apology. I could quote examples, but it would be of no further consequence. The man is dead, Mr Stern, and if I'm honest, I'm not happy with what I've said already."

"I think I've got the picture, Doctor." Stern thought for a moment. "I assume other members of your staff felt the same way?"

"Well, it would be wrong of me to speak for others," the doctor conceded. "I can only tell you that it wasn't uncommon for other members of the team to come to me with similar complaints. Those at his level hated working with him and his subordinates were scared of him. He was a big strong man and his tantrums could be pretty intimidating to the junior staff."

"To your knowledge, was there anyone in particular that disliked him more than the others, maybe bore a particular grudge for some reason or other?"

It took a second or two, but Lancaster realised the implication of Stern's question. "Oh no, Mr Stern. If you're implying that anyone here could have..." He gave a vigorous shake of his head. "Unthinkable, Mr Stern. Unthinkable."

"I'm implying nothing at all, Doctor. I'm merely asking routine questions so as to familiarise myself with the murdered man and his movements. You should read nothing into my questions other than that. Anyway," Stern pushed himself out of the chair. "that will do for the time being. If I need to talk to you again, I'll call and make an appointment." He reached the door and turned. "By the way, during the time he was with you did you ever hear Dasti mention the name Martin Baldwin?"

Lancaster shook his head. "It's not a name I recall."

"Thank you, Doctor." He pulled open the door and left.

Eighteen

Stern had a lot on his mind and sleep hadn't come easily. He spent most of the night awake, or so it felt, his thoughts ricocheting among the three interviews he'd carried out the previous day. Dasti's father admitting to the rebellious side of his son, bitter to the point of completely disowning him and possibly more, and the haunting, wrecked eyes of his distraught wife peering from the other end of the hallway. Then there was the Brigadier, happily confirming Dasti's powerful personality, praising him as perfect officer material, and Dr Lancaster describing the dead man as the most obnoxious individual he'd ever met in his entire life, a view it seemed held by the rest of the clinic staff.

If all this wasn't bad enough, from time to time the overpowering image of Frank Runcie came to the fore. Had Stern really agreed to work for him? And there had also been the occasional digression to Melanie Campbell. He had to admit she'd impressed him, left her mark. In fact he couldn't remember thinking about a female, other than Annie, in the way he was thinking of Melanie

Campbell right now. He'd tried not to dwell, pushing guilty thoughts from his mind.

At six he'd given up, thrown off the duvet and dragged himself out of bed. A vigorous, sweaty half an hour on the rowing machine followed by a shower and a leisurely breakfast had seen him in the office just before eight. Now he had the old chair rocked back as far as it would go, his heels resting on the edge of the desk. Thinking mode. Well, wondering more than thinking.

Wondering how the hell, in the blink of an eye, he'd suddenly found himself embroiled in a triangle of events that, although on the face of it appeared separate, were, as far as he was concerned anyway, intrinsically linked. Andrew's missing friend, Martin Baldwin, was certainly linked to the disappearance of Cain Engineering's designs and Melanie's sighting in the Cain car park pretty well confirmed he was also linked to Atif Dasti, the man found drowned in the ditch.

But that wasn't all he was wondering…as well as succumbing to Runcie's pleas, he'd also allowed himself to be coerced into accepting a secondment to the Norfolk Police Force. Stern back on the force; how the dickens had that happened? Okay, if he were honest, even after all this time, he still missed true authoritative policing. He guessed he always would. It was one of the reasons why he so enjoyed his association with David O'Connor. But he wasn't sure his decision to accept O'Connor's offer of officially being part of it all again had been wise. Sure it was only for a limited period and only on the case he was working anyway, but he still wasn't sure. He'd grown too used to being a free agent, calling his own tune. Even when he was in the Met, he'd been known as a bit of a loose cannon, often openly rebelling against the strangling bureaucracy and petty politics that clogged the system. Still, it was done now, so hopefully during this secondment he'd be able to use David as a buffer and stay well away from all that rubbish.

He turned his mind back to the case in hand and what he had learned from yesterday's visits. Dasti's father had made it clear his son had committed a cardinal sin, crossed an irretrievable line and even if he had lived there, would have been no turning back, no reconciliation. Now he would do the right thing; he would pay for the funeral, but that was all…his son would be history.

The discussions with the Brigadier and Doctor Lancaster had revealed plenty about Dasti himself, particularly about the murdered man's character. The Brigadier saw it from a military man's perspective. He appreciated the dominant spirit, saw it as a positive attribute. Not so with Dasti's workmates, who obviously felt threatened, first by Dasti's advanced expertise in his field, but mostly, Stern felt, by his arrogant, demanding attitude. So two questions: Could Dasti's father have gone as far as murdering his son for his transgressions? Or could Dasti have upset someone at the clinic severely enough for them to have killed him?

Neither could be ruled out and each should be investigated further. But there was a fly in the ointment, something that led Stern to believe that neither of the options was likely. He dropped his feet to the floor and pulled the old chair up to the desk. As he reached for the piece of paper lying there…the piece of paper he'd found being used as a book marker in Dasti's pharmaceutical text book at his flat…he heard the sound of the outer office door quietly opening and closing again.

He glanced down at his watch, twenty past eight. Most mornings Cherry was in before him, but twenty past eight was pushing it, even for her. Maybe with Rob's recent proposal uppermost in her mind she hadn't been able to sleep. Kept waking up and looking at that big sparkly thing on her finger. He smiled at the silly thought. But then there was silence, not the usual rattle across the office of those ridiculous spikes she wore on her feet.

"Hello?" The voice was male and tentative.

Stern climbed out of the chair and crossed to the door and peered into the outer office. The man was standing uncertainly inside the outer door. He was six two at least and built like a barn. His fair hair was cut short, but not quite a crew cut and bright eyes shone from a pale, chubby face. He was dressed in dark blue chinos and a leather jacket. He was holding a folder.

"Can I help you?"

"I'm Keen, sir."

Stern couldn't help the tease. "I'm pleased for you, but who are you and what d'you want?"

The man gave an uncertain smile. "You can't imagine how many times I've had that thrown at me, sir."

Stern instantly regretted the crack. "Yeah, I guess so. Suffered it myself in the past. So your name is Keen?"

"Yes, sir." A troubled frown creased his forehead.

"Detective Constable Colin Keen." He came forward and handed the folder to Stern, almost standing to attention. "Inspector O'Connor sent me, sir. Didn't he tell you I was coming?"

Stern shook his head. "No, it must have slipped his mind." So this was the surprise David had promised. He studied Keen for a moment or two, noting the young man's uncertainty, the past coming back. Maybe he understood. "How long have you been out of uniform, Constable?"

Keen looked down at his boots. "This is my second week, sir."

Bingo. Stern gave a slow, knowing nod of his head. "Guessed so." He'd seen it all before, even done it himself in the past. Nobody wants a rookie. Send him to someone else to break in.

David, you crafty bastard. Thanks a bunch.

Stern held up the folder. "What's this?"

"It's for your information, sir. A breakdown of my service so far, together with details of the case I've been sent to help you with. Oh, and a warrant card authorising your position with CID."

Stern looked up into the sparkling, earnest eyes. "Right, Keen, whether you'll be staying or not is debateable, but one thing's for sure, I haven't got my knighthood yet, so for a start you cut out the 'sir' thing, okay?" Shaking his head, he turned back into his office. "And if you once call me 'Guv,' as big as you are, I'll kick your arse out of here, got it?"

Twenty minutes later, the outer door sounded again. This time the familiar clatter of those heels across the wooden floor announced Cherry's arrival. Seeing his office door ajar she called out, "Morning boss. What's up, the old insomnia set in again?" She poked her head through the office door and saw Keen. "Oh, sorry I didn't know..."

Stern grinned. "Cherry, come and meet Detective Constable Colin Keen. David sent him over to solve all our problems."

As Cherry approached, the colour had already started to creep up Keen's neck.

Later, having instructed Cherry to take Keen into the outer office on the pretence of showing him the Stern Investigations ropes, Stern punched the buttons on the phone.

"O'Connor."

"David, its Theo."

"Theo, I was about to call you..."

"I bet you were, you crafty sod," Stern weighed in. "What on earth made you think I'd want this lad you've sent over?"

"He's a good lad, Theo. You read his record?"

"'Course I have and yes, he sounds okay, but I thought it was you who were short staffed, not me. For crying out loud, David, that's why you recruited me, wasn't it?"

"Yes I know, but it's active help I need, Theo. I was really pissed off when he turned up here. What my Super was thinking of when he okayed Division to lumber me with him I don't know. Right now the last thing I need is the responsibility of breaking in a rookie. There just isn't time. But it's different with you; he'll be your key into wherever you go. He's a serving detective..."

"You mean, instead of a temporary lackey," Stern broke in sharply.

"Okay, if you like, but listen, Theo, he's Keen by name and super keen by nature. Believe me, there's nothing he won't tackle and he'll benefit so much from just being alongside you for a while. A few days, well maybe a week or two under your wing and he might even be of some use to me. But enough about Keen, that wasn't what I was going to call you about..."

"Maybe not, but I still don't think it's right you just sending him over here like this. You might have..."

"*Theo*, will you put a sock in it for just a minute, for God's sake. I'm trying to tell you there's been another one. It's happened again."

"What?" Stern was stunned by O'Connor's unusually sharp words.

"It's happened again, Theo. Same MO...back of the head bashed in, then drowned and nothing on him, stripped of all he possessed."

All thoughts of the young man in the next office were instantly erased. "When did this happen?"

"Some time last evening. Another dog walker. Found the body around nine."

"Male?"

"Yup."

"Where?"

"Eastfield Park, Northampton.

Northampton?" Stern reached forward and picked up the piece of paper he was studying when interrupted by Keen's arrival. He read it again, then said, "David, I think we have a major problem here. We need to talk."

Nineteen

Lisa Armitage was young, Stern suspected, not yet thirty and small even before the tragedy that a few hours before had destroyed her life. Now, a shrunken, terrified wreck, she was curled into the corner of a sofa seemingly a million sizes too big for her. Constantly dabbing at swollen, tear destroyed eyes with a long since sodden wodge of tissues, she clutched the hand of the WPC Family Liaison Officer sitting alongside her. It couldn't be true, could it? Yesterday morning she'd lain comfortably in her bed, her little boy curled into her side, both receiving a cheerful kiss from her husband as he left for work. A normal day in her normal happy life. Now, less than twenty four hours later, that same life was in shreds and only hell and all its terrors lay ahead. She stared out into the room, uncomprehending, totally and utterly punch drunk.

Stern had seen it many times before; lives shattered by violent acts, people totally destroyed by the unexpected loss of a loved one. He'd also faced the heartrending task of delivering the news, taken that first unbelieving volley from a totally unsuspecting recipient. Yes, he'd faced it many times, but that was a million years ago, in a different life. Now with all those old feelings again rushing through him, he just wanted to be somewhere else. Anywhere but here.

Through his Superintendent, O'Connor had made the contact and again received authorisation for Stern to make the trip, to record a statement from the wife, survey the murder scene and talk to the locals on the ground. "Get there as soon as you can, Theo," David had instructed. "And take young Keen with you. He needs blooding and this'll certainly do that. We'll tie up when you get back."

It was just past four when they arrived, the hundred and fifteen miles having taken a little over three hours. True to O'Connor's word, the local Detective Inspector, a heavy set, bearded Scot named Buchanan, was waiting for them. Buchanan, a gnarled lifelong street copper, had shaken Stern's hand showing no resentment to an outsider poking his nose into the local investigation. He had made it clear, however, that he would take the lead when questioning the wife. Stern had no objections. He was being tolerated here, a favour from one brass to another...he knew his place. Besides, it was bad enough being in the same room as the distraught young wife without having to lead the questioning.

As instructed, notebook at the ready, Keen took up a position standing quietly in the farthest corner of the room. For some reason the family Labrador chose to tuck itself against his legs, its ears flat against its head, looking as if solemnly considering itself the cause of all the trouble.

"Mrs Armitage," Buchanan began, his voice surprisingly soft and gentle for such a big man. "First I must say how sorry we all are for your tragic loss. And I apologise for having to put you through this so soon after such a devastating blow. But timing is important and the first few hours after such a crime are the most important of all. I do hope you can understand and can bear with us. I really will be as brief as possible."

The woman stared at him with glazed eyes and Stern wondered how much they were going to get from her at this early stage. But Buchanan was right; the first few hours after any such crime were the most important. The longer time went on, the farther away the perpetrator would be able to move. Every scrap of available evidence had to be coordinated as early after the event as possible.

The WPC eased the wet soggy mess from the young woman's fingers and replaced it with a fresh, dry wodge of tissue, giving the hand a gentle squeeze. "Take your time, Lisa," she whispered.

Buchanan paused for a few moments, aware it was taking time for things to sink in, for their words to penetrate, before cautiously continuing. "Just try to remember exactly what happened last evening," he said gently. "I mean after your husband got home from work."

Lisa Armitage clutched the fresh tissues between her hands as if in prayer, a deep frown of concentration corrugating her young forehead. "He got in around six," she said, her voice little more than a croaking whisper. "He gave us all a hug, then went upstairs to change." Her eyes sought Buchanan's as if what she was about to say was important. "You see he always does that as soon as he gets in. He says he can't wait to get out of his working clothes."

Buchanan smiled. "I think most of us feel that way after a hard day. Did he seem okay? Not troubled or maybe worried about anything?"

"No, he seemed fine. Maybe a little tired, but nothing unusual. He changed and we had dinner, then he played with Timmy for a while..." She stopped, jerking forward, her eyes flicking fearfully round the room. "Where is Timmy, what's happened to Timmy?"

The WPC laid her hand gently on the girl's arm. "Don't worry, Lisa. Timmy's fast asleep in his room and we have someone looking over him. Your mum and dad are on their way, remember? They'll be here soon."

Sinking back in the chair, she gave a huge, shuddering sigh and dabbed at sore red-rimmed eyes.

"You were telling us about when your husband came home," Buchanan prompted softly. "You said he seemed okay, no worries."

"That's right. It was only later, when I told him about the call. He seemed to change then."

"Call? What call are we talking about?"

She screwed her eyes shut, straining to concentrate, to remember. "I don't know, I think maybe an hour before he got home. It was a call from one of his colleagues at work. They asked if he was at home. I told them he hadn't arrived yet. They said that was a pity because there was something important he should know, something he would have to sort out for the following day."

"Did they say what this something was?"

She shook her head. "No, just that he needed the information because he may have to work on it during the evening."

"Did he usually work during the evenings?"

"Sometimes, when he was snowed under at work. Then I would leave him alone in the other room so he could... He could..." The words faltered on trembling lips.

"It's okay, Lisa." the WPC eyeballed Buchanan and reached for a glass of water standing on the side. The big man took the hint and relaxed back in the chair.

Lisa Armitage took the water, whispered her thanks and drank gratefully.

They sat in tense silence for several minutes, waiting, giving her time. Eventually she looked again to Buchanan. "I'm okay now."

"Good girl," Buchanan soothed. "Just a few more questions and we'll be done. Now, about this call?"

Lisa took a breath, her fingers clasped tightly around the half empty glass. "They seemed concerned and said if Ralph had a mobile they would make contact and give him the information. I said that would be okay because Ralph has a mobile and even if he was in the car he would answer because he has hands free."

"So you gave them his mobile number?"

"Yes, I..." She stopped, eyes widening, her mouth dropping open. "I didn't mean... It wasn't because I gave them...?"

Buchanan quickly held up a beefy hand. "No, no, Lisa, don't worry. I'm sure the call had nothing at all to do with what happened to your husband. But we need to know just so we can check with Ralph's workplace and see who it was that called. It's all just routine." He gave a reassuring smile.

Stern caught Buchanan's eye, tilting his head toward the girl, requesting a word. Buchanan nodded his approval.

"Lisa," Stern said softly. "Could I ask if your husband had recently received a letter or note that may have concerned him at all?"

She looked confused. "A letter?"

"Yes. Anything that may have come through the post, or maybe have been dropped through the letterbox, anything unusual, out of the ordinary?"

She shook her head. "I deal with all the mail. Even when it's early, Ralph always brings it to me. He always has."

"And there's been nothing that's puzzled you at all?"

"No, nothing."

Stern smiled reassuringly and deferred back to Buchanan.

"Okay, Lisa," Buchanan came back. "Just one last thing. You said your husband changed when you told him about the call. How did he change?"

Again the deep frown. "I don't know really. He just became quiet, seemed thoughtful. I asked him if he was okay and he told me he was fine. He said he was just thinking about work."

"Okay, then what happened?"

Her face crumpling, her eyes scanning the room, finally resting on the dog at Keen's feet. "Then he said it was time to take Mabel for her walk. I told him she was okay because I'd taken her out earlier, but he insisted."

"Do you remember what time this was, Lisa?"

Her brow wrinkled, thinking difficult. "Yes, it was just before nine," she said after some seconds. "I remember reminding him he would miss *New Tricks*. It was his favourite programme, always made him laugh. He said not to worry he'd just give Mabel a quick walk so she could relieve herself." She gave a sad resigned shrug of her narrow shaking shoulders. "They went out and that was the last I..." She dropped her face into her hands and began to sob uncontrollably.

~ * ~

The three of them were standing inside the blue and white taped off area of lakeside. The body was gone, but a number of uniforms were scouring the immediate area. Stern turned his back to the lake and looked into the thick bushes running down to the water's edge.

"Hidden in there, you think?"

"Ay, it looks that way. The wife said he went out around nine. The light would have been fading fast." He pointed to the thickest shrubbery. "Tucked away in there he'd never be seen."

Stern nodded his agreement. "And a round blunt instrument, right?" He looked across at Keen, ensuring he was still taking notes.

"Ay, back of the head. Poor sod wouldn't have known what hit him. After a blow like that, it wouldn't have taken much effort to hold his head under the water, just to finish him off."

"And he was cleaned out?"

"So he was. Not so much as a penny piece on the man. The wife said he had his mobile with him when he left the house. Never went anywhere without it. She gave us the number and we tried calling it."

Stern gave a knowing smile. "Switched off."

"Ay and we wouldn't expect anything else, would we?" He turned and studied Stern for a moment. "What was all that about a note or letter?"

Stern knew Buchanan would ask the question. "You know I'm here because we think there could be a link to a death we're investigating in Norfolk?"

"Ay."

"Well, I'm flying a kite here, but something I found at the Norfolk victim's flat leads me to believe it's possible he may have been threatened before he was killed."

"You mean a threatening note or letter?"

Stern searched through his pockets, finally producing the piece of paper he'd found being used as a page marker in the pharmaceutical book on Dasti's desk.

Buchanan scanned the words. "Think it's relevant?"

Stern gave a shrug. "Right now I've no idea, but it's certainly a threat and for that reason alone it has to be checked. It's an outside chance, I know, but it could mean our Norfolk victim was warned before he was killed."

"And because this one has similarities you think it's worth checking for a note here, too?"

"A bit of a punt, but yes."

Buchanan gave a thoughtful nod of his head. "A punt, maybe, but I agree it's worth checking. I'll keep my eyes open at this end."

"Thanks, I'd appreciate it. You realise if the two are linked, we could be facing something pretty nasty here."

"It had crossed my mind." Buchanan pulled out a packet of cigarettes and lit up. He looked out across the lake and took a lungful, exhaling slowly. "When they said you were coming, told me your name, it rang a bell. Then I remembered; it was all over the papers, way back...Manchester and the stabbing."

Stern gave a tight lipped smile. "Two thousand and three, would you believe? Feels like a lifetime ago."

"But they put you out to grass."

"They did that."

"So why this then? Why are you here?"

Stern explained how, after being dumped from the Met, he'd moved to Norfolk and set up Stern Investigations. Then he related how Andrew's call about his friend Martin Baldwin had led to the link with the murdered Atif Dasti and subsequently to this.

Buchanan gave a beefy grin. "So, for a bit anyway, you're back on the payroll."

"I am, but I'm not sure if it's such a good move," Stern mused.

The grin widened. "Bollocks, who're you kidding, man? It's still there, inside I mean. You know as well as I do, wild horses wouldn't have made you refuse such an offer."

The bugger of it was, Stern had to admit, the old veteran was right; it was a battle between head and heart...and in this case the head hadn't stood a chance.

Twenty

O'Connor had kept to his word and driven from Norwich so Stern didn't have to attend the station. Now the four of them were settled in Stern's office for the debrief. Stern ensured Cherry was involved, not wanting her to feel ousted by the new arrival. She was sitting alongside Keen, both with notebooks at the ready. Competition? Stern had yet to see how Keen performed, but guessed he'd have to go some to keep up with Cherry.

As Stern had made the trip to Northampton and seen the situation first hand, O'Connor was happy to defer the proceedings to him. It brought back memories of debriefings back then; not a room full of people with photos pinned up and white boards covered in relevant notes, but still more formal than the usual laid back Stern Investigations, 'grab a cup of tea and we'll have a chat' he'd grown so used to with Cherry.

"Okay, there's no doubt it's murder," he began. "And the MO appears to be the same as for Atif Dasti."

"Incapacitated then drowned," O'Connor confirmed.

"Yes, a blow to the back of the head, then,

unconscious, he was held under the water. The doc at the scene said her first guess at the weapon would be a hammer. Maybe the reverse side of a ball pein. She was cautious about that though, warned us not to take it as gospel. Said she'd be able to confirm more, give a full report after the autopsy. George Buchanan said he'd keep me informed."

"No problems with the local lads then?" O'Connor again.

"No, Buchanan's a good man," Stern confirmed. "He's done the rounds, knows the score. I gave him the full SP up front and we were good from square one."

O'Connor gave a satisfied nod. "Excellent. So Armitage then...no sign of resistance? No fight?"

Stern shook his head. "After a smack on the head like he got, there wouldn't have been. He wouldn't have known what hit him. After that, all the killer had to do was drag him to the water and hold him under. Job done."

Pen poised, Cherry chimed in. "Was all his stuff taken like Dasti?"

"Yup, clean as a whistle."

"So could it be robbery?"

"It's a thought," Stern conceded. "Except for Dasti. Sure the two murders are geographically miles apart, but I don't believe it's a coincidence they're so similar. They look to be more like specific targets, not just random robberies."

"I'll go with that," O'Connor said. "I don't know why everything was taken from these two, but whatever the reason, I think it was secondary to the killing. Anyway, if you've knocked someone unconscious and all you want to do is rob him, why kill him?"

Cherry came back quickly. "Maybe because he knows who you are."

"Good point," Keen ventured tentatively. "Just because he was hit from behind, it doesn't mean he didn't know who it was. Remember how keen he was to take the dog out, even though his wife had already walked it."

"Maybe an arranged meet, you mean? The phone call, right?" Stern said.

"Yes." Keen looked pleased with himself.

O'Connor glanced from one to the other. "What phone call?"

Stern described the phone call received by Lisa Armitage asking for her husband's mobile number. "The caller said they were calling from work," he explained. "But Buchanan checked; nobody from the company admitted to making the call."

O'Connor scratched thoughtfully at his chin. "I see. You're saying, having got the wife to hand over the mobile number, the killer called Armitage and arranged a meet in the park."

"That's what Colin's inferring," Stern said. "And if he's right, it could mean being hit from behind doesn't necessarily mean Armitage didn't know his killer. I mean, it's more likely you'd agree to meet someone you know, rather than a strange voice over the phone, isn't it?"

"Of course," O'Connor agreed. "And although, in Dasti's case, we don't know of any phone calls, he could have been lured to a meet in the same way. It would corroborate our theory of the two cases being linked, even though they're some distance apart."

"A serial killer?" Cherry said with trepidation.

"Whoa." O'Connor gave a vigorous shake of the head. "Christ, Cherry, don't go down that road. The mere suggestion there might be a serial killer out there will send the tabloids into orbit. It don't bear thinking about."

"But with so much looking similar in each case, it can't be ruled out, can it?" Cherry insisted.

"No, of course not, but until we're sure, we don't even say the word."

Stern was pulling thoughtfully at his bottom lip. "Maybe not, but there is one thing." He pulled the piece of paper from his pocket and handed it to O'Connor, who first read it silently to himself then again out loud.

Murderers all four
A killer every one
One by one you have to pay
Justice will be done

All eyes turned toward Stern. "Where the hell did this come from?" O'Connor asked.

"When I was at Dasti's flat, I was looking through one of his pharmaceutical text books," he explained. "At first this looked to be a folded scrap of paper he'd used as a book mark. It was when I opened it at the page and read what was written on it I realised it could be important. I palmed it just in case. I was going to tell you about it when you hit me with the Armitage thing, and insisted I went straight to Northampton. It may have nothing to do with anything, but..."

"But you don't believe that," O'Connor cut in.

"No. I don't. I asked the question in Northampton, asked the wife if maybe her husband had received a note or letter. She knew of nothing."

"Doesn't mean her husband didn't get one."

"No it doesn't," Stern agreed. "And it is possible. His wife told us he was an early bird, always up first in the morning, especially now she's pregnant. Which meant he got to see the post first. According to her, he took little notice of it, just handed it over for her to deal with later."

"But if he'd seen something suspicious, he could have pocketed it before handing over the rest," O'Connor broke in.

"Exactly my thoughts," Stern came back. "And if somehow we can establish that, it will give us a convincing link between the two killings. Anyway, I showed the note to Buchanan; he thought it was possible, too. Promised to let me know immediately if he came up with anything."

"Good," O'Connor said. "It's what we need to prove our hypothesis, to give us a solid link between Dasti and Armitage."

"If there is one," Cherry ventured.

"There is. I'd lay money on it," Stern insisted. "And d'you know what? Baldwin's in there somewhere, too."

"You could be right, Theo," O'Connor agreed. "But seeing as Baldwin is out of the loop right now, we'll have to work on what we've got."

"Agreed," Stern said. "Which means digging out more about Dasti and Armitage, look into their background and see if we find that link." He looked across the office. "Colin, you take Dasti, and Cherry, you see what more you can find out about Armitage." Glancing again toward O'Connor, he said, "In the meantime, let's hope Baldwin doesn't suddenly turn up like the other two."

~ * ~

It was late afternoon when O'Connor left. The day had begun cool, but slowly the temperature had risen and even now there was still a comfortable spring heat in the low sun. Leaving the office, Stern strolled with O'Connor along the high street to the car park where he'd left his car. Stern wanted a few moments alone with his friend and new boss.

"So what's the score with young Keen?" he asked as they weaved their way through meandering late shoppers.

"Score?"

"Oh c'mon David, no bullshit, please. One minute you're so short of staff you come to an oldie like me for help, next you've got a surplus you can't cope with." He didn't wait for an answer. "Tell you what; let me have a guess. Keen is the son, or maybe the nephew or grandson of a friend of your Super who wants him looked after, broken in gently. And with you lot up to your earlobes, he sees me as an easy option." He glanced across at his friend. "How am I doing?"

Reaching the car park, they strolled over to the car. O'Connor wrinkled his nose distastefully, the acrid smoke of a gently chugging North Norfolk Preservation line steam locomotive drifting across the car park. "Now I know why they changed to diesel and electric," he said. "What a stink."

Stern laughed. "Don't knock it...it's part of our heritage. That station's been there since eighteen eighty-seven, I'll have you know. A lot of people work hard to keep it going."

O'Connor hit the remote and pulled open the car door. "They shouldn't bother. We're supposed to be cutting back on pollution, aren't we?"

Stern held onto his friend's arm, preventing him from sliding onto the car. "You're avoiding my question, David. I want to know who Keen belongs to. Come clean or he's back with you tomorrow and I pull out of the case."

That would never happen and they both knew it, but O'Connor knew Stern wasn't going to let this rest. With a sigh he leaned back against the car. "You are one definite pain in the arse, Theo, you know that?"

Stern grinned. "I know, but I bet I'm not far wrong, am I?"

"You are, my friend, very wrong. And your memory's crap too."

"Memory? What's that supposed to mean?"

O'Connor gave a sad shake of the head, holding Stern's gaze for just a moment before saying simply, "Jimmy Keen?"

"Jimmy Keen? What the hell..." The smile dropped from Stern's face as slowly, very slowly, an ancient event tucked away in the deepest cavity of his mind, a place where 'things best forgotten' were buried, clawed its way to the surface. "Oh bollocks." He closed his eyes and took a very deep breath, letting out a mammoth sigh. "It never registered. Not for a second."

"Obviously not and it would have been best left alone," O'Connor admonished.

"But why me?"

O'Connor rested his hand on Stern's arm. "I asked myself that very same question when he was foisted on me, but I had explicit instructions, I had no say in the matter, and anyway I didn't know the history, did I? It was all before my time. So I looked it up in the archives. Then I understood. You were there, Theo. It was you who held him, had his head in your lap, talked him through those last moments. You were the last person Jimmy Keen ever saw in this life."

Stern felt his heart lurch at his friend's words, the memory, thought to be buried forever, forcing its way inexorably to the fore. Sharp sounds and images, the bile in his throat, returning with a rush. He swallowed hard and gritted his teeth. "So tell me."

O'Connor held up his hands, a defensive gesture. "Don't shoot the messenger, Theo. I only know what the brass chose to tell me."

"And that was?"

"It was his wife; she never forgot. When her boy insisted in following in his father's boots, she promised herself, when the time was right, he should meet the man who risked everything in an attempt to save his father's life. The man she said her son should aspire to."

"Shit."

"Jimmy Keen's Queen's Gallantry Medal still holds sway, Theo. She went to the very top, asked the right people. Now son Colin is sitting in your office. Not a thing I could do about it."

"But I didn't, did I? I didn't save his life."

"No you didn't, but the record shows you nearly lost your own trying. But for you he would have died alone. His wife never forgot that."

"I know, she sent me a letter; words that could break your heart." He gave a heavy sigh at the memory. "Does the boy know?"

"No. The mother asked for advice on that one. The brass decided no. Frightened of hero worship, I guess. As far as Keen is concerned, you're just someone loaded with experience he can gain from."

"Good, that's something anyway." He thought for a quiet moment then said, "Hey, wait a minute, does this mean I was only recruited so I could babysit young Keen?"

O'Connor slid into the car. "As far as I was concerned, absolutely not. I shoved my request to recruit you up the chain before I knew anything about Keen." He started to pull the door closed. "Mind you, whether it had anything to do with my request being accepted so quickly, I don't know." He grinned up at Stern. "Doubt it though; that would be too much of a coincidence, and you don't believe in coincidence, do you, Theo?" He pulled the door closed before Stern could answer.

Stern stood for some time after O'Connor had driven

off. He watched as the old hissing steam train, smoke billowing, shunted away from the station, but his mind was elsewhere, in a different place a lifetime ago. It was some seconds before he became aware of his mobile warbling its heart out. He quickly pulled it from his pocket.

"Stern."

"Theo, it's Melanie Campbell."

The call dragging him away from the disturbing past, Stern crossed the car park and headed back along the high street. "Melanie. This is a surprise."

"Am I interrupting anything?"

"No, not at all. It's nice to hear from you. Is anything wrong?"

"No nothing wrong at all." There was a short silence then, "Theo, you're going to think me dreadfully forward, but I enjoyed our evening together so much I wondered if maybe you'd like to do it again?"

Instantly transported to a happier state of mind, thoughts of past unhappy times and of the young detective constable waiting in the office evaporated. Since their evening together the previous week, he'd several times almost picked up the phone and called to ask her out again. Each time he'd backed away and he didn't really know why. Was he afraid of rejection, or was Annie, as far away as she was, still pulling the strings? Well now he knew he had no fears of rejection, at least.

"Theo, please say if it's not convenient or if..."

"No, far from it," he said quickly. "I would like to do it again, really." He'd reached the bakery and, pushing his way inside, he squeezed passed several customers and made his way up the short stairway to the office. "When would you like to meet?"

"I'm free this evening. Is that too soon?"

"No, that would be great. What time shall I pick you up?"

Cherry and Keen, enjoying a coffee at Cherry's desk, glanced up as he came through the door. Cherry heard the last few words of the conversation and wondered why the boss had that silly grin on his face.

Twenty-one

Mo Rahman sat staring at the plate, his food hardly touched.

"Mo? Are you alright? Is something the matter?"

Mo looked up and saw his mother viewing him with concern. She was as vigilant as ever, her four children, even in adulthood, still the centre of her universe, He forced a smile. "No, Mum, I'm fine. I was just thinking about the shop."

"Well, don't look so worried," his father chimed in. "Haven't I already said the shop looks fine. It's probably the best it's ever been. You've done a good job, son."

"Is it the wedding? Are you worried about the wedding?" His mother again, frowning, seeing beyond his weak excuse.

The business was not his mother's domain. She was not expected, nor did she want to have anything to do with the chain of shops her now wealthy husband had built up in the fifty years since he had first come to the country. Her job was family, her children. The three daughters had left the fold, had established families of their own and were producing the expected grandchildren. Only Mo was still at home. He had followed in his father's footsteps, qualifying as a pharmacist and moving into the family business. He was running just the one shop right now, but the future had already been laid out for him. The marriage, an arranged coupling, was programmed to happen in six months' time and Mo knew well enough he would have to do what was necessary to continue the Rahman dynasty.

But that was okay by Mo. The young woman he'd had chosen for him was a beauty and there had been a spark from the very first meeting. He had no doubt their future would be blissful and productive. That would make his father happy and if Dad was happy, then all was well in Mo's world.

And so it had been until the postman had called two days before.

He pushed the worrying thoughts from his mind. "The wedding? No, of course not, Mother. Why would I be worried? I can't wait to be married."

"What then?" His mother may have nothing to do with the business, but she had everything to do with her offspring, and she could read every one of them like a book, particularly Mo. He could see she was suspicious of his weak excuse and knew when she got her teeth into something she shook it till it rattled. Or in her children's case, until she got to the truth. He had to come up with a more plausible story.

"It's really nothing. I just think, as good as the shop has turned out, I think one of the displays could be better placed. It's just a small change but I was thinking I could do it after work one evening."

His father gave a happy chuckle. "There's a chip off the old block, Mother. It's business, business, business with our Mo. Thank goodness we managed one boy in our brood. After the first three, I thought we would have to go on forever."

It was a struggle but under the still suspicious eye of his mother, Mo managed to finish his meal. He excused himself and retired to his room on the pretence of contacting his bride-to-be and sending some emails. In his room, he pulled out the note he had received at the shop and read it for the hundredth time.

Murderers all four
A killer every one
One by one you have to pay
Justice will be done
Number 1. The local North Norfolk Newspaper tells the story
Number 2 soon.
Guess who's Number 3?

Mo laid the note to one side and fired up his laptop. He called up the search engine and started looking. He'd had the note for two days and this was the first chance he'd had to react to it. His days had been totally consumed at the shop and his evenings spent dealing with the demands of his family and his intended. Tonight the pressure was off; his parents were about to leave for a visit with friends and his soon to be wife was having a girlie night in. He would phone her, of course, it was expected, but that would be later. Right now the time was his.

When he'd first read the note, he hadn't understood. He'd even checked the address on the envelope; maybe the postman had delivered it in error. But there was no stamp, no postmark, just his name and the address of the shop. The note must have been delivered by hand, dropped into the shop's post box, maybe before the postman had arrived, before any of them had arrived.

And it read like a threat. Initially a frightening thought had invaded his mind. So much so, he'd completely forgotten the time and his assistant, Sally, had come to find him, her sudden appearance in the little back room of the shop jolting him from his troubled reverie. It had never happened before and, guilt ridden, he'd had to push such ridiculous thoughts from his mind, telling himself too much time had passed, it couldn't possibly be. He'd tucked the note away and forced himself to concentrate on the job.

But frequently over the last two days, the threatening words on the note had worryingly invaded his mind. He'd tried to appease himself by asking why anyone would want to threaten him. He was a good, clean living, law abiding citizen. He was conscientious about his work, doing whatever he could to help his customers, frequently receiving praise for his dedication and compassion. So why him? And why a local Norfolk newspaper? Not just Norfolk, but North Norfolk. Mo had never been to Norfolk, didn't even know anyone living there. He'd been born and raised here in Bradford, any excursions away from the City being brief, his father totally dedicated to building the business, fearful of anything less than a twenty-four-seven effort would jeopardise the family future. So, no, Norfolk had never even been on the family radar.

But it seemed Norfolk was where the answer lay. He'd had no option but to wait until he could find time to follow the instruction and read what he guessed had to be a back issue of some obscure local North Norfolk newspaper. That wouldn't be easy, because he didn't know which newspaper he was looking for and even if he did, he had no idea which issue he was supposed to read.

Hearing his parents leave the house, his mother calling her goodbyes from the bottom of the stairs, he knew he could be certain of no interruptions. He settled down to search the web for local North Norfolk newspapers.

He quickly found there to be one prominent title. It was at least a place to start. Checking the e-papers section, he established that after downloading a free app, the paper offered five days during which back issues could be viewed for free. Fifteen minutes later he had the relevant details on the screen. But what was he looking for? Other than talking numbers and hinting he was next, it told him nothing. But there had to be something. Okay, so how far back should he go? Four editions? Five? He decided on a full week. After all, how long would it take to quickly scan the headlines of a local rag?

Twenty minutes later, when the image of the front page of the third paper appeared, the breath was taken from Mohamed Rahman's body. He sat frozen, his fingers clenched around the computer's mouse, his mouth hanging loosely, a dribble of unnoticed saliva slithering from its corner. A bombshell had exploded in Mo's head destroying all logical thought, the words in front of him engulfing the whole of his consciousness.

IDENTITY OF MAN FOUND IN DITCH REVEALED.

The identity of the man found in a water-filled ditch in a remote Norfolk lane on the outskirts of Reepham on Wednesday last was revealed by the police today. The dead man is believed to be Atif Dasti. At the moment the police are unable to reveal further details other than that Dasti is a British citizen of Pakistani descent. The police are treating his death as suspicious.

Mo stared at the report, his eyes drifting from the familiar name to the last sentence: *the police are treating his death as suspicious.* Finally, tearing his eyes away from the screen, he looked again at the note lying alongside the laptop, knowing now what it really meant.

Number 2 soon.
Guess who's Number 3?

Sitting dumbstruck in the quiet of his room, the past thundering back into his head, Mo felt himself begin to shake, his every limb weakening, the feeling of helplessness returning exactly as it had back then. It should never have happened. It wouldn't have either, if only they'd been stronger. But they hadn't...they'd been weak, and when disaster struck they'd panicked and fled. Now someone was making them pay. The trembling increased as the stark realization dawned. One by one, someone was going to kill them all.

Twenty-two

Given the option of choosing where they went, Melanie Campbell had deferred to Stern's greater knowledge of the area's hostelries. He had been happy to oblige and this time had chosen a typical Norfolk pub in Salthouse, a tiny village situated on the coast road a few miles to the west of Sheringham. The pub claimed its aspiration was to be a pub that served good food— not a restaurant that happened to have a bar. In Stern's experience, the claim was well justified. The food was indeed excellent with a bonus, in Stern's eyes anyway, of a fine selection of real ales on tap.

It was a little after nine-thirty when, the meal finished, they sat contentedly chatting over coffee. Stern studied her across the table. She was wearing a simple blue dress, close fitting, accentuating her slim figure and the same gold heart at her throat. As before she wore just lightly applied makeup and her hair was less formal this time, casually combed, fluffier about her face. He liked that.

"Theo Stern, am I wrong or are you staring at me?"

He smiled self-consciously. "Sorry, but something just occurred to me."

"What?"

"This is our third date."

Melanie cocked her head questioningly. "Is that good?"

"As far as I'm concerned, it's good. How about you?"

"Well, you may remember, it was me who asked you out this time, wasn't it?" She leaned toward him. "And as I've never ever asked a man out on a date in the whole of my life and since losing my husband haven't been on three dates with any man...that might just give you a clue."

Stern felt a sudden unusual glow inside. "So on a scale of bad to good, I can rate that sort of somewhere up there?"

Leaning back, she lowered her hands and picked up her coffee, her eyes never leaving his. "What do you think?"

"I'm glad."

"So am I. I just feel there's something there, Theo. Something nice."

Stern knew what she meant. "Me too."

She took a sip of coffee. "So is this conversation getting a little serious, Mister Stern? Maybe even a little soft?"

He followed suit with the coffee then shook his head. "Me serious? Soft? Nah, never."

A discerning smile formed. "No, of course not. This is the hardnosed, ex-detective inspector I'm talking to here, isn't it?"

Stern couldn't remember the last time he'd been tongue tied, but under that knowing gaze he could feel he was coming close to it now.

She helped him out by changing the subject. "Have you made any progress with your search for Martin?"

Earlier, in the newspaper, Stern had read the police statement revealing Atif Dasti as the man found in the ditch. But there had been no mention of the Jaguar found abandoned, so he guessed, even if she'd read the account, Melanie wouldn't have linked Dasti with the man she'd seen with Baldwin in the car park. Not that she needed to. Her interest was simply as someone curious about the sudden disappearance of an acquaintance. "Nothing. After my visit to Baldwin's old lodgings and Cain's, I had nowhere else to go. How about you? Hear anything at work?"

She dropped her eyes, slowly stirring the remnants of her coffee. "No change. Things are going on as usual."

"No more mention of Baldwin then?"

"No. As I told you before, it seems as if everyone has been sworn to silence. I've asked a couple of people, those I know better than others, but they insist they know nothing. One minute he was there, then he was gone and silence reigns. It's like he didn't exist in the first place."

Stern wasn't about to make any mention of Frank Runcie's visit to Stern Investigations or his own acceptance to work for the big man. Client confidentiality ruled. He gave a nonchalant shrug. "Looks like it's case closed, then. For Andrew's sake, I'll keep my ear to the ground just in case anything pops up, but that's about it."

Stern steered the conversation away from Baldwin and the mysterious silence Melanie was encountering at Cain Engineering and for the next hour they chatted happily, drifting from one subject to another. It was well after eleven when Stern drew up outside Melanie's cottage.

She leaned across and kissed him on the cheek. "Thanks for another lovely evening," she said softly, her lips close to his ear. "Would you like to come in? Like I said, it's been a long time, but I think the usual term is 'for a nightcap,' isn't it?"

A sudden panic welled up inside Stern, his mind plunging into a flat spin. He'd met and fallen in love with Annie in nineteen eighty...thirty three years ago, and since that time hadn't even looked at another woman, let alone been invited in for a nightcap by one. What the hell would he do if she got him inside and expected... Well, so what? Annie was gone, wasn't she? She'd chosen another country in preference to him. He might be fifty nine, but he was a free man, no ties, and everything still worked. Let's face it, he still had needs. Sitting alongside him was a very attractive woman making him an offer he couldn't refuse. Could he?

"There's nothing I'd like more," he heard himself say. "But I have to be on the road at the crack of dawn to meet a client. It's an important case, otherwise..."

Melanie seemed completely unfazed by the rejection. She smiled and kissed him again, this time softly, lingering, on the lips. "I understand," she whispered. "Maybe next time." She pushed open the door and climbed out, her perfume still hanging tantalisingly behind her. Before closing the door, she leaned down and looked in at him, her lips parting in that same knowing smile. "I don't bite, Theo, I promise."

He was hardly out of second gear when he found himself punching the steering wheel. "You prat," he growled. "You absolute five star prat."

He was still seething when he pulled the up-and-over door of the garage closed and stomped his way round to the flat.

Twenty-three

Martin Baldwin left the bungalow and made his way toward the busy little main street of Mordialloc. It was a pleasant morning, the temperature a comfortable twenty degrees, and since being here he had grown to enjoy the daily twenty minute morning walk. He'd found the tiny café cum sandwich shop, halfway along the Mordialloc high street, the first time he'd ventured into the town. The formidable array of sandwich fillings and various coffee blends had been too much to ignore. Since then, the daily pilgrimage to the little establishment for breakfast had become a must, the little oriental lady proprietor, a refugee from the atrocities of the Cambodian carnage, happy to concoct any sandwich filling he chose from the vast range displayed.

But today's trip wasn't just about breakfast. Today was about much more.

Before absconding from Cain Engineering and leaving the UK, he'd gleaned several contacts from the Cain customer records. They were contacts he knew had no particular allegiance to Cain, one in particular whose marketing man, after crossing swords with Runcie, had broken ties with the company altogether. In conversation, Rupert Cain had admitted the loss of the contract had hurt the company. Business was at an all-time low and they could ill afford to lose further contracts.

Baldwin felt no sympathy for Cain's plight. Neither did he have any regrets, or feel any guilt, about jumping ship. Nor was he surprised that Runcie's tactics had led to the loss of a contract. Indeed it was amazing it hadn't happened before. Runcie was nothing but a pig, ignorant, overpowering barrow boy. Were it not for Rupert Cain he would probably be emptying bins in some low class, run down urban district. As it was he was a millionaire who treated everybody like shit. Everybody but Cain, of course; if nothing else, Runcie knew on which side his bread was buttered.

Runcie was the prime reason for Baldwin making his move. Time after time he'd seen Runcie treat the people who kept the company afloat, the people who were solid experts in their field, like dirt, while all the time he'd stashed the cash. Almost as aggravating was the way Rupert Cain, so closeted in his own little design world, allowed it to happen. It was one thing to work on Cain products, designs coming from others within the company. It was another to let that ignorant fat piece of crap grow even richer on the back of his own design. A design that was probably the most advanced in its field anywhere in the world.

That wasn't to say he didn't have some misgivings. Rupert Cain was a nice man and to desert him hadn't been easy. But nice as he was, Cain contributed to the problem by turning a blind eye, condoning his partner's bullying tactics. So those misgivings hadn't plagued Baldwin for long. Cain, he'd soon decided, was only reaping what he had sown over the years.

Baldwin had been here in Mordialloc for a little over two weeks and so far things were working well. Living was expensive here, but the part time maintenance job was supplementing the savings he'd brought with him and he was scraping through. He'd budgeted for twelve months max, but with luck it wouldn't take anywhere near that long. If he played his cards right, he could be living on easy street long before then. To that end he'd worked every second he could find to ensure his baby was ready.

The biggest fear on releasing any design was that it was not complete, that you'd forgotten something or made a miscalculation and, in short, the thing just didn't work. Sure, under normal circumstances Research and Development trials would take place, updates and modifications made. But this was about as far from normal circumstances as you could get. This was totally down to him alone and it had to be spot on. It had to hit the customer and show its potential from the get go. Not doing that would make it about as lucrative as an expired credit card. That wouldn't happen, of course, because he knew it would work. He'd been over it a thousand times, and since being here, a thousand times more.

Even so, as he approached the sandwich shop and noted his usual pavement table was vacant, he gave a little shudder. The time was now. He'd taken a huge risk and today would tell whether that risk had been worthwhile. Today, while sitting at the little pavement table, he was about to find out whether Martin Baldwin's life was to change forever.

Fifteen minutes later he was sipping piping hot coffee, a three inch thick ham and salad sandwich balanced precariously on the plate in front of him. He'd made sure he was early, giving himself time to enjoy his breakfast— as much as the rising tension inside him would allow— before facing what he knew would be the most important confrontation he would ever have to endure. Determined to relax, he took his time, carefully dissecting the sandwich into bite size portions and forcing himself to chew slowly, washing the remnants down with the coffee.

Almost half an hour later, his breakfast finished, a fresh coffee in front of him, he opened the newspaper he'd bought on his way here. He turned the pages, slowly reading each news item. There were no major catastrophes to speak of, the main headline being about the disgraceful abuse suffered by the country's lady Prime Minister from the opposition; the so-called Australian macho man culture showing its shameful face at the highest level. Baldwin recalled how in the past he'd thought how infantile the behaviour of some UK politicians could be. Reading as he did today he realised they didn't hold a candle to this lot. A smile broke as he thought how Maggie, the Iron Lady, would have made mincemeat of 'em all.

"Mr Baldwin?"

The voice jolted him back to where he was and the

realisation that time had passed quickly. The short dapper man standing in front of him was immaculately dressed, the suit pinstriped, the shoes gleaming. His jet black hair was perfectly groomed, slicked back above a rotund, healthily tanned face radiating a confident, amused smile that looked like it already held a secret. He was carrying a document case casually in one hand.

A million butterflies took control as Baldwin dropped the newspaper onto the table and leaped to his feet, offering his hand to his Chinese visitor. "Mr Li, it's nice to meet you at last."

Li gave a tiny bow and took Baldwin's hand, the handshake light and brief. He turned and surveyed the surroundings; the traffic buzzing to and fro, the pavements busy with shoppers. "Distracting noise," he said, the smile still in place. "Perfect for confidential discussion." He pulled out the chair on the other side of the table and sat.

The little lady, always on the lookout for customers, appeared at his side.

Li looked up at her and smiled. "Tea, no milk, no sugar, please."

A few minutes later, the tea in front of him, Li surveyed Baldwin for a long silent moment. "So, is this your permanent home now?" he asked finally.

Baldwin shook his head. The butterflies had halved now, but under the Chinaman's probing gaze, the muscles in the back of his neck still felt taut. "No, just a temporary measure."

"Mmmm, maybe I can understand that." He took a

delicate sip of tea, the cup little more than touching his lips. "So much depends on our discussion."

"Yes it does."

"So, before we discuss your offer, I would like to establish a few facts."

"Go ahead."

"You were under contract to Cain Engineering, I understand?"

"Yes I was."

"Which means what you are offering is in fact not yours to offer."

Baldwin hadn't been sure what exactly would be thrown at him today, but this was one question he had prepared himself for. Design was his thing and it felt good to be one step ahead. The tension eased even more. "Not so," he said. "The design I was working on at Cain was unfinished. It was unfinished because I realised I was on the wrong track. That design would not have been successful and was discarded. What I'm offering you is a completely new design developed since I left Cain Engineering." It wasn't true and he could see by Li's expression he suspected as much.

"So have you covered yourself? A patent or some other protection against theft?"

"Nope, and neither do I intend to."

"Oh?"

"Mr Li, I intend to sign my design over to the highest bidder and relinquishing all rights in the process. Whoever the successful bidder is can claim it as his own and do with it as he will."

Li's tapered eyes narrowed further. "Are you telling me you have offered this to others as well as ourselves?"

Seeing the concern in the Chinaman's eyes, Baldwin's confidence soared. No more tension; the butterflies had flown. "At this time absolutely not, "he said, holding Li's searching gaze. "At this time, my design has gone only to you. But I can assure you there are others. Hopefully I have a long life ahead of me, Mr Li, and my expectations are high. Having studied the protocol, you have, I am sure, carried out your own research. That being the case, you will know that right now there is nothing else in the world that can match what I'm offering you. Its applications are endless, both civil and, maybe more importantly, military. Its potential worldwide is mammoth, profits astronomical. If your company's offer meets my expectations, I will hand everything over, lock stock and barrel. If not, then I will be forced to go elsewhere."

The smile was back. "My company also has high expectations, Mr Baldwin, and so far you've given us little more than an outline design and the protocol. Your design incorporates both electronic and mechanical components and is complicated to the extreme. It will be hugely expensive to manufacture and we only have your word that the final product will be as lucrative as you profess."

Baldwin was flying now. Whatever Li said, however he pussyfooted around, he wouldn't have been sent all the way from China if the company hadn't seen the huge potential in what they were being offered. "It will work," he said simply. "And I don't think you would be here if after scrutinising what I gave you, your technical people didn't think that was the case."

There was that look again; a long, hard, decision-making stare then, "Okay, Mr. Baldwin, so tell me, what are your expectations?"

Twenty-four

"Dad, you mean his own boss was having him followed?"

"Yes, it was as simple as that." Stern sat in front of the TV, the sound muted, a ready meal Madras straight out of the microwave and a bottle of London Pride on a tray on his lap, the phone wedged between shoulder and ear. "Martin's boss, a stroppy individual called Runcie, thought your friend was up to something so he had him followed." Stern forked in a mouthful, the pleasantly sweet heat radiating as he swallowed, sweat, as always, forming on the top of his head. "As it turns out, he was right." He took a swig of cooling beer from the bottle. "Seems your mate has done a runner with one of Cain's top designs."

"What? That doesn't sound like Martin, Dad. As far as I knew, he was a pretty straight and honest guy."

"He may have been, son, but right now everything points to him absconding with some pretty valuable company property."

"Are the police involved?"

"As far as the company is concerned, no. They're in a pretty delicate situation at the moment and it would do them no good for their competitors to know one of their employees had walked off with some top design information." Stern refrained from mentioning that on behalf of the company he had agreed to look for Baldwin. "But the police do have an interest."

"What sort of interest?"

Stern briefed his son on his temporary secondment to O'Connor's team and the belief that Baldwin could be connected with another crime.

"Anything serious?"

"No nothing serious. It just looks like Martin could have known an individual we're investigating," Stern explained, not wanting to worry his son with the fact that it looked like his friend could be linked closely with one, maybe even two murder victims. "Probably nothing, but you know how it is, they have to check everything."

"Nothing to do with the other business then?"

"Not that I can see."

"So, working for David means you're still involved, right?"

"Yes it does." Stern scraped the last of the curry from the plate and wiped up the residue with the remaining piece of bread.

"Real policing again, Dad. Is that what you want?"

Stern washed the last mouthful down with a heavy pull at the bottle. "Don't read anything into it, son. It's just a couple of weeks because David's team is at an all-time low. But in answer to your question...no it's not what I want. Cherry and I are happy with our little lot here, and anyway I'm too old for real policing now."

"I'm glad to hear it. Can you imagine what Mum would say if she knew?" There was a short pause. "By the way, have you spoken to Mum recently?"

There it was again, and Stern knew it would come. It did every time they spoke. One way or another, his son would always bring Annie into the conversation. "No, not recently," he admitted. "Your mum's a busy lady now, son."

"Bet you haven't tried, though, have you?"

Stern felt a familiar annoyance rise within him, but he held it back, not wanting to upset his son. "No, I haven't, but don't push, Andrew. The situation is as it is. I know you want us to stay in touch and we will. But we have to do it our own way. Mum made a choice, it was what she wanted and we have to work with that. However hard you try, you won't change things. Just relax and go with it. In the long term, whatever will be will be, okay?"

"Yeah, I guess you're right. Would be nice for us all to get together sometimes though, wouldn't it?"

The annoyance was replaced by an instant sadness. "Yes it would and maybe we will. Let's just see, shall we?"

"Okay Dad, you win."

Stern felt he could hear the same sadness in his son's resigned acceptance. "I'll let you know if I have any joy with Martin, okay?"

"Okay, Dad, speak again soon."

Stern terminated the call and dropped the phone down onto the cushion beside him. He sat for some moments, the depression, always there after talking with his son, heavier than usual. Andrew was an adult now, but his constant attempts to reunite his mother and father brought back memories of when he was a child and never happier than when they were all together. Regrettably, because of Stern's total dedication to the job, those times were all too infrequent which was why Andrew had cherished them so much and probably why even now he constantly tried to rekindle the flame. The sad truth was; no one had wanted to rekindle that flame more than Stern himself. Even now, all these years later, the thought of how things could have been still triggered a sickening feeling of sadness and regret. If he could turn back the clock, he'd do it in a heartbeat.

Stern lifted the bottle and swallowed the last dregs, his eyes drifting to the clock on the wall. The time, ten-thirty, prompted the now automatic calculation: three hours back and at the other end of the day. It would be half seven in the morning in Melbourne. He had her number on quick dial. It would take just one push. At least then, when they next spoke, he could honestly tell Andrew he'd tried. He almost reached again for the phone, but pulled back. Probably she'd already left for work, couldn't wait to get at it. Yeah, that would be it. But then the ultimate stupid thought; just suppose she hadn't, suppose she was still there, maybe still in bed, and suppose someone else answered. Just for that instant a brick settled in his stomach. He jerked out of the chair and headed for the kitchen, the fridge and another London Pride.

A couple of swallows and common sense returned. Hadn't she told him long since; it wasn't *them* anymore, it was *him* and it was *her*, two separate people with two separate lives. And hadn't she demonstrated this by buggering off to the other side of the world? So it didn't matter a single toss who answered the phone, did it? But it did matter that he made his son happy by at least keeping in touch. He slumped back in the chair and reached for the phone, his fingers barely closing round the instrument when it sprang into life. The sudden sound made him jump and he hesitated, his hand hovering, a thought suddenly crossing his mind. In the early, happy days Annie always said they were in tune with each other, knew what each other was thinking. Could it possibly be...? He picked up the phone, apprehensive. "Stern."

"Hi."

Soft and feminine and just for a moment he thought... But then he realised. "Melanie?"

"It's not too late, is it?"

"No, of course not."

There was an awkward pause before she said, "It's about last night."

"Oh?"

"I haven't been able to stop thinking about it."

"About what?"

"About asking you in like that. I shouldn't have. I've felt cheap ever since, like some sort of..."

"Whoa, hang on, Melanie," he broke in. "I never for one moment thought of you as cheap. What on earth gave you that impression?"

"The way you looked at me. I could have died. I haven't been able to get it out of my mind."

He thought he detected a hic in her speech, as if she were close to tears. He gave a short laugh, forced, lighten the mood. "Don't be silly. Anyway I can't be responsible for my looks, can I? I was born like it. But the last thing to cross my mind was cheap."

"But you didn't have a client the following the morning, did you?"

She had him there. "No I didn't," he admitted. "But you read me all wrong. I didn't refuse your offer because I thought it cheap. Far from it."

"So why...?"

It was his turn to pause. The truth or another fabrication. It came out of its own accord. "I lost my nerve." He hoped she'd say something. She didn't. "I told you I was divorced. What I didn't tell you was Annie and I met in our teens and she's..." Shit this was difficult. "Well, truth is she's the only... It's only ever been..." He stammered to a halt.

"Oh, I'm so sorry. I didn't realise."

He took a long swig of beer. "Not such a hardnosed cop after all, eh?"

"We've all got our soft side, Theo, and you can't imagine how much better I feel now."

"I'm glad about that anyway."

"And it doesn't mean we can't carry on seeing each other, does it? Like you said, she did choose Australia over you. I mean you're here and I'm here and there was something, wasn't there?"

"Yes there was."

"So?"

"Can I ring you?"

"Soon?"

"Soon."

The call ended, Stern sunk gratefully back into the chair. It was true; he did enjoy being with her. Let's face it…she was a very attractive woman and he wasn't proud of himself for bottling out when he'd had the chance to do what he'd thought about doing more than once since he'd met her. He took another long pull at the bottle. No point in just thinking about it, though, was there? Time to stand up and be counted, Stern. Well maybe lie down and be counted, whichever. He grinned at the silly joke. One thing was certain: Melanie's call had convinced him. It was time to let go of the past and get on with his life. Uplifted, he drained the bottle and pushed himself out of the chair. A quick wash, brush his teeth and bed. How did it go? Tomorrow would be the first day of the rest of his life?

He'd taken only a single step when the phone, still lying on the cushion he'd just vacated, again burbled into life.

He spun round and picked it up. "Stern."

There was a short delay then, "If the mountain won't come to Mohammed."

Soft and feminine again, this time instantly recognizable and his heart leapt.

Twenty-five

Never, in all the time he'd run the shop, had Mo ever made a mistake on a prescription, let alone mix two prescriptions up. It was fortunate Sally had been her usual vigilant self. The prescriptions had been for the two extreme ends of the spectrum; one for the elderly, one for the young. Had Sally not checked every detail as she always did, as she had been trained to do by Mo himself, the result could have been serious. And grateful as he was, he hadn't found it in himself to be able to apologise as he should have, just mumbled how he was under pressure with an instruction for his assistant to keep the customer happy until he'd put things right.

Then later there was the angry snap at the youngster for handling stuff on one of the lower, newly laid out shelves. The mother had been furious, berating him crossly for being so cruel to her five year old, who by that time was in floods of tears. He'd tried to apologise but too late. He felt sure that was one customer he'd lost for good.

The shop closed, Mo sat in the little back room, his head in his hands. He knew how badly he'd behaved today, knew how sharp and irritable he'd been with Sally, and worse, with the customers. He'd been so relieved when he'd closed the door behind Sally and thrown the bolts. Now all he could think of was what on earth his father would say if he knew just the half of it.

But that mustn't happen.

To his father the business was life itself. He had come to this country a young penniless immigrant determined to succeed, prepared to carry out any task that would enable him to squirrel away enough money to eventually pay for an education. Sometimes those tasks were at the lowest end of the scale, sometimes not even legal, but he had persevered, stuck resolutely to the plan, and eventually achieved his goal. His first shop, situated in a rundown area, had been tiny: newspapers, cigarettes and sweets mostly. But at the back there was a small section of over the counter drugs. It had been the start and his father had frequently boasted, despite the racist attitude of the minority, no other country in the world would have given him the same opportunities. He had from the start vowed to show his appreciation by serving the British people faithfully through his business. "The customer is always right, son," he would say, waving a warning finger. "And you must never forget it."

Before now, Mo had never forgotten and he dreaded to think what would happen if his father ever got wind of what a disaster today had been. But never before had he felt quite so uptight, so... so scared. And he had good reason; he was being threatened with his life. He had no idea who was making the threat, but after seeing the report of Dasti's death, he knew why. Only once in his life had he allowed himself to be led by the nose into doing something utterly stupid, something that had ended in disaster. Even worse, he'd allowed himself to be persuaded to walk away, to say nothing of the catastrophic consequences. Now, all this time later, after the memory had almost faded and a good, happy life lay ahead, someone was intent on making him pay the ultimate price for that one mistake, that one stupid moment in an otherwise blameless existence.

He'd racked his brain all last night after finding the Norfolk newspaper report, and again today at the expense of the business, trying to find a way, something, anything that might help him find out who had sent the note. But it was no good. He had long since broken all links with the others. He had no idea where they were or how to make contact.

He had considered contacting the police...he was being threatened and needed protection, but after much thought, long into the night, had discarded the idea. It would be too complicated. It would mean concocting a story, one not involving the past. He couldn't let the past come into it under any circumstances. Would he be able to do that? At first he'd thought maybe, if he played the race card, suggested it could be someone out there jealous of the family success. His father would be distraught, of course. The Rahmans were respected business people in the community and there had been no significant sign of discrimination in the area for years. Under those circumstances, the police would probably see it more as an individual with an axe to grind for some reason or other, maybe not take it too seriously. But they would be involved and with a couple of quiet phone calls, he could ensure a headline or two in the newspapers saying so. He'd thought it could act as a deterrent. If whoever had sent the note saw that the police were involved, they might just back off. Maybe, maybe not, but after a sleepless night, it had been the best he could come up with.

Not now, though. Now, after a day of further torment, it seemed the most ridiculous of plans. He would have to show the police the note, wouldn't he? And the note did more than just make a threat. *Murderers all four*, it said. *Killers every one.* What would the police make of that? He could feign ignorance, of course, swear he didn't know what it was all about. But what about the quote: *'The local North Norfolk Newspaper tells the story'?* After reading it the police would do exactly as he had, wouldn't they? They'd search the Norfolk newspaper headlines, maybe find the story about Dasti's killing and contact their Norfolk colleagues who would search for a link. There was a link, too. A long time ago, maybe, but there was one and the police had unlimited resources; they would find it.

So no, the police must not be involved. But what, then? Did he just have to wait until someone attempted to kill him? Hope when that time came, he could do something about it, somehow protect himself? He remembered Dasti...all powerful, arrogantly confident and the cause of all the trouble. If Dasti hadn't been able to protect himself, what chance did he have?

He lifted himself out of the chair and stood looking around him, the hopelessness, as it had last night, again coursing through him. Leaving the room, he wandered down the passage and emerged into the shop, moving across to the counter and leaning on his elbows, surveying the new layout. He'd put a lot of effort into it and had been pleased with the result. Even his father liked it, said it was probably the best yet. One shop now, he'd said, but Mo my son, before you know it, it will all be yours. Mo had revelled in that thought. He had a good loyal family, a wonderful bride-to-be and a happy, fruitful future ahead. What more could a man ask? But... He thumped his fist angrily down on the counter, frustrated to the extreme. An attempt on his life was somewhere ahead and he just couldn't do anything about it.

He took a deep breath and looked at the clock on the wall. His mother would have a meal ready, she would be wondering where he'd got to. As he turned back toward the passage and the little room where his coat and bag hung, the telephone rang. Mo frowned; he couldn't remember the last time someone had called after closing time. His brow cleared as he remembered he was late. Mother would be on the prowl.

"Hello." He purposely refrained from using the business name after hours.

"Did you know Ralph Armitage used to live in Northampton?" The voice was male and soft, an amused edge to the words.

He heard the words, every one, the name in particular,

but somehow they seemed to stick somewhere between hearing and recognition. "What?"

"And did you notice I used the words *used to*?

Mo Rahman felt his legs weaken, begin to sag. "Who is this?"

There was a chuckle and the line died.

Twenty-six

Stern leaned back in the old chair and linked his hands behind his head. "Okay, let's take it from the top and see if we've missed anything."

It was Tuesday morning, first thing, with nothing else particularly important on the books and the Baldwin case, as it had been christened at Stern Investigations, at a standstill.

Cherry and Colin Keen sat opposite. Cherry was first off the mark. "The more I think about it, the more I ask myself if the two murders are really linked? I know they were both hit from behind and forensics say they were both drowned. But so far that's all the two cases have in common. Is that enough?"

"I know what you mean," Keen agreed. "There's something like a hundred and thirty odd miles between them, too." He looked across at Stern, his head tilting questioningly. "Would you take the method of both killings sufficient to link them, boss, or is it possible it's just coincidence?"

Stern smiled inwardly at how quickly the young

constable had picked up on Cherry's use of 'boss.' "Well, officially, the M.O., on its own, no, but we mustn't disregard it. We have to look at it alongside anything and everything else we uncover. For instance; something that might link the two locations."

"You mean something that Reepham here in Norfolk and Northampton might have in common?"

Stern unlinked his hands and leaned forward. "That's right. For instance, as has happened in the past, if our killer was a lorry driver who had regular runs between the two places." He held up a warning finger. "As for coincidence; in my opinion that's a no go. If two things, like we're looking at here, look to be related, then it's a damn fair bet they are."

Cherry studied her boss across the desk, a half smile forming. Sixteen years ago he'd ridden into her life like the proverbial knight in shining armour. In those sixteen years, she believed she'd come to know him better than anyone alive, even she would argue, his ex, Annie. That was apart from the more personal aspects, of course. Certainly, now, she was sure she knew what he was thinking. "The M.O. does it for you, doesn't it?"

Colin Keen looked from Cherry to Stern, noting the knowing eye contact, the obvious connection between the two. It made him feel one apart, on the outside.

Stern couldn't contain the grin. "It certainly does, kid. As far as I'm concerned, the similarity between the two killings is no coincidence."

"So, you're sure it's the same killer, right?"

Stern eyeballed Keen. "I know what you're thinking,

Colin, but remember I said *officially* we couldn't link the two on that basis alone. That doesn't mean we can't have our own opinions, our own beliefs." He turned, looking back at Cherry. "Sometimes I think madam here knows me too damn well. But what I believe mustn't cloud our judgement. We can only work on the facts. Like I said, we look at everything, however unlikely, okay?" He looked across at Cherry. "Same goes for you, miss-clever-clogs. Everything, get it?"

Cherry primly dropped her eyes, but grinning. "Yes, boss, whatever you say, boss."

"Right, let's go over things again." He looked to Keen. "What more did you find out about Dasti?"

"Not much more than you found out on your visit," Keen admitted. "He was born and raised in Nottingham to a devout Muslim family. His father's a doctor, but I couldn't find a thing about his mother."

"Knowing the culture, that's not surprising," Stern said. "Historically, the women have taken a back seat."

Keen scrutinised his notebook further. "Dasti was educated at Liverpool University where he gained a first in Pharmacy. I called Liverpool, couldn't get hold of any of the tutors, but I was lucky; I managed to talk to a secretary who's been in the department for years. She remembered Dasti, said he was one of those students that stood out among the rest. Seems he sailed through his studies, excelled at just about everything he touched, and that included sport. He was a big guy, bags of muscle. He played just about every sport and excelled in most of them; had a bucket load of trophies according to the sec.

Seems the girls went for him big time, too."

"Regular Superman." Stern rubbed his nose with the back of his hand. "What about friends?"

"Yeah, I asked about that. The secretary thought Dasti was probably more respected than liked by most of his peers, but he did regularly hang out with the same group of three or four regulars."

"Any names?"

Keen shook his head. "No, she couldn't remember specific names. She told me every so often, in any intake, there'd be one that stood out like Dasti. The rest just came and went. It does confirm what you learned on your visit, though. The doctor at the clinic said how good Dasti was, didn't he? And what was it the Brigadier said about him?"

"Excellent officer material or just a plain bully, it depends how you look at it," Stern mused. He was quiet for a moment, then turned to Cherry. "Interesting he got his degree in Liverpool, though, don't you think?

"Why's that?" Keen asked.

"He wouldn't make the connection, boss," Cherry came in quickly. "He wasn't here at the start." She grinned across at the confused Keen. "Don't forget he only came in to solve the Dasti murder for us."

"That's true," Stern agreed, turning back to Keen. "One or two things did happen before you came here, so I'd better explain." Stern reiterated how things had started with a phone call from his son about a troubled friend and a stalker, outlining how it had escalated to the connection with Dasti in the Cain car park and Dasti's killing.

"So your son, and his friend, er...?

"Martin Baldwin," Cherry helped him out.

"Right, Martin Baldwin and now Dasti, all went to Liverpool University?"

"That's right. Which leaves Armitage." Stern turned to Cherry. "Got anything on him?

"Yes I have and I'm sorry to break the chain, but Armitage didn't attend Liverpool. He did accountancy at Bristol."

"You're sure?"

"Positive. See, our Ralph was a great Facebook fan and there's not much you can't find out about someone from their bio on their Facebook page."

"And you're on this Facebook thingy, of course?" Stern said.

"Of course." Cherry looked across at Keen and raised her eyebrows questioningly.

"Too right," Keen agreed. "Been on it for ages." He tried to suppress the grin, not very successfully. "Aren't you on it, boss?"

Stern said nothing, just wrinkled his nose and pushed himself back in the old chair.

"Okay," Cherry went on quickly. "Armitage did three years at Bristol University and got himself a two one in Economics and Finance. He graduated in two thousand and five. His aim was to become a Chartered Accountant and, according to his own account on his Facebook page, he was lucky to get a job with a firm of accountants almost straight away."

"This at the Northampton Company?" Stern broke in.

Cherry nodded. "Yup, it looks that way. It was also

where he met his wife, too. They're still at the same house they bought when they were married."

Stern rubbed thoughtfully at his chin. "No link with Liverpool then?"

"Not that I can see."

"So as far as Armitage is concerned, we do only have the M.O." The room was silent and for some time Stern stared into the middle distance, thinking. Finally he said, "Well call it what you like; copper's nose, intuition, whatever, I'll lay money there's a link there somewhere." He leaned forward and rested his elbows on the desk. "This Facebook gizmo; you guys don't tell everybody everything about yourselves, do you?"

Cherry smiled. "It's called social networking, boss. Brings people together. Sure, in some cases people do reveal too much, say what they shouldn't and it gets them into trouble. Mostly, though, it's general, everyday gossipy stuff, trivia."

"Right, so you won't get everything on there, will you? What I'm saying is, if someone had something to hide, they wouldn't put it out there, would they?" He didn't wait for an answer. "And there is that something, trust me. It's just a matter of looking deeper and finding it." He looked from Keen to Cherry. "So I need the pair of you to drag your backsides off those chairs and show me what a fantastic couple of investigators you really are. Find the link, guys. It's there, I know it."

Cherry looked at Keen and nodded toward the door. "Right, we'll spread the search and check out those on Armitage's Facebook contact list. See if there's someone tucked away there who might link him to Liverpool."

"You never know," Keen said, heaving himself up. "We might even find Dasti."

"And in the meantime, what're you going to do, boss?"

"Me? I'm going to have another little chat with a certain busty landlady."

Twenty-seven

Martin Baldwin was ecstatic. It was past midnight but sleep was impossible. In fact right now he felt as if he'd never ever be able to sleep again. He'd pulled it off. After all those months of planning, of intense, brain searing work, he'd just clinched the most mind blowing deal of his life. He still found it hard to believe he'd had the audacity, the nerve to go through with it.

But he had, and now a life of unending fun and leisure lay before him. He couldn't help wondering if this was how Bill Gates had felt when he made that first daring approach to the mighty IBM.

The idea had germinated on that very first day, the day he realised he'd come upon something very special, something that could take the world by storm. It had taken months, both during the working day at Cain's and again every waking hour at home, to slowly and carefully pull together his ground breaking design and, most importantly, to confirm it would actually work. A stroke of utter brilliance, even if he did say it himself.

On that very first day, that eureka moment, he knew he

could never hand over what he had created to Cain Engineering. He'd decided there and then what he had to do, and finally today it had happened. Today he had become Martin Baldwin, multi-millionaire.

There were no signatures yet, nothing to make it legal and binding, and he didn't intend to move an inch further until there were. But that was just a formality; it would happen, he was sure of it. He'd seen it in Li's eyes, as clear as day. There was no doubt about it, it was in the bag as sure as he was hanging onto this glass of scotch. Twenty million, the figure was so huge he'd almost choked on the two simple words, the so often practised demand almost sticking in his throat. But he'd made that demand and to his utter amazement, Li hadn't so much as blinked.

He knew Li's company would make more, much more, over the years…probably billions, but he cared not about that. He, Martin Baldwin, not yet thirty years old, would immediately be richer to the tune of ten million. Then in twelve months' time, after helping validate and ratify his design at the company's factory on the outskirts of Beijing, he would be handed another ten million. Added to that there would be share options which he would certainly go for. With luck, in the longer term, the appreciation of shares in such a successful company could net him an astronomical sum. It was all just too mind-blowing to contemplate. Runcie, you fat slob, eat your heart out

It was a full sixteen hours since Li had shaken his hand and left him sitting, stunned, at the little café on the high street, and still his heart pounded, his stomach lurched each time the realisation of what he'd done dawned afresh.

It dampened the euphoria a little that he was alone with no one to share his joy, but he could cope with that. Time would pass quickly and before he knew it, he would be enjoying a life full of freedom and pleasure, answerable to no one with nothing out of reach. He drained the glass and reached again for the bottle, pouring himself another generous measure.

It might not all be plain sailing, he reminded himself. His departure from Cain Engineering hadn't actually been by mutual consent. He'd dumped them with a note of resignation and run. That was after stealing information from their confidential client list. Runcie would be steaming, he was certain of that, and, with the design so important to the company, might decide to get the police on the job after all. But that was what was so beautiful about the whole thing. Firstly it could never be proven he'd stolen anything. He'd been careful not to access the company confidential client files via his own terminal; he was pretty sure this would be traceable and his position with Cain's gave him no authority to do so. But he hadn't had to. Working late, as he so often did, had its benefits. Particularly when you worked for someone so laid back as Rupert Cain, who seldom bothered to turn his own terminal off from one day to the next.

Then there was his design, his very own masterpiece. How stupid of them not to keep track of that, ask him for regular updates on the design concept, demand progress reports, all the usual, expected things. Runcie would have wanted such things, he was sure of that, but Cain, his usual trusting, laissez-faire attitude coming to the fore, hadn't bothered; he'd just allowed things to breeze along with nothing more than an occasional 'how y'doin'. In any other, larger, more controlled company it would have been unthinkable. But this was Cain Engineering...small, specialised and, as he had used to his own advantage, with lackadaisical in-house control. In that regard, Baldwin guaranteed things would change after this episode. He smiled to himself, the words 'stable door' and 'bolting horse' coming to mind.

So, even if Runcie did find him and bring charges, what could he be charged with? He stole nothing and who was to say the design he had just sold to the Chinese was anything to do with what he was working on at Cain's? He was a brilliant design engineer, but sadly had come to realise the work he was doing for Cain Engineering was not a viable design. It had always been his dream to go freelance, so he had left and started again on his own. It was this, his very own new design, he had handed over to the Chinese company. How could anyone prove otherwise?

He dragged himself back to the present, looking across the room at the two envelopes lying on the table, reminding himself there could be a potential pitfall in the trouble-free life he saw ahead. He checked the time and did a quick mental calculation. It would be evening in the UK; coming on half past nine and there was one person he could talk to, one person he knew would be delighted to hear from him. It was important he maintained contact, for the time being anyway, though there was obviously no long term future in the association. When he had his fortune, when he had the world at his fingertips, he would quietly slip away, but for now, if he wanted to know what was going on at home, and those two notes told him he most definitely did, then contact was essential.

Two packages of mail had arrived since he'd been here, but he'd been too absorbed in his work, too focussed on his goal to even open them. Only earlier this evening, his work finished, his future assured, had he decided to go through them. Most had been junk, ending up in the bin, but not the two he could see still lying on the table. He climbed from the chair and crossed the room, picking up the first envelope, the one dated the week he had left the UK. He pulled out the note and read it again.

Murderers all four
A killer every one
One by one you have to pay
Justice will be done

The words again brought back the memory of that day. He hadn't seen any of them for years then, out of the blue, Atif Dasti was there, standing in the car park waiting for him. Dasti's timing couldn't have been worse; he'd chosen the very day Baldwin had walked away from the company, tickets tucked in his pocket for a dawn flight to Australia the very next morning.

He remembered how Dasti had seemed nervous. He'd

tried to play it down, but then Dasti would; it never had been in the big man's nature to show anything other than powerful confidence. But Baldwin had seen it in his eyes, a tense uneasiness he was unable to completely disguise. He'd received a note, he'd said, a note threatening them all, saying they were all murderers and would have to pay for what they had done back then. He didn't know who the note was from, just that he felt sure it was genuine. Someone knew the truth and was coming after them. He'd taken time off to come and see Baldwin and explain, but he believed the others should be told; they should all meet and decide what to do.

But on that day Baldwin had been on a higher plane. The following morning he was going to fly out of this place and who knew when he would be back, if ever. He had a mission, one he'd worked on for far too long to jeopardize for the sake of a silly note that was more than likely a hoax, someone playing silly buggers. He remembered how Mo Rahman was always the jester, always up for a laugh. He'd said as much to Dasti, told him to check with Mo before going off half-cocked. Baldwin had no idea where Mo Rahman was, neither did he care. All that mattered was getting home and making those final preparations. He was being driven to Heathrow at some silly hour in the morning. He had to be ready. But Dasti wasn't to be shaken off easily and finally, just to get rid of him, Baldwin had agreed to meet him that evening. Then they would decide what to do. He'd no intention of keeping the appointment, of course, and neither had he.

At that time he wasn't to know a similar note was already on its way to him and wouldn't reach him until all this time later. Neither would he have been aware that later still a second note had also been sent. He dropped the first one onto the table and slid the second out of its envelope.

Your time has come, it must be said
Ask Atif and Ralph
Oh no, you can't
THEY'RE BOTH DEAD!

A chill ran through him as he read the note a second time. Those last two lines, mocking. Both dead? It couldn't be true, could it? He tried to calculate how long he'd been out of the UK. Three weeks? Yes that was it, around three, maybe four weeks. In that time the two notes had reached him; one in the first package forwarded from home then this, the latest, in the second. So if it were true, in the last three weeks someone had killed both Armitage and Dasti.

Suddenly, as he reached for the telephone, Baldwin didn't feel so euphoric.

Twenty-eight

She must have seen him arrive because the door was opened before he had a chance to ring the bell and it could have been a different woman. The heavy makeup was all but gone, replaced with little more than a pale lipstick. The black eyebrows were no more, as were the spikes and highlights in her hair. The struggling t-shirt and tights had been replaced with a loose blouse and slacks. Only the bright smile was unchanged. Marge Saunders looked as she should have looked...a pleasantly attractive, forty something lady.

"Hello dear, it's you again."

He gave her his best smile. "D'you think we could have another chat?"

She didn't hesitate. "Of course." She pulled the door fully open and stood back. "Come in and I'll make tea."

Tea!

She left him in the sitting room and made for the kitchen. Stern wandered across to the same armchair he'd occupied on his last visit, scanning the room as he went, noting right away that what looked the same as last time was not quite. The glass fronted sideboard now housed an array of china figurines. There wasn't a bottle or glass to be seen.

He settled himself in the chair and a few minutes later Marge returned with a tray. She placed it on the table between them and sat opposite. Stern clocked the tea service, everything gleaming white, all the same design, homely. Something had happened to sexy Marge since his last visit, that's for sure.

Marge poured the tea and handed him the cup and saucer. Cup and saucer? It felt awkward in his hand and he tried to remember the last time he'd taken tea from anything other than a mug. He couldn't.

"So, what do want to talk about?" She cradled the cup and saucer easily in front of her, the smile still there, but softer now, not pushy and definitely not suggestive as before.

"I'd like to ask a couple more questions about Martin Baldwin, if that's alright with you."

"Well yes, it's alright, but I don't think I can tell you any more than last time."

"Maybe not, but bear with me, if you will. Martin told you he was leaving because things were getting awkward. That's right, isn't it?"

"Yes."

"But he didn't say why, didn't say what was getting awkward?"

"No. As I told you before, I did ask because I thought it might be something to do with me, or the way things were here. Martin assured me that wasn't the case. It was something else, but he wouldn't say what."

"And he didn't leave a forwarding address?"

She shook her head. "No."

Was there something a little too positive about that shake of the head? "Did Martin have a car?"

"Yes he did."

"Good, that's something. Maybe that could help me locate him. I'll check with the DVLA, maybe get his new address from them."

Her eyes left his, flicking quickly down to the cup and saucer in her hand. "Well, no."

"Oh, why's that?"

"Well he..." The hesitation was short but obvious. "You see he sold it. Just before he left, he got rid of it."

"D'you know why he did that?"

She shrugged her ample shoulders. "He just said he wouldn't need it anymore."

"So on that day, the day he left this house, he didn't actually have a car, didn't have any means of transport?"

Marge was finding the cup and saucer ever more interesting. "No."

Stern leaned a little closer. Not too close, but enough to up the tension just a tad. "I assume he had luggage. So he would have needed transport of some kind."

"I think he ordered a taxi."

"I see. You don't happen to remember which cab company, do you?"

Now she looked up and there was no mistaking the moist eyes. "No, I don't really remember anything about that day. I was a little upset about him leaving." She took a deep breath.

"Look, do you have to keep asking these questions? I really can't tell you anything more than before and I find it upsetting. I'd rather you didn't carry on."

Stern carefully placed the cup and saucer on the table. He'd been through this loop so many times over the years. There was an art to lying, or not telling the whole truth, and not many people could pull it off, not for any length of time, anyway. The eyes were a dead giveaway in every case. Some so-called experts in human behaviour would tell you that by studying the direction of the eye movement you could tell exactly what was going on. Stern doubted it could possibly be so precise, but one thing was certain...in his opinion whichever way the eyes travelled, they were the giveaway, always. Right now, though, he had to be careful. Since his last visit there had been a drastic change here, and unless he was very much mistaken, the lady sitting opposite was in a very fragile state. It wasn't the time for the big push. Not yet anyway, so softly does it.

He leaned forward a little further, elbows on knees, keeping his voice low, his tone gentle. "Marge, it's true I am working for the police, but I want you to understand I'm not the enemy here. I'm not out to harm Martin in any way; in fact quite the opposite."

"Then why all these questions?"

The slight tremble in her voice didn't escape him. "Because there have already been two murders and we believe Martin..."

"*Murders.*" Her eyes widened. "No, you're not suggesting Martin could possibly..."

He raised a hand, stopping her. "No, I'm not suggesting anything at all. But I do believe Martin was in some way associated with two people that have been killed. There is also a possibility that Martin may be in danger himself." He let the statement hang, watching her closely, recognising an uncertainty churning in her.

She placed the cup and saucer carefully down on the table, her hand shaking. "I didn't know anything about...murders."

"There's no reason why you should have," he soothed. "But maybe now you can understand why I'm trying to find Martin." He retained his position, leaning toward her, a confidential, one-to-one pose. Time to dig deeper, but slowly. "Marge, were you and Martin close? I mean really close?"

For a long moment, her back held straight, she held his questioning gaze, her mouth a determined tight line. But there was an inner battle raging and it was a battle she couldn't possibly win. Inevitably her shoulders sagged and the tears came. "It would never have happened," she sobbed, "if my husband hadn't... I was so stupid. Even after Martin left, I still tried to..." She pulled out a handkerchief and dabbed at quickly reddening eyes. "I acted like a common tart, Mr Stern... So ashamed."

Stern reached across and laid his hand on her shaking arm. "No need to feel ashamed, Marge. In times of extreme stress, most of us are capable of almost anything." He gave her arm a gentle squeeze then relaxed back in the chair, giving her space. He was sure he'd broken through, but he would give her time.

It was some moments before she regained her composure, before she raised her eyes and was able to face him. "There's no fool like an old fool, is there, Mr Stern?"

"So they say." He gave her what he hoped was a reassuring smile. "But if we're bandying quotes they also say; 'there, but for the grace of God, go I.' So take it from me, whatever you did has been done untold times before. By the way, it's Theo. Never could get on with the 'Mr' business."

She just managed a faltering smile. "Thank you, Theo. The sad thing was, my husband had started to lose interest in me some time before Martin came on the scene," she said, studying the damp handkerchief clutched in her hands. "I just hung on, didn't want to admit it." She lifted her eyes and held his. "We'd been married for twenty years. It was hard, difficult to come to terms with, you know?"

Oh yes, he knew. How he knew. But he said nothing, just held the silence, knowing there was more to come.

"The times when he worked late became more frequent," she went on finally. "Then that first time, when he said he'd been called to head office in London. Said the meeting was late and it wasn't worth coming home, he would book into a local Holiday Inn or motel, come home the following morning. Something told me then... I mean there was a time when it didn't matter where he was or how late it was, he would always come home."

Stern was no agony aunt and this was not what he had come for, but experience told him he would have to go this way to get what he wanted. "You said it was his secretary."

"That's right. Stupid old fool."

"You were sure?"

She gave a tight lipped, determined nod. "Oh I was sure, alright. The old fool was stupid enough to leave his mobile lying around while he was having a bath." She gave a sad smile. "I trolled through the texts. They told me all I wanted to know."

"And that's when you and Martin...?

Again she looked down, colour beginning to creep into her neck. "All I could think of was my husband in some seedy motel with this..." Her fingers were strangling the handkerchief now. "I was so angry I just wanted to hurt him and to my shame I didn't care how." She picked up the cup, draining the remains of cold tea then took a deep breath. "Martin hadn't been with us very long and until then he was just a pleasant young man, our lodger, nothing more than that. I knew he was working hard on something. He seemed to be preoccupied, under pressure. I took little notice, assumed it was his work and anyway it was none of my business.

"But things changed, I changed, the day I read those texts and confirmed my husband was playing away. I waited until he told me there was another so-called meeting in London and I knew he wouldn't be back until the following day. Even now I don't know what came over me, how I did it, but I tarted myself up as I've never done before, grabbed a bottle and two glasses and went up to Martin's room." She swallowed heavily and shook her head slowly, sadly. "He didn't seem the least surprised. It was as if he were just waiting, as if he were expecting me."

"And it started from there," Stern interrupted, not wanting to hear more.

"Yes. Whenever my husband was away, Martin and I came together."

"And your husband never knew?"

"No. One day he came to me and said he thought he needed a break, a trial separation. He said he was going through a bad time and needed to get his head straight. I still never let on that I knew about the other woman, just told him to do what he wanted. By that time I was totally enchanted with Martin and couldn't have cared less what my husband did. He packed his bag and left the next day."

"Then Martin did the same."

"It was a while after, but yes he did. And in my heart I knew sooner or later he would, though I didn't want to admit it. We were having a great time but there was no future in it and I think we both knew that."

All intriguing stuff, but Stern had come for a different reason and now was the time to get what he wanted. Time for that push. "So when Martin left, even though you had become very close, he never said why or where he was going?"

"No, like I told you..."

Stern slowly shook his head. "Wrong answer, Marge." Again he leaned forward, more aggressively this time, his face now a hard mask. "When Martin Baldwin left Cain Engineering, he took with him important information to which he had no right. That makes him a criminal, Marge, and anyone who helps a criminal can be charged with aiding and abetting. You should think hard about that. But that's not all. We also know that two of Baldwin's known associates have been murdered.

"Now we don't know how or even *if* Martin was involved in any way with those killings, or even if he may himself be in danger." He let the following silence hang for a long moment, let his words sink home, then stood and looked down at Marge. "Now you got close to Baldwin, very close, and I believe you know more than you are telling me. I'm about to walk out of here, Marge, and when I do, one of two things will happen. Either I leave with all the information you can give me, and I mean everything. In that case you'll hear no more about this. Or, the next thing you know a police car will be here to take you to the station to be questioned under a formal caution. It's up to you, Marge. It's your call." He watched her closely, silently, allowing the magnitude of his words to hit home. "Now let's start again, shall we?

Twenty-nine

Things had come together in the most unexpected way and now confusion and uncertainty reigned supreme. After returning from interviewing Marge Saunders, Stern had briefed Cherry and Keen. He'd then called Frank Runcie and brought him up to date. Runcie hadn't hesitated for a second.

"Great work, Stern. All you have to do now is go get the bastard."

"What? Now hang on..."

"Oh come on, Stern, you might as well finish the job. Cost no object, first class all the way. Get what I want and there'll be a bonus in it, too. What d'you say?"

"But now you know where he is, surely you must finish the job properly. You have to involve the authorities, have him brought back and formally charged."

"No absolutely not," Runcie growled harshly. "No way do I want the law in on this. Let them get their claws into things and you never know what they'll dig up. You know the drill; you were one of 'em once."

"I was. You should remember that."

"I do, of course I do. But there's nothing iffy about what I'm asking you to do, is there? It's simple. Just make the trip and see if you can persuade him to return the design. That's it. Look, I've discussed this with Rupert Cain. We both want you to keep going and finish this for us. To that end we've come to an agreement."

"An agreement?"

"Yes. Even with what little Rupert already knows about the design, he believes it to be a world-beater. He thinks it could put us on the map for the foreseeable future. So we're prepared to offer Baldwin a deal. If he returns the design to Cain Engineering who, you can remind him, is its rightful owner anyway, we are prepared to offer him shares in the company. And, if the design really turns out to be as revolutionary as it seems, he's got himself a partnership."

Even over the phone, Stern could hear how difficult it was for Runcie to say the words. "Cain really believes it's that good, eh?"

"He does. If it were up to me I'd cut the little runt's balls off and feed them to the seagulls. But, yes, Rupert's convinced the design is that special. Which means Baldwin is special too." He gave a heavy sigh. "So, that being the case, if he comes back with the design, he has Rupert Cain's word the deal will be on the table."

Stern hadn't promised, he'd just said he'd think about it. He could understand Runcie's reluctance to involve the law; the man was a wheeler dealer and probably had more than one skeleton he didn't want dragged out of his cupboard. Besides, despite disliking Runcie himself, Stern couldn't dispute that Baldwin had turned the firm over. If Baldwin's design was as important to Cain Engineering as Runcie had led him to believe, then bully boy tactics or not the big man had every right to bring Baldwin to book. Whether Runcie would honour any of those fancy promises if and when he got his mitts on the goods was another matter. So taking everything into consideration, did he want to accede to Runcie's request and finish the job? It seemed a simple question.

But it wasn't as simple as that and now, at the end of the day, with a fully briefed Cherry and Keen having left for home, Stern sat alone in the office. Rocked back in the old chair, heels perched on the desk, he was thinking hard. There was plenty to think about and it wasn't only his successful interviewing of Marge Saunders and Frank Runcie's reaction that was bugging him.

Under the threat of the police and the prospect of her ex-lover being targeted by a killer, Marge Saunders had broken her silence. Yes, Baldwin had admitted taking information from Cain Engineering, but he'd told her it was his own stuff; it legally belonged to him not the company. But, he'd said, Runcie, who he hated and who hated him, would try to prove otherwise, would try to steal his special design and make huge profits for himself. He'd had to get it out of Runcie's reach, he'd told her, and he could only do that by leaving the country, getting as far away as possible. Marge had finally admitted that at the crack of dawn on the morning following the day Baldwin had walked away from Cain Engineering, she had driven him to Heathrow and watched him board a plane for

Australia. She had also confirmed she had spoken to him several times on the telephone since.

Stern had quizzed her about Baldwin's mail; did she know if he may have received anything through the post that may have worried him?

Marge wasn't aware of anything, but then she had never been privy to any of Baldwin's mail. As far as she knew, his only worry was Runcie. Though she had, since Baldwin had left the country, forwarded two batches of mail to him. Unopened of course.

Then she had an address.

Becoming upset, Marge had initially refused to reveal the address. It was the one thing she would not do. The night before he left, she'd promised her young lover, given her word. Stern had persisted; he would not reveal it to another soul, but if Baldwin were the target of a ruthless killer, he at least should be warned, given the chance to take protective measures. Finally she had succumbed to Stern's continued pressure. Baldwin was living in a bungalow in a suburb of Melbourne, a place called Mordialloc. Melbourne, Australia. Sometimes, Stern thought, life had a way of throwing an unexpected fast ball that was difficult, if not impossible, to avoid.

Since the day Annie had left the country, Andrew had kept up the pressure for him to visit her in Melbourne. So far he had resisted strongly. He needed to move on, forge a new life. And now someone had come into his life that could make that possible. Melanie Campbell was right; there was something, something they both felt and immediately on putting down the phone after their last conversation he'd been determined to make that move, to take the relationship a step further.

But within a second of ending Melanie's call, the phone had rung again and he'd heard the voice he'd cherished for so many years.

"If the mountain won't come to Mohamed."

They'd talked for almost an hour, at first the exchange awkward and stinted, but slowly, the tension had eased, the conversation becoming more relaxed, as it always had been. Annie was doing well running the new Melbourne store and her brother had kept his word; the paperwork for her partnership was being drawn up as they spoke. Stern had congratulated her warmly. Despite everything, he was genuinely pleased things had turned out right and she was happy. He in turn had confirmed all was well in Norfolk and Stern Investigations was still thriving. Then, inevitably, their son had come into the conversation.

"Have you spoken to Andrew?" Annie had asked.

"A couple of times in the last week," he was pleased to be able to say truthfully.

"Has he mentioned about coming over?"

Stern couldn't help the chuckle. "Does he ever not?"

"And?"

"Annie, you know the score."

"So tell me."

He sighed, irritated now. "Annie, you said it yourself, told me more than once; it's not *us* anymore, it's you and it's me, two separate people with separate lives. It also may have slipped your notice we're something like ten thousand miles or more apart."

"That doesn't mean you can't come and see me. We're still friends, aren't we?"

"Of course we are." Stern felt the pressure rising in him. He'd said it all before, thought he'd made her understand; he didn't want just friends, couldn't take just friends. He'd loved her all his life, still did. For him it had to be all or nothing. Friends was not an option. To visit, to be close to her, hold her again would only open the wound he was still desperately trying to heal. "Like I said; you know the score."

Annie was quiet for a long time, her breathing strangely audible across the line. Finally she said, "You remember how I used to say what a pain in the butt you were?"

He felt relieved, she'd given up, taken a different tack. "Frequently, sometimes with venom."

"Well that pain isn't there anymore, Theo."

He thought those last words sounded strained, her voice tight. He could think only to say, "Good, I'm glad."

"But I do miss it. I miss it such an awful lot."

Before he could say a word, there was a click and the line died.

That night he'd lain staring at the ceiling, sleep impossible, all thoughts of Melanie Campbell and his determination to further the relationship now forgotten. Only Annie's last words churned over and over in his head. What had she meant and why had she hung up so quickly afterwards? He could, if he chose, fantasise, interpreting her words as meaning she wanted him back. Maybe six months away from him had convinced her they should be together again. But, no, he couldn't do that, he dared not, it would be reading far too much into just a few, probably throwaway words.

So what then?

Well it just happened a very large man had offered him a genuine reason, a golden opportunity, to make a trip that before the phone call, before Annie had spoken those last few emotionally sounding words, he'd vowed never to undertake. Even now he couldn't be certain. Sure, the prime reason would be to locate Martin Baldwin and hopefully convince him to return his design to Cain Engineering. But would he be able to go all that way and not see Annie? And if he did see her, what would he be faced with?

Dragging himself back from the night of the call and Runcie's earlier demands, Stern dropped his feet to the floor and eased himself wearily out of the chair. It was true; sometimes life did have a way of throwing an unexpected fastball that was difficult, if not impossible, to avoid. Right now he wasn't sure how he was going to avoid this one. One thing was for sure though; a pint would help.

Thirty

The call had been taken at the police station adjacent to the Bolling Road. The time was nine-seventeen in the morning. The young woman sounded anxious, saying her boss hadn't turned up for work, which was unheard of, and looking through the shop window she was sure she could see water on the shop floor. It was approx two and a half miles from the closest police station to the address given by the girl; a chemist shop on the Tong Road, and under normal conditions, the drive from the station would have taken around seven minutes. However, this particular morning things were far from normal. Two vehicles in a head-on collision, and a cyclist mown down by a car in the early rush hour hadn't been the best of starts for the boys in blue. Add to that two burglaries reported in quick succession and the duty Sergeant's day had been made almost before it started.

The police car arrived at Mo Rahman's Pharmacy a little after ten-fifteen. As a result of Sally Buckingham's second call, Rahman senior's BMW pulled into the curb just a few minutes later. His timely arrival, with a spare set of keys, prevented the two patrolmen from battering in the front door of the shop.

It was as well the senior of the two police officers was firm in his instruction that everyone, including Rahman senior, stay outside the shop until he and his colleague had confirmed the premises were safe to enter.

~ * ~

"*Bradford?* Are you sure?"

O'Connor gave a positive nod of his head. "As near certain as we can be at this stage."

It was coming on lunchtime and O'Connor's unexpected arrival at the Stern Investigations office had taken them all by surprise. Stern had planned to call O'Connor anyway because the way things had developed they needed to talk.

Now, though, the case had taken another pace forward. Stern had immediately ushered O'Connor out of the office and into his local where, pints in front of them, they were tucked away at a corner table.

Stern raked his fingers through his unruly grey thatch. "Norfolk, Northampton and now Bradford. Just trying to get my head around the geography of this lot."

"Already been down that route, Theo."

"Nothing?"

O'Connor shook his head. "Not that I can see anyway. There has to be a link, I know, but as far as I can see, whatever ties this lot together has nothing to do with the locations."

"Okay…so tell me, when did it happen?"

"The local lads got the call first thing yesterday morning."

Stern gave a low, soft whistle. "Yesterday? Christ, you guys were quick off the ground. How the hell d'you pick it up from Bradford so fast?"

"Can't take the credit for that," O'Connor admitted. "It was a hawkeyed detective sergeant in the Bradford CID. You know we already believed there had to be a link, even though the Norfolk and Northampton murders were carried out some distance apart, right?"

Nodding, Stern reached for the pint. "The MO did it for me."

"And me, and as much as I won't let anyone else even mention the word, my gut keeps telling me we've got a serial killer on our hands."

"Yup, I'll go with that, too."

"Right, so I red-flagged the MO on the national data base, just in case."

"And this guy in Bradford picked it up?"

"He did. Thing is, though, there is one difference. No ponds or ditches this time, Theo. This was an indoor job and I'm sorry, mate, but I need you over there as soon as possible."

They'd agreed he would go first thing in the morning. It would give O'Connor time to contact the Bradford nick and, as they had with Northampton and the others, organise a contact for Stern to liaise with.

Before leaving the pub, Stern had briefed O'Connor on his visit to Marge Saunders and how he'd established that Baldwin was in Australia. O'Connor had listened and taken it all in, but it was obvious his mind was firmly fixed on the murders and, Stern thought, rightly so.

Baldwin's only connection to O'Connor's present problem was Melanie Campbell's account of the meeting with Atif Dasti in the Cain Engineering car park. Baldwin was now in Australia, so even if initially it might have been thought he could have been involved in Dasti's murder, the same couldn't be said of the others. So if the MO pointed to the killer being the same for all the killings, they could almost certainly rule out Baldwin as a suspect. That being the case, though Stern still had an interest through his own involvement with Runcie and Cain Engineering, he wasn't surprised that, as far as O'Connor's current investigations went, Baldwin wasn't a priority.

He knew the information would be logged, tucked away at the back of his friend's mind, filed for future reference if required, but right now O'Connor needed to concentrate. Someone out there was knocking over victims with impunity and O'Connor's bosses would be very unhappy about that. They would also be letting him know of their unhappiness in no uncertain terms.

Back in the office, Stern brought Cherry and Keen up to speed, instructing the latter to be ready to roll with an overnight bag at eight-thirty the following morning and Cherry to book a B&B for two as close as she could to the Bradford police station.

It was approaching five when, arrangements set for the following day, Stern decided to shut up shop and head back to the flat. The evening was cool and as he often did during his return stroll along the promenade, he stopped and leaned on the sea wall, scanning the North Sea. His eyes drifted to the recently completed offshore wind farm, just visible on a shimmering horizon. He'd read somewhere its eighty-eight gently turning turbines could produce enough clean energy to power over two hundred thousand homes and save something like five hundred thousand tonnes of CO_2 every year. It sounded a lot but as always there were two sides to every story and opponents said, whatever the saving, it wasn't worth the cost and disruption and no one would benefit from cheaper bills. Stern didn't have much of an opinion; he guessed only time would tell.

He eased himself away from the wall at the same time as he felt the vibration. He pulled the phone from his pocket and checked the screen. He thought the number was familiar, but wasn't sure.

"Stern."

"You said I could call again soon."

"Melanie."

"I've got some nibbles and a passable bottle of wine here. Wondered if you fancied a quiet evening in."

For some reason the sound of her voice created an instant recall of his conversation with Annie, those last words resounding in his brain. *'You remember how I used to say what a pain in the butt you were? I miss it such an awful lot.'* He couldn't understand why, but the thought had him suddenly gripping the phone tightly, holding it hard against his ear, his mouth moving, but an answer slow to come, the hesitation obvious.

"Just to talk, as friends," Melanie added quickly.

He found his voice. "Sorry, bit awkward to talk here,

others close by," he lied. "Er, yes that would be nice, but..."

"You have an early call in the morning," she came in quickly. There was no rancour in her voice, just a soft sadness.

"No, not at all..." He paused, stopping another lie in its tracks. "Well yes, if I'm honest, I do have to be away early in the morning; a trip to Bradford, but that doesn't mean I can't come over for an hour or two. Is that okay?"

"That would be lovely. You can tell me all about your trip and I promise I won't keep you late."

~ * ~

He arrived at the cottage at seven and parked on the grass verge across the lane. By the time he reached the front door, she was waiting. She showed him into a small, cosy sitting room with just enough space to fit the essentials: a couple of arm chairs, one either side of a rustic brick fireplace, a settee against the far wall and a sideboard tucked directly behind the door. A small television sitting on the sideboard was positioned so as to be comfortably viewed from one of the arm chairs. Several small dishes containing crisps, nuts and other finger snacks stood with a bottle of wine and two glasses alongside the television.

Melanie waved Stern to one of the arm chairs and as he lowered himself he noticed the framed photograph sitting on the mantelpiece above the fireplace. It was of a smiling couple standing together on a rock, a glistening blue sea behind. They were both in swim suits, Melanie, shapely in a black one piece and a tall, heavy set man, handsome, smiling confidently, his arm around her waist, holding her to him. The photograph stood alone, the rest of the shelf barren, with no other photos or ornaments anywhere near. Scanning the room, Stern couldn't help noticing how sparse it also was. There were no other photographs to be seen, no pictures on the walls and none of the ornaments usually seen dotted around a sitting room.

Retrieving a couple of dishes from the sideboard, Melanie balanced one on the arm of each chair. "Sorry," she apologised. "I suppose I should have a coffee table or something to put these on. Don't get many visitors and I've never got round to it." Back at the sideboard she poured two glasses of wine, returning, she handed him one. "Hope you like red, it's all I have, I'm afraid." She eased herself into the chair opposite and Stern couldn't help noting how a pair of close fitting jeans and a simple blouse, the two top buttons casually undone, can be so enhanced by a shapely figure.

"You look nice." The words seemed appropriate as she couldn't have helped noticing his wandering eyes.

"Thank you. I'm glad you approve."

He turned his head toward the solitary photo. "Your husband?"

"Yes, it was taken on one of the Greek islands. I think Zakynthos, maybe Kos, for the life of me I can't remember which. Joe and I visited several over the years."

"He was a handsome fella."

"Yes he was." She gave a little cough and took a sip of the wine, pulling her eyes away from the photograph. "Now tell me, what's dragging you all the way to Bradford tomorrow?"

She'd told him before, it was six years since she'd lost her husband, but Stern could see it still hurt. He was happy to go along with the change of subject.

"I'm back in harness for a bit; a short term contract, you might say, helping out the local lads."

"The local police?"

"Yes. They're under pressure right now, sickness and what have you. I'm just giving them a hand."

"And what's happening in Bradford?"

He took a sip of the wine, considering how much he could tell her, deciding it was okay, but not too much detail. "It's a murder."

Her eyes widened. "Really? How exciting." She paused, a little frown forming. "Maybe not for you, though. Before, when you were with the Met, were you involved with murders then?"

"Yes, I did other things in other places, but the majority of my career was spent with the murder squad."

"So this is nothing new?"

"It wouldn't have been back then, but it's been a long time."

"Yes I can understand that." She thought for a moment. "But how come Bradford? I mean, if you're helping out the Norfolk police?"

"It's complicated." He hesitated, not wanting to reveal too much, conscious of the serial killer aspect. "Let's just say there's a possibility of a link. It's only a possibility," he followed up quickly, "But it's felt we should check it out anyway."

"You mean a link with Norfolk?"

Stern smiled. Typical woman, she wasn't about to let it go easy. He drank more wine, then said, "Sort of."

Now she was leaning forward, eyes twinkling excitedly. "You don't mean *someone* in Norfolk?"

It had gone far enough. The smile still in place, he held up a hand. "Sorry, Miss Marple, I can't tell you anymore."

She feigned a heavy pout. "Spoilsport, I was hoping to get all the grizzly details." The pout quickly changed to a bright smile. "Sorry, Theo, reading a good crime thriller is about the most excitement I get these days. And," she pushed herself up from the chair and leaned across, pecking him gently on the lips, "I'm naturally a nosy woman, right?" she collected his glass and headed toward the sideboard.

Stern laughed. "I didn't say that, did I?"

"Maybe not, but I bet you thought it." She refilled the glasses and returned to the chair, handing his across and lowering herself down. "Okay, no more talk of murder and mayhem. What else has been happening in your busy life? With everything else going on, I don't suppose there's been any sign of poor Martin, has there?"

The feel of the tender kiss had stayed with him, as had the soft sweet aroma of her perfume still lingering. Had it been spontaneous, or was it planned; the two buttons of the blouse deliberately left undone with that rehearsed, revealing lean forward and gentle kiss in mind? The way she sat now, prim and proper, her questioning eyes innocently searching his, gave nothing away and Stern wasn't experienced enough in these matters to know. This was when the great super-sleuth realised that over thirty years with one woman put him at a distinct disadvantage when thrown back into the dating game. Best not dwell on it, just answer the question. With Baldwin pretty much out of the loop, he felt he could, though with no details and certainly with no mention of his own involvement with Runcie.

"Well as it happens there has. It seems our friend Baldwin has decamped and headed for Australia."

Thirty-one

They'd cut west across country on the A17 until they'd picked up the A1(M) heading north, finally breaking away onto the M6 then the A650 into Bradford. Google maps had said three hours fifty minutes. It had actually taken four hours twenty. They pulled up outside the guest house at half past twelve.

During the drive, Keen's several attempts at making conversation had been met in the main with short cryptic answers, Stern seemingly unwilling to engage for any length of time. The young DC could be forgiven for thinking his boss's silence was as a result of something he had said or done. Such a thought would have been far from the truth. The real reason for Stern's silence was guilt, bucket loads of guilt about something *he* had done.

Just to talk, she'd said. As friends, she'd said, and like an innocent lamb to the slaughter, that's exactly what he'd expected. A glass of wine, a few nibbles and a friendly chat. So how the bloody hell had it managed to end up where it had? Christ, he hadn't climbed back into his car until the early hours and he hadn't slept a wink since. The four hour drive had been purgatory and even if he'd wanted to talk, which he didn't, he couldn't have held a sensible conversation anyway. For the whole journey, only one thing, one question had dominated his mind: how had he let a couple of glasses of wine, a carefully unbuttoned blouse and a soft kiss on the lips lead to where it had? And why did he feel so soddin' guilty about it? Yeah, okay, that was two questions, but the second was just supplementary to the first, wasn't it?

He kept reminding himself it was Annie who'd done the runner, buggered off to the other side of the world. So that was it then, wasn't it? He was his own man, a free agent. He could do what he liked, see who he wanted. That's exactly what he'd done, right? It wasn't as if he hadn't enjoyed it either, he had, and some. Probably, more than anything, that's what was fuelling the bloody guilt. That and until only a few hours ago he'd known only one woman, physically that was, for the whole of his life.

Now they were here, though, he had to push it from his mind. The rest of the day still lay ahead and he was due to meet his contact in the local nick at three. Then the afternoon would be taken up reviewing the crime scene. With his brain about to close down and half a ton of grit infesting his eyes, he doubted he'd be able to see anything clearly, let alone make any sensible conclusions unless he got some rest. Lucky he had some time before his meet at the local nick. He'd try and get his head down for a couple of hours.

Total fatigue had won the day and a still fully clothed consciousness had only returned with the tentative but persistent tapping on his bedroom door. He forced glued eyelids apart and peered down at his watch. Half past two.

"Yeah, I hear you. I'm on my way."

He peeled himself out of his clothes and staggered into the shower. Every room with en suite; well done, Cherry. Ten minutes later, feeling almost human, he was out front where he found Keen leaning patiently against the Hyundai. He smiled, the best he could do, hoping it made up just a tad for four plus hours of almost constant silence his young sidekick had had to endure on the way here. "Okay, let's see what we can come up with, shall we?"

Their contact this time was a young DC called Roberts who could have been no more than a couple of years older than Keen. He had in tow the senior of the two uniformed constables who had responded to Sally Buckingham's emergency call. He'd been the first to wade through an inch of water to the back room, the first to see the carnage there.

Roberts was quick and on the ball, fully briefed, and with a car at his disposal. Half an hour after arriving at the nick and parking the Hyundai, they were pulling up outside Mo Rahman's closed and sealed pharmacy. Again, full marks to O'Connor, or someone on his behalf, for making the right contact, and to the locals for their instant cooperation. Nationwide, Stern thought, the police liaison and collaboration was better than ever.

A uniformed constable was guarding the taped-off front of the premises. Their access, Roberts informed them, would be through a rear entrance. From the street they made their way along a short alleyway leading to a small square yard. A green wheelie bin stood to one side of a doorway into the back of the shop. The door was open and two individuals clad in white coveralls were at work inside. Stopping at the door, Roberts turned to Stern. "Instructions are not to..."

Stern nodded. "Yeah, I know the score; no one in until the SOCOs say so, right."

"Sorry, I forgot, you've done all this before, haven't you?"

"Once or twice."

Roberts gave a little self-conscious cough. "By the way, Mr Stern. Just for the record, they prefer to be called CSIs now. Crime Scene Investigators."

"Really? Thanks for the update. Has the job changed?"

Roberts shook his head. "Not that I know of."

Smiling, Stern gave a little shrug. "Oh well, a change is as good as a rest, I suppose."

Keen leaned in close and whispered in Robert's ear. "Take a look at DI Stern's record." Stern heard the comment, noting his elevation back to DI, but said nothing. He did wonder if it meant Keen had himself looked him up, studied his record, and if so, did he already know about Stern's connection with his father?

If he did, he'd certainly shown no sign of it. Stern pushed the thought from his mind...now was not the time.

He stood on the threshold looking into the room. Old habits die hard. For all those years his own little routine, still not forgotten; the first few minutes on an initial visit to any crime scene always spent on the outside, standing back looking in. An overall scan, before closing in and studying detail. Surprising what you can spot from a distance that might blur up close, he would maintain to any subordinate willing to listen.

The room was small. It had no windows and a single unshaded bulb hanging from the centre of the ceiling would normally be the only source of light. Now, though, the Scene Of Crime Officer's powerful lamps supported high on a tripod in one corner of the room starkly illuminated every nook and cranny.

In addition to the one they were standing in, there were two other doorways leading from the room. Both stood open. Stern looked from one to the other, noting the first to be a toilet. The second led into the passage which he guessed ran through to the shop itself. The floor was still soaking wet with puddles filling its irregularities, saturating the lower half of several cardboard boxes stacked against the far wall.

In the middle of the room a video monitor lay on its side, its screen shattered, the glass fragments scattered across the floor glistening in the wetness. To his immediate right a table stood directly in front of an old style ceramic, Belfast sink, its outer face stained by pale brown rivulets. Above the sink a large brass tap dripped occasionally. An upturned wooden kitchen chair, its back broken, lay alongside the table.

After some scrutiny, Stern turned to the uniformed constable standing at his right shoulder. "As it was when you first came in?"

"Exactly. Well, except there was the body, of course."

"Okay, so paint me a picture."

"When we arrived, the young woman who'd phoned it in was waiting," the constable explained. "She's the pharmacist's assistant, name of Sally Buckingham. Seems she'd arrived for work at the usual time and found the place still locked, something that had never happened before. Then when she looks through the window she sees the shop is flooded. We didn't know about this back door and were about to break in the front when Mr Rahman Senior turned up. Turns out the girl had phoned him as well."

"Mr Rahman?"

"Yeah, he owns a string of pharmacies. His son managed this one."

Stern looked to Roberts. "The son was the victim?"

"Yes, Mohamed Rahman. Twenty-nine years old. Single, but due to marry in a few months' time. The Rahmans had daughters but Mohamed was the only son. He was a qualified pharmacist and was being groomed to take over the family business when Rahman senior retired."

Stern thought for some moments then again

addressed the uniformed PC. "You say you didn't know about this door?"

"No." Shaking his head, the constable took a breath. "In hindsight, maybe we should have."

Stern gave a dismissive shrug of the shoulders. "Don't know why. Knowing or not knowing wouldn't have made any difference to what happened here, would it?"

"No, I guess not." The constable seemed relieved to hear the words.

Stern wasn't letting him off that easy, though. "Mind you, you wouldn't have been flavour of the month if, with everything open at the back here, you'd caved the bloody front door in." He ignored grins on the faces of the others, and carried on surveying the room, finally running his eyes over the door and the door jamb. "No forced entry."

"No," Roberts concurred. "But we think the girl gave us the answer to that one. Seems Rahman was meticulous, had a strict routine. He was here before eight every morning. He checked out the shop, making sure all was well, even went over it with a broom if he thought it necessary. Then he cleaned up back here, collected the rubbish from the previous day...old containers, empty boxes from deliveries...that sort of thing, and took them out to the wheelie bin outside."

Tight lipped, Stern nodded. "Same thing every day."

"That's what the girl told us," Roberts confirmed. "Every day exactly the same routine. Seems he was with everything he did. Seems you could set your watch to him. By the time she arrived every morning just before nine, the place would be spotless. Always the same."

"So it would have been easy for someone studying this routine for a while to know exactly when to be out back waiting for the door to be unlocked," Stern said. "And at such an early hour, tucked away back here, no one would be any the wiser." He turned back to the uniformed constable. "Okay, go on."

"Well I got my partner to stay outside. He made sure no one came in while I waded through the shop to find where the water was coming from. Thought it was a burst pipe somewhere. Didn't expect to find what I did." He took a breath. "With the stuff all over the place, it looked like there'd been a fight." He pointed to the broken monitor and chair. "Looked even worse then. With the water and all."

"So where was the body?"

"Well, that was what was so weird. It looked like it had been staged."

"Staged?"

"Yeah, well maybe staged is the wrong word, but," he indicated the table drawn up to the sink. "I mean normally you'd never have a table in front of a sink like that, would you?"

"Put there for a purpose you mean?"

"It certainly was. See, the plug was in the sink so it was full of water, overflowing in fact, and the tap was still running. The body was lying on its back across the table. I remember the legs were together, bent at the knees, hanging over the end of the table. The arms were dropped down either side and tied together under the table. When I looked closer, I could see the legs had been pulled back under the table, too, and the ankles were tied to the hands. The guy couldn't have moved an inch if he'd tried."

"What was used to tie the hands and feet together?" Stern asked.

"Plastic banding, we assume from one of the packages at the back there." He pointed at the boxes stacked at the rear of the room."

"Okay, go on."

"Well it was the head." The PC swallowed heavily, the memory returning. "I couldn't see the head because it was hanging back over the edge of the sink. It was completely under water."

Thirty-two

Back at the Bradford nick they'd been given the chance to talk to a member of the SOCO team and the doctor who'd attended the murder scene. It was made clear, particularly by the doctor, a world-weary old hand, that any comments were first thoughts only, based on his initial inspection at the scene. Nothing could be certain until the official post mortem had been carried out. He'd said it so often before, particularly to pushy DIs concerned with making headway in those important early hours, it came out like a practiced mantra.

However, two things did seem clear: first there appeared to have been a fight during which, as well as several minor cuts and bruises, the deceased had received two severe blows. The first was to the face; the doctor's first impression suggesting the damage being consistent with a blow from a fist. The second: a heavy blow to the head, probably from the broken chair, on which there was a good amount of blood, had been severe enough to render Rahman unconscious. Also, based on that initial examination, the doctor did believe death had been the result of drowning. Analysis of the blood on the chair would confirm the former and drowning would be verified during the post mortem. He refused to commit himself further.

It was gone seven when they finally left the station. Stern thought about driving straight back to Norfolk but decided against it. His eyes were already beginning to droop and considering the previous night, he wasn't surprised. Besides, the room was booked, no point in wasting it.

The guest house only provided breakfast so it was necessary to arrange an evening meal. The desk sergeant at the nick pointed the way; a pub within walking distance of the guest house supposedly served up good pub grub until nine. They were standing at the bar just after eight thirty and tucking into liver and bacon with creamy mashed potatoes and thick brown gravy by a few minutes before nine.

Twenty minutes later, his plate clean, Stern watched Keen scrape the last morsel of potato from his plate. He reached for his glass and drained the final dregs. "Good, eh?"

Keen leaned back with a sigh. "Yes, very good. Didn't realise how hungry I was."

"And me." Stern held up the empty glass. "One more and bed, right?"

Keen followed suit, emptying his glass and handing it to Stern. "Sounds good to me."

Stern returned to the table with two fresh pints and dropped into the chair. "So, any thoughts?"

Keen took a mouthful of beer, wiping the fresh froth from his lip with the back of his hand. "Well, if it is the same killer, he had his work cut out this time. He couldn't sneak up behind like it seems he did with the other two. He had to take this one head-on."

"Which would explain the fight," Stern agreed. "The doc said the severe bruising to the face looked like he'd been punched, so maybe the attacker hit Rahman as soon as he opened the door to put the rubbish out. But if that wasn't enough, he had to finish him off with whatever was at hand."

"The chair."

"Looks like it. They'll confirm that when they match the blood on the chair to the victim's blood. Wouldn't bet against it, though."

Keen ran his finger thoughtfully around the rim of the glass. "So now the killer has his victim unconscious, he needs to carry out the drowning."

"Yes and that's going to be difficult. He can fill the sink okay, but then he has to haul the body, dead weight, and hold the head under water. What if his victim starts to regain consciousness while he's trying to do this? No, much easier to pull the table up to the sink and lift the body onto it while his man is out cold. Lay him on his back, tie his hands and feet together under the table and let the head drop backwards into the sink. Any reaction, any resistance and he could sit on the body and hold the head down with one hand. Couldn't be simpler."

Stern took a long pull at the beer. "Anyway, Roberts is going to update us as soon as the pathologist has done his bit and they know more. They're also going to interview Rahman's family. We'll get a briefing on that too. Best we can do right now, so business over for the day." He raised his glass again. "Finish this and get some shuteye. To be honest I could do with it."

Keen watched Stern take another drink. "Can I ask you something, Mr Stern?"

"Sure."

"What was my dad really like?"

Considering Keen's earlier suggestion to Roberts that he should study Stern's record, maybe he should have been prepared. But he wasn't. It was the last thing he expected and caught him totally unawares. Tight lipped, he slowly lowered the glass to the table, his mind searching for the right response. "Don't you remember him?" It was a pathetic answer, a question for a question, but it gave him time to think.

"I was four when he was killed."

"Of course, I'm forgetting how long ago it was." Stern thought back, dragging the memory up from the deep, remembering nineteen ninety-six, seventeen years ago. "Didn't your mum tell you anything about him?"

The young DC smiled softly. "Yes, of course she did, often. But Dad was Mum's hero, her superman." He eyed Stern closely across the table. "She only ever told me how wonderful he was. But that's natural, isn't it? Couldn't expect anything else from his wife, could I? She didn't even tell me about you, how you were there when Dad was killed."

So, the young detective had done his homework; he did

know about Stern's involvement in his father's case. "When did you learn this?"

"After I was assigned to you. I couldn't understand why, after only a couple of weeks in plain clothes, I was handed over to a private investigator. It didn't make sense. I asked DI O'Connor and he said it was to broaden my horizons, said you were the absolute best in your time. To be honest, it sounded like a bit of a fudge to me, but he painted such a glowing picture I just had to look up your record. I read every word, including your own report about that night. You were there, weren't you? You did try to help my dad?

Stern was silent for a long moment. The bright-eyed young man sitting opposite was asking the wrong person the wrong question. From the age of four he'd been led to believe his father was a hero, someone who, unarmed, had tackled one of the most ruthless, East London killers of the day, single handed, and paid for it with his life. For that he was awarded the Queen's Gallantry Medal. A hero indeed.

Now seventeen years later, he was asking the question of the only man on the planet who knew the truth about Jimmy Keen. And that truth was the single reason why Stern had been there in the freezing early hours when Jimmy Keen had met his maker. Yes it was true, and on record, that Stern had held the dying man, cradled his head in his lap, comforted him as best he could while desperately hoping the ambulance would arrive soon. But it hadn't, and Stern had helplessly watched Jimmy Keen's eyes glaze and his life slowly ebb away.

Now, as a result of that single act seventeen years before, a grateful mother had chosen him as the living legend to which her son should aspire. But what wasn't recorded and what Stern had kept locked away for all those years was how on that bitter night he had also become a father confessor. As a result, then and there, he'd decided no one could benefit from the truth that was Jimmy Keen, and right now, all these years later, it would be the last thing the anxious young man sitting opposite would want to hear.

"D'you know, Colin, I didn't know your dad very well at all," he lied. "Yes, I was there on that night and I was able to give him some comfort, but that's about it, I'm afraid."

"But you did take care of Raker, didn't you?"

Stern gave a heavy resigned sigh. "Okay, yes I did. You must remember Raker was a maniac, public enemy number one of the day. He was into drugs, prostitution and anything else his filthy hands could get hold of. He'd been in and out of jail since he was a kid and always for violent offences. He was obsessed by handguns and was always armed to the teeth. We were sure he was responsible for at least two murders; both rivals who had disappeared without a trace, their bodies never found. Though, until then, we hadn't been able to prove it. It's true I did take care of him, but that night luck was on my side. Unlike your father, I was armed.

"I didn't know it when I first arrived, but Raker had already shot your father. He was heading out of the building toward his car. I called for him to stop, but he just swung round and started firing. Like I said, luck was on my side because it was bitterly cold and the road was icy. As Raker turned and fired at me, he slipped on the ice. The first shot took a chunk out of my shoulder, the second missed completely. I fired just once. As we were taught, I aimed at the biggest part of the body, the torso. Luck again, Colin lad, my shot went straight through his heart. Raker was dead before he hit the ground."

"That's when you went inside and found my dad?"

"Yes."

Keen frowned, troubled lines breaking his forehead. "One thing I could never figure," he said, his finger continuing to trace that slow line around the rim of his glass. "The record says Dad was acting on a tipoff. But if that was the case, why was he on his own and why wasn't he armed like you were?"

There it was, Stern thought, a young astute mind going instantly to the heart of the problem. Stern was desperately tired and could do without this, but Keen was hungry for answers; he wasn't about to let this go.

"Look, you have to remember things were different then," Stern said, his tired brain thinking on the hoof. "Particularly in London. We all had snouts…informers who we paid for information. Sometimes they came up with details of some hit or other going down, or, as in the case of your dad, the whereabouts of a known villain. When this happened you had to act fast. If you didn't, you'd miss the chance. So you'd go for it and call for backup if and when you needed it. Don't forget we didn't all have mobile phones tucked in our pockets in those days."

Keen gave a slow thoughtful nod of understanding, sort of. "So Dad must have called you from the house, right?"

"Called me?"

"Yes. The report said you arrived as backup, but my father had already been shot. So I assume he must have somehow managed to call you. Like you say, you didn't have mobiles so I can only assume it was from the house."

Stern felt young questioning eyes closely scrutinising him across the table. It had been a long time and, weary as he was, for a moment he'd forgotten the minor details. At the time it seemed everyone was having a go at the police: wrongful arrests, brutality in police station prison cells, you name it, they were doing it wrong. The true reason for Stern being there that night, which was certainly not as a result of a call from Jimmy Keen, would have only fuelled an already well-stoked fire. Stern wasn't about to let that happen. For the same reason, those in office were happy to accept his version of events, questionable as it was, without hesitation, even taking the opportunity to improve police ratings by creating a hero of their own.

"Yeah, well, of course I never did know where he called from," he said, trying to cover the obvious hesitation his initial confusion had caused. "After the run-in with Raker, I was too busy trying to help your father. By the time it was all over, there was no way for me to find out."

Keen pulled a long sober sigh. "There was no one left to ask."

"Yup. Sorry, but that's how it was."

They were both silent for a long time before, without

raising his eyes, Keen spoke again, his words soft, as if directed at himself. "I just want to be a good copper, Mr Stern."

Stern was relieved the interrogation was over. "I'm sure you will be, lad."

The young detective looked up, his face a serious, a concerned mask. "I should say I want to be like my father, shouldn't I?"

Stern frowned, his brain stalling, at first confused by the question, then suddenly, alert to what Keen could be asking. Could he possibly suspect, or even somehow know the truth behind his father's demise? And if so, how the hell had he found out? Stern knew he had been the only other person there that night and he'd spoken to no one.

In all the seventeen years since, not one soul had questioned his report of the incident. So no, not possible. He had to be reading Keen's question wrongly. He gave a casual shrug of his shoulders. "Of course you should. Your father was a good copper, and you should be proud to be like him." It was a lie, but on this matter Stern had been lying for the past seventeen years. He wasn't about to stop now.

Thirty-three

Martin had spoken to Marge, first telling her how well things were going. then, with the threatening notes in mind, asking if there had been any other developments. To his dismay she'd admitted talking to a private investigator, and worse, revealing where he was living.

"You've told someone where I am?" he'd exclaimed incredulously. "But why would you do that? I told you I would do the deal, then send for you. I promised, didn't I?"

"Oh c'mon, my love, you and I both know you were never going to keep that promise."

There was something in her tone; something very different, sombre, older sounding, a mother reprimanding her child. "I was there and so were you. For different reasons the time was right for both of us. We had needs and it was great fun while it lasted, and for a little while I even believed what you were telling me. I could say you used me, dear, but that would be unfair because, if I'm honest, I used you just as much. But there's no future for us, Martin. There never was. I was an old fool for a while,

246

but even old fools come to their senses sometimes."

He felt exposed, found out, and he didn't like the feeling. But she was right; he'd had no intention of telling her his plans, certainly not that for the next twelve months he'd be hiding away in China. He'd figured not knowing where he was and a year's total silence would have spelled it out for her. But this wasn't the breathy, sexy voiced old tart that'd been unable to keep her hands off him as soon as her husband walked out the door. Who'd given him such a good time and in their most intimate moments had him believing he was the greatest thing since sliced bread. No, this was a softly spoken mature lady who was making him feel immature and inadequate, dirty even.

"I'm sorry, Marge, I didn't mean to..."

"Oh of course you did, Martin, but don't apologise, it's not necessary. Let's face it...you didn't have to beat me into submission, did you?"

Each word made him feel more of a heel and for a moment the shock of being exposed to a private eye working for the police was forgotten. "Maybe not, but please don't think I did it just to..."

"I really don't care why you did it, Martin," she broke in again. "It's over, forgotten. What's important now is why I chose to reveal your whereabouts."

She had given him chapter and verse about the private investigator's two visits, including the suggestion that Baldwin may be at risk, particularly if he'd received threatening notes. When she'd asked if there had been anything of the sort in the two bundles she'd sent him, he'd denied it, insisting most had been junk mail. What was to say this investigator character wouldn't be back, probing for more? Marge had let out enough, too much already; he wasn't about to expose himself further.

Now he sat staring down at the two notes lying in front of him and wondering. The one delivered in the first bundle was worded exactly as Atif had explained. Back then, in Cain's car park, he'd asked to see the note, but Atif hadn't been able to produce it. He'd driven straight to Norfolk from the clinic where he worked, he'd insisted, forgetting the note was tucked in one of his books back at his flat. But that didn't matter because it was a rhyme and he'd memorised it.

Murderers all four
A killer every one
One by one you have to pay
Justice will be done

Atif had been so sure; he knew what it said. More frightening still, he knew what it meant and if Atif were right in his construal of the note, so did Baldwin. But it was so long ago. Back then an agreement had been reached and they had all remained tight lipped ever since; not a word in seven long years. Besides, at the time Atif had confronted him in the car park, Baldwin had been on the move.

There was a fortune waiting for him on the other side of the world and he wasn't about to jeopardise it for some cranky note Atif had put his own interpretation to. Sure, it could mean exactly what Atif was so sure it meant, but then again it could mean nothing of the sort. Hell, the words he quoted could mean anything. Besides, he'd told himself, in twenty-four hours he would be on the other side of the world. Even if the threat were genuine as Atif had feared, whoever sent it would have to go some to hurt him ten thousand miles away.

But now he had seen the second note, the one that had come in the second bundle posted to him by Marge.

Three have paid the price
There's just one to go
Your time has come, it must be so

Could his old university friends really be dead? All of them? Had Atif's interpretation of that first note been right after all? It certainly looked like it. But if that were the case, who was making these threats and if the words of the second note were true, who had killed his old friends?

He tried to relax, reminding himself again that even if it were true and someone had killed his friends, here, on the other side of the world, he should still be safe, shouldn't he? For just a moment that thought gave him some comfort, but then, chillingly, the truth dawned. That might have been the case, but not now. Now Marge had told a private investigator where he was. Now his whereabouts were out there, known in the UK. Marge had said the PI was working for the police and had assured her any information she gave him would go no further; all he wanted to know was that Martin was alive and well. But what if the man wasn't a PI at all? What if he were the person who had carried out the killings and was masquerading as a PI? Baldwin's heart skipped a beat at another alarming thought. If that were true, right now someone could be on their way to kill him as they had his friends.

He looked across the room at the lone calendar hanging on the wall. Each day until today had been struck through with bold marker pen. A day, five days from now, was circled in red. Just five days till the day he jumped on another aircraft and headed first class, courtesy of Mr Li's company, for China. But could it be five days during which, at any time, the killer could arrive at his door?

He shuddered at the thought. Maybe he should move out, go and live somewhere else, tuck himself away for the next five days. It would make sense. But no, he stopped himself short. He mustn't panic, mustn't let his imagination run riot. He had no proof that his old friends had been killed and anyway he'd put too much into this to let himself be frightened now. He just had to be super careful for the next five days. There was twenty million at stake here and he'd worked his butt off for too long to let silly panic distract him now. Once in China, he was worth too much to Mr Li's company for them to let anything happen to him. No, all he had to do was keep his eyes peeled, make sure there were no strangers in the area, be careful who he opened the door to, that sort of thing. Then he'd be up and away.

Thirty-four

An early breakfast had seen Stern, together with a bleary eyed Keen, leaving Bradford around nine. They'd grabbed a quick bite en-route and arrived at the office just before two. During the journey, they'd called Cherry and kept her up to date with their progress. When they arrived, she was waiting, eyes gleaming, coffee at the ready.

They settled in Stern's office and his rear had hardly touched the seat of the old chair when the phone rang.

Stern picked up. "So, when are you going?" Sod it, he should have let Cherry take the call.

"I didn't actually say I was going, did I? I said I'd think about it."

"Yes, yes, I know what you said, but this is critical, Stern." Runcie's growl of frustration echoed down the line. "Good grief, man, I told you once I wouldn't beg, but if that's what it's going to take..."

"There's no need for that."

"You think not? Well let me tell you, this could be make-or-break time for Cain Engineering and I'll do whatever it takes to get that design back."

"Except go to the police."

Another growl of aggravation. "Yes, except that. For the moment, anyway. You're a man of the world, Stern. You know the way things work. I'm not a criminal; I've never actually broken the law. But sometimes to make things work, you have to sail close to the wind. If you want to get on, achieve your aim, it's the way it has to be, it will always be that way. Let's just say the police could make things awkward here, and I'd prefer that not to be the case."

Never broken the law? Yeah right. Stern knew, in legal terms, there was a fine line between honesty and dishonesty and he doubted any of the so called honest rich hadn't at some time or other strayed well below that line. They probably wouldn't be rich if they hadn't. He said nothing.

"I'm being honest, Stern," Runcie ploughed on. "I hope you can appreciate that and work with me here. The simple fact is Baldwin had a contract committing him and his work to Cain Engineering. He's broken that contract and stolen what is legally ours. Truth is, without it we could even go to the wall." There was a long pause Runcie's heavy, agitated breathing rasping on the line for some moments before he spoke again. "You may not like me, Stern," he continued finally. "Not many people do because sometimes, to get what I want, I do use bully boy tactics. I'm also well aware it might be because of me Baldwin ran like he did. But regardless of that, regardless of what you or anyone else thinks of me, the guys at Cain, particularly Rupert Cain himself, don't deserve this. They're a brilliant bunch and they've worked hard for years to build the company. It's not their fault that things are tight and it's certainly not their fault the future of the company is being put at risk by one greedy little toe-rag."

"Greedy?"

"That's right. Why d'you think I'm panicking about this? It's obvious what he's up to; he's out there right now trying to sell our design to the highest bidder."

"In Australia?"

Runcie gave an impatient snort. "Ever heard of sequential or successional switching?"

"No."

"No, neither had I and probably, in the terms applied to Baldwin's design, neither would anyone else. In layman's terms, which is how Rupert had to explain it to me, it's a multi-switching device that can control any amount of functions, electrical or mechanical, at a phenomenal speed. Rupert Cain only saw the initial design, the protocol, but still as far as he's concerned, it could be a worldwide first. Its applications are endless...in weapons systems in particular it could be revolutionary. Everyone will want it. So it matters not one toss where Baldwin is skulking away. He could be sitting on top of Everest and the treacherous little bastard would still be surrounded with offers."

Stern gave it some thought. "But how would he sell something like that out there on his own? He would need to make contact with governments, wouldn't he? Or at least large companies contracted to governments."

"Rupert Cain had every faith in Baldwin." Now there was a soft, almost sad edge to Runcie's words. "He could see him as the future of the company, trusted him implicitly; gave him a free hand. As a result, Baldwin worked all hours, sometimes late at night. We can't prove it, but we believe at some time, when he was alone in the place, he broke into our company customer records. In the past we've dealt with companies all over the world; he could have taken his pick."

"Sounds like he planned this all along," Stern said.

"He must have," Runcie agreed. "And if he'd stayed with us, if his design is as good as Rupert Cain believes it is, Baldwin would have been made."

"But not made as much as if he sells the design himself," Stern mused. "From what you say it could pull him millions."

"That's true," Runcie admitted reluctantly. "But don't you see, it's not his to sell."

"Okay, assuming I do agree to go and I do find him, what if I can't change his mind, can't persuade him to come back?"

"Then we could be in serious trouble and maybe the law would have to be my last resort after all. But something tells me, with you working with us, that won't happen. So what d'you say? Will you do it?"

Mixed thoughts were rushing through Stern's head. He couldn't possibly go to Australia, Melbourne even, without seeing Annie. Neither she nor Andrew would ever forgive him. Yet the night spent with Melanie had been special, bringing them even closer together, closer than he'd have previously thought possible with anyone other than Annie. So how would he feel, seeing Annie so soon afterwards? Would it only create more confusion in his already torn mind?

But Baldwin had broken a contract and if the loss of his design could be as devastating to Cain Engineering as Runcie intimated, whatever he thought of Runcie himself, the rest of the company didn't deserve to go down because of one man's breach of contract. Also, through Atif Dasti, there was always Baldwin's possible connection to the murders. It was a speculative connection to say the least, but if by talking to Baldwin there was the remotest chance of throwing some light on the case, that in itself would be worth the trip.

Stern took a deep breath. "Okay, but first class all the way," he growled through gritted teeth. "And a hefty bonus if I get him back."

He dropped the phone back in its cradle and looked from Cherry to Keen. "Well, it looks like I'm going to Australia."

Both Cherry and Keen had listened intently to the telephone conversation, trying desperately to interpret its content from Stern's words only. Keen was first in, grinning.

"Well it's obvious, isn't it; you're going to need someone to look after you, boss. Think you could wangle me a ticket, too?"

Cherry hit back. "Whoa, hang on sunshine. After me, you're first."

Stern waved a hand. "Sorry guys. This has to be a one man show, all expenses paid and, as the big man said, first class all the way. Tell you what, though, when I get back

I'll treat you both to a slap up fish and chip supper."

"That's what I love about my boss, generous to a fault."

They were interrupted by the telephone again springing into life.

Cherry picked up. "Stern Investigations." She listened for a beat then, her hand cupped over the mouthpiece, said: "It's Inspector Buchanan, Northamptonshire CID."

Stern took the phone. "Buchanan, how y'doin'? Yeah, I'm good. You got something for me?" He listened for a moment, then pulled open the desk drawer, rifling around until he found a piece of paper. "Where'd they find it?" Again he listened, nodding. "Read it to me, would you?" Another short pause. "Yup, exactly the same words. That does it, right? Closes the link? Yeah, I agree. Oh and by the way, there's been another one, this time in Bradford.

"That's right, slightly different...indoors job this time, but the same MO. We need to pull this lot together and establish what links the three victims." From the corner of his eye, he glimpsed Cherry's raised hand but waved it down, listening again to Buchanan. "Yeah, I agree," he carried on. "I'll talk to O'Connor, see if we can set up a face-to-face. I think we could do with it, don't you?" Another pause. "Okay, sounds good to me. The sooner the better. Cheers, I'll get back to you. And thanks again for the info." He placed the phone back in its cradle and looked from Cherry to Keen. "They were clearing out Ralph Armitage's work desk and found the note."

"The same?"

He held up the piece of paper he'd pulled from the

drawer, the note he'd found tucked inside the book in Atif Dasti's flat. "Yup, Buchanan read it to me. Exactly the same words." He gave Keen the eye. "Colin, I want you to brief Cherry on the Bradford visit. She can then update our records."

Keen pushed himself out of the chair. "Okay, will do."

Cherry stayed put. "I was just trying to tell you I have some updating to do, too," she said, unable to keep the eager edge from her voice.

"Ah, I'm sorry," Stern apologised. "But you have to excuse me. See, I'm tired and I'm not a woman. I can only concentrate on one thing at a time."

Cherry gave an exaggerated sigh. "How on earth did you ever make Detective Inspector?"

Keen glanced apprehensively toward Stern. He still had a lot to learn about the banter that went on at Stern Investigations.

Stern grinned. "I lied a lot." He'd noticed the excited tension in Cherry's demeanour when they'd first arrived back at the office, but the call from Runcie, and now again from Buchanan, had overtaken things. Now, though, seeing that gleam still in her eye, her bottom fidgeting on the chair...typical Cherry agitation, he knew something was up. He relaxed back in the chair, nodding for Keen to do the same. He had learned long since that when Cherry looked this excited, whatever she had bottled up would be worth hearing. "Okay, kid, let's hear it."

Her grin was wider than usual. "I've found another link between Dasti and Rahman."

Stern leaned forward in the chair. "Go on."

"Well, we knew they were both pharmacists, but what we didn't know was they both qualified out of Liverpool University, and both in the same year, two thousand and six."

Keen gave a low whistle. "Which means they almost certainly knew each other."

Giving a slow nod of his head, Stern studied Cherry, a slow smile spreading across his face. "And that's not all, is it Sherlock?"

"No it's not, because we already know that Martin Baldwin qualified a year earlier than son Andrew, don't we?

"And Andrew qualified in two thousand and seven," Stern confirmed.

"Which means Baldwin finished in two thousand and six, the same year as the other two."

"Bloody hell," Keen breathed. "That's three out of the four. That just leaves Armitage."

"Still nothing on him then?" Stern asked.

"Not yet, no," Cherry admitted.

"Well, he may not have been at Liverpool," Stern mused, "but we know he's in the mix somewhere because he also received a note." He looked from one to the other. "Keep digging…it's there somewhere. In the meantime I need to talk to David."

The two were almost out of the office door when he remembered. "Oh, and Cherry, see if you can book me a seat on a flight to Melbourne, say day after tomorrow, give me time to get myself ready. And remember, it has to be first class."

Thirty-five

"*Australia!* Theo, are you out of your mind? We've got a triple murder enquiry going on here, and the brass are so far up my back it feels like my arse is on fire. And what have I got? Bugger all but dead bodies. I need you here, Theo, not gallivanting off to the other side of the world." He paused, but only for a beat. "It's about Annie, isn't it? You're going to see her."

Stern held the phone a little farther from his ear. He could almost hear the steam pumping from O'Connor's ears. "Hang on, David; no it's not about Annie, and I'm not gallivanting anywhere. It's all part of the enquiry."

"Well correct me if I'm wrong, Theo, but I don't remember any of these murders taking place in the bloody outback."

The sheer tension in his friend's voice indicated the pressure he was under and Stern understood it. He'd been there himself. He excused the sarcasm. "No, of course not, but I believe the answer could well be over there."

"How, for Christ sake?"

Stern explained how originally Cherry had been able to

tie Dasti and Rahman to Liverpool University at the same time. "And, if you remember, Andrew, my son, also knew Martin Baldwin at Liverpool. We already know Baldwin met Dasti in the Cain Engineering car park, don't we? That links the two of them. Now, what clever old Cherry has also established is not only did Baldwin, Dasti and Rahman all attend Liverpool, but they were all there at exactly the same time. Now, Dasti and Rahman are both dead, so doesn't it make sense for us to get our hands on the only one that's still alive?"

O'Connor was silent for a long time, his mind collating Stern's words. Eventually he said, "What about Armitage?"

"We know Ralph Armitage qualified out of Bristol University in two thousand and five. But so far we can't find anything linking him with Liverpool. He certainly didn't go to university there," Stern admitted. "But Buchanan has now confirmed he received a similar threatening note as Dasti. That ties him to the others. But there has to be more and I've got Cherry and Keen working to find out where he fits in. I know Baldwin is in Australia. I even know where he's living, or was, up till a few days ago. Okay, we don't know if he's been threatened like the others, but we do know he was closely associated with them. That's got to be worth a trip surely."

The silence was long, only O'Connor's hoarse breathing audible. "What about expenses?" he finally said, a grudging edge to the words. "My budget won't stretch to much more than a cup of tea at the airport."

"Forget expenses, they're covered."

"What? Don't tell me you're paying for yourself?"

This was the awkward part. It could be construed he was using the case as an excuse to get away, to carry out a paid Stern Investigation job. But he had no option; he wasn't about to lie to his friend. Well, only a small white one anyway. He explained how he had agreed to find Baldwin for Runcie and how Runcie was willing to fund the trip. "Believe me, David, it sounds like I'm pulling a fast one, but I can assure you I'm not. I was on the point of turning Runcie down when Cherry told me about her findings, how it was obvious Baldwin was linked to the other two via the university." Stern was glad O'Connor couldn't see the crossed fingers. "That clinched it for me…two problems, one man. Best part, it's not going to cost you a penny."

"How long d'you think?"

"A day out, maybe two or three days max and a day back. That's if he's still at the same address. A little longer if I have to root him out. A week at most."

"When d'you plan on going."

"Don't know. Cherry's setting it up for me right now. I'm aiming for the day after tomorrow, if she can get me a seat. Don't forget, Keen and Cherry will still be here."

"Okay, but get this, Theo; I want to hear from you every day, right?"

"You got it."

~ * ~

Cherry had managed to get him a return upper class seat on Virgin leaving Heathrow at lunchtime the day after next. A twenty-four hour flight with one short stop in

Singapore. Cost four thousand pounds. She had also booked a return trip with the local taxi firm to and from Heathrow. Duration three hours each way, cost three hundred pounds. Within minutes of making the bookings, she told Stern, grinning widely, an invoice was winging its way to the fat pig.

Alone at the flat that evening, the memory of his last meeting with Melanie Campbell wouldn't leave Stern. The initial guilt over what had happened that night had faded and the urge to see her again was strong. Sure he was going to Australia and he would undoubtedly see Annie, but as he'd told himself untold times, Annie had made her choice and was ten thousand miles away. Melanie was here, now. Melanie was available. He couldn't help reaching for the phone. She answered almost immediately.

"Wondered if you fancied accompanying a beat up old retired cop for a drink?"

She laughed softly into the phone. "If I remember correctly, that old cop didn't feel so beat up last time I was with him."

Despite only being on the phone, he felt himself flush. "Just wanted to see you again," was all he could think of saying. God, this courting business was bloody difficult when you got older.

"The feeling is mutual," she said softly. "Tonight?"

"Pick you up in an hour?"

"Wonderful."

When reading an old romance novel, it would probably be described as 'light hearted'. He doubted modern day authors would use it, choosing a much more contemporary term. But right now, as he climbed into the Hyundai, shaved, showered and sprayed with his best underarm smelly, light hearted was the term he felt best described his mood. A couple of weeks back he was in a black hole. Stern Investigations was going through its leanest patch ever and worse, Annie was gone. Now he was back in harness, albeit only temporarily, and he was dealing with the most challenging case since he'd left the force. But best of all, he'd met Melanie Campbell and, particularly since their last union, he felt differently...hell he felt... Well, he felt positively lighthearted. So maybe that hole had closed just a little.

He'd chosen a small pub sitting almost on the beach a few miles outside Sheringham. It was quiet with just a few customers. The table, directly alongside a window, gave an uninterrupted view of the coastline, at the moment the high tide completely engulfed the sand, its rollers breaking gently at the edge of the dunes.

There was no tantalising, strategically unbuttoned blouse this evening. Just a soft, light blue, V-necked t-shirt over a pair of jeans. Make-up a minimal light pastel, with a touch of lipstick. Stern had taken it all in within thirty seconds of seeing her and felt good about it.

They'd chatted happily about nothing in particular for ten minutes before he broke the news. "I'm going to be away for a few days, maybe a week."

She looked surprised. "Oh, when?"

"Day after tomorrow. I'm off to Australia."

"Ah, I see."

The surprise had turned to what he saw as disappointment. It took him a moment before it clicked. He reached across and laid his hand on hers. "No, this has nothing to do with my ex. You remember I told you Martin Baldwin had gone to Australia? Well I'm going to find him."

Her lips parted in surprise. "You mean you know where he lives? His actual address?"

"I do."

She shook her head, a smile breaking. "Well, you said he'd gone to Australia, but you never said you knew exactly where. How on earth did you find out?"

Stern touched the side of his nose. "We have our methods."

Elbows on the table, Melanie rested her chin on steepled hands and leaned closer. "You are one very clever policeman, Theo Stern."

"It has been said."

"So you leave the day after tomorrow?"

"Yes, three o'clock out of Heathrow. Virgin Atlantic."

"Sydney?"

"Initially, yes, but then I have to get an internal to Melbourne."

"So Martin is actually living in Melbourne, is he?" She gave a shake of the head. "Well I never."

Stern smiled. "It's not actually Melbourne. It's a place called Mordialloc. It's a suburb of Melbourne."

"A strange name."

"Yeah, it is," Stern said. "I Googled it and apparently it comes from an Aboriginal term meaning Muddy Creek."

He grinned. "Don't forget we're talking Australia here."

She took a sip from her glass, her eyes lowered. "I'll miss you."

"It's only for a few days; with luck less than a week."

She studied him closely for a moment before saying, "Will you see your ex while you're there?"

Stern shrugged. "She is running one of her brother's stores in Melbourne. I couldn't go all that way without seeing her. Firstly, if I did, my son would never speak to me again. He's constantly on about how we should keep in touch." He turned his glass between his fingers. "And I guess he's right. We were together for an awful long time. Just because we've split it doesn't mean we shouldn't stay in touch, still be friends. So if I'm in town, I should look her up, shouldn't I?"

"Yes, you should." There was a pause, Melanie also fingering her glass. "How long ago did she leave?"

"Seven, maybe eight weeks ago."

"Do you miss her?"

He thought for only a second. "We split in two thousand and three." He gave a sigh. "My fault; gave more time to the job than I did Annie."

"From what I've heard, you wouldn't be the first policeman that's happened to."

"No, you're right there. Anyway I got myself wounded and invalided out of the force. Annie was making a new life for herself here in Norfolk and I didn't have anywhere else to go. My head wasn't in a good place at the time and the next thing I knew, I was here too."

"When was that?"

He scratched his head, thinking back. "Must have been two thousand and four."

"And you've been around each other ever since?"

"Yes we have, but just as friends." Stern refrained from saying just how friendly he and Annie had been at times. "We were finally divorced in two thousand and eight, but we still saw each other fairly regularly. So in answer to your question…yes, when she left I did miss her, I missed her a great deal."

"And now?"

Stern held her penetrating gaze. He knew what the question implied. Was he still pining for Annie? What would happen when he saw her again? Was there a chance of reconciliation with this ex who had been part of his life for so long? And she was right to ask. The last time they met, their relationship had taken a major step forward. They'd committed themselves totally, both emotionally and physically. On that night Melanie had cried into his shoulder, tearfully revealed it being the first time she'd given herself to any man since losing her husband. So, yes, she had every right to know if the relationship had a future.

"When I left to pick you up this evening, I tried to think how I felt," he said. "I could only think of one term that really described my feelings. It was 'lighthearted.' It's old fashioned and some would say soppy, 'specially for a hardnosed ex-London copper. But it described my feelings perfectly and I can tell you I haven't felt that way for a very long time."

Her eyes moistened and she reached into her pocket for a handkerchief. "You know, for a hardnosed ex-London copper, you sometimes say some really soppy things."

He reached across and again took her hand. "Never say anything I don't mean, though."

"Will you allow me my own silly proviso?"

"Name it."

"You must tell me where you're staying, give me the phone number because I don't think I'll be able to cope without talking to you every day."

He felt his heart swell.

Thirty-six

First class, or Upper Class, as Virgin called it, was good, very good. But however comfortable and however well you were looked after, the journey couldn't be shortened. Twenty-four hours was twenty-four hours, however you looked at it. Okay, you could grab some sleep, and some passengers seemed to be able to do that from the time they sat down. Not so with Stern. He was a bad flyer. He wasn't nervous, not at all, but he was a doer and to be locked away in a flying tube with nothing to do but read, eat and maybe watch a film, was not his favourite way of passing twenty-four hours.

The short stop at Singapore eased things a little, but only a little and by the time they made the final approach into Kingsford Smith, Sydney, Stern had long since had enough. He had a couple of hours' wait for the onward flight to Melbourne and made good use of the first class lounge facilities to enjoy a long shower and change of clothes. It was after 11:00 pm and even though he wasn't hungry, he still grabbed a sandwich and a couple of cups of strong coffee.

By the time he staggered off the Virgin Blue in Tullamarine, Melbourne, it was well past two in the morning and Stern was running on empty. The fifty minute drive from the airport to Mordialloc and the small hotel Cherry had booked for him was a complete blur. He couldn't have been more pleased to see the burly night porter who immediately took control of his bags, escorting him to his room with the words, "Don't worry, mate, you've gotta be bushed. They'll do the necessary later."

Leaving a pile of clothes on the floor beside the bed, he checked his watch for the last time. It showed 3:27 a.m.. He slid beneath the duvet and died.

Jet lag affects different people in different ways. Some suffer more going east to west, others the reverse. Stern had no idea how he would react, but was amazed when he came to and checked his watch again. 11.45 a.m....he'd been out cold for over eight hours. He felt pretty good, too. Using the facilities in the room, he made himself tea then relaxed back on the bed and surveyed his surroundings.

The room was spacious enough to accommodate the king size bed, a wide dressing table along one wall and a round coffee table with an easy chair either side taking centre stage. To one side of the dressing table was a door which, while waiting for the kettle to boil, he'd poked his head through. The en suite housed a double shower, a large corner bath, a hand basin and toilet, and a bidet. Stern grinned; he'd never used one before, but when in Rome...

Still cradling the half-finished tea, he eased himself off

the bed. Wandering across the room, he pulled open the curtains covering a window at least six feet wide. He stopped short, mouth open. He didn't know how much research Cherry had carried out into finding the hotel, but whether by luck or design she'd hit a winner. Outside, the sun was sparkling on the bluest sea he'd ever seen and a pure white sandy beach stretching as far as he could see in both directions. He swallowed the last of the tea and headed for the en suite.

"We were beginning to wonder if you'd ever wake up. Thought we might have to let ourselves in, see if you were still breathing." She was small, fifty plus with the widest, most mischievous smile and whitest teeth he'd ever seen.

He gave her his best in return. "Not surprised, I don't sleep as well as that at home."

"There you go then," she said, swivelling the visitor's book around for him to sign. "Like we tell all our visiting Poms...choose the best hotel and you get your best night's sleep."

He liked the way she'd slipped in the Pom. Signing the register, he took up the challenge. "Only the Poms?"

Her eyes sparkled impishly. "Of course, they're the only ones that matter." She offered a small hand, a ring on every finger. "I'm Grace, by the way. Anything you need, just let me know. You staying for lunch?"

Her handshake was cool and firm and in answer to her question Stern glanced up at the impressive sunburst clock hanging behind the reception desk. It showed a little after one. "Must admit, I'm hungry," he admitted

"Not surprised after sleeping that long." She pointed to

a door to their right. "Dining room in there and I'll need your passport."

He'd expected it and pulled the passport from his back pocket, handing it across.

The meal was good, as was the glass of Australian wine accompanying it. When he re-emerged into the reception area, Grace was still in position behind the reception desk.

"Better now?" The smile was still in place, teeth gleaming like beacons.

Stern had heard of the ceramic covers some celebrities had cemented to discoloured teeth, but he didn't think this was the case with Grace. He considered asking which toothpaste she used, but thought better of it. Pulling his notebook from his pocket, he wandered across. "Yeah, much better. Thought I'd be spaced out today, but so far so good."

Grace laughed. "It'll get you some time. You can count on it." She looked down at the book in front of her on the desk. "Says here three days with a question mark. Think you might stay longer?"

"I'm here on business," he lied, "and it depends on how available people are. I'm hoping to wrap it up in three days, but I might have to beg a couple of extra days."

"I'm sure we'll be able to fit you in somewhere." Her eyes twinkled playfully. "We can always bung a camp bed down in the basement."

Stern chuckled. "Sounds good to me. Have to admit, I've had worse."

"You ain't seen our basement, mate."

He laughed, flicking through the pages of the book, finding what he was looking for. "Got any idea how far away this address is, Grace? An old mate lives there, thought I'd look him up while I'm here."

She looked at the address for a moment then rummaged around under the reception desk, pulling out a book of street maps. "No probs with that, mate," she said after a moment's search. "You could walk there in twenty minutes." She swivelled the map round to face him. "Left out of here, over the bridge then follow the road round." She traced a route with her finger, indicating a turning leading left from the main road. "Twenty minutes max. Ten if you run."

"Thanks, Grace," he said grinning. "Walking's good."

Grace shook her head. "I dunno, you Poms. No sense of adventure."

She was right; the walk took almost exactly twenty minutes. Turning off the main road Stern found himself in a pleasant bungalow-lined street. Everywhere looked neat and tidy, well maintained. But front gardens were small and buildings seemed close together, cramped even. He couldn't help wondering why in such a huge country they didn't space themselves out more.

He stood for a moment checking if he had the right address. It was a bungalow with just enough room to park a small car on a front, gravel covered area. A drive ran down one side, past the bungalow to another larger building squeezed in at its rear. He swivelled round, looking up and down the street. It was eerily quiet and there wasn't a soul to be seen, completely different to what he was used to in bustling little Sheringham. Everyone at work, he thought, and the perfect place to tuck yourself away and not be noticed. Was that why Baldwin had chosen it? He gave a shrug and wandered up to the front door. There was a bell push to one side. He gave it a shove and heard the chimes react inside.

A few minutes and a couple more presses on the bell push and he had to accept there was no one at home. He wasn't too surprised. He knew nothing of Baldwin's circumstances; couldn't be sure he still lived here even. If he did, then he'd probably be working. That being the case, he would only be available in the evening. So it would have to be a return trip later.

As he turned to leave, the voice came as if from nowhere. "He's only there evenings and weekends."

Stern spun round to see the small, round oriental face peering over the fence. "Thanks. It is Mr Baldwin who lives here, isn't it?"

The little man gave a shake of the head. "Dunno what his name is, I've only spoken to him a couple of times, just to say hello. Keeps himself to himself. When he's not working he hardly comes out."

"But he is a Brit, right?"

"Oh yeah, he's a Brit alright. In some sort of trouble, is he?"

Stern gave his best, he hoped reassuring smile. "No, far from it. He's an old friend."

"Well, if you want to see him, he gets in about six every evening."

"You don't happen to know where he's working, do you?"

Another shake of the head. "No idea."

Stern thanked the neighbour and wandered back the way he had come. His watch told him it was approaching three and he remembered, as he left the hotel earlier, spotting a small café with tables on the pavement farther along the high street. A cuppa would go down well right now. Before reaching the main road, he passed a young mum trying to control her little boy weaving erratically along the pavement on a scooter, and a man, long hair pulled back into a ponytail, jogging steadily in the opposite direction. He smiled to himself; including the little man on the other side of the fence, that was four. So the place was inhabited after all.

Thirty-seven

It was a beautiful afternoon. The sun was shining from a totally cloudless sky yet the temperature wasn't too high, comfortable enough to sit in the full sunlight without baking. Stern reminded himself it was April, autumn in this part of the world. Sitting at the little pavement table he sipped his tea and watched the comings and goings of people up and down the high street. He wondered what he would do if he spotted Baldwin. The photograph, taken from the Cain Engineering personnel records and given him by Runcie was recent so he was pretty sure he would recognise his quarry. He doubted it would happen, though. He'd resigned himself to another visit to the bungalow this evening. Meanwhile he had a decision to make.

The mobile phone in his pocket was fully set for worldwide roaming. It had been supplied, courtesy of Runcie, with the proviso Stern kept the big man informed on a daily basis. He smiled to himself; it seemed everyone back home expected him to report daily. O'Connor was definitely on his case, Runcie had even supplied the means and Melanie had told him she also needed to hear his voice every day. Only Cherry, bless her, had told him to look after himself, she would see him when he got back. Truth was Cherry seldom got the option of running the office on her own. She probably relished the opportunity and was glad to get him out of her hair for a few days. He guaranteed there would have been some changes made around the office when he got back.

He considered his options. There was no point phoning either O'Connor or Runcie because he had nothing to report. He checked his watch and did a quick mental calculation, and anyway it would be 7:00 a.m. in the UK. Still a bit early. He pulled the phone and his notebook from his pocket. He'd made a list of the relevant numbers, including codes before he left home. He keyed in the number.

"Hello." The response was much quicker than he'd expected and the reception clear enough to be heard above the passing traffic.

"G'day from Australia," he said.

"Theo, you called." Melanie sounded genuinely pleased.

"I said I would."

"I thought maybe once you got there... You know, with everything... Are you okay?"

"Yup, everything's good. Haven't done much yet, but I'm all set to go."

"So you haven't seen Martin yet?"

"No. I've been to his place, but he wasn't at home. I'm going again this evening."

"How was the flight?"

"Bone aching, but it got me here."

"And you're at the hotel you told me about?"

"Yes."

"How is it?"

"Fine. Comfortable room and the grub's good too."

They talked for a few more minutes before he said he'd better sign off. "I'll break Runcie's bank if I carry on."

She laughed. "I miss you already," she told him. "Keep in touch, won't you?"

He promised he would and said goodbye.

For some moments, he hesitantly cradled the phone in his hand before doing what he knew he had to and again punching the key pad, this time a local mobile number.

"Ann Reynolds." The answer was officious, business-like.

"So it's Ann now, is it?"

There was a long pause before a tentative, "Theo?"

"Last time we spoke you accused Mohamed of not coming to the mountain. Thought I'd make an appearance this time."

Another pause, then a very cautious, "Theo, where are you?"

During all the years they'd been together, Annie had always called him Stern. There was no disrespect, quite the opposite. It had been her way of making him special to her; something only she did. Only during their most intimate moments, times when they were as close as any couple could possibly be, when no one else could hear, did she use his first name. Now, though, she'd used it twice in as many minutes. "I woke up this morning and

277

found myself in a place called Mordialloc," he said. "Where the hell it is and how I got here God only knows. Still, the sun's shining so I suppose that's a bonus."

Her gasp was loud in his ear. "You're here?"

"You catch on quick, kid."

"But why, I mean, what made you... I can't believe..." She finally ran out of words.

"Blimey, *Ann Reynolds*." He put the emphasis on the name. "It's not like you to get your tongue in a knot."

"Are you serious? Are you really here?"

"Yup, just couldn't keep away."

"Oh Theo." Only two words, but unless he was very mistaken, there was joy in every syllable. "When can I see you?"

"Well I know you businesswomen are tied up all the time. Didn't know if you could spare me a few minutes in the next day or so."

"The next day or so? Is that all we have?"

He noticed the 'we' and liked it. "Afraid so."

The line was silent for a while and he could almost hear her brain working. Finally she said, "You're not here just to see me, are you?"

No point in lying; she would spot it in an instant. "No, love, I'm not. But you were a major factor behind me coming." Well that was sort of true.

"A case?"

"Yes." He heard the disappointed sigh "But that's better than not coming at all, isn't it?"

"Have I ever told you what a shit you are, Stern?"

Now that was more like his Annie. He smiled.

"Frequently, but I do remember you telling me once I was a lovable shit."

Another sigh. "So when?"

"Well to kick off with, I'm yours all day tomorrow if you'll have me."

"All day?"

"Every minute."

"Okay, be at my place at eight."

It was a challenge and reminded him of how, in the early days, she'd fought so valiantly for every minute of his spare time. And how, because of his uncompromising dedication to the job, she'd invariably lost the battle. He had to push the sad memory to one side. "Blimey, as late as that. I thought we were going to have a whole day together." He hoped the sudden sadness he'd felt hadn't shown in his words. Annie had always been able to read his mood in a heartbeat.

"Okay, smart arse, why don't you come over tonight?"

He hadn't expected her to ramp up the challenge. He thought quickly. "Love to, but it might be later. Would that be okay?"

"How late?"

"Don't know. I have to see someone here in Mordialloc. Could take no time at all, but again it could go on a bit."

"You always did have to see someone or do something."

She was right and there was a sadness in her words that cut him deeply. He couldn't argue. "I know, love, but I am here now and I do want to see you."

"You got my address?"

"Of course."

"I'll be here."

"And I'll be as early as I can."

"You'd bloody well better be, Stern."

After ending the call, Stern ordered more tea. He sat for a long time thinking, the thoughts little more than a confused mess. He'd met Annie in nineteen eighty when he was a geeky twenty-six year old with only one ambition; he was determined to become a super sleuth and rid the world of all evil. So single minded was he that even Annie would admit *she* had to chase *him*. She'd caught him, too, and five years later they were married.

The conflict between family and work had started almost immediately, but regardless of that, Annie had been the only woman in his life. For over thirty years he hadn't even thought of looking at another woman. So close was that tie that even now, just to hear her voice brought a lump to his throat. Worse too, even after divorce, even after Annie putting a whole world between them, he still housed a huge feeling of guilt about his association with Melanie Campbell; still felt he'd committed the ultimate betrayal.

It was after four when he left the café and strolled casually along the high street. He hadn't resolved the conflict swimming around his insides and he guessed he never would. How could he? You couldn't be singularly part of someone for thirty odd years then unemotionally cut yourself off just like that, could you? Not possible, not as far as he was concerned anyway.

Now what was eating at him more than anything was how he would feel when he came face to face with Annie again. Would he be able to keep from telling her about Melanie? Would she guess? She'd always been able to read him like a book, so would she suspect, see something in his demeanour that was a giveaway? He became angry with himself. So what if she did? Why did he have to keep reminding himself they were no longer married, not even a couple? Why should he worry? Well he knew why, didn't he? And that was the trouble.

Pushing the thoughts from his mind, he concentrated on the case. If the neighbour was correct, there were still a couple of hours before Baldwin would be home. He was feeling weary now; maybe the jetlag was beginning to catch up. He decided to head back to the hotel and get his head down for a couple of hours.

As he made his way toward the hotel, Stern glanced across the street, spotting a man jogging easily back toward the town. The red vest, the ponytail; it had to be the same guy he saw earlier? And why not? The guy had a slow, comfortable, loping style that Stern guessed he could have kept up for hours without any problems. It reminded him of his own morning runs along the Sheringham beach. Not quite such a languid, energy conserving style as the man already disappearing up the road, but nonetheless satisfying. The thought brought back the view he'd seen from his hotel window earlier, the superb white beach stretching for miles in either direction. Maybe, instead of trying to sleep, he should go for a run, stretch his legs and get some sea air in his lungs. He gave it some long consideration; about thirty seconds, before deciding sleep would be best. He had a feeling it was going to be a long night...he would need all the rest he could get.

Thirty-eight

The hotel room was warm and he'd stripped before relaxing on the bed. His mind was awhirl with thoughts of everything that had happened over the last few weeks and he didn't think he would sleep. How wrong can you be? It was well after eight when he again dragged sticky eyelids apart and squinted at his watch. Half an hour and a lingering shower later had him feeling refreshed and ready to go. A further thirty minutes and he was again leaning on the bell push alongside Baldwin's front door. It took some moments and he was beginning to wonder if he'd had another wasted journey when the door opened only a few inches, a solid looking chain holding the door firmly to the door frame. A face peered cautiously out. It wasn't the face Stern had expected to see. For a start, the hair was the wrong colour and a neatly trimmed but full beard all but covered any features he could compare with the photo sitting in his pocket. He scrutinised the face hard, trying to look beyond the beard.

"Yes?"

"Mr Baldwin?"

The man said nothing, just held Stern's questioning gaze.

"It is Mr Baldwin, isn't it?" Stern repeated.

"Who are you?"

Stern couldn't be absolutely sure, but something in the man's wariness, the way he protectively held the door in front of him, was enough. He ploughed on. "Name's Stern, I'm Andrew Stern's father. You remember, your friend at university?" He'd decided to start with the personal approach, using Andrew as his entry ticket, tackling the other business once he was in.

Baldwin's mouth fell open, but he said nothing.

"I know it must be a surprise to see me, but Andrew called, said he was worried about you, said you were being followed and could be in trouble. He told me you sounded scared, asked if I could help."

Confusion shrouded Baldwin's eyes. "Andrew's father?"

"That's right."

"Andrew Stern?"

"Yup."

Baldwin clutched the door with both hands, knuckles white, holding it firmly in place. Slowly he shook his head. "No, I don't believe that. I haven't spoken to Andrew for..."

"I know," Stern broke in. "It's because he couldn't contact you he asked me to investigate."

The last word seemed to trigger something in Baldwin. "Investigate?"

"Yes. I don't know if Andrew told you, but I'm a private investigator."

Baldwin thought for a long moment, his brow wrinkled, confusion showing. Then he gave a slow nod of his head. "Yes, I remember now. Andrew did tell me about you. You used to be with the London Met."

"Yes I did. I retired and moved to Norfolk. Started my own private investigation firm."

Baldwin studied Stern some more before he slowly shook his head. "No, you don't really expect me to believe you came all this way just because Andrew was worried about me?"

"No, you're right. It's not only because of Andrew, but..."

"Wait a minute. Stern." A light dawned in Baldwin's eye. "Of course, it was you who spoke to Marge Saunders. I remember now, she told me your name, but I didn't link it with Andrew. I should have remembered."

"No reason why you should have," Stern said. "If I remember correctly, we only met once and if you haven't spoken to Andrew for a while..." He gave a shrug, leaving the sentence unfinished, but giving it his best friendly smile. The door was still only open a fraction and the chain was still firmly in place. Somehow he needed to rectify that and get inside.

"So this is nothing to do with Andrew at all?"

Stern shook his head. "That's not strictly true. Truth is, if it weren't for Andrew I probably wouldn't be here."

"What's that supposed to mean?"

Stern gave a sigh. "It's complicated. D'you think I could come in and explain?"

Baldwin gave a decisive shake of the head. "No. I

don't even know if you are who you say you are."

"I can understand that," Stern conceded. He reached into his pocket and withdrew the warrant card supplied by O'Connor, holding it in front of Baldwin's face. "This is my temporary warrant card issued by the Norfolk police. I truly am Andrew's dad, Martin, and he did ask me to try and find you. But I am also temporarily seconded to the Norfolk police force. I'm working on a particular case that I'm convinced also involves you. Things have been happening in the UK you should know about. I don't think you have any idea what's going on back there, and if you think you're safe by running away, you have to think again. Three people have died already and I believe for some reason you're in someone's sights to be the fourth. The world's a small place now and if that person's determined enough, he'll get to you, believe me. You need to talk to me, Martin. I believe your life could depend on it." He watched Baldwin closely, allowing his warning words to sink home.

"Marge did tell me you're working for the police."

"And it's true, but please don't let that worry you, because I'm not here to hurt you. I'm here to help."

"But how can I be sure? That card could be a forgery. You say people have been killed; how do I know you're not the one..."

Stern quickly held up his hand. "Hold on." He reached into his pocket and produced the passport he'd retrieved earlier from Grace on the pretence of needing it for business purposes. "This identifies me," he said. Baldwin hesitantly took it from him and scrutinised it closely, suspiciously. "And if you're not happy with that," Stern pushed, holding out his mobile. "Take this. It has a full roaming facility. Call the UK Norfolk police. Ask for Detective Inspector David O'Connor. He'll verify that I am who I say and why I'm here."

Eventually, with a heavy sigh, Baldwin handed back the passport. "No need for that," he said resignedly. He closed the door and Stern heard the chain being removed.

In the sitting room, Baldwin motioned Stern to a chair. "D'you want a beer?"

After the tension created by the doorstep confrontation, the offer was appreciated. "Thanks. That would be good."

A minute later, Baldwin returned from the kitchen carrying two bottles. He handed one to Stern and dropped into a facing chair cradling the other between his hands.

Stern took a long pull from the bottle. It was ice cold and tasted delicious. "That's good," he said, raising the bottle in salute. "Cheers."

Baldwin half-heartedly returned the gesture before himself drinking deeply from the bottle. Relaxing back in the chair, he lowered the bottle, clasping it between both hands in his lap. "I don't know what this is all about, Mr Stern, but are you really telling me three people have been murdered?"

"Yes, I'm afraid I am. But it didn't start that way. Andrew did phone and tell me about you being followed. He told me you didn't want to talk to the police and asked if I could help. I didn't understand what it was all about then, but I think I now know why you didn't want the police involved. It was because of what you were up to at Cain's. Am I right?"

Baldwin stiffened, his face clouding. "I don't know what you're inferring. I wasn't *up* to anything..."

Stern raised a hand, stopping him in his tracks. "No, c'mon, Martin, don't let's waste time with bullshit here. I know all about what you did at Cain's so there's no point in arguing about it. We might just as well be honest with each other and get that out of the way from the start. Because let me tell you, the Cain business is only half your problem and it's the lesser half at that."

Baldwin held a defiant pose. "I've done nothing wrong, nothing to be ashamed of."

"You were contracted to Cain Engineering, Martin. Your contract said anything you designed was theirs. Legally speaking you've stolen from them, it's as simple as that."

Baldwin leaned forward. "That's not true. What I have now is mine. I designed it after I left the company."

Stern waved the comment away. "Maybe, maybe not, and anyway, I'm not qualified to argue about that. One thing you can be sure of is Frank Runcie's adamant it's their property."

Baldwin's mouth fell open. "Runcie? What have you got to do with Frank Runcie?"

"Like I said, it's complicated," Stern admitted. "You see, as well as working with the police, I also agreed to bring you a message from Runcie."

Baldwin shook his head in bewilderment. "Christ, man, what the hell is happening here? How could you be with the police and...? "

Stern held up a hand, cutting him short. "It's confusing,

I know, but let me explain." He quickly outlined how, as well as Andrew being concerned about his friend, Stern had also been recruited by David O'Connor and Frank Runcie."

"So you are working for Runcie as well?"

"Sort of, yes. But only because he was willing to fund the trip. You see, I needed to get to see you, Martin, because I genuinely believe you could be in danger. Even if you're not, I'm convinced you can help us with our enquiries into three killings."

It seemed Baldwin hadn't heard the second part of the sentence. "Runcie is a bastard."

"Maybe, but he believes you're about to make yourself filthy rich by putting your design out there on the open market, flogging it to the highest bidder." He studied Baldwin's face closely. "He's not far wrong either, is he?"

Baldwin took a deep breath. "He's a fat obnoxious bastard."

Stern gave a wry grin. "You should talk to my assistant."

"What?"

"Never mind. I take it you don't get on with Runcie then?"

"I hate him. He's just a cheap barrow boy. He'd be nothing without Rupert and the rest of the team. They do all the work and he trumpets his way around making it look as if everything revolves around him. Rupert's as soft as a bag of lights, too. He lets Runcie get away with it." He snorted angrily. "They deserve each other."

"But they don't deserve your design?"

Saying nothing, Baldwin stood and headed for the kitchen, returning with two more bottles. He handed one to Stern then moved across to the table and picked up something lying alongside a laptop computer before returning to his chair. "I believe what I've designed is unique, Mr Stern, a once in a lifetime thing. I'll probably never design anything as good ever again. Can you understand that?"

"I guess so."

Baldwin held up the small memory stick he'd picked up from the table. "It's two and a half inches long, but have you any idea what it's worth?"

Stern shook his head. "Not a clue."

"Twenty million." Jaw clenched, he held the stick in front of him, a triumphant light in his eyes. "Twenty million and all my own work. Not Rupert Cain's or that obnoxious fat gorilla Runcie's, but mine, Mr Stern, all mine." He took a deep shuddering breath, lowering his hand still clasping the memory stick protectively. "And what would I have got if I'd stayed with them, eh? I'd have carried on getting my measly pay cheque and fatso would have put a few more million in his own bank account. No, I deserve more than that, Mr Stern, and this way I'll get it. As far as I'm concerned, Cain Engineering can whistle."

Stern drained the first bottle and stood it on the floor beside him. "Okay, as I've already said, I'm not qualified to argue about this, so I'm simply going to do as I was asked by Runcie."

Baldwin stopped, the bottle hovering close to his lips.

"Don't think I want to hear anything Runcie has to say."

Stern waved a warning finger. "Now listen to me, Martin. You need to get off that high horse and start to see reason because, like I said before, Cain Engineering could be only half your problem. The other reason I came is by far the most important. But just calm down and listen to the Runcie bit first, right?"

Baldwin gave a grudging nod. "If I must."

"You must, believe me." Stern went on to explain how Andrew's call had prompted him to visit Marge Saunders and Cain Engineering. He told of his confrontation with Robert Chapman who suspiciously had refused to give him any information and how subsequently Runcie had turned up at his office. He described how it was Runcie who, with earlier suspicions of Baldwin's intentions, had had him followed. Finally, and most importantly, he told of how Runcie had admitted to Cain Engineering being in financial difficulties and how important Baldwin's design was to secure the future of the company.

"So it was Runcie who had me followed?"

"Yes. Seems he paid an out of work friend to try and find out what you were up to."

"The devious bastard."

"He may be devious." Stern waved a warning finger. "He may even be a bastard, but he was right, wasn't he? You were up to something."

Baldwin took a morose swig at the bottle, using it as an excuse not to answer.

"Listen," Stern went on. "I can't say I liked the bloke much myself, but we can't blame him for feathering his own nest. Isn't that what you're trying to do right now?"

Baldwin looked sullen. "Maybe, but I have a right. This is my design. It belongs to me."

Stern gave a dismissive shake of his head. "That's debateable, Martin, and you know it. Besides, what you probably don't know is Runcie has sunk a lot of his own money into Cain's and for what it's worth, I think he genuinely has the company at heart." He raised both hands. "Not that what I think is worth anything and anyway that's not what I'm here for. What I'm here to tell you is both Runcie and Rupert Cain are willing to forgive and forget. They're even prepared to offer you shares, even a partnership in the company if you return with the design."

Baldwin's eyes widened. "Are you kidding me?"

"Nope. That's exactly what he said—go back with the design and they'll offer you shares in the company. Plus, if the design is as successful as you claim, a partnership."

Baldwin puffed out his cheeks and let out a low whistle. "Well…I'll be buggered."

Stern held up a hand. "However, there is a flip side. Runcie told me to warn you if you don't return the design, he'll have you hunted down and dragged through whatever international court is necessary to bring you to justice." He watched Baldwin's face drop. "And he meant it, Martin, I can assure you he did. He's got all the documentation including your signed employment contract. I don't know much about employment law, but it looks to me like one way or another, wherever you run, eventually he'll have your arse in a sling."

Baldwin took a swig from the bottle, nervously running the back of his hand across his mouth. "Shit."

Stern suddenly realised. "You've already sold it, haven't you?"

Staring down at the bottle, Baldwin gave a tight lipped nod.

"Who?

"The Chinese."

"*The Chinese?* You've sold a potential world-beater to the bloody Chinese?"

Baldwin finally looked up and held Stern's accusing glare. "Twenty million, Mr Stern. Need I say more?"

Stern gave a resigned sigh. "No I suppose not." He thought for a moment, then said, "Have you signed anything yet?"

"No, but I've shaken the man's hand."

"Then, my old son, you've still got a decision to make."

Baldwin gave a sad smile. "And you say this is the least of my worries."

"It is, Martin. Believe me, it really is."

Thirty-nine

"I need time to think." Baldwin had gulped down the remains of the second bottle of beer and sat looking down at his hands twisting nervously in his lap.

"I can understand that," Stern said. "But while you're thinking, talk to me about Atif Dasti."

Baldwin slowly raised his eyes, Stern's words provoking a huge sigh. "That's really why you're here, isn't it? That's the real reason."

"I told you...the business with Cain Engineering is only half your problem."

Baldwin closed his eyes and drew a hand across his forehead. "What do you want to know?"

"Start from the beginning," Stern said. "On the day you left Cain's you met Dasti in the car park. Why?"

Baldwin looked surprised. "How did you know that?"

"When I came to Cain's, I spoke to Melanie Campbell. She told me she spotted you and Dasti that day in the car park."

"Ah, I see. Melanie. She was nice. I liked her."

"I'm glad, but what about Dasti?"

Baldwin screwed up his eyes, ran his hand roughly across his forehead. "Atif had received a note through the post. He was worried."

"A threatening note?"

"Yes."

"About what?" Stern already knew the content of the note. What he didn't know was why it had been sent, why the victims warranted *'justice being done.'*

Baldwin held Stern's demanding glare silently for too long.

"C'mon Martin," Stern urged impatiently. "Three people have been murdered recently and I believe all for the same reason. We found notes on two of those people and both said the same thing. So I know what the notes said. What I don't know is why they were sent. I believe you do."

Baldwin shook his head. "No, when I spoke to Atif in the car park I didn't know... Well, what I mean is, I couldn't be sure what they meant, why they were sent, not then anyway."

"But Dasti was sure, wasn't he? He must have been to have driven down to see you about it."

Baldwin gave a grudging nod. "Yes." Again he silently studied his hands.

Jesus, Stern thought, *this is like pulling teeth.* "The note said murderers all four, didn't it?"

Another almost imperceptible nod of the head. "Yes."

"And we've had three murders: Dasti, Ralph Armitage and Mohamed Rahman. We know notes were sent to Dasti and Armitage. Given time I'm sure we'll establish

Rahman received one as well." He leaned forward, elbows on knees, closing the gap, more pressure. "So tell me, Martin, did you receive a note? Are you the fourth person?"

Baldwin pushed himself angrily out of the chair, moving away from Stern's imposing presence, across the room to the table. He picked up the two envelopes lying there. "It's not fair," he grumbled, returning and handing them to Stern. "It wasn't my idea. The idiot brought it on himself."

As he took the envelopes, Stern had no idea what those last words meant, but he knew he had broken through. Now it was only a matter of time. He studied both notes closely. The first was familiar; he'd seen it before, the second not so.

Three have paid the price
There's just one to go.
Your time has come, it must be so

These both came in the mail sent by Marge, right?"
"Yes, first one then the other."
"So, at the time they were sent, the killer knew where you lived. What he didn't know was, you were about to hotfoot it out of the country and come here."

Baldwin looked defiantly down at Stern's upturned face. "Given a couple more days and I wouldn't be here either."

Stern didn't pursue the remark. He wasn't interested in Baldwin's plans for the future; he'd already dealt with that side of things. Now it was all about the past. He needed to know what the four men had done that was so bad it had brought the wrath of a killer down on their heads. Holding Baldwin's challenging glare he said: "Sit down, Martin. I think it's time you got something off your chest."

Baldwin sighed heavily. "It's not fair," he muttered for the second time. "I had it all. Now this could ruin everything." He sat, head bowed, for a long moment before looking back at Stern. "I thought it was cut and dried, but now... First Runcie, then this. Everything's ruined." He again drifted into silence.

Stern needed to keep him focussed. Letting him wallow in self-pity wouldn't help. "No, you don't know that," he snapped. "And whining on about what might have been will do you no good at all. So come on, tell me what happened back then. Tell me what the four of you did to spark this off?"

Baldwin sank back in the chair and ran his fingers through his hair. "It was all such a long time ago," he said, his voice little more than a whisper. "And really I had nothing to do with starting it. It was Atif...he just couldn't bear to be challenged. I just went along because of the others." Frowning, he shook his head slowly. "And he had such a powerful personality. Looking back, I can't understand how it happened, but then he somehow dominated us, seemed able to make us dance to his tune."

Stern could see Baldwin about to start rambling again. It wasn't what he wanted. "Start from the beginning, Martin," he insisted. "Tell me how it all began."

Baldwin crunched up his eyes, remembering. "His

name was Simon, Simon Wright and it was me who asked him in."

"Asked him in?"

"Yes. I'd met him at a party earlier and we got chatting. He was a year below us but there was something about him I liked. He seemed good fun so I invited him to another party that was coming up. It was supposed to be a sort of early graduation do, but like these things everyone was invited. Anyway on the night Simon latched onto our group, four of us that were always together, particularly at parties and at the pub."

Stern held up a hand. He felt sure he knew the answer to the question he was about to ask, but he needed Baldwin to confirm it. "We're talking university here, aren't we?"

"Yes, Liverpool, two thousand and six, the year we graduated."

"Okay, go on."

Baldwin puffed out his cheeks and exhaled, unhappily dragging back a memory he'd prefer to forget. "As I remember, it was a good night, though I do recall Atif not being too happy with Simon hooking up with us. See, the four of us had known each other since day one and almost from the start Atif had held sway over the rest of us. I guess he wasn't sure about an interloper. He didn't say much though and Simon wasn't pushy, so there didn't seem to be a problem. Well, that is, not until much later."

"So what happened later?"

"Well like I said, Simon wasn't pushy. In fact most of the time he just sat there enjoying himself. He drank his beer, laughed at our jokes and mostly spoke only when he was spoken to. And, if I'm honest, the rest of us left it at that. We didn't know much about him at all really. Didn't even ask."

"Did you know what he was studying?"

"Oh yes he did tell us that. He was up for a BSc in anatomy and human biology. But that was about it." He stopped and thought for a second. "Thinking back, though, I did wonder if he was studying us more than we were him."

"How do you mean?"

"Well sometimes, particularly when Atif was in brag mode, which he was a good deal of the time, Simon would have a peculiar look on his face. Can't explain it, but it was as if he were having an inner laugh, as if he had the measure of Atif." He thought for a beat. "Thinking about it, maybe he had the measure of us all."

"So what happened?" Stern pushed.

"Graduation was coming up fast and the excitement was building, probably some of us were nervous; I know I was. Anyway, it must have been around midnight, if not later, and there weren't many of us left at the party. Atif had had a few and was really giving it all that. Seems the day before he'd done God knows how many lengths in the local swimming pool and was letting everybody know it."

"He was a good swimmer then?"

"He was, very good. Senior member of the Liverpool swimming club, Varsity team, top of division two in the Northern University League...he was well up there. Trouble was, he couldn't help going on about it. Him and Ralph were always at each other's throats."

"Why was that?"

"Well Ralph wasn't at university, you see. He worked on the financial side of a large company based in Liverpool. The company had a sports and social club with its own swimming team and Ralph and Atif met through friendly competitions; you know, some of the university guys taking on a team of outsiders. It was all unofficial and friendly, but the competitive edge was just the same. Anyway, Ralph and Atif got on well and as a result Ralph became one of the gang when we got together. They were always going on about what they'd done and who was better than who. It was all in good fun, but sometimes Atif went over the top."

Another piece of the jigsaw fell into place, explaining why Cherry had been unable to find any trace of Armitage at Liverpool University. Stern remained quiet, giving Baldwin time to collect his thoughts.

"Well, like I said, Atif was really in high gear, going on and on about this swim he'd done the day before, when out of the blue up pipes Simon. I can tell you we were all stunned. The last person we expected to challenge Atif was Simon."

"What did he say?"

"I can't remember the exact words, of course, but the gist of it was what Atif was going on about was no big deal. He reckoned swimming in a pool was the easy option. Said if Atif was going to brag, he might as well do something worth bragging about. Atif was livid. Like I said, Atif had been unhappy about Simon joining the group in the first place. He hadn't said two words to him all evening, virtually ignored him in fact. I remember him asking me on the side why I'd invited the nerd to join us. Said he was an interloper, not really one of us, wasn't even part of our intake."

"He wouldn't have been best pleased to be challenged by the interloper then?"

"Best pleased? He was furious." Baldwin paused, grinding knuckles into his eyes trying hard to remember. "D'you know I honestly can't recall how the hell it happened, who said what, but suddenly the challenge was out there and before we knew it, Atif had us all involved." Suddenly his eyes flooded and his voice became hoarse. "God, if I'd had the slightest inkling of what was going to happen that night I would have had nothing to do with it. I mean, I can't even swim. But that didn't bother Atif. Oh no, he couldn't bear to leave one of us out. He decided I had to row the boat."

"The boat?"

"Yes. Atif said there should be a boat just in case anyone got into difficulty. To be honest I don't think he gave a toss whether anyone got into trouble or not. It was just his way of making sure he had us all involved." He gave a sad smile. "So knowing I was alright Jack, like a little puppet I agreed." He lowered his face into his hands. "How's that for being a selfish bastard?"

Stern could see the emotion building as the memory flooded back, but he wasn't finished…he needed to know exactly what happened. "So what was the challenge, Martin? And what happened that night?"

Forty

Stern managed to get a taxi, knowing that, at eleven, it was going to cost him an arm and a leg. But that didn't matter; it would all go on Runcie's bill. Thing was, the lengthy discussion with Baldwin, the questions and explanations, had consumed more time than he'd expected. He'd had no time to return to the hotel and collect things for an overnight stay with Annie. It was fortunate he'd showered and changed after sleeping earlier in the evening. The taxi driver, having looked at the address, had confirmed it to be a forty-five minute drive from Mordialloc to Annie's place. It would be close to midnight before he got there. He slumped down in the back seat of the cab and closed his eyes. Seemed like nothing ever changed; however hard he tried, he was destined to keep Annie waiting.

When he arrived, the lights were on at one window. He climbed from the taxi, paid the driver and as the cab moved away stood letting his eyes become accustomed to the low light. He couldn't determine much, other than it was a house, not a bungalow, and it appeared to sit in more ground than those he'd seen in Mordialloc. There was an open front garden with a driveway to a garage at the side and a path leading to the front door. Before he reached the house, the porch light came on and the front door opened.

He stopped short, not expecting the sight of his ex, after only a little over a month's absence, to have the effect it did. She had on a pair of white slacks with a casual loose fitting top. Her bare feet were slipped into flip-flops and her hair had been cut shorter than he'd ever seen. In the artificial light of the porch, her makeup free, tanned skin glowed. He had no control over the way his heart rate increased or his throat instantly restricted. They'd been married twenty three years and divorced for five and yet still she took his breath away. For the zillionth time he asked himself how the hell he'd let her go.

He raised both hands, palms out. "Sorry." If he'd tried more than the one word, it would have stuck in his throat.

Annie didn't say a word; she just came to him, took him in her arms and hugged him close. He wrapped his arms around her and felt tears sting his cheeks. Some hardnosed ex-cop, eh?

She'd made tea and they sat at the kitchen table, Annie, a mug in one hand, her other hand holding his across the table. In the full light he could see just how tanned and healthy she looked. But she looked tired, he could only assume from the rigours of running a store. Back in the UK, after the separation, Annie had left London and returned to her roots in Norfolk. There she had built a small estate agents business in the tiny Georgian town of Holt. Though eventually successful, initially it had been hard work and for some time Stern could remember seeing the same tiredness in her eyes then.

"You look tired," he said, then smiling, "Just as sexy, but tired."

Annie sipped her tea. "Thanks for the sexy bit anyway."

He followed suit with the tea then said, "Hard work, eh?"

"It has been. I think we're beginning to turn the corner now, though. We're up and running and I'm getting the hang of things. It's a bit different to the one man band I had in Holt. How's it going, by the way? Susie tells me it's good."

When she left for Australia, Annie had left Susie, her assistant, running the show; the plan being there would be something to return to if the Melbourne venture failed.

"Yeah, she's doing okay," Stern confirmed. "I pop in there from time to time, just to see how things are. There's the recession, so the house market is slow, but Susie's holding her own and enjoying every minute of it. Proper little manager now. Even dresses the part."

Smiling softly Annie looked down at her cup. "I'm glad."

Stern eased his hand out of hers and, elbows resting on the table, cradled the mug in both hands. "So, how about you? Are you happy?"

She gave a tentative nod of the head. "Yes. It can be lonely at times, but I'm getting there, I think."

Annie's migration to Australia had been at the request of her brother. He already owned a very successful store in Western Australia and had decided to expand to the other side of the country. He'd chosen Melbourne and had asked Annie to manage the shop for him. He'd painted a glowing picture, citing the weather and the prospects of a successful life in a country he had come to love. Annie had succumbed to his pleas. Stern had wished her all the luck in the world, but her leaving had torn him apart.

"Think?"

She looked up, holding his questioning eyes. "It's really too early to say," she admitted. "It's only been a month or so and I haven't had time to make friends." She grinned. "The weather's not all Harry cracked it up to be either. Melbourne's not Perth, that's for sure."

"Didn't I read somewhere that you could have every season in one day here?" Stern asked.

"You can. I've already seen it." She looked across the table, studying him for some long time. "I meant it, you know," she said softly. "What I said on the phone; I do miss you terribly."

His heart turned in his chest and he felt an overpowering urge to push the table out from between them, pick her up and take her home. Instead he reached across and took her hand back in his, doing his best to give what he hoped was an encouraging smile. "It's just early home sickness, love. Like you said, it's only been a month. You haven't given yourself time to settle."

"Do you miss me?"

Did he miss her? She had no idea. "Of course I miss

you, but we've been through this before, haven't we? You chose to come here and I appreciate why. It was too good an offer to turn down and I understood that, I really did. I'm sure, given time, you'll settle." Grinning, he cocked his head to one side. "You see, you'll meet some huge Australian hunk and life will be all sweetness and light."

Annie didn't share his smile…instead she stood and came round to his side of the table, holding out her hand. "We have all tomorrow to talk," she whispered. "But now I'm tired."

Stern hadn't known what to expect, what sort of reception he would be given, but later, lying in Annie's arms as he had so many times before, his whole being was once again flooded with guilt, Melanie Campbell's face hovering over him. It was a long time before sleep finally came.

~ * ~

It had been only twenty minutes after Stern had left when the front door bell rang again. Martin Baldwin had checked the time: twenty past eleven. He frowned, concerned, and sidled up to the front window, squinting between the curtains. He could see nothing, whoever it was must be standing to the other side of the door. He made his way cautiously to the front door, wishing he had one of those peephole things that enabled you to see who was on the other side of the door. He stood for a while listening, but could hear nothing.

"Hello, who's there?"

"Martin, it's Theo Stern," the muffled reply came. "I'm sorry to come back so soon, but there's something I forgot to ask you. Something I need to think about before we meet again tomorrow."

Baldwin let out a sigh. Since the earlier discussion with Stern, he'd felt more uncertain than ever. He knew he was being silly because he now knew Marge had only revealed his whereabouts to Stern and there was nothing to fear from that direction. Quite the opposite…he was sure Stern had his best interest at heart. He let out a relieved sigh and pulled open the door.

"You had me worried there for a minute," he said to the figure standing on the darkened step. "I thought…"

Forty-one

The day had been a huge success. The sun had shone from a cloudless sky and they hadn't stopped from the time they left the house to when they collapsed back in Annie's sitting room at well after ten that night. The first stop had been Annie's store around which he'd been given the grand tour. From there they'd explored Melbourne city, lunching at Cumulus Inc on Flinders Lane, Annie insisting it to be one of the top five eating houses in Melbourne and her very favourite. The rest of the afternoon and evening had been spent exploring the city. It had been like their early days together, when they relaxed and enjoyed each other's company, laughing lots, frequently holding hands, not even conscious of doing so. Back at Annie's she hit him with the question he knew had to come.

"When do you have to leave?"

"I'm booked to fly out on Saturday," he told her.

"Tomorrow's only Thursday," she said hopefully. "My assistant manager is quite capable of looking after things for a couple of days. Besides I'm always on the end of the phone if she needs me. We could maybe take a couple of trips out; see Philip Island, have a day on the beach somewhere."

Stern had met Annie's number two, Pam, during his visit to the store earlier. She was certainly a sharp cookie and, he was sure, perfectly capable of covering things. But it wasn't quite as easy as that. "I have a meeting tomorrow morning," he said. "Everything depends on how that goes."

"Oh."

The disappointment was obvious and Stern could understand why. Annie had been in the country for such a short time. She hadn't yet had a chance to make any real friends. It was obvious she would try and make the most of his unexpected visit. "Look," he said, reaching across. "Let me get the meeting out of the way, then I'll know. If all goes well, maybe we can spend tomorrow evening and Friday together."

~ * ~

He'd left Annie's early, calling a taxi before eight and arriving back at the hotel just after nine. The timing suited the arrangement made with Martin Baldwin, who had agreed to take the morning off. They'd arranged for Stern to be there around eleven and in the intervening period he would think hard about what he wanted to do regarding Frank Runcie's offer.

Waving a good morning to Grace, eyeing him suspiciously from behind the reception desk, he made his way to his room. Half an hour, a shower and a welcome change of clothes later saw him back down in reception.

"So who's a dirty stop-out," she greeted him with a grin.

"You don't miss much, do you, Grace?"

She tilted her head to one side, squinting one eye. "Two nights away? What's to miss, mate?"

"Breakfast on?"

"You mean she never fed you, before she kicked you out? Blimey, mate, you picked a wrong 'un there."

He headed toward the restaurant door, throwing over his shoulder, "You've got a dirty mind, Grace." He heard her cackle as he pushed his way through the door and into breakfast.

It was a completely different day from yesterday. The temperature was down at least a couple of degrees and a thin layer of cloud gave the sun little chance. Rain looked unlikely, though, so stretching his legs on the brisk walk from the hotel to Baldwin's bungalow felt good. As before, the road was quiet; not even the mum with her scootering son or the ponytailed jogger this morning.

It was a little after eleven when he leaned on the bell push. There was no immediate response and a couple more pushes later it seemed there wasn't going to be. He wondered why. They'd agreed eleven so why wasn't Baldwin there? Then it dawned on Stern. Had he agreed to the meeting just to get rid of him, to give himself time to do an overnight runner? He'd admitted that's what he'd done to Dasti when he'd left the UK, so why not again now?

"Damn." At the time, because he was anxious to get to Annie's, he'd been happy to agree to reconvene this morning. Now Stern cursed himself for letting it happen, for not nailing Baldwin when he had him. Teeth angrily gritted, he was standing uncertainly, trying to decide his next move when he noticed it; the door was pulled closed, but it wasn't latched shut. He tentatively pushed it open an inch or two and called through the gap. "Martin, it's Theo Stern."

He waited some more, thinking maybe he was wrong in his assumption that Baldwin had skipped. He could be in the bathroom or maybe outside in the back garden. If there was a back garden. After a while, he gave another call and still with no response pushed the door fully open and moved inside. The silence continued as he moved down the hallway toward the door which he knew from his last visit led to the sitting room. Easing the door open, he peered inside.

"Martin, you there?" Nothing. He scanned the room. Everything looked the same as it had when he'd been here before. He crossed to the table, his eyes searching the seemingly untouched scattered paperwork and laptop, the discarded, innocent looking memory stick lying alongside. He paused at the sight of the tiny instrument, remembering; twenty million pounds. He moved across the room and peered into the kitchen from where he recalled Baldwin collecting the welcomed cold beers. The four empty bottles from the night before stood on the worktop alongside the sink.

Leaving the sitting room, Stern crossed to one of the other two doors leading from the hallway. The bedroom was tidy, the bed made and a pair of shoes standing neatly side-by-side in front of the wardrobe. So, the front door on the latch and the bed already being made, so had Baldwin popped out, maybe to get a newspaper or fresh milk maybe, intending not to be long.

Stern left the bedroom and closed the door quietly behind him thinking maybe he should wait outside for a while. If Baldwin did return, it wouldn't look good him raking around the guy's pad uninvited. He hesitated for a moment, his brow furrowing, concentrating, his subconscious trying to tell him something. He realised then, from the moment he'd pushed open the front door it had been there, but so subdued, so muffled it had been absorbed into the overwhelming silence. Now, though, as his eyes moved to the farthest door, the only other door he hadn't opened, it came with a rush. He moved quickly, noticing the squelch, the sodden carpet made beneath his feet as he approached the door and pushed it open. The bathroom, the sound of running water now obvious. He peered inside, the words uttered sharp, spontaneous.

"Oh bloody hell."

Forty-two

His name was Marcus and he was a senior detective out of the Melbourne Crime Investigation Unit based on the St Kilda road. He looked to be in his mid-forties and though he didn't quite make six feet, he was heavy set with a short thick neck and broad shoulders that together gave him an American football player stance. As they faced each other across the table in the interview room, Stern got the distinct impression that Marcus didn't like him one bit. Certainly, after listening to Stern's explanation of the situation, the doubt was obvious.

"Okay, so let's go through it one more time, shall we?" he said, his words dripping with cynicism. "You used to be with the London Metropolitan Police, but now you're a private dick."

"Yes."

Marcus held up the warrant card David O'Connor had supplied. "And now you're also working for the police in..." He scrutinised the card closely. "Norfolk, is that right?"

Stern felt the irritation rising fast, but he held back.

Confrontation would do him no good at all. "Yes, that's right."

"So, on behalf of the Norfolk police, you made the trip 'specially to see the deceased because you thought he could help you with a case back in the UK?"

"Right again."

"And you just happened to be around when the poor bugger had his face bashed in and for some bizarre reason was dumped in a bath of water."

"Look, we've been all through this once and I told you...I wasn't there when it happened. I was due to meet him this morning and when I got to the bungalow the door was open. I called several times and there was no response so I went in. That's when I found him. I called you guys straight away."

"And you think you know why he was killed and dumped in a bath."

Stern gave an exasperated sigh, his irritation beginning to show. "You don't listen, do you? I've already told you he wasn't killed then dumped in the bath. He was knocked unconscious then drowned in the bath."

"But, see, this is where I get confused," Marcus said, his mouth turning down sceptically. "How would you know that if you weren't there when it happened?"

Stern shook his head and smiled. "Okay, I'll play your game, shall I? You ask me the same question umpteen times and I'll give you the same answer every time. That way we can waste as much time as you like and you can book for overtime, right?"

Marcus didn't move an inch, but a sudden tension

radiated from him, his clenched jaw muscles standing out like steel rods.

Stern realised he'd pushed the boundary hard, maybe too hard. Raising both hands, he backed off. "Okay, okay. I know because I have established a link between Baldwin and three other victims murdered in the UK. The MO for all three UK murders was exactly the same as this one. All were knocked unconscious and, one way or another, drowned. I believe your pathologist will confirm the same happened here. That's how I know."

"So how d'you come to be back with the police?"

Stern smiled inwardly. The sudden, unsettling change of tack he'd done the same a million times. Hell, he'd almost invented it "It's just a short term contract," he said calmly. "The local force found itself understaffed so..."

"Why?" Marcus interrupted bluntly. Another tactic; harsh interruptions to knock an individual off course.

"Why what?" Unblinking, Stern held the other man's hard-eyed glare. He knew very well what the Inspector was asking, but what the hell, he could play the game as well as anyone. Marcus gave an impatient, exaggerated harrumph. "Why were they short of staff?"

"The police in the UK are under pressure," Stern said calmly. "As I'm sure you guys are, too. The recession, the cutbacks have hit everything hard. Right now the Norfolk team has also been hit by unprecedented sickness. They needed help and I happened to be handy."

"Well I dunno about you Poms, but you're right about us being under pressure," Marcus admitted. "That's why I could do without this shit. But why you? Tell me what's so special about an old drongo like you?"

That did it. Stern didn't know much about Australian slang, but he had a shrewd idea that drongo wasn't a term of endearment. Anyway, he was only willing to grit his teeth for so long. Resting his elbows on the table, he leaned forward. "Let's just say this old drongo, as you put it, has probably handled more shit than you'll come across in your whole career," he said softly. "And if you want to see the scars, I'll happily show you." He let the words sink home for a second then, as Marcus opened his mouth to reply, he continued, "You may not like us Brits, Inspector, and you may not like me in particular, but that doesn't mean you have a right to let your pig ignorance loose on me. Right now I'm an official member of the UK police force." He pointed at the card still held by Marcus. "You should at least respect that. And it might be an idea if you give Detective Inspector O'Connor a call before we go any further. I really do want to co-operate, but it's going to be difficult if you carry on acting like a complete arsehole."

For a while their eyes sparked across the table, then just the trace of a smile touched the corners of Marcus's lips. "Spiky old git, ain't ya?" He didn't wait for an answer but stood and headed for the door. He looked to the constable standing guard there. "Keep your eye on him while I'm gone, but for Christ sake, don't upset him or he's likely to bite your goolies off."

Fifteen minutes later he was back. He flopped back into the chair opposite Stern and folded his arms across his barrel chest. "Okay, so you've done a bit in your time.

According to O'Connor, you're quite a hero back there. Still don't give you an excuse not to contact us when you arrived here and started poking around."

For a second time, Stern held up his hands submissively. "Guilty as charged, Inspector, and for that I do apologise. But I had no idea it would come to this. As far as I was concerned, it was to be a quick chat to see if Baldwin could help us with our enquiries at home then back on the plane. Two or three days tops." Stern had no intention of mentioning Baldwin's involvement with Cain Engineering. As David O'Connor had made clear before he left; the police had not been involved, therefore it was none of their business.

"And you did get to speak to him?"

"Yes I did. I talked with him on Tuesday. We agreed to speak again today."

Marcus thought for a moment. "So what happened to Wednesday? Why didn't you finish with him then?"

"Baldwin said he needed time to think back, to try and remember anything he may have forgotten." It wasn't the truth, not the real reason for Baldwin asking for time, but it was plausible. "He asked for twenty-four hours to think it over." Stern gave a shrug. "Didn't seem unreasonable to me. And if I'm honest I had things to do anyway."

"Things to do? I thought you said you were here just to see Baldwin."

"I was, but..." He gave a heavy sigh. Why was everything so complicated? "You see I spent the day with my ex-wife." He went on to explain the situation with Annie; their background and how he had made the most of the visit, being with her, spending the day exploring the city.

To Stern's surprise there was an immediate softening in the Marcus attitude. "It's a bugger, right?"

Stern read the sign. "Been there, have you?"

"With knobs on, mate. Couple of years back. Still struggling with it."

"We're not the first and we won't be the last. It's a copper's lot, I'm afraid."

"You can say that again." Marcus dropped his eyes for a silent, reflective moment then gave a sharp cough and squared his shoulders. "So, from what you've told me, the guy was able to help."

"Yes, thankfully he was. It seems the problem started back in two thousand and six." He related the story told to him by Baldwin.

"Revenge then?"

"Seems that way, but all the way over here. Can't imagine how they got to him here."

"Yeah, it does seem a bit of a stretch. But if what you say is true, this Baldwin character is the last of the group, right?"

"Yes, it seems that way. It's what Baldwin told me anyway. There were five to start with; he was the last."

"So that should be the end of it then?"

"I hope so."

"Bit of a bugger," Marcus harrumphed. "He might at least have got himself topped before he left the UK. Save me the bloody paperwork."

Giving a wan smile, Stern pondered the point for a while. "Something tells me, but for a stroke of luck, he might well have. As it happened, that luck ran out here in Mordialloc."

The rest of the day had disappeared in a blur. The interview with Marcus had continued for some time, though considerably more convivial than when it started, and the local superintendent, a robust, red faced man called Roper, had also joined the party, taking Stern through the whole episode again. A statement had to be written and reviewed, and e-mails flashed back and forth between Flinders Lane and Bethel Street station in Norwich. Also, even though Stern was able to produce his passport as means of identification, Roper, a committed belt and braces man, insisted Stern's full details, including a recent photograph, be faxed securely to him. As further backup still, he arranged a Skype discussion involving himself and Marcus at this end and O'Connor and his super in Norwich. Only then was he happy to release Stern.

Marcus's offer of a police vehicle to take him back to the hotel was gratefully accepted. It was after 10:00 p.m. and, other than a sandwich at lunchtime, Stern hadn't eaten since breakfast. Now, after two late nights with Annie and the intensity of the day, he was hungry and tired.

Back in the hotel room, he made himself tea and gobbled the several small packets of courtesy peanuts and biscuits left daily. Checking his watch, he did a quick mental calculation; it would be around lunch time in the UK. He could imagine Cherry at her desk munching her healthy packed lunch and reading the latest paperback she'd picked up from the local charity shop. He wondered if Colin Keen would be with her. He hoped so. He hadn't been allowed to

take part in any of the communications between Flinders
Lane and Bethel Street, but he knew those conversations had
concentrated in the main on validating his authenticity and
credentials. He'd been the last to see Baldwin alive; he had
also found the body...therefore the first priority for the local
police would have been to eliminate him as a suspect. That
done, the detailed investigation would concentrate on the
murder itself and there was no doubt, after his explanation as
to how there was a direct link to three previous killings in the
UK, the interface between Marcus and O'Connor would
continue at a pace. But he also needed to talk to O'Connor,
to update him with the details from his point of view and get
the ball rolling with further investigations in the UK. He also
wanted to ensure all was well at Stern Investigations. Maybe
he could kill two birds with one stone by updating Keen,
who would then bring O'Connor up to speed.

"Stern Investigations," Cherry answered immediately.

"Let me guess," he said. "Wholemeal bread, salad and
some mucky, fat free cheese."

"You're only jealous."

"No way. Is Colin there?"

"Yes he is. I'll put you on the speaker."

He waited until Keen confirmed they could both hear
him. "Okay, I'll bring you up to date. Then, Colin, I want
you to brief Inspector O'Connor."

Forty-three

With the four huge 747 engines throbbing in the background, Stern thought about what a hotchpotch of a day Friday had been. It had started with an early call to Annie, who had bluntly confirmed, as he hadn't had the decency to phone her the day before, she had arranged meetings which precluded her from seeing him during the day. The best she could do was leave work early so they could spend a couple of hours together that evening. He'd considered trying to explain, but immediately discarded the idea. He'd spent a lifetime trying to explain. The problem was compounded by his flight from Melbourne back to Sydney being at some ungodly hour the following morning. That meant an early night, their time together being shortened even further. Grudgingly, Annie had agreed to be home by four. He said he'd be there. And he had fully intended to.

He'd set the ball rolling back home and there was nothing for him to do except wait. He had been released by the Melbourne police on the proviso that he would make himself available to them at any time if required in the future, even if it meant returning from the UK. This to be reinforced by a written assurance from the Norfolk Constabulary. Which it was. Roper certainly liked things tied nice and tight. So, tomorrow he would fly back to Sydney and on to the UK. It was there he was sure the end game would be played out.

After an extended morning stroll, he'd eaten a slow lunch and was relaxing in the hotel lounge when his mobile vibrated into life.

"Stern."

"G'day Stern, it's Marcus. Where are you?"

"At the hotel, why?"

"Need you back at the station, mate. I'll send a car."

"Now?"

"'Fraid so."

Instinctively, Stern looked at his watch. It was approaching two. "Is there a problem?"

"Tell you when you get here."

A familiar knot started to form in his stomach. How many times had this happened over the years? "Will it take long? I'm supposed to meet my ex at four."

There was a short pause. "Sorry, mate, I'll do my best, but it's Roper."

"Oh, 'nough said."

"It's a copper's lot, mate, right?"

"Tell me about it." Stern sighed. "Okay, I'll be here."

The post-mortem had been carried out and the pathologist had confirmed Baldwin had drowned. Stern had been right and Superintendent Roper, having finally accepted his legitimacy, insisted he needed more time with Stern before he returned to the UK.

It had been little more than a repeat run of the previous day, but this time with the added emphasis on details of the previous killings in the UK and lengthy, detailed discussion aimed at convincing Roper, who unusually attended throughout, that the killing was indeed an extension of what had been happening in England.

They had also discussed the necessary future actions, including finding and informing Baldwin's family of his death. Only then would they conclude what to do with the body and the victim's belongings. Stern had taken the task on board, promising to locate Baldwin's family and put them in touch with Marcus.

Finally, satisfied, Roper had authorised the case to be put on hold until Stern had returned to the UK with the information he'd gleaned from his discussion with Baldwin. That, Stern had advised, together with what they already knew about the other murders, could well lead to a conclusion. If it did, no further action would be required by the Melbourne police. Thinking of his paperwork, Marcus was happy to accept that.

By the time they'd finished, it was almost 5:00 p.m. Stern had begged a police car to take him to Annie's place, no more than a fifteen minute drive from the station. Marcus had driven himself. As they arrived, Annie pulled open the door. She stood, slowly shaking her head, but she was smiling. Maybe Marcus's use of the car's strobing lights and sirens had had the desired effect.

~ * ~

Stern had phoned and ordered the taxi for eleven. At

five the following morning, he had been back in another taxi heading for the airport. That had been almost twenty-six hours ago. Now, the Singapore stopover done and dusted, he was on the last leg into Heathrow. The last few hectic days, together with the late nights spent with Annie, had taken their toll and in the comfort of his first class seat, Stern had slept deeply for a good deal of the journey. Now, with just a few hours to run, he felt surprisingly rested. He thought again about the events of the last few days and how what had happened back there in Mordialloc linked in with the killings in the UK.

He hoped Cherry and Colin Keen had carried out the necessary investigations as instructed. Knowing what he did, he was convinced there would be no more killings. Still, the killer had to be brought to justice and that might not be easy. It all depended on what Cherry and Keen had been able to uncover. He kept running the name Simon Wright through his memory bank. He knew what had happened back in two thousand and six; Baldwin had told him the whole story, but he couldn't remember seeing a report of it. Maybe, because it was local to Liverpool, it hadn't been reported in the nationals, just the local rags. If that were the case, Cherry would have to dig deep to find the details. However, knowing his assistant as he did, he felt sure she wouldn't rest until she'd got the goods. One thing was certain…Stern was absolutely certain he knew the 'why' and the 'how.' Now he needed to establish the 'who.'

Frustrated that, imprisoned in a steel tube thirty-nine thousand feet above the earth he could only bide his time and be as patient as possible, his mind inevitably turned to Annie. Truth was, it didn't matter what he was thinking about...she was never far away. She had, he thought, been homesick, there was little doubt of that. She had taken him to her bed as if it were a given and for a moment, the pillow talk had even drifted to the likelihood of her returning to the UK if things didn't go right there.

Shortly before he left, she had also mentioned the possibility of a return visit. All hints that maybe all was not lost. Or was he just grasping at straws? Maybe his showing up unexpectedly as he had just triggered a little homesickness that otherwise would never have occurred. Like he'd reminded her: she'd only been there a month or so. She was bound to feel alone and probably vulnerable too. His sudden appearance couldn't have helped.

But, hey, what the hell was he thinking about? Hadn't he already taken to another woman's bed? And hadn't he enjoyed it immensely? And despite that side of things, hadn't Melanie endeared herself to him in other respects; hadn't he felt the connection she herself had spoken of? And hadn't he already convinced himself the new relationship signalled the final break with Annie? He gave an angry shake of his head. Final break with Annie? Who was he kidding? If that were the case, why, when she'd first appeared at her front door, had Annie stopped his heart? And why, when at Sydney airport, had he phoned Annie to say a final catch-in-the-throat goodbye, but couldn't bring himself to call Melanie to say he was on his way home? No, Annie was part of him. There were thirty-three years of her imprinted on his soul.

Stern saw the stewardess approach along the aisle. He beckoned her over and ordered a double scotch, the last indulgence on Runcie's bill. He sipped it very slowly, confirming not for the first time in his life that it was a fact...when it chose to be, life could be an absolute bitch.

Forty-four

Jet lag had him by the throat, and it wasn't just tiredness. It was much more than that; in fact, he felt like he was going down with something pretty serious. He knew he wasn't, of course; he'd read about how some were affected by long distance air travel more than others, but it certainly felt that way. Maybe he shouldn't have tried to continue yesterday as he had. When they'd touched down in Heathrow, he hadn't felt too bad and the taxi had been waiting as arranged. But as soon as he settled into the back seat of the car, it hit him like a brick. The driver had tried to engage him in conversation, but after the first twenty minutes, realising Stern was no longer with him, had given up.

Three hours later, still half asleep, he'd staggered from the taxi and into his flat. He'd remembered someone saying, faced with this situation, trying to sleep was a bad idea. The best advice was to try and stay awake for the rest of the day. That way you get back into the correct time zone and sleep at the proper time. Well, for some maybe. He'd hung on until well after eleven, but was still wide awake, staring at the ceiling in the early hours, sleep not an option.

He'd tried to make this morning like the start of a normal day…a shave, shower and a couple of cups of strong coffee. Somehow he couldn't manage food, but he'd arrived at the office looking, it seemed, as bad as he felt.

Dressed in a smart skirt and crisp white blouse, Cherry, looking her usual fresh self, didn't help. "Blimey, boss, long haul flights don't do you any favours, do they?"

"Just keep the coffee coming, kid, and give me a kick if I doze off."

Cherry hadn't needed telling…as soon as she'd heard his footsteps on the stairs leading up to the office, the brew was on its way to the mugs. They assumed their usual positions in Stern's office and after the obligatory question and answer session about the trip, Cherry giving him the third degree about Annie, Stern noticed the absence of Keen.

"Where's Colin?"

In the chair opposite, after kicking off the lethal high heels, Cherry curled her legs beneath her. "David was called to a meeting with the brass, reckons it will take best part of the day. There was something he needed doing while he was away and Colin was all he had spare. Said he should be back tomorrow morning."

"Pity, I'd have liked him and David here this morning." He drank some coffee, extra strong and lots of sugar. Cherry didn't approve, but knew what he liked. He smacked his lips and raised the mug. "Good stuff. I missed it."

Cherry smiled. Truth was, though it had only been a few

days, she'd missed him too. It was good to have him back. She followed suit and sipped her coffee...decaf, no sugar. Then, holding the mug in one hand, she flipped open her notebook with the other. "So, how d'you want to play it?"

"Well, before he was killed, Baldwin told me basically what happened back in two thousand and six. I'll kick off with that and you can fill in the details as we go." He closed his eyes and eased himself back in the old chair, its familiar groaning complaint comforting. "A young guy called Simon Wright," he began, "was a student at Liverpool University."

Cherry referred to her notes. "He was doing a BSc in anatomy and human biology."

"Yes, that's what Baldwin told me," Stern confirmed. Wright and Baldwin met for the first time at a party. Seems Wright was a year behind Baldwin, but for some reason the two of them hit it off. So much so, Baldwin invited Wright to another party, 'a sort of early graduation do' was how Baldwin described it. Anyway, Baldwin was one of a group of four guys who'd known each other since their enrolment and who hung out together most of the time. The four guys in the group were Martin Baldwin, Ralph Armitage, Mohamed Rahman and Atif Dasti." He eyed Cherry across the desk. "Getting the picture?"

"Yup." Another glance at her note pad. "Three of them at Liverpool University," she read. "Rahman and Dasti doing pharmacy, Baldwin engineering." She paused, frowning, chewing her bottom lip. "But that still leaves Armitage. He was at Bristol. So how did he come to get involved?"

"Swimming."

"Swimming?"

Stern waved her question away. "Yeah, swimming, but don't worry about it, we'll get to that in a minute." He took a quick sip of coffee before continuing. "See, it was at the second party, the so called graduation do, that Wright latched onto Baldwin's group of mates. Now according to Baldwin, that was okay with everyone except Dasti, who took exception. Looks like he ruled the roost in the group and resented any gate crasher who might upset the balance of power. Now, here's where the swimming comes in. If you remember, Colin already established that Dasti was a top swimmer at the university, remember?"

"Yes."

"Well, what we weren't able to establish, even through your Facebook thingy, was that Armitage's first job after university was not in Northampton."

"No?"

"No. It was with a company in Liverpool. Seems he worked there for a year or more before moving to Northampton. Now, the Liverpool company had a thriving sports and social club and, more importantly, its own swimming team."

Cherry nodded slowly. "I think I'm beginning to get the message."

"I'm sure you are," Stern said. "It turns out that this swimming team competed in friendly competitions against the guys at the university. Dasti and Armitage often swam against each other and as a result became friends."

"I see, so that's how Armitage became part of the group?"

"Exactly."

Thinking for a moment, Cherry took another look at her notes. "So that's another link, then."

"Why?"

"Well when you called us from Oz and asked us to look into the name, Simon Wright, I Googled him."

"And?"

"Two thousand and six he was drowned in the River Mersey. The body was spotted wedged behind a pier. I looked up all the reports. Seems no one could figure how it happened, though there were the usual theories. It was suggested he might have had a few drinks and fallen in, but the autopsy showed no sign of alcohol in his system. Then it was said he could have tried to swim the river and got into trouble. That was also played down because, with the river as busy as it always is, the river authorities said he would never have done it without being seen."

"That would have been the case," Stern said. "Unless he tried it at night."

Cherry looked up from her notes. "What?"

"As they said, he would have been seen," Stern repeated. "Unless he'd tried to swim the river at night."

"Oh now that's just..."

"Which is exactly what he did," Stern cut in.

Cherry stalled for a beat, holding his gaze. "You actually know that?"

"Yes I do. Baldwin confirmed it. It wasn't only Wright, either. They all had a go."

Cherry gave a confused shake of her head. "You mean the Baldwin crowd?"

"Yup."

"They all tried to swim across the Mersey? At night?"

"Yes they did and other than Wright, they all succeeded. Except Baldwin, that is. He rowed the boat."

"Boat?" Cherry held up a hand. "Where does a boat come into this?" She gave a heavy sigh. "You always do this to me, don't you? Just when I think I've got a handle on something, you throw in a ruddy great spanner. Nothing was reported about anyone else being involved. Certainly not a boat. The reports I read concluded Wright somehow got himself into the river and drowned. The final coroner's report tagged it as accidental death. End of story."

Stern was into the meat of things now, all tiredness forgotten. "Yes, but that wasn't what happened. The truth is it was all about a stupid bet. From what Baldwin told me, it all started when Dasti was bragging about how good he was in the swimming pool. Simon Wright challenged him, said swimming in a pool was easy. Dasti took offence and the next thing anyone knew, Dasti had challenged Wright to a race across the Mersey at night.

"But Dasti wasn't happy unless he involved them all. Like I said, at the time he held sway over the group so they agreed. Baldwin couldn't swim, so he was given the task of pinching a rowing boat and acting as the safety boat in case anyone got into trouble. Other than Wright, it was the group's graduation year, so Dasti came up with the idea it would be their leaving gesture, something for them to be remembered by. The truth of it was he just couldn't take being challenged by Wright. According to

Baldwin, neither Dasti nor Wright really intended it to happen…it was just bravado, a face off. But once the challenge was out there, neither of them would back down."

"But that's just stupid."

"I know that," Stern agreed. "But we're talking young blood here. Testosterone city."

"We're talking idiocy," Cherry snorted.

"Maybe, but they went ahead with it anyway. They chose a night when there was a slack tide and swam from the Albert Dock to Monks Ferry, two adjacent points either side of the river. Seems they all made it except Wright. Baldwin told me part way across he heard a shout, but he couldn't be sure whether someone was in trouble or not. He said he rowed toward where he thought the shout came from, but he couldn't see anything so he carried on to the other side of the river."

Cherry ran her fingers thoughtfully through her hair. "None of the reports mentioned anyone else being involved." Again she referred to her notes. "And I couldn't find any reference to anyone reporting the incident, either. Just the chap on the bank spotting the body. They did say, though, that Wright had some damage to his head. Problem was they couldn't be sure whether it was done before or after he died."

"My guess is it happened before. In fact it may well have been the cause of him drowning."

"You mean he was hit by something?"

"Could be. A chunk of flotsam maybe. And the reason you couldn't find anything other than the body being discovered was because that is all that was reported."

Cherry's mouth dropped open. "You mean none of the others reported him missing?"

"No they didn't. Baldwin told me that when they met at the other side and Wright didn't appear, Dasti was over the moon. He'd won and that was all that mattered to him. Baldwin told them about the shout he'd heard, but Dasti just brushed it aside, said as he'd expected Wright had bottled and given up, probably swum back to the other side. Seems Rahman did suggest they look for Wright, maybe even alert someone, but Dasti vetoed the idea. He reminded them it was their last year and they could be in serious trouble if it were found out they'd tried such a stunt." Stern shook his head sadly. "One thing has become very clear here...Dasti held immense sway over the group. In the main, what he said went. So, being so late, there wasn't much more they could do but head back to their digs."

"So they didn't know what had happened to him until they heard about the body being found in the river?"

"That's right."

"But then surely they would have..." She stopped short, seeing Stern shaking his head.

"No, Cherry, that's where they made their big mistake. They chose to say nothing. They figured none of them was responsible for Wright's death. Dasti actually said as far as he was concerned, it just proved Wright wasn't a good enough swimmer, just couldn't hack it."

"In other words, he'd won the challenge."

"Seems he was that sort of bloke."

"A nasty piece of work, you mean."

Stern nodded. "Looks like it. Everyone I've spoken to has said the same about him." He gave a dismissive shrug. "Anyway, for whatever reason, they all agreed it would be in everyone's interest to keep schtum."

"And for all these years they've said nothing?"

"That's right, and now I believe every one of them has paid the price for that silence."

"Jeez, boss, that's one heck of a price to pay."

Stern sat thoughtfully, saying nothing for a moment, then, "Of course, we only have Baldwin's word that that's how it happened."

"Do I detect some doubt there?"

"I'm not sure," Stern mused. "If I'm honest, I would tend to believe Baldwin's account of events that night." He paused for a moment. "As far as I can see, he had no reason to lie to me. Besides, what reason could a bunch of students have for murdering someone?" Another pause. "It's just those notes."

"You mean the threatening notes they received?"

"Yes. They used the word murderers and insisted justice had to be done."

"So you're thinking whoever wrote the notes knows something more. Something Baldwin never told you?"

"Could be. They certainly know something because if, as Baldwin said, none of the victims ever mentioned their involvement in the swim, how did the note writer know they were there?"

"So you think between two thousand and six and now someone must have said or done something to trigger the killings."

"I do," Stern agreed. "I also think whatever it was happened fairly recently. Otherwise why would the killer have waited all this time before making his move?"

"Geez, boss, it gets more complicated by the minute."

"It always does, kid. Now we have to ask ourselves who it was that made these guys pay the ultimate price and, after all this time, what happened to kick it off?" He grinned at Cherry's puzzled expression. "No pressure then?"

Forty-five

Stern had set Cherry the task of finding out as much as she could about the Wright family; who they were, where they came from, close friends of the family, etc. It seemed logical that if the murders were revenge killings, it was likely to be a member of the family or someone close. Meanwhile he'd called an eager Frank Runcie and agreed a meet at Cain Engineering first thing after lunch. It would also be the ideal opportunity to see Melanie and arrange a meeting.

He needed to make a decision once and for all and could only do that by confirming Melanie's intensions for the future. On their previous meetings, she'd said all the right things, her actions substantiating her words twice in the bedroom. But he couldn't put out of his mind that when asked about staying in Norfolk, maybe buying the cottage, she'd been vague, saying *if* she stayed in Norfolk she *might* get around to buying it. Before Australia he thought he'd had it cracked. Now everything was up in the air again.

Being with Annie had rekindled the old flame and he'd

seen the doubt in her. Was that because she hadn't been there five minutes, hadn't settled, given herself time? Or was she having real doubts about the move, maybe even being away from him? So should he even consider there was a chance of her coming home, even of them getting back together? He would truly give anything for that to happen. But if that were out of the question, he still had a life to live and a life alone was not something he'd wish on his worst enemy. The jet lag wasn't helping, but Stern couldn't remember ever feeling so confused, so uncertain.

At just after two, he parked in the Cain car park and made his way into the reception area. Melanie was at her desk as she had been on his first visit. She gave him a warm smile as he approached.

"You're back."

"Sorry I should have called. It's been a little hectic."

She shook her head. "Don't worry; I guessed you'd be busy."

"I've got a session with Runcie," he said. "Can we talk afterwards? Arrange something?"

"Of course, I'd like that." She lowered her voice, even though there was no one else near. "It's seemed an age. I've missed you."

"Me too." Saying the words somehow made him feel uncomfortable.

"Good." She picked up the telephone receiver and pushed a button on the switchboard in front of her. After listening for a moment, she said, "Mr Stern is here." She replaced the receiver. "He's on his way down." She raised her eyebrows. "He sounded keen."

Runcie bounced through the door on the other side of reception and headed toward Stern, hand outstretched. He was grinning broadly. "Good to see you back, Stern." They shook hands. "Come through." He steered Stern back through the door and, as Robert Chapman had done on Stern's last visit, up the stairs to the upper floor. Passing Chapman's office, Runcie led Stern to the end of the corridor and into a small outer office where a young woman sat working a word processor.

Runcie turned to Stern. "Coffee or tea?" He gave a grin. "Maybe something stronger?"

Stern shook his head. "No, coffee'll be good."

Runcie indicated toward another door to the left of the young woman's desk. "Right, it's two coffees then, Brenda." He ushered Stern through the door and into a much larger room, Runcie's domain. A large desk sat at the far end with a heavily padded, high backed leather chair behind. In the centre of the room a long conference table was surrounded by a dozen chairs. Wide windows overlooking the car park and beyond, stretched along almost all of the outer wall and a highly polished mahogany and glass cocktail cabinet held pride of place opposite. Runcie waved Stern to one of the chairs at the table and parked himself opposite. As he did so, the door opened and Brenda, carrying a silver tray, appeared. A cafetiére surrounded by two silver sugar bowls, one carrying white the other Demerara sugar crystals, together with an equally shiny silver milk jug sat alongside two gleaming white cups and saucers. A plate carried an assortment of biscuits. Once again, Stern thought about the two mugs and the jar of instant coffee used at Stern Investigations. How the other half.

"Would you like me to pour?" Brenda asked.

Runcie gave a shake of his huge head. "No thanks, we'll manage." He waited until the door closed behind the girl before again focussing beady eyes on Stern. "So, how'd it go?"

"Baldwin's dead," Stern said simply.

"*What?*"

"Yup, he was murdered."

Runcie's mouth dropped open. "You've got to be kidding me."

Stern shook his head. "Wish I were. Someone got to him while I was out there."

"But why? Surely it was nothing to do with this. I mean, his design... It had nothing to do with his design, did it?"

Stern couldn't help but notice how Runcie had conceded to calling it Baldwin's design. "No, it had nothing to do with the design at all. It was because of something else, something that happened a long time ago."

"So are you telling me you know why he was killed?"

"Yes I believe I do, but it has nothing to do with you or Cain Engineering." He held up a hand. "And before you ask, it's something I can't talk to you about."

"Oh, I see." The flabby face dropped, the disappointment obvious.

"I did talk to him, though," Stern continued. "In fact he was killed only a short time after I left him."

"You talked to him about our business?"

"Yes I did and he confided in me that he had already agreed to sell his design."

Runcie gave a sad shake of his head. "I knew that's what he was up to. Who got it?"

"Well, the agreement he made was with the Chinese."

Saying nothing, Runcie sat perfectly still for a long moment, his eyes fixed on Stern. Finally he said, "Big money, eh?"

"Twenty million."

The big man took a huge intake of breath and let out an enormous sigh. "That's it then. If they've got it, we're dead in the water."

"Maybe, maybe not," Stern said. "Baldwin told me that, although he'd agreed to sell to the Chinese, he'd only shaken someone's hand. A guy he called Mr Li."

Instant recognition showed on Runcie's face. "Yes I know him. He's a high profile procurement executive. We almost did business with his lot some time back." He screwed up his nose as if there was a bad smell. "Can't remember details, but it went pear-shaped. Got a feeling I upset him somehow."

Why am I not surprised at that? Stern thought. "Well, as it turns out, Baldwin never actually signed anything," he said. "Seems the Chinese reviewed the design protocol just like your Mr Cain did. They saw the same potential and offered him a deal: fifty percent up front, the remaining fifty percent after he'd worked with them at their factory for twelve months and proved the design, which by the way he was certain he would do. Sadly he was killed just a couple of days before he was due to leave for China and a very wealthy future."

Eyes closed, Runcie rubbed roughly at his forehead. "Damn, damn, damn."

Stern reached into his pocket. "Now I could never blame Baldwin for doing what he did. That amount of money was enough to tempt anyone. But I believe you were right when you said, having signed a contract with Cain, Baldwin's design technically belonged to the company. Pulling his hand from his pocket, he held up a small memory stick. "I don't know what's on this, so it could be of no use to you whatsoever. I should also make clear that removing anything from a crime scene before the authorities arrive is strictly against the law. Therefore, if I am ever asked, I will swear I've never seen this before. Is that clear?"

Runcie stared at the tiny item held in front of him. "I'm not sure I understand. Is that...?"

"I said, is that clear?" Stern snapped harshly.

"Yes, yes of course, anything you say. I can't believe..."

Stern placed the stick on the table in front of Runcie and pushed himself up from the chair. He turned and made his way across the room. At the door he turned. "Don't think I've done this for you, Runcie, because I most certainly have not. I think you're an obnoxious arse who could do with a lesson in manners and humility." He paused, enjoying Runcie's stunned, open-mouthed astonishment.

"Were it not for your selfish, bullying tactics, I don't

think Baldwin would have even considered doing what he did. Maybe you should reflect on that and learn something. You just happen to be fortunate in that I still fervently believe in justice. So, regardless of all else, Baldwin's design did legally belong to the company. I am also a true patriot and believe what is truly British should stay in Britain." He paused for just a second longer before saying, "My bill will be in the post."

Downstairs he found Melanie still at her desk. "Everything okay?" she asked.

"Yeah, no problems." Hands resting on her desk, he leaned toward her, lowering his voice. "When can I see you?"

There was a second's hesitation. "Can I call you?"

It wasn't the answer he'd expected. He pulled back. "Sure, is there a problem?"

"No, not at all," she said quickly. "I'm sorry…it's just that I've had an old friend staying for a day or two. She's due to leave in the morning." She smiled up at him. "I'll call you as soon as she's left. Is that okay?"

"Sure." He hesitated uncertainly before turning to go. "I'll hear from you then."

As he headed across the car park, he couldn't help a deep feeling of disappointment. His brain was already in turmoil and Melanie's reaction hadn't helped one bit. Okay, she had someone staying with her, he understood that, but there was something else, something about the way she hesitated when he asked to see her. Or had he imagined it? He stabbed the remote and unlocked the car. He really needed to get some sleep, get his head straight.

As he climbed into the car, it came to him that he hadn't got to sample the coffee so nicely prepared by Brenda.

By the time he got back to the office, it was approaching four. Cherry was studying her laptop closely. He perched himself on the corner of her desk.

"Any luck?"

She looked disappointed. "Not much. I tried to trace the family back through Simon, but it's difficult. He was staying in halls at the university, so there wasn't any family address readily available."

"There's no point in asking the university," Stern confirmed. "Even if they still have an address after all this time, they would never give it to us. Data protection and all that."

"And as we have no idea where he lived...?" She didn't need to finish the sentence.

Stern eased himself off the desk and looked at his watch. "Did Colin leave a contact number?"

"No, but I have his mobile number."

"See if you can raise him for me, will you?"

Cherry punched a number into her phone and moments later said, "Colin, it's Cherry, I've got the boss here. He wants a word." She handed the receiver to Stern. "He's still at the nick."

"Good. Hello Colin, when are you expecting Inspector O'Connor back?" He listened for a moment. "Okay, that's good because we need a bit of official clout. When he comes in, ask him to contact his opposite number at the Liverpool nick. I think it's imperative we know Simon

Wright's family address back in two thousand and six, when he was at the university. The university would never give it to us, but a bit of pressure from the law could do it. Also tell him we need to get together soonest. Are you back with us tomorrow morning? That's good. See if the inspector can get over here, too. Okay I'll see you then." He handed the receiver back to Cherry. "Best we can do right now, so I'm off home before I fall over. Tell you what, why don't you shut up shop, call it a day? Give that fiancé of yours a surprise."

Cherry automatically looked down at the sparkle on her finger and grinned sheepishly. She was still getting used to the idea.

Forty-six

Stern didn't remember where, but he'd heard that a single antihistamine tablet could help you sleep. He'd also remembered seeing a packet of Boot's allergy relief tablets in the bathroom cabinet. He had no idea why they were there and, like most of the stuff in his cabinet, they were probably well out of date. Still, anything was worth a try. He was right on both counts...the warning on the box confirmed the tablets might cause drowsiness and they were a couple of years out of date.

He popped one anyway, figuring, together with the couple of shots of malt he'd enjoyed before, they could only help. After sitting comatose-like in front of the television for a couple of hours, he'd climbed under the duvet well before nine. When he next forced lead heavy eyelids apart and squinted at the bedside clock, it was six-forty-five. He closed his eyes and squirmed back down, trying to do the calculation...nine-thirty to six-thirty? Wasn't that nine hours? Half an hour later, as he dragged himself heavy-eyed out of bed, he determined not to dump the antihistamine tablets.

The weather was fine with the temperature sitting at around nineteen and a gentle onshore breeze. Light rain was forecast later, but then just a few fluffy clouds drifted across the crisp morning sky. He left the flat and crossed the green down to the steps leading to the promenade and the beach. The tide was low and by half seven, the moist sand compacting beneath his trainers, he was plodding eastward. As he jogged along, he recalled Australia and the view from his hotel window. He had to admit it was pretty spectacular, but then so was this and there was no doubt in his mind which he preferred. He breathed in a huge lungful of fresh, brine-soaked air and increased his stride.

This morning he was feeling good and his mind was clear. He still didn't know how his love-life would turn out. Annie was putting out mixed messages and now Melanie had put him on hold. Still, there was nothing he could do about any of that right now, and if he were honest, for the moment anyway, he was happy to put it out of his mind. His first priority had to be the case and he was fairly sure he finally had a handle on that.

If Baldwin had been telling the truth, Wright's drowning had been a tragic accident, the result of a stupid dare, and because they'd all remained silent, that had been the final, official conclusion. But someone must have learned of the conspiracy, probably recently. Why else had it taken so long for the killer to reap retribution?

And whatever had been discovered must have been pretty telling, because it had led to the four men's silence being interpreted as one of guilt, proof that for some reason they were responsible for Simon Wright's death. But what had come to light after all this time had driven someone to take such drastic revenge?

First to send those frightening notes to the victims warning them of their impending fate, then to carry out the killings, bizarrely ensuring each died in exactly the same way as Simon Wright? Stern had yet to establish what had prompted the killing spree, but of one thing he was sure: the culprit had to be someone very close to Simon. Therefore logic said he had to start with the family.

He arrived at the office at nine and as usual Cherry was already there. So was Colin Keen. Cherry had previously told Stern that Colin had confided to her that he enjoyed being there with them more than being at the station in Norwich. Stern had advised Cherry to tell the young constable not to make himself too comfortable. The association wasn't going to last.

They congregated in Stern's office and Stern looked toward Keen. "No Inspector O'Connor then?"

"No, he apologises for not being able to make it. Said to tell you he was up to his earlobes, being driven like a donkey. Told me you'd understand."

Stern did, absolutely. "How about the address?"

Keen flicked open his notebook. "Yes, he got that before he left last night." He looked across at Stern, his lips turned down. "That was after ten, by the way. He kept me there, too."

Stern grinned. "Comes with the territory, son. Nobody forced you to join."

Keen gave a broad smile. "No complaints, boss. I love it, really. You never know, could be, some way down the line, I'll be doing the same to some poor sprog."

"Maybe, but you've a long way to go before then," Stern warned. "And my guess is you won't get that far unless you give me that flippin' address."

"Oh, right, yes," Keen stuttered, looking back down at his notes. "It's in West Sussex, a place called Wright House."

"Novel choice, considering," Stern said. "Whereabouts in West Sussex?"

Grinning at the two men's exchange, Cherry piped up, "It's on the eastern fringe of Horsham. We Googled it just before you arrived. You come off the M23 onto the A264, the Horsham road. A couple of roundabouts later you break left onto a 'B' road, the 2195. Then you take another left onto New Moorhead Drive. It's down there. From here about a hundred and eighty miles, best part of a four hour drive. That's if you're thinking of driving. You have become a bit of a gadabout lately."

Stern wrinkled his nose at the jibe. "Never know, clever dick, I might just send you." He thought for a moment. "Don't suppose you got a telephone number by any chance?"

Cherry looked across at Keen. "Funny you should ask that."

Keen immediately tore a page from his pad and crossed to the desk, dropping it in front of Stern.

Stern looked up from the number written on the paper, glancing from one to the other. "I think I've got a couple of smart arses with me this morning."

Cherry was enjoying herself. "They call it efficiency, boss. Mind you, getting in early helps."

He gave her a withering look. "So this address came from the university archives and is the one given by Simon Wright back in two thousand and six, right?"

"That's right," Keen confirmed. "They took a bit of persuading, but DI O'Connor can turn on the heat when he wants to."

"And I'm guessing he got hold of the phone number at the same time."

"Yes. Bit of luck that."

"Problem is, even though the house has retained the name and number, we can't be sure the Wrights still live there."

"No we can't."

Stern picked up the phone. "Better give it a call and find out then, hadn't I?"

The call was answered after a couple rings. A male voice. "Hello"

"Is that the Wright residence?" Stern asked.

"Yes." A cautious edge.

Stern's mind flashed to two thousand and six when Simon Wright would have been eighteen or nineteen. Therefore his father at that time would have probably been in his forties. That would put him in his fifties now. The voice on the end of the phone was younger. "Would it be possible to have a word with Mr Wright?" he asked. "Mr Wright senior, I mean."

"No."

"He's not there?"

"He's dead." Blunt and to the point.

"Oh, I'm so sorry."

"Don't be, it was a long time ago."

"Could I speak to Mrs Wright then, please?"

"She's not here."

"Do you know when she'll be back?"

"No, and whatever you're selling, we don't want it."

This person, whoever he was, had no intention of being helpful. "I can assure you I'm not selling anything."

"That's what you all say."

"In this case, it happens to be true, so could you please tell me who I'm speaking to?"

"No, wrong way round, mate. You need to tell *me* who *I'm* talking to. Who the hell are you and what do you want?"

Stern thought quickly. "I'm a detective inspector with the Liverpool constabulary cold case squad. We have recently unearthed fresh evidence relating to the death of Simon Wright back in two thousand and six. I would just like to..."

There was a click and the line died.

Stern held the phone away from his ear. "He hung up on me."

All three were silent for some time before Stern said, "So, Wright senior is dead and Mrs Wright is not available," he mused. "And as soon as I mentioned Simon's death and the police, the guy hangs up on me. Now why would he do that?" He rubbed thoughtfully at his chin. "Right, we need to look at the electoral roll."

Cherry cocked her head questioningly. "The what?"

"The electoral roll," Stern repeated. "It tells you who lived where and when."

"Is it on the web?"

"I'll be surprised if it isn't."

Cherry wrinkled her nose. "Okay, but what are we looking for?"

"We're looking for more information about the Wright family," Stern said.

Cherry gave a dismissive shrug. "Why don't we just get the local police round the house?"

Stern gave an emphatic shake of his head. "No, that won't do. That call tells me we need to be cautious. You can see what effect just the mention of Simon's name and the police did. That proves we mustn't push. We need to know more about the family before we go barging in."

"That makes sense," Keen came in. "Don't forget, back in two thousand and six, this family lost a son."

"And, from what the guy said, also a father," Stern said. "Start opening up old wounds before we're sure what we're up to and we could be in real trouble."

"Okay, so what d'you want me to do?" Cherry asked.

"We know the name and we know the address," Stern said. "What we don't know is who lived at that address in two thousand and six and, maybe more importantly, who lives there now. So grab that laptop of yours and see if you can find the electoral roll for the Horsham area."

Cherry thought for a moment then said, "If it's anything like other search sites, the genealogy sites for instance, it'll probably cost us."

Stern pulled his wallet from his pocket and retrieved a credit card. "Okay, use this."

Cherry took the card. "Got it." She headed for the door.

Stern turned to Keen. "Get hold of Inspector O'Connor a soon as you can and arrange a meeting at his earliest convenience. Today if possible. Either here or at the nick, whichever suits him best. Tell him it's now imperative we talk as soon as possible."

Forty-seven

It was nearing lunchtime when, alone in the office, Stern picked up the phone. Andrew would be at work, but it was important for him to speak to his son. He hoped he would be available to talk. He was relieved when Andrew picked up after only a couple of rings.

"Andrew Stern."

"Hi son, it's Dad. Sorry to get you at work, but it's important. Can you talk?"

"Er, sure, but can I get back to you? Two minutes."

A few minutes later, Andrew came back. "Sorry about that, Dad, but my desk was surrounded. You sounded serious so I got out of there. I was due a break anyway, so I've grabbed myself a coffee and I'm outside now on the mobile."

"Hope I didn't interrupt anything."

"Nah, just a planning thing. Mainly rubbish talk. I'm not involved in most of it anyway. So what are you after?"

No point in beating about the bush. "Well, son, to start with I'm sorry to have to tell you that your friend Martin is dead."

"*Dead?*"

"Yes. I know it must be a bit of a shock. Worse still, I'm afraid he was murdered."

"But when? I mean, how?"

Stern outlined what had happened in Australia.

"You mean you went all the way to Australia? But surely not because of me?"

"No, it's a lot more complicated than that, son. Your friend was involved in a couple of things, either of which could have got him into serious hot water. I went to Australia partly on behalf of the company he worked for and partly for the police. Like I say; it's complicated and unfortunately I haven't the time to go into detail right now. When this is over, we'll get together and I'll explain everything."

"But what had he got himself into that led to him being murdered?" Andrew insisted.

"Something I believe happened way back, when he was at university."

"But how can that be? What on earth could he have done back then that got him killed now?"

Stern ignored the question. "Andrew, do you remember a lad called Simon Wright back then?"

There was no hesitation. "You mean the guy that drowned in the Mersey?"

"That's him. Did you know him back then, or know anything about him?"

"No, not really. I recall he was in the same year as me, but if I remember, he was studying one of the sciences. I never had anything to do with him. Can't ever remember meeting him. Why d'you ask?"

Again Stern chose not to answer the question. "What about after he was drowned? Was there any talk among the students? You know, the usual conjecture about how it happened, maybe conspiracy theories even?"

"*Conspiracy theories?* Christ, Dad, what the hell do you mean?"

"It's a simple question, son. After Wright was drowned, did you hear anyone at all speculate about his death being anything other than an accident?"

"No, nothing. It was a shock at the time, but the inquest came up with accidental death, didn't it? Everyone just accepted it. Look, Dad, what's this all about? You're not suggesting Martin had anything to do with Wright being drowned, are you?"

"I'm not suggesting anything at the moment," Stern hedged. "But I will tell you everything when I've got it sorted." Before his son could come back at him again, Stern went on quickly. "By the way, you'll be pleased to know I met up with your mum while I was in Melbourne. We spent a couple of days together. When she calls, she'll probably tell you all about it." *Well, not quite everything, I hope*, he thought.

"That's great, Dad. How did you get on?"

"Smashing. We had a good couple of days."

The mention of his mother had had the desired effect, deflecting Andrew away from Baldwin and further questions. "I'm pleased. It's good to know you guys still get on."

"You should know by now, son, whatever else, your mum and I will always be friends. Anyway I must let you go now. As soon as I can, I'll bring you up to date on things, okay?"

"Okay, Dad. Thanks for letting me know. But I still don't understand..."

"Don't worry yourself about it," Stern cut him off. "Like I said, when I know the full story, we'll get together."

Stern had at last managed to ease himself away from his son's constant questions and end the conversation. He looked at his watch, noting it was almost one. Leaving his chair, he wandered into the outer office. Cherry and Keen were bent close, studying the laptop screen. They both looked up as he entered.

"Any luck?" he asked.

"Almost there," Cherry said. "You were right; we had to register. We've checked out several, but I think we've got hold of the best now. Just setting it up."

"Still no joy with the inspector," Keen said. "But I've left a message and I'll keep at it. Maybe get him after lunch."

"Good. I'm going to grab a bite, be about an hour. Anything turns up, I've got my mobile on."

~ * ~

In the pub Stern ordered a pint and a ploughman's and settled himself at a table. He thought about the strange response he'd got when he called the Wright house. He wondered who it was had answered the phone, and why he had reacted by hanging up when Simon's name and the police had been mentioned. Keen was correct when he'd talked about opening old wounds. One foot wrong these days and there were lawyers by the score who would revel in taking a harassment action against the police. Stern had to remember, right now, even though it was only temporary, he was a member of the police force. So it was important they were cautious when approaching the Wright family.

There was, of course, no reason to believe the Wrights had anything to do with the killings. Nevertheless, he still believed it was the place to start. Historical statistics confirmed, in the majority of such cases, a member of the family or someone close would in some capacity be in the mix somewhere. Certainly he would have to eliminate the involvement of family and even close friends before moving on.

Knowing what he knew now, however, he felt sure the killing spree was over. If Martin Baldwin had told him the truth, and he had no reason to believe otherwise, there had been just five people involved in this tragic saga. One had died in the murky waters of the Mersey River and he felt sure, the other four had been killed as a result of that death. Revenge killings, it had to be. Each had received a threatening note warning them of their impending fate; each was made to die in exactly the way as the unfortunate Simon Wright.

But what about the intervening quiet period between 2006 and now? If they were indeed revenge killings, why had the killer taken so long to act? What had happened relatively recently to kick off the murders? As the plate of cheese, pickles and crusty bread was laid in front of him, Stern thought if he knew that, he'd pretty well know it all.

He plodded his way through the food, the first pint disappearing before he knew it. He ordered another and again mentally, methodically ran through the facts, analysing every detail, looking for anything he may have missed that might throw further light on things. He came up with nothing. He felt sure he knew what had happened back in two thousand and six and, as a result, why the murders had been committed. Right now what had sparked the killings so long after the event was unimportant. His first priority was to find the killer. Then, with luck, the whole story would be revealed.

It was approaching two when he left the pub. As he strolled back along the promenade toward the high street, his mobile rang. He smiled, remembering she had promised to phone as soon as her visitor had left. He was disappointed.

"Theo, it's David. Look, I'm sorry I haven't been able to get to you sooner, but so much crap has been hitting the fan I've been running like a lunatic just to stand still. Anyway I've just managed to drag myself away from a bone-aching meeting and, providing no one with pips on his shoulder nails me again before I get to the car, I should be with you in half an hour. Is that okay?"

"Yeah, that's good. We'll be waiting." Ending the call, Stern looked down at the mobile for a thoughtful moment. Didn't Melanie say her visitor would be leaving first thing? He tapped out the number and let it ring for some time before giving up with a grimace. He wasn't enjoying this; it was all too complicated. Before, with just Annie, even when they were separated, he knew where he stood.

He could concentrate on the job, whatever case he had going. Now he didn't know where the hell he stood and it made him angry. He determined that if Melanie hadn't called by close of play today, he'd go round there anyway. He slipped the phone back in his pocket and headed back to the office.

Forty-eight

Cherry and Keen had managed to get the information Stern had requested, but he'd suggested they put it on hold until O'Connor got there. He arrived, weary eyed, just before three. He gratefully accepted the mug of coffee offered by Cherry and slumped down opposite Stern. On chairs brought in from the outer office, Cherry and Keen took up station either side of Stern's desk. Primarily for O'Connor's benefit, Stern related details of his trip to Australia, in particular the story told by Martin Baldwin of the events in two thousand and six.

O'Connor was quick with the questions. "He could have been onto millions then?"

"Looked like that," Stern said. "That's if his design was as good as he said it was. Certainly, from what they'd offered him, the Chinese seemed to think it was. It would have been simple for them to make one or two minor changes and claim it to be their own design. Cain Engineering wouldn't have stood a chance of getting it back. Mind you, after we'd talked, I had the feeling he was considering coming back."

"What about now?"

"About the design, you mean?"

O'Connor nodded.

Stern gave an innocent shrug of his shoulders. "I guess the Ozzies will hand Baldwin's stuff over to his family. What happens then I don't know. That's not our concern though, is it?"

"No, I guess not." O'Connor drank some coffee and thought for a moment. "So do you believe Baldwin's story?"

"I have no reason not to. The facts tie up and when you consider they were all youngsters, all full of vim and vigour, it's plausible. On the face of it, the only thing that might sound a bit iffy is the hold Dasti seemed to have over the others at the time. But having talked to those who associated with him since university, and knowing what an arrogant, dominating individual he was, it's not impossible."

"Okay, so let's say we believe the story. Does that mean the killing is over?"

"Yes, I think it is," Stern said. "The killer, whoever it is, was determined to make sure that everyone involved in that sorry saga was dealt with right down to the way they died. Norfolk, Northampton, Bradford. Hell, he even managed to find Baldwin in Australia and despatch him in the same way."

"Any idea how the murderer traced Baldwin to Australia?"

"Not a clue. He knew where Baldwin lived in Norwich, because that's where he sent the threatening notes, but how he traced him to Oz...?"

"What about the landlady you told me about?"

"Marge Saunders?" Stern gave it some thought. "Possible, I suppose, but somehow I don't think so. While Baldwin was at her place she had a good time with him. She really liked him. I somehow don't think she would have betrayed him like that."

"She told you where he was," O'Connor reminded him.

"I know, but I was the police, remember. She believed I was trying to help him." Stern paused. "Still, like I said, it's not impossible."

"And now it's not important either," O'Connor mused. "What we now have to concentrate on is who killed these people." He drained the mug of the last of the coffee. "So where do we stand, Theo?"

"My belief is it has to be someone who was close to Wright."

"Family?"

"Or close friend, yes. We've established the family still live in the same house as they did back in two thousand and six. It's on the outskirts of Horsham, West Sussex. I gave them a call to check out the current situation there. Got a bit of a strange reaction." Stern outlined what had happened when he called the Wright House. "I did consider calling in the local lads, but decided to wait until we'd made a few more enquiries and talked to you. I asked Cherry and Colin to check who lived in the house at the time of Simon Wright's death, and again now."

"Makes sense," O'Connor agreed. He looked from Cherry to Keen. "What did you find?"

Keen gave a nod, deferring to Cherry, who looked to her notebook. "We did a scan of the Electoral Roll and established four people lived at the Wright House in two thousand and six. They were Mr and Mrs Wright and their two sons, Simon and Alec. At that time, both sons were said to be nineteen."

"And now?"

"Now there's just Mrs Wright and son Alec."

"Son Alec," Stern pondered. "That figures. Nineteen in two thousand and six would make him twenty-six now. The voice on the phone; that would fit. He did say the father had been dead for some time."

"Yes, we checked on that too," Keen came in. "We could see the father was there in two thousand and six but not now, so we trawled through the intervening years. He disappeared off the roll in two thousand and eight."

O'Connor scratched pensively at his chin. "Two sons the same age...twins then?"

"If the ages on the roll are correct, yes, it looks that way," Keen agreed.

O'Connor looked across at Stern. "So, what d'you think, Theo?"

"Well, before I made that call, I felt it important we spoke to the family, see if there was anything going on there. Now, after the reaction I got from that call, and from what the guys have found out, I think it's even more important we speak to them."

"So do I." O'Connor thought for a long moment. "Could do the same as with the others. I could contact my opposite number down there, explain the situation, let them know you're coming to their patch. No need for them to get involved initially; you're only having a chat. But they'll insist you report anything untoward, maybe insist you show your face at the local nick regardless."

"No problem with that," Stern said. "I'd have done the same in my time."

"Tomorrow then?"

Stern gave a shrug. "That's okay by me. I'll kick off early and take Colin with me. That okay with you?"

O'Connor pushed himself out of the chair. "Wouldn't have it any other way. Now I'd better get back before him upstairs realises I'm missing and goes into overdrive."

~ * ~

It was just after six when, having sent Cherry and Colin on their way, once again warning Keen of the early morning start tomorrow, Stern wandered down the high street to the front and back along the promenade toward the flat. As he did most mornings, he'd left the car in the lock-up and the promised rain hadn't materialised, so it was nice to stretch his legs in the mild evening air. His mind, just for the moment, drifting away from the case, he remembered Melanie still hadn't called as promised. He relaxed against the promenade wall and dialled her number. Again there was no reply. He stood for a moment gazing out across the North Sea, recalling again her hesitation at Cain Engineering, when he'd asked to see her. The story of a friend staying with her sounded plausible and was a good enough reason for her not wanting him there. Yet there was something about the way she'd reacted; the hesitancy, the body language. Was it that policeman's nose again? Suspicious, always on the lookout for that tiny inconsistency that said something was wrong. Or did he really detect a coolness, a barely perceptible backing off? As he made his way up the steps and across the seven green to the flats, Stern decided there was only one way to find out.

After a quick shower and a change of clothes, he left the flat and made his way around to the rear of the building and the row of lock-ups. A few minutes later, he'd left Sheringham and was cruising past the extensive grounds of the National Trust's 17th century country house, Felbrigg Hall, on his way to Aylsham.

He pulled the car onto the verge opposite the cottage and made his way down the path to the front door. Hanging on the bell push, he prepared the smile he was about to throw at her as soon as she appeared. That smile was not needed because after the second lengthy push, it became obvious there was no one at home. He paused for a moment, considering whether he should hang around for a while. Reminding himself of the early start tomorrow, he decided against it and wandered back across the lane, pulling open the car door. He heard the call as he was about to slide behind the wheel.

"Hello there."

Stern eased himself upright and looked back across the lane. The elderly man had appeared from a tiny bungalow two doors down. Stern closed the car door and re-crossed the lane.

"You looked like you were waiting for the lady in the cottage," the man said as Stern approached.

Stern could imagine the man living alone, most of the time at the window, missing nothing, glad to grab any opportunity for a chat. "You're right, I was. D'you happen to know where she might be?"

The man shook his head. "No idea where she is, but I do know she's not there anymore."

Stern smiled tolerantly; after all, the man was knocking on a bit. "Yes I know she's not there. I realised that when she didn't answer the bell. I just wondered..."

The man waved a scrawny hand. "No, you don't understand. I mean she's not there anymore at all. She's gone, mate, headed out, left the area."

"Are you sure?"

The old guy dangled a bunch of keys in front of Stern's face. "Considering she banged on my door early this morning and gave these to hand back to the landlord, yeah I'm pretty sure." He gave a knowing grin. "He'll have a new tenant in there within a week, I'll lay my pension on it. No flies on him and that's a fact."

Forty-nine

Stern had collected Keen soon after seven and they'd made good time, Stern enjoying being able to give the Hyundai its head for a change. Keen was bent on talking, enthusiastically going over the facts of the case, probing Stern for his thoughts on the situation. Unlike their last trip together, when they travelled to Bradford, Stern was more inclined to let the youngster have his head, genuinely becoming involved in discussion, answering questions and giving his opinion. However, during the occasional quiet moment, his mind drifted to the mystery of Melanie's sudden evacuation of the cottage. The move had obviously been planned beforehand, therefore she had to have known she was on the move when he'd spoken to her at Cain Engineering. But why, when before she had been so keen, saying more than once she felt there was something between them? Had she suddenly realised how serious things were becoming and lost her nerve, unable to accept the possibility of a permanent, long term relationship?

Stern recalled the overpowering guilt, the huge sense of betrayal he'd felt after the first time he'd slept with Melanie. Even though he and Annie were no longer together. So had Melanie felt the same? Her husband was no more, but she had admitted not having a serious relationship since his death. So was she feeling a similar guilt and was she not able to handle it, choosing to run sooner than face Stern with a rejection? The thoughts whirred around his head, the endless cycle broken only by Colin Keen's frequent question and answer sessions.

The M25 had been kind and there had been no holdups on the Dartford crossing. The traffic had started to increase when they left the M25 and headed south on the M23, but even so they still found themselves joining the Horsham road well before ten thirty.

"A good run, boss," Keen commented. "She goes well."

"Nice to be able to open her up," Stern said. "Normally it's just trundling around locally. So what happens now?"

"Second roundabout we make a left onto the B2195. Soon after it's another left into New Moorland Drive. Ten, fifteen minutes max."

There were some nice properties in Moorland Drive and the Wright House was no exception. Set well back from the road, it was a large, double-fronted building with wide bay windows either side of a central front door. A well-clipped hedge bordered an extensive front garden simply laid out with flower beds surrounding a square lawn. A metal gate led to a slabbed path running straight down one side between the flowered border and the lawn before branching diagonally across to the front door. A wooden stake driven into the earth just behind the front hedge displayed a for sale notice.

Stern spotted a short lay-by on the opposite side of the road to the house and eased the car into a position that gave him the clearest view of the property. He pointed at the for sale sign.

"Looks like the Wrights are on the move. May be just as well we came."

"Nice place," Keen commented. "Fetch a bob or two."

"Mmmm, when you checked out the father, did it say what his occupation was?"

"No, it's pretty restricted. The best you get is who lived where and when."

Stern checked the dashboard clock. "I'm just thinking we'll be lucky to find anyone in at this time. Probably Mum and son both at work."

"Could be. D'you want me to go and give them a knock?"

Stern shook his head. "Not just yet. Let's watch for a while, see if there's any sign of life."

Keen grinned. "Strikes me it could be a long day."

"It's not out of the question, but if push comes to shove, I did clock the Premier Inn back there."

"Great," Keen harrumphed. "And there was me on a promise tonight."

"Like I said before, it goes with the territory, son."

Stern glanced sideways and saw the grin on Keen's face. "And you know as well as I do where you'd rather be. Am I right?"

"Damn right you are, boss."

Smirking contentedly to himself, Stern eased himself down in the seat.

~ * ~

"Hey up!"

Less than half an hour had passed and Stern was resting his eyes when Keen's sharp retort brought him to full alertness. The front door of the Wright house had opened and a man carrying a large cardboard box had appeared. He moved round to the side of the house and a moment or two later returned empty-handed. Without looking around, he went back into the house and closed the door behind him.

"Late twenties?" Stern murmured.

"And chunky with it," Keen responded.

"Has to be our Alec, don't you think?"

"Looks that way. How d'you want to play it?"

Stern gave the question some thought. "One of us, I think. Something tells me it would be wise for one of us to stay out of it."

"You're not expecting trouble, are you?"

Stern shook his head. "No I don't think so. As I see it, if they've had nothing to do with any of this, they can only be grateful that we're looking into things again. I mean, Baldwin's story sounds kosher, but who knows, a few questions here could throw a whole different light on things. It's only the response I got on the phone that's making me cautious. Besides a few questions to a mum and her son don't need two of us, does it?" He flipped open the door and left the car.

Acting as casual as he could, Stern strolled across the road and up to the house. Easing open the gate, he wandered down the path to the front door. A quick glance confirmed there was no bell push, but positioned centrally on the heavy wooden door was an old fashioned wrought iron knocker in the shape of a stag's head. Stern couldn't remember the last time he'd had to use one of these. He lifted it and brought it down twice with a hard rap. Seconds later, the door was pulled open by the young man they'd seen carrying the box round to the side of the house. He stopped short, a scowl instantly clouding his face. Not a great start.

"Mr Wright?"

"What do you want?" The scowl stayed firmly in place.

"You are Mr Wright?" Stern repeated.

"Who wants to know?"

It was the same voice and the same belligerent response he'd had on the phone the previous day and Stern realised to even mention the police would be a bad move. Somehow he had to get to the mother and he could see that wasn't going to be easy. This was a big lad who for some reason did not welcome visitors and was not going to give way easily. There was something about him, too. Something that... Stern pushed the thought away. Not now. Now he had to concentrate, figure a different tactic.

"It's Alec, isn't it?"

At the mention of his name, the young man's face dropped and for a second confusion filled his eyes. Then with a heave, he tried to slam the door closed.

He didn't know why; maybe the eyes telegraphed the move, or maybe it was just because Stern had been in so many similar situations before. Whatever, he saw it coming. Ramming his shoulder forward, he jammed his foot into the quickly closing gap at the bottom of the door. Fortunately for his foot, the shoulder took the brunt of the weight. Nevertheless he grunted as the heavy door crunched against his foot and the pain shot through his ankle and up his leg.

"Don't be stupid, boy," he gasped, pushing his whole body weight against the door, only just managing to maintain a big enough gap to speak through. "I just want to talk to your mother. There's nothing to be afraid of."

But there was no let-up on the pressure against his shoulder and screaming foot, but he heard Alec shout. *"Mother!"*

"Who is it, Alec?" The female voice came from the back of the house and footsteps quickly approached the front door. "What on earth is going on?"

Again it was Alec's anguished words. "It's him, mother. It's him."

"It's who? For goodness sake, Alec, open the door."

For a tense moment nothing happened, then Stern felt the pressure ease and the door once again slowly opened. He staggered back, gently easing the crushed foot to the ground, thankfully realising, though sore, it could still take his weight. No broken bones.

Alec Wright stood wide-eyed, his back to the wall as the woman came into view striding down the hallway toward the open front door.

Stern's gaze moved from the anguished face of the son to the mother coming toward him and in an instant his heart stopped dead in his chest. His mouth fell open and it was an agonising age before, through an almost totally restricted throat, he could utter the single word.

"Melanie?"

Fifty

Eyes locked, the two stood in stunned silence, each utterly shocked at coming face to face with the other. Finally it was Melanie, her face a taut, determined mask, who spoke first, saying simply, "What do you want?"

"What do I want?" Stern managed incredulously. "Are you kidding?"

Alec stood like stone, his eyes flicking from one to the other. "It's him, Mother?" he said for the second time

Melanie ignored her son. "You shouldn't be here. I don't want you here," she snapped through gritted teeth.

Stern threw up his arms. "You don't want me here? What the hell is that supposed to mean? What's going on here, Melanie? What are you doing...?" He drifted into silence, looking from mother to son, a frightening mental picture forming, the true horror of the situation slowly becoming clear. He shook his head from side to side. "No, no, surely not. Not you?"

"Mother?" Alec repeated, a deep, worried frown creasing his forehead.

Melanie held up an impatient hand, motioning her son

to silence. For several seconds she held Stern's accusing stare, her hand still aloft. Then, taking a huge breath, her shoulders sagged. "You fool," she breathed softly. "Why did you have to come here?"

Stern held out both hands submissively. "I didn't know. How was I supposed to..."

Without letting him finish, she took a pace back and beckoned him inside. "You'd better come in."

The first door on the right led them into a large sitting room fronted by one of the wide bay windows. The room was almost empty; a tea chest sat in one corner and two heavy wooden kitchen chairs were pushed haphazardly against one wall. Newspapers piled in one corner were being used to wrap plates and other items of crockery dotted about the floor. There were no pictures on the walls, just the dark outlines of where they had been.

Stern turned and faced the woman and her son, for the first time scrutinising Melanie closely. She had on a faded t-shirt and stained jeans and wore no make-up at all. Her hair was pulled severely back, held in place by a red elastic band. It didn't slip his notice that Alec, also dressed in jeans, a red vest pulled over a t-shirt, had taken up a position in front of the door. An innocent coincidence? Maybe, but Stern didn't believe in coincidence. The atmosphere in the room was chilled and Stern couldn't help feeling just a little apprehensive. But he'd had years of practice hiding apprehension. He pulled back his shoulders and crossed his arms confidently over his chest.

"So, you going to tell me about it?" he said bluntly.

The soft-eyed, loving face he'd grown used to over the past weeks was no more. Instead a hard, tight jawed expression, enhanced even more by the lack of make-up, faced him across the room. "You were a fool to come here," she said. "It was over, done. You should have left it that way."

Stern fought desperately to hold onto the confident 'ex-hardnosed copper, I've seen it all before' stance, but his stomach was churning and his brain was in absolute turmoil. This was a woman he'd lain with, even envisaged as a life partner, replacing his beloved Annie. Now here she was...a harsh, totally different person and the more his chaotic brain slowly collated the facts, recalled almost forgotten images and drew everything together, the more it became clear. He, Theo Stern, ex-super cop, had been taken for the biggest ride of his life. So much so he'd become complicit in murder. The anger building, he swallowed hard, trying to clear the increasing bile from a raw throat. He must hold it in, display the image and hope he didn't falter. He turned to the young man standing by the door.

"So, how's the jogging going, Alec?"

Alec Wright jerked forward, every muscle in his body tightening menacingly.

Melanie saw the signs and spoke sharply. "*No.* Stay where you are, Alec." She turned back to Stern with sad eyes. "Still got the policeman's powers of observation, Theo?"

"A photographic memory helps," he said. "The red vest...same one, is it?"

She ignored the question, posing one of her own. "They know where you are, don't they?"

"Of course they do. They always do."

She gave a slow nod of her head, for a second the hard, determined expression replaced with a tight, wan smile. "Theo Stern, ever the policeman." She studied her long shapely fingernails. "And to think tomorrow we would have been gone."

Stern could feel the anger beginning to creep away, leaving him feeling sad and weary. But he knew he must not succumb to it. He needed to confirm he was actually standing face to face with a woman he now believed to have cruelly orchestrated the killing of not one but four innocent men. "Gone where? Where did you think you could hide?"

In an instant, Melanie's face had again hardened, her lips tightening determinedly. "Oh, Theo, my love, you have no idea. This was all planned a very long time ago." She made a point of looking down at her watch. "And after all this time, it would have been over. Justice would have been done and tomorrow we would have been away." Shrugging her shoulders, she looked toward her son. "But now...?"

Suddenly the atmosphere had become increasingly tense and Stern saw muscles constrict on the broad shoulders of Alec. He was big and powerful, and he was poised, just waiting on a single word from his mother. Stern could see that if he didn't act quickly, something bad was about to happen. But it was crucial for him to extract the ultimate confession. Then he would know; then he could be sure.

"But why?" he blurted out. "Why would you do such a thing?"

Her mouth twisting angrily, Melanie spun back to face Stern. "Why? You ask me why?"

Alec, coiled, ready for action, realised his mother had been distracted. "Mother, we have to do something. Don't let him..."

"Shut up, Alec." Her blazing eyes hadn't left Stern for a second. "Okay, I'll tell you why. Because they destroyed my whole family, that's why."

From the corner of his eye, Stern could see Alec's restraint was hanging by a thread. Just a single word from his mother was all it needed for him to break. Somehow he had to hold her attention, had to keep her talking. "But, Melanie, they didn't. It was an..."

"They didn't?" she spat at him. "How dare you? What do you know?"

"I know you had no right to take the law into your own hands, no right to kill four innocent young men."

"Innocent? You know nothing," she snapped. She spun round, an arm outstretched. "D'you see this room, this house? It once held a family, a happy family. It was all I ever wanted...my lovely husband and my two beautiful boys." She paced nearer to Stern, peering up at him, her face contorted with rage, spots of saliva beginning to creep from the corners of her mouth. Her eyes blazed crazily and before this moment Stern could never have believed it possible for her to look this way. "You whinged pathetically to me about your lost woman," she said, the pitch of her voice becoming higher, more resonant. "But that was your own stupid fault. You told me yourself; you had every chance; you could have done something about it." She jabbed a finger at his chest. *"You lost her."* Tears flooded her eyes. "But me, I did nothing, I was blameless. Yet still those four animals gave me no chance; they took away my sons, my wonderful husband, and they destroyed me."

Stern shook his head. "But you don't know that. You can't be sure..."

Suddenly her expression changed. Gone was the angry, challenging face...now it was an ugly wide-mouthed, tooth-baring grin. The trembling hand, the finger waved under his nose. "Oh I can, I really can and do you know why? Because he told us, that's why. My Simon told us. From the grave he told us what they did."

It was an involuntary, knee jerk reaction, done before he realised what he was doing. She had become unstable and he reached forward, taking her gently by the shoulders. "No, this is silly, you must..." But that one move was a grave mistake because in doing so, not only had he taken his eyes off Alec, he had also laid his hands on the boy's mother.

"Nooo," was all he heard before a huge force crashed into him. He felt himself propelled violently across the room, crashing on his back, his head ricocheting agonisingly off something solid. He could just distinguish the huge blurred shape of Alec over him, an arm raised and in an ever darkening grey mist he raised his arms, flailing his fists in a desperate attempt to protect his face.

There was a roaring in his head. Was it in his head, or was it coming from his attacker? And the higher pitched screeching sound. What the hell was that? He couldn't be sure and in the following split second, it didn't matter anyway, because something crashed into his face and the grey turned to instant blackness.

Fifty-one

He felt so comfortable, more relaxed than he'd felt for a very long time, his whole body seeming to sink into the bed, every muscle like lead. Christ, to feel like this he must have had one helluva night's sleep. He decided not to open his eyes until he had confirmed what was on the books for today. He was feeling so good that if there were nothing important, he would stay here, just for once have a lay in. But that was difficult because he couldn't remember what day today was.

Okay, don't panic, just think. Start with yesterday. What happened yesterday? Had he downed a few too many malts before turning in last night? Was that why he couldn't remember? No, that couldn't be so, because there was no headache. Too many malts and there was always a headache. He decided he would, after all, have to open his eyes. That was difficult, though, because it felt like his eyelids had been super-glued shut. Concern started to well up inside him. This was daft; he could hardly move a muscle and he couldn't open his eyes. No, he wasn't having this, he had to move, something was telling him it was very important for him to move.

"Ah, at last, he's back with us."

The voice was muffled, indistinct, but he could just make out the words. But who was it and who they were talking about; who was back? He had no idea. Then another realisation; someone was holding onto his hand very tightly? He tried to move his arm, pull his hand away, but there was no response. Now arms encircled him, pulling him up, lifting him into a sitting position. And words were being whispered into his ear. "There, that's better. Come on, Mr Stern, let's see those eyes open."

Well, whoever you are, don't go on, because I'm trying, I'm trying bloody hard.

The hand still clutched his tightly, and now another voice...female, afraid sounding. "Is he okay? Will he be alright?"

"Give him a moment. It's been a while."

At last the supreme effort was rewarded and heavy eyelids were forced apart. Blinding light flooded in and as if in unison the pain came, soaring within him. *Jesus Christ.* The subconscious euphoria instantly drained and in a single heartbeat his head was throbbing abominably and every muscle, every sinew, every bone in his body began to cry out. He tried to fill his lungs with clean air, but stopped instantly, the effort sending pain scything through his chest.

He groaned. "Bloody hell, that hurts." The words came out as a dried up, guttural mumble.

A soft hand gently on his cheek. "Shh, don't try to talk,

Mr Stern. Just lie still and I'll feed you some fluid." Slowly his vision cleared and he could see she was a big lady, dressed in blue and immaculate white, and as he looked up at her, trying desperately to assess the situation, to drag himself into the here and now, she fed a tube into the corner of his mouth. "Suck gently," she instructed. "Not too much now."

He did as he was told and drew the sweetest, coolest water he'd ever tasted into his foul, filth-lined mouth. Too soon the tube was withdrawn and he closed his eyes, rested his head gratefully back against the pillows and swilled the water around his mouth before swallowing. It was all coming back now...the house, Melanie and her son, the attack.

"Boss?" The words were spoken softly, hesitant.

Again he levered his eyes open, this time squinting down the bed, blinking, focussing slowly. Cherry sat on a chair alongside the bed. She was clasping his hand in hers, her face pale, her eyes red rimmed.

He tried to smile. It didn't work.

"There, I told you he'd be okay, didn't I?" From the other side of the bed, the big lady, a nurse. "Don't forget, now, he mustn't try to talk." She turned to leave the room. "The doctor will be doing her rounds soon, probably half an hour or so. Push the button if you need me."

Stern waited until the door had closed behind the nurse before he tried to do exactly as he was told not to. But in doing so he realised he could hardly move his jaw and an attempt to do so shot hot lances of pain through the whole of his face. "Arghh."

Still holding his hand, Cherry jumped to her feet, her pale face bathed in concern. "No, no, please, boss. Don't try to speak. You'll only hurt yourself. Your jaw is broken. They've wired it together." She reached for the bottle on the bedside cabinet, again carefully inserting the tube into the corner of his mouth. He sucked gratefully on the cool liquid for some time before nodding for her to remove the tube. "Probably gave you too much there," she said uncertainly. "Are you okay?"

Stern this time did manage a semblance of a smile.

Cherry slowly lowered herself back onto the chair. "Just let me talk. I'll tell you what's been going on, okay?" She pulled the chair closer to the bed. "You're in a private ward in the Horsham hospital. Today is Saturday and you've been here for three days. Everyone's been worried sick."

Three days? He couldn't help jerking forward at the news. He instantly wished he hadn't, because the sudden movement sent a fresh set of sharp, red hot spears probing from his back to his chest and up into his neck.

Cherry understood the move and saw the pain etched on his face. "Yeah, you shouldn't try to move too much either, boss. They reckon you've got a few broken bits in there."

He cocked his head to one side and raised his eyebrows as best he could. The gesture he hoped referring to a question.

Cherry was quick to understand and shook her head. "Sorry, I've not been able to talk to the doctor, so I don't know all the details. But according to the nurse, you have a fractured skull, severe concussion and a broken jaw. And that's only your head." Her eyes moistened. "Honest, boss, I thought I'd lost you." She swallowed back the obvious emotion. "If it hadn't been for Colin... He said you had actually stopped breathing. If he hadn't been there, I'm sure that animal would have killed you."

He did the cocking head and raised eyebrow bit again.

"Colin told me, at the house, when you went up to the front door, he saw you have some trouble with the guy, so he got out of the car to come and help you. But then he saw the woman appear and let you in, so he stayed back. He waited for you all to go inside and sneaked up to the front of the house. He stood to one side of the bay window and watched you talking to them. He told me the woman seemed to get more agitated by the minute. Then he saw you reach out for her. He didn't know why you did it, but as soon as you did the guy launched himself across the room at you.

"Colin said it happened in a blink of an eye. He knew he couldn't get through the heavy front door so he rushed round the back. As luck would have it, the back door was unlocked. As he ran through the kitchen and into the hallway, he could hear the man roaring like a wild animal and the woman screaming blue murder. By the time he got to the front room, the man had already knocked you to the floor and was standing over you kicking you to bits. Colin saw a couple chairs against the wall so he grabbed one and smashed it across the guy's back. He said, even then the guy kept punching and kicking you. So he hit him again twice before he went down and stayed down." For a second a smile broke. "Colin said it made a real mess of the chair. Anyway, it seems the woman just stood there screaming, so Colin hit her too. He laid her out cold. They reckon he could be in a bit of trouble for that."

Stern fluttered crooked fingers, beckoning her to carry on.

She knew what he was asking, but hesitated before carrying on. "I don't know much more, boss. Maybe you should wait for the doctor."

He frowned, eyeing her suspiciously.

"Look, boss, I'm not supposed to..." She stopped, looking to the door as it opened and a young, white coated woman came into the room followed by the nurse. The woman came to the side of the bed and looked at Stern. She slowly shook her head. "You know, Mr Stern, a man of your age should know better than to get involved in this sort of thing," she said.

She had the advantage; he couldn't answer back, so he just gave a resigned shrug. Even that hurt. He grimaced.

"In pain?"

He nodded...a small, cautious movement.

"Headache?"

He lifted his hand and pointed to his head and his chest.

"I understand. Do you have any stomach problems? I mean before this happened...ulcers or the like?"

A very slow shake of the head.

The doctor turned to the nurse. "Oxycodone, I think, nurse. Just to take him through the worst. Turning back to Stern, she said, "Right, Mr Stern, I'm Dr Armstrong and I guess I don't have to tell you, you've taken a bit of a beating. You have a fractured skull and the concussion that comes with it. Hence the head pain. Fortunately, the fracture is not severe and the concussion, though grade two, should clear in twenty-four to forty-eight hours. We will, of course, keep you here under observation.

"You also have a broken jaw, which has already been repaired. This means we have wired your top and bottom jaw together. To do this, we have put wires around your teeth. Not very comfortable, I'm afraid. You will have already realised you can't open your mouth which means for a while you will have to be fed through a straw." She smiled. "Soups and smoothies for you, Mr Stern. I would also recommend baby food. I know that sounds strange, but it will provide you with more nutrition and is something different.

"Believe me, even if you like them, you'll soon get sick of smoothies. Your jaw will be wired shut for four to eight weeks, by the way. Now, the pain in your chest is caused by several cracked ribs. X-rays confirm there are no fragments and the ribs are still in position which means, apart from the strapping you already have, we'll leave the rest to nature. I know breathing is painful, but do what you can to breathe naturally. Too much shallow breathing is not good for you, okay? Your ribs will probably take a couple of months to heal properly. Maybe longer, don't forget you're not as young as you used to be, and we must not forget as well as everything else you did need CPR at the scene.

"We believe your heart stalled as a result of severe trauma, the shock of the brutal beating. But we need to be sure so there are one or two more tests to be carried out and further observation. I estimate you to be with us for up to a week, maybe longer, depending on the tests and how you progress." She waved a warning finger at him. "But even after you leave us, you will need to rest, Mr. Stern. I mean at least several weeks, probably even months. Even putting the cardiac arrest to one side, a fractured skull, broken jaw and cracked ribs, not to mention the extensive soft tissue damage means rest, lots of it." She paused, relaxing a little, and there was that mischievous smile again. "But, d'you know what? Other than that, there's not an awful lot wrong with you."

Fifty-two

He'd passed the rest of Saturday in a semi-conscious state, drifting between nodding off as the pain killers kicked in to waking uncomfortably as their effect wore off. Cherry, who'd left him only for food and comfort breaks, had filled him in with more info during the waking periods.

She told him that, after overpowering Melanie and her son, Colin had called in the local police. A good deal of explaining had been needed, but fortunately O'Connor had already informed his opposite number in Horsham that they were in the area, promising they would report as soon as they'd interviewed those at Wright House. After Melanie and her son had been taken into custody, Keen had called Cherry. She had immediately closed up shop, thrown a few things in a bag and hit the road. She'd been there ever since, lodging at a small B&B a short distance from the hospital.

Through a series of painful grunted words, Stern had gently chastised her for leaving her fiancé for so long, insisting that tomorrow, Sunday, she must return home.

Cherry agreed but only, she was adamant, after the meeting.

Meeting?

Cherry explained O'Connor had been in the area since the day after the attack. He hadn't visited the hospital because, together with local detectives, he had spent long hours questioning both Melanie and her son. But his superiors had insisted he return on Monday. He had contacted Cherry to inform her he would be visiting to update Stern on Sunday.

~ * ~

Sunday dawned and Stern felt marginally better. Everything still hurt, but to his relief the screaming, debilitating headache had subsided. Just a tad, but it made all the difference. When O'Connor, accompanied by Keen, arrived, he at least felt he could concentrate on what they had to tell him. Most of the time anyway. Cherry came through the door first, followed ten minutes later by O'Connor and Keen.

O'Connor stopped short inside the door. "Bloody hell, Theo, what a mess!"

"What?" Surprisingly, Stern had found this morning, if he was careful and didn't move his jaw more than a fraction, and used his lips, he could actually form words. Maybe, as the nurse had told, it was because some of the swelling had gone down overnight.

Cherry jumped in protectively. "The boss hasn't looked in the mirror yet."

O'Connor whistled softly. "Don't let him, then."

Stern looked at Cherry and did the eyebrow thing.

"Don't worry, boss, you're still a bit swollen, that's all. One or two bruises. Nurse says it'll soon go."

O'Connor didn't let go easily. "A bit swollen? One or two bruises? His face looks like a bloody truck's hit it."

Stern sighed. "Thanks, David. I feel a lot better now," he burbled.

"Oh, sorry mate, I didn't mean to, but... Well you do look a bit of a mess."

Stern looked from O'Connor to Colin Keen. "Without you, it could have been worse."

The words sounded strung together and indistinct, but Keen understood and moved self-consciously. "I was only pleased I left the car when I did. If I hadn't, I'd have had no idea what was going on."

"And CPR too." The CPR came out as *sheepier*. It was the best he could do and thankfully just understandable.

"All part of the training, boss. Anyway, the rapid response guys were there in no time. Defrib, the lot. It was their call, really."

"Maybe, but thank you anyway." There was an awkward silence for a moment or two before Stern looked again to O'Connor and raised his eyebrows.

O'Connor understood. "I think we've got everything now," he said. "The boy has shut down completely, hasn't said a single word since he came round in custody. My guess is, other than a mental institution, he won't be going anywhere for a very long time. The mother's a totally different kettle of fish. She's confessed to the whole thing, given us all we need and more. She hasn't stopped talking since we took her in. This has been with her for years and now it's over, all she wants is to get everything off her chest. The woman's been a time bomb since two thousand and six, Theo. Her life must have been hell. Even so, she has no regrets and still fervently believes the legal system let her and her family down big time. So much so she decided to do the business herself." He paused. "Sounds crazy, but having heard the whole story, though nothing can justify what she did, I can't help sympathizing with her."

"She said her family was destroyed," Stern hissed through clenched teeth.

O'Connor nodded. "It was, too. Melanie and her husband were very close and when she was told she was about to have twins, she was overjoyed. But when the boys were born there was a problem... one of them, the youngest, Alec, wasn't quite right. Turns out he took longer to materialize and was starved of oxygen. So whereas Simon was the bright spark, Alec was introverted, brilliant in some respects, but deep and sometimes unpredictable. He doted on his brother and from day one depended a great deal on Simon's support and guidance. And, it seems, Simon responded by always being there for him. So when Simon left for Liverpool, the effect on Alec was dramatic. He turned even more inward and at the slightest upset had a tendency toward violence. Melanie and her husband sought advice and slowly, with a great deal of effort from them and some special psychiatric treatment, Alec began to revert to his old self. Then, out of the blue, came the news that Simon had been found floating face down in the Mersey."

"That must have been awful," Cherry breathed.

"Awful hardly covers it," O'Connor said. "As well as facing the trauma themselves, they had to cope with Alec, who on being told went ballistic. He became totally unpredictable and prone to violent rages at the least little upset. So much so that before two thousand and six was out, they had no option but to have him sectioned."

"So they lost both sons." Cherry sighed

"Yes they did, but even then, for Melanie, the horrors weren't over. Her husband, who had always found it more difficult to cope with Alec than Melanie, went into decline. He took to the bottle more and more until one day early the following year, she came home to find he'd taken a bottle of vodka to the bath and cut both his wrists."

Cherry's hand went to her mouth. "Oh, my God."

"See what I mean when I say awful hardly covers it?" O'Connor repeated. "And to make things worse, the husband left a note. It was a scribbled, rambling thing, but in it he said he'd been warned and had done nothing about it. Said he couldn't face the shame of letting them all down."

"What did he mean about being warned?" Cherry asked.

"At the time, nobody could understand. But he'd put away a full bottle of vodka so they could only put it down to him being out of his head with the drink."

Cherry shook her head. "Blimey, it's enough to send anyone over the edge."

O'Connor gave a sad smile. "You couldn't be more

right, Cherry, because that's exactly what it did. Melanie had a total mental breakdown and had to be taken into care herself. It was two thousand and eleven before the psychos decided she was okay to be released into society again."

Stern held up a hand. "Is that when she changed her name?" He was getting used to speaking through clenched teeth, forming his words slowly and carefully.

"She didn't change her name, Theo. Not then, anyway."

Stern frowned. "I don't understand."

"Hang on and you will," O'Connor said. "You see, Melanie had come to terms with the fact that her son had died in a tragic accident; the enquiry's final report had said so. Now, after dragging herself up out of a nightmare, she knew she had to accept it, just as she'd have to accept her husband's suicide.

"She had to build herself a new life. She told me, at that time she was feeling strong and was determined to try and put things behind her and make a fresh start. For some months she lived in a B&B, unable to return to Wright House, the memories still too harsh. But eventually she plucked up the courage to make a decision; she would not only return to the house, but she would also convince the authorities to release Alec back into her care. He was all she had left in the world and if she were to make that fresh start, she felt he should be with her. It took time, but eventually she succeeded and at first, she told me, it worked.

"Alec was on medication and much more controlled,

and slowly she was coming to terms with her new life. In their absence, the house had declined considerably, but slowly they brought it back to life...they had a builder repair the outside damage and deterioration and redecorated the whole of the inside, even had that bathroom gutted to a shell and refitted with new stuff."

Stern was becoming impatient. He could feel a huge 'but' about to come. "So what went wrong?" he urged.

O'Connor lifted a warning hand. "This is complicated, Theo. Don't try to rush me."

"Sorry."

"Eventually they'd had the whole house done. Except for one room," O'Connor continued. "The husband's study. It hadn't been touched since his death and, Melanie told me, she knew as soon as she opened the door she would see all his things, smell the old familiar smell, his smell. It was months before she was able to force herself into that room."

"But she did, she eventually did," Stern pushed again.

O'Connor took a deep breath and exhaled slowly. "Oh yes, she did. That's when it all went belly up." O'Connor stopped and looked from Cherry to Stern, both their faces anxious and expectant. Then he turned to Keen. "Looks like I've been doing all the talking so far, Constable. Have you got the printout?"

"Yes, I have." Keen reached into his pocket and pulled out a folded sheet of paper.

O'Connor gave him a nod. "Okay then. You were with me at the interview, so why don't you take it from here."

Keen enthusiastically pulled his chair closer to the bed.

"The study was exactly as it had been left by her husband, including his laptop, still open, sitting on the desk. Melanie told us that she ignored it, concentrating more on clearing out the rest of the room. It was Alec who picked it up. You see, like we said, he was brilliant at some things and computers was one of those things. He knew, after all this time, the battery would be flat and it was only his intention to recharge it. But once the thing was plugged in and fired up, he couldn't resist clicking on some of the icons on the desktop, including e-mails." Keen stopped and unfolded the sheet of paper and handed it to Stern. "This is a printout of an e-mail he found there."

Stern took the sheet of paper and beckoned Cherry alongside him. Together they started to read:

SimonWright@gmail.co.uk
To: Dad

Hi Dad.

Just thought I'd let you know about a piece of extracurricular excitement I've got myself involved in. Last week a guy I've got to know invited me to a party. His name's Martin Baldwin and he's graduating this year...

Fifty-three

Stern lowered the sheet of paper and looked up at O'Connor. "This kicked it off?"

"Yes it did. You see, we mustn't forget what they'd been through. It was true...she'd managed to fight her way back into the real world, but even so, after everything that had gone before, both mother and son were still in a pretty fragile state. Then, just when she must have thought she was at last starting to build a new life for herself and her son, they found that." He pointed to the printout in Stern's hand. "Can you imagine the impact it must have had?"

Cherry let out a soft whistle. "Now I understand why you said you felt sympathy for her."

"Wouldn't anyone?" Keen agreed. "The last few words on that e-mail could lead anyone to believe Simon's death was not an accident. To someone in her state of mind it must have been proof positive."

"Right, and now I understand why Melanie said her son had told her what had happened from the grave," Stern hissed through clenched teeth. "Bloody hell."

"It also explains why the father said in his suicide note that he had been warned and could have done something to save his son," Keen broke in. "Let's face it, a phone call advising Simon not to be stupid, to back out, would have probably done the trick. Instead he did nothing and his son died."

"But maybe, even if he had tried, he wouldn't have been able to stop it," O'Connor came back. "Because what he knew, and Dasti and his cronies didn't, was his son was a prominent tri-athlete. In fact, Simon Wright had competed, and had considerable success, in any number of top triathlons. A swim across the Mersey, day or night, would have seemed a doddle to him. From the e-mail, you can see he was obviously convinced none of them could match him. He said it, didn't he…they'll have to catch me first. Except something," he shrugged his shoulders. "Who knows, maybe a chunk of heavy flotsam, happened to turn up in the same place at the same time as him."

"You believe that's what happened?" Stern mumbled.

O'Connor shrugged his shoulders. "If we believe what Baldwin told you, then, yes, we have to. It would seem to be the only logical answer."

Keen reached across and took the printed e-mail from Stern. "But it was this that sent Melanie back over the edge. She told us, there and then, she decided she would put right what the system had got wrong. She had the motivation; she was absolutely convinced the four students had somehow orchestrated her son's death. And she had the means…son Alec.

"She'd discovered over the years that he had an almost

infallible photographic memory. Alec may have been dependent on her guidance, but motivate him and give him detailed instructions and they stuck, nothing would stop him carrying them out to the letter. And motivation was not a problem; Alec would do anything to avenge his brother's murder and, crucially, without his medication he was a virtual killing machine." He looked at Stern. "You for one can vouch for that, right boss?"

"Yeah, suppose I can," Stern muttered. "It's still hard to believe… I mean, that woman… Thought I knew her."

"I know…it's hard to believe," O'Connor said. "But we have the signed confession to prove it and believe me, it was no mean task. You can see each of the four students…Baldwin, Dasti, Rahman and Armitage, were conveniently named in the e-mail. So she had her targets. Also, in the e-mail her son said they were all on their last graduation year, so she also had a timescale to work with. She admitted it took her a while, but using that information and the internet, she eventually identified them. She had a dossier on each: background, present address, even a photograph. First she sent them all a threatening note. Perversely, in her warped mind, she felt it only fair to warn them that they were about to die. After all, she told us at interview, her son could have walked away from them, so they should at least have the chance of escaping her." O'Connor gave a slow, sad shake of his head. "She was, and still is, one very disturbed lady."

"And she decided they should all die in the same manner as her son," Keen said. He looked toward O'Connor, who motioned for him to carry on. "Baldwin was her first. She found out he was living in Norfolk and working at Cains Engineering, so she rented a local cottage and wangled herself the receptionist job at Cain's. Then she set about getting to know Baldwin, confirming his address and his movements." He glanced across at Stern. "That's where the name change came in. She didn't think it likely her name would mean anything to Baldwin after all that time, but just in case, she used her maiden name: Campbell."

Stern took a breath, resignedly nodding his understanding. "Ah."

"She was about to call in her executioner son, Alec, when up pops Dasti."

"The meeting in the car park," Cherry said.

"That's right. It was too good a chance to miss, so she put Baldwin to one side and set Alec to follow Dasti. You know what happened there."

"How did he take Dasti?" Cherry asked.

"I don't think we'll ever get to know the true detail of that," Keen said. "The boy hasn't spoken a word since his arrest and from what we know, he never told his mother much either. All she can tell us is her son admitted to getting Dasti by flagging him down in his car, feigning to need a lift. And, truth be told, she didn't care much how he did it. His instructions were to somehow get Dasti and drown him. That's what he did. We can only assume, after flagging Dasti down, he overpowered him and tied him up. Then he must have driven the Jag out to where he found a waterlogged ditch and finished the job. After that, all he had to do was dump the car and head home."

Cherry gave a shake of the head. "You couldn't make it up, could you?"

"Thing was," Keen went on, "Melanie didn't know that Baldwin was on the point of leaving the country, and by diverting to Dasti, she missed him. She wasn't happy about that but it didn't stop her. She just kept Baldwin on hold while she did the necessary for Alec to deal with the others. From her cottage here in Norfolk, she arranged everything for her son to travel from Horsham to Bradford and Northampton. All Alec had to do was turn up, finish the job then hotfoot it back home. From what Melanie told us, he was never in the killing area for more than twenty-four hours. There and gone...a real will-o-the-wisp. She was proud of that."

"And," O'Connor came back, "he had to improvise the drownings with whatever was on hand at the scene. He sure as hell did that."

"Why did he take everything from the bodies?" Stern asked.

"That was the boy's idea," Keen said. "He had some twisted notion that said if he took everything from them, it stripped them of their identity, made them a no-one, a nothing. He told his mother he felt good about that."

Cherry was frowning. "Okay, I understand all that, but how did she eventually find out Baldwin was in Australia?"

For a moment nothing was said, but both O'Connor and Keen turned toward Stern.

Stern, seeing their reaction, slowly lowered his head into his hands. "She told you, didn't she?" he mumbled through his fingers.

"Sorry, Theo, but yes she did," O'Connor said softly. "She gave us the details. She even crowed about how clever she'd been."

"So how?"

O'Connor shook his head. "Theo, there's nothing to be gained by..."

"Tell me, David." The sharp words, forced through gritted teeth, sent a flash of white hot pain shooting through his clamped jaw. "Jesus!"

"Okay, okay," O'Connor conceded. "But I see no point in this."

"Just tell me, David."

O'Connor gave a heavy, resigned sigh. "The last time you saw her, she got you to tell her all about the trip...where you were going, even where you were staying. Within an hour of you leaving her, she had the boy booked on exactly the same flight as you were on."

"He was that close?"

"He was in cattle class, a few yards behind you," O'Conner said. "He even followed you across from Sidney to Melbourne and on to Mordialloc. Christ, Theo, he stayed in a joint not two hundred yards from your hotel. Posing as a jogger, he just watched and waited until you went to Baldwin's place. I got Marcus to check the Virgin Blue bookings." He hesitated, not liking what he was having to tell his friend. "The boy was on his way back to Sydney even before you found Baldwin's body."

Stern held O'Connor's sorrowful eyes. "The devious bitch," he whispered.

"It's cold comfort, I know," O'Connor continued, "but she did say deceiving you was the one thing she wasn't happy about. Said she felt like a Mata Hari."

"She seemed happy enough at the time," Stern ground through clenched teeth.

The frown had deepened on Cherry's brow. "Boss? What are we talking about here?"

Stern lifted his head and faced her searching eyes. There was no hiding place. "It was me, luv," he said, his voice little more than a hoarse whisper. "She found out about Baldwin from me."

Cherry chuckled. "Yeah, right. You, give out client confidential info? I don't think so. You'd never do that. You'd have to be…" She stopped, at last seeing the guilt flooding her boss's already battered, black and blue features. She looked back at O'Connor. "Did you say Mata Hari?"

O'Connor took a deep breath and dropped his eyes. He was hating this.

Cherry turned back at Stern. "You don't mean you…?"

The look on her face was the final straw. The effects of the anesthetic, the pain killers and severe trauma at last overran all else. Stern dropped his head into his hands and the tears came.

Fifty-four

August had arrived and the three months since Stern had been released from hospital had not been a happy time. The sign pasted on the front door of the Sheringham bakery explained that, due to illness, Stern Investigations would not be operating for the foreseeable future. Dave, the baker and Stern's landlord, had spent a good deal of time fending off questions about the absence of the town's favourite gumshoe.

Cherry was not a happy bunny, either. She was engaged to be married, it was true, and under different circumstances may well have welcomed the time off. But, as it was, time spent on wedding plans would not happen for a good while yet. There was an awful lot of saving to be done before a wedding could be considered, so time hung as heavy on Cherry as it did on Stern.

Stern, though, had a lot more to deal with. The concussion had passed as expected and the skull fracture had healed with no complications. But that was about the only good news. It had taken more than a month for the extensive bruising covering a large percentage of his body to recede, though even now some darker shades remained, and muscle aches, particularly at night, still persisted.

The jaw, too, hadn't healed well; a week or so after the attack, an infection had set in and a return to hospital and further surgery had to be undertaken. As if that weren't enough, the ribs had also taken their time. Indeed, even now, a twist in the wrong direction or a sharp breath when turning in a particular way could make him wince. The result of all this meant, under strict doctor's orders, he'd had to spend an inordinate amount of frustrating time sitting on his backside.

His fitness had deteriorated to a level where a walk round the block had him out of puff and, until now, the usual beach run that had been so much a part of his daily routine had been out of the question. Cherry had visited regularly, sometimes with fiancé Rob, sometimes alone, and from time to time they had ventured out for lunch or an evening meal. Those visits, together with the occasional very slow stroll to the pub, had been the only respite from the excruciating boredom.

Today, though, the tide was right and he was determined; the fight back would begin in earnest. At 6:00 a.m., when he left the flat, all was quiet on the Sheringham seafront. It was cool but there was hardly a breeze and the North Sea lay flat calm. On the beach, he carried out some preliminary, very cautious stretches, calves and thigh muscles complaining bitterly, before setting off on little more than a very slow jog. After only a few yards, he knew it was not going to be easy, but he persevered, stopping from time to time to ease laboured breathing and slow the heart rate. He was determined, though. Sure, he was fifty-nine years old and a severe beating followed by a forced three month lay-off had wreaked havoc. Losing fitness was a hell of a lot easier, and quicker, than getting it back. But that didn't mean it couldn't be done.

He'd aimed at an hour and it was an hour later, almost to the minute, when, exhausted and sweating profusely, he climbed the steps from the beach and made his way across the green, past the children's play area, to the small block of flats. As he approached, he was surprised to see the figure leaning languidly against the wall alongside the front door. Even more surprised when he recognized who it was.

He glanced at his watch. "Seven o'clock; you wet the bed or something?"

Colin Keen grinned. "Thought I'd come and see how you were doing."

"At this time in the morning?"

Keen shrugged. "It's my day off. Like to make use of it. When I got no response from your flat, I wandered across to the cliff top. Saw this lone figure plodding back along the beach. Guessed it had to be you."

Stern knew there had to be more to it than that, but he didn't pursue it. "Better come in then. You can make the coffee while I pull myself together."

Twenty minutes later, showered and feeling at least half human, he joined Keen waiting patiently in the sitting room, two large mugs of coffee on the side. He grabbed a mug, eased himself into the armchair opposite the young detective constable and waited.

Keen picked up the other mug. "So how are you?"

"I'm getting there, but it's slow. First run this morning. Bloody exhausting."

"I can imagine." He drank some coffee. "Office still closed?"

"Yes, will be for a while yet."

"Bet Cherry's pulling her hair out. Have you seen her?"

"Yeah, she's been in and out. She wants to open up just so she can be there and answer queries. I told her there's no point; we can't take a case, so we might just as well stay closed."

Looking down, Keen ran his forefinger thoughtfully around the rim of the mug.

Stern gave an impatient sigh. "Okay, we've established that I'm getting better and Cherry's impatient to get back to work. So now why don't you tell me why you're really here, eh?"

Keen put the coffee mug down and rubbed his hands together. "Don't miss much, do you, boss?"

"No I don't. So c'mon, out with it."

"Well, it really is my day off, and I did mention to Inspector O'Connor I wanted to come and see you. He asked me to pass a message while I was here."

Stern said nothing, just took a swig of coffee and waited, his eyes holding Keen's anxious gaze.

Keen swallowed hard. "My dad was bent, wasn't he?"

Stern was absolutely stunned. It was the last thing he expected to hear. "What? I thought you said David had asked you to…"

"No, I said I wanted to come and see you...and this is why. He was, wasn't he? My dad?"

Collecting his thoughts, Stern gave it a try, already knowing, from the determined look in Keen's eye, he was wasting his time. "What on earth gave you that idea?"

Keen stood up and paced over to the window, standing with his back to Stern. "You know, I've listened to my mum's story any number of times," he said softly. "I've also studied every line, every word of the official report. I've also checked the newspapers, the back copies." He turned to face Stern. "I've always thought there was something not quite right, but I could never put my finger on it."

"You shouldn't try," Stern interrupted. "Your dad got himself the Queen's Gallantry Medal, Colin. Accept it and be proud."

Keen shook his head angrily. "No, I can't do that. I'm a police officer and I want to be a good one, the best. Justice is based on the truth and that's of paramount importance to me. If my father died a hero, then I will be proud, but if he didn't, if he was bent, I must know. I just have to."

"But you can have no reason to believe..."

"Yes I can. You see, I've also been back through police records. I've seen who was involved in what at the time." He hesitated for a beat, as if intimidated by what he was about to say. "The Raker case...it was yours, wasn't it?"

"Well, yes it was, but..."

"Not my father's?"

"Look, Colin, this can do no one any good. It's the past, it's over."

Keen shook his head slowly. "Not for me it isn't." For a long moment he studied Stern closely, eyes dark, challenging. "The Raker case was nothing to do with my father and yet that night he was with Raker at that house. Why was that?"

Stern broke eye contact, determined not to answer.

"I'll tell you why. My dad was on the take, wasn't he? And you must have known because that's why you went there that night. You also knew how dangerous Raker was. That's why you were armed. My father wasn't armed because there was no need for him to be, was there? He wasn't there as a policeman, was he? He was there as an informant, to get paid dirty money by some lowlife scumbag." His eyes were blazing, his cheeks ruddy with anger.

Stern pushed himself up from the chair. "Now you stop right there," he growled. "I didn't know your father. I'd never worked with him before. But, yes, I did get a tipoff that he was involved in something at the house that night. You're also right about me knowing Raker was a psychopath. That is why I armed myself. The rest of what I told you was the truth.

"Raker was leaving the house as I arrived and after he shot at me, I returned fire and killed him. When I got inside, I found your father had been shot in the neck. He was bleeding profusely and I knew he was dying. I called for an ambulance, but I knew it was already too late so I cradled your dad in my arms until the end came."

He was breathing heavy now, the horror of that night again climbing from the depths of his memory, crystal clear in his head. "In the short time left to him, your father continuously begged me to forgive him, kept asking me to tell your mother how sorry he was. *Me*," he snapped into Keen's face. "He asked *me* to forgive him. Shit, at that time I didn't even know what he'd done wrong."

He turned away from Keen and sunk, spent, back into the chair, reaching for the cooling coffee, swigging down the dregs. "Before your father died, I told him there was nothing to forgive. I told him he'd led me to Raker who I'd dealt with, so he could rest easy; he'd done his job well. Your father died in my arms, Colin. Sure he'd made a mistake…he'd been weak, been turned, but at that time, at any time, even now, there but for the grace of God could go any police officer on our streets. You should know that, boy. You read the newspapers, don't you|?"

"But you said nothing of that. Your report stated my father had been killed during a brave, unarmed attempt to apprehend Raker. You even let them award him the medal."

"Yes, for the greater good, of course I did. You have to remember it was a time when whatever the police did, whichever way they jumped, they were being slated; the do-gooders constantly shouting police harassment, the newspapers endlessly claiming incompetence. And, yes, there were other cases of bent policemen. There still are.

Like I said, read the bloody newspapers. But what your father had done was done. It couldn't be undone and more to the point he wasn't around anymore to be punished. And don't forget there was an innocent grieving wife and child to consider." He stopped and waved a warning finger. "Understand one thing, though. I was a copper and truth and justice meant as much to me then as it does to you right now. So if your father hadn't been hurt, if I'd been able to bring him and Raker to justice in one piece, I would have done it in a heartbeat. As it was, there was nothing to be gained by my shouting about it. A vicious criminal had been taken out. That's what mattered. I made my report and the police media people took it from there. Just for once they had a hero...they weren't on the back foot trying to defend the force."

Keen ran his fingers through his hair. "You're a one off, Mr Stern, d'you know that? My father didn't deserve what you did for him, but my mother and I owe you a huge debt of gratitude."

Stern shook his head. "D'you know, son, history has a way of repeating itself. A few months ago you came to my aid in exactly the same way as I did your father. Okay, the circumstances were different and so was the outcome, but on that day, when you rescued me from that goon and pumped the life back into me, any debt you think you may have owed me was paid back twofold." He gave Keen the hard eye. "But hear this and hear it good. If you try to pursue this further, mention this conversation to anyone at all, I'll brand you an outright liar and swear an oath it never took place. Now do we understand each other?"

Keen took a huge breath, gave a heavy sigh. "I guess so."

Stern climbed stiffly out of the chair again. "Don't look so gloomy, son. Take a piece of advice from an old salt; it's history...put it all behind you and let it rest. I don't know…and I don't want to know what turned your father, but I would gamble when he first joined the Force he was every bit as honest and as dedicated as you are now. Whatever happens, Colin, try not to lose that dedication. Try and be the best of the best…it's the only way. Do that and you'll more than make up for whatever mistake your dad made all that time ago." He gave Keen a gentle punch on the arm. "Now, why don't you let me put some shoes on and I'll take you to my local café for the best fry-up you'll ever have? Oh, and while we're there, you can give me that message from the inspector."

Epilogue

Midnight had long since gone, but Stern, sitting alone at the little round table on the balcony of the flat, the heavy crystal tumbler of malt whiskey in front of him, hadn't noticed. It was a mild, calm night with hardly a breeze; the only sound the waves gently rolling the pebbles to and fro on the beach below. In the blackness that was the North Sea, only the twinkling lights of the far out wind farm were visible. Stern, however, was seeing nothing; his mind was a million miles from the present.

The week before, he'd been surprised to see Colin Keen waiting for him on his return from his beach run. He was even more shocked at the young detective constable's revelations about his father. But the surprises kept coming when, over breakfast, Keen related the message sent by O'Connor. From her cell in the Bronzefield Category 'A' women's prison in Surrey, Melanie Wright had made several requests for Stern to visit her.

Under the instructions of police hierarchy, Keen had told him, the earlier requests had been refused on the grounds that Stern was not fit enough. But she had persisted and now it was felt he should be told of the woman's wish. There was no other information given, no reason why she was making the request, just that she wished to see him.

Alec Wright was in Broadmoor and would be for a very long time, probably the rest of his natural, but pre-trial psychological tests on his mother had concluded, though temporarily disturbed by the trauma of the family tragedies, she was considered sane. She was able to stand trial. She had been at Bronzefield for almost three months. Stern had thought long and hard before finally making his decision.

Knowing he faced a three and a half hour journey each way, he'd booked an early visit, calculating, with a seven o'clock start, eleven would be about right. In the event, he'd arrived with fifteen minutes to spare.

In prison garb, with no makeup, she looked pale and tired. But she was smiling and there was calmness about her as she approached the table and lowered herself onto the chair opposite.

She studied him softly for some time before she spoke. "Hello, Theo, how are you now?"

"I'm okay." He was conscious he hadn't returned the question; hadn't asked her how she was. Somehow he couldn't bring himself to do so. Notwithstanding what he had suffered at the hands of her manic son, she had orchestrated the murder of four young men. Could he really care too much about how she was?

Her eyes clouded and the smile drifted from her face. "You're still angry with me and I can't blame you for that."

Poker faced, he held her gaze for a long moment. "What do you want, Melanie?"

"I wanted to see for myself that you were okay, that you had recovered. But more than that, I wanted to explain..."

"You had four innocent young men murdered," he broke in. "What's more you conned me into helping you do it. What's to explain?"

"No, it's not about the others," she said passively, not reacting to his harsh words. "I'll never be able to explain that, and even if I tried you could never understand. You see, Theo, no one can ever comprehend the true meaning of *'while the balance of the mind was disturbed'* unless you've been there, unless that mind was your own." She gave a gentle, dismissive wave of her hand. "But I'm not making excuses; we did what we did and now we're paying the price." She closed her eyes and ran her long fingers through her hair. "But it's you I'm talking about. You were different; I grew very fond of you and it torments me that I hurt you. I would have done anything to prevent that."

"Really," he harrumphed. "You and your butcher son had a hell of a strange way of showing it."

She shook her head sharply, clearly agitated by his words. "No, stop. Please let me explain."

Recognizing the trauma in her, the sudden bowstring tightening of her posture, he leaned back in the chair and waited.

"Yes, we killed four men, and you call them innocent, but I will never accept that," she said, her voice little more than a shaky whisper. "I believe they deserved what they got and not for one single moment have I regretted doing what we did. But, though I can't expect you to believe me, I do bitterly regret the way I treated you."

Stony faced, Stern gave a slow shake of his head. "Bullshit, I was nothing more to you than a means of getting to Baldwin."

"Maybe, to start with yes, but..."

"But nothing," he snapped. Stern hadn't seen her since the day her son bludgeoned him into unconsciousness. Now, facing her, looking into her dark eyes, he realized the true reason for making the long drive this morning; he needed to shed what had been eating away at his insides since that day, needed to vent his spleen on her, to her face.

"When Dasti unexpectedly turned up at Cain's, it was too good an opportunity to miss," he went on before she could respond. "So you put Baldwin on hold and dealt with Dasti first. But you didn't know Baldwin was on the move and by the time you were ready for him, he'd disappeared. That meant you had to set your pet gorilla onto the other two victims, knowing all the time Baldwin had eluded you. That upset your plan.

"But not to worry, because out of the blue a gullible private detective appears." His lips twisted into an angry sneer. "What luck...he's also looking for Baldwin, so why not get him to do your dirty work for you? No problem; all you have to do is leave a couple of buttons undone, show him what you had on offer and give him a load of bullshit about there being something there, something special."

417

He stopped, swallowing the bitterness that had invaded his throat, his heart thudding against his chest. "You even went the whole hog, didn't you? You let him have what you knew would clinch it, what would ensure he gave you the information you needed." He stopped again, the outburst leaving him feeling hopeless and spent. "Yes, I'm sure you bitterly regret every moment."

Throughout the tirade, she held his angry gaze, patiently waiting for the furious outburst to subside. "All true," she said softly. "And I wish with all my heart that things had been different, that we had met under different circumstances. When I was with you it was like I was in a different world, a different time. There really was something special between us, Theo; you felt it as much as I did, you know you did. You won't believe me, but I cherished those times and when I was with you, I truly meant every word I said. But then, when you weren't there anymore, the hate always returned. It was like a fever and however hard I tried not to, I had to keep going, had to finish what I'd started."

"Even using me to lead your son to Baldwin?"

"Yes I admit it. I would never have found him otherwise."

"And now?"

"I've already said you could never understand, Theo. One minute there's a perfectly happy family...a doting husband and wife and two beautiful boys. Then mayhem descends and in what seems a blink of an eye, everything is torn apart, everything dear to you taken in a way you could never comprehend."

She was shaking and wringing her hands before her, the effect of her last words obvious. "Can you imagine your own dear son perishing in the filthy waters of that river, then your loving Annie, the bath red from her life's blood pumping from ugly gashes...?" The words died on her trembling lips and she held his eyes, her breath coming in short little gasps. "But even after all that, I tried, I really did. Nothing would ever be the same, I knew that, but I still had Alec and if for that reason alone, I had to make a new life. I nearly did, too." She paused, her eyes darkening.

"But when we found the laptop, read the email, it was too much. My mind was turned and I lost all track of reality. All I could see was someone out there was responsible for the devastation that had shattered my whole life. They had to pay, Theo. They had to suffer in exactly the same way as my poor Simon had suffered. From that point on, I couldn't stop until it was done." She held up her hands in a submissive gesture. "My son and I will go down in criminal history as vicious killers, Theo, but I doubt the truth of it will ever be known."

Melanie's words had truly unsettled Stern, but still he couldn't bring himself to condone the killing of four young men who had done nothing more than enter into a stupid bet. "The truth is you and your son slaughtered four innocent young men."

Melanie gave a heavy sigh. "You see, as I told you, you'll never understand. No one ever will. And you will persist in using the innocent word. But can you be sure your interpretation of what happened the night my Simon was killed is the truth?"

"Baldwin told me the whole story."

The soft smile returned. "And that makes it the truth, does it?" She shook her head. "No, Theo, Martin Baldwin's confession to you can no more be relied on as being the truth than my interpretation of Simon's e-mail to his father. It just depends on which one you choose to believe."

"So you still believe your son was murdered?"

Melanie put her hands together as if praying. "Of course I do. I will always believe it. Why else would I have taken the lives of the perpetrators?"

Stern pushed the chair back. "It's time I left."

Melanie reached quickly across and grabbed his hand. "Wait, Theo. I have no doubt that I will never see you again and there is one last, very important thing I must say."

Stern eased back in the chair.

Still gripping his hand, she leaned toward him, her eyes fervently holding his. "In a split second, my family moved from being a perfectly normal loving family to a total catastrophe. There were a million things I never got to say to my husband or my sons, things that now invade my mind every waking minute. Now it's all too late and those unsaid memories will haunt me to my dying day."

Stern moved uncomfortably in the chair. "I don't want to hear…"

She crushed his hand in hers. "Annie," she whispered hoarsely. "When we were together, when you spoke of her, I could hear it in your words, see it in your eyes.

Don't lose her, Theo. Don't end up regretting all those things you should have said, should have done, and never did. Don't wait for something to happen that takes it out of your hands and ends it all. Whatever you have to do, whatever sacrifice you have to make to be with her, make it." Her crushing grip on his fingers remained for long silent seconds before suddenly she released his hand and abruptly stood, looking round to a watching guard. "I'm finished here," she called.

Melanie Wright, nee Campbell, never once looked back as she was escorted from the room.

~ * ~

Now, sitting on his little balcony staring into the blackness, those words still ringing in his ears, Stern raised the crystal tumbler to his lips and sipped tentatively at its contents. The peaty harshness turned to fire as it slid down his dry throat. He gave a cough and drank some more, swilling it around his mouth before swallowing. The effect was softer, less harsh.

He looked down at his watch, noting the time as 1:45 a.m. He calculated as best his tired brain could manage, coming up with 12:30 p.m. in Melbourne. He thought for a few moments more before pushing himself out of the chair and moving back through the glass doors to the sitting room. Slumping down on the settee, he picked up the phone. She would be at the store, but that didn't matter...she was the boss, wasn't she? He was glad she knew nothing of his latest escapades, his injuries; he'd put off the promised meeting with Andrew until at least the outward signs of his wounds had faded and threatened

Cherry with her very life if for any reason she said a word about it. It rang four or five times before it was picked up. "Anne Reynolds' office."

The voice was female and he thought he recognized the sharp tone of Annie's assistant manager. "Is she there?"

"Who's calling?"

"It's Theo, Theo Stern."

"Oh g'day, Theo. This is Pam...we met when you were over."

"Hi, Pam, how are you?"

"I'm good, Theo. Hang on there and I'll drag her over."

A couple of minutes later, Annie came to the phone. "Stern? You okay?"

"Yeah, I'm fine. Just thought I'd like a chat."

There was a long pause before she said, "Have I got this wrong or is it almost two in the morning there?"

He smiled into the phone. "No, you're right. It's a few minutes to."

"So what the hell do you want to chat about at this hour?"

"I needed to ask you something?"

"At two in the morning?"

"Yup, it's important."

"Stern, you've got me worried now. Are you sure you're alright?"

"Positive. I just wanted to know if it would be okay for me to visit again."

This time a shocked silence, then, "Well, of course it would, but..." Another pause. "Hang on, have you got another job here or something?"

The smile was broadening. "Nope. This time it'll be just me to you, a proper holiday."

"When?" He could hear the excitement in the single word.

"The sooner the better."

"Well yes, of course, any time, you know I'd love it, but... I mean for how long this time?"

"Oh I don't know; I was thinking maybe for the rest of my life."

Meet

A. W. LAMBERT

A.W. Lambert was born and raised in Battersea, South London, England. After completing his National Military Service, during which time he was engaged in active service in the EOKA terrorist conflict on the island of Cyprus, he embarked on an engineering career in the British aircraft industry where he also became a qualified pilot. In 1992 he retired from industry to follow his two main passions: the playing of his favourite music, traditional New Orleans Jazz and Creative Writing. After studying with The Writer's Bureau, he developed extensive experience achieving success in magazine article and short story writing before moving into the field of full length Action/ Adventure. A Treacherous Past, his first published novel, introduced retired London Metropolitan Police Inspector, now private investigator, Theo Stern for the first time. Since then follow up novels have seen Stern and AW's other absorbing characters, involved in increasingly intriguing and dangerous scenarios.

After raising two sons; one now living in Boston, USA, the other in Melbourne, Australia, A.W. lives with his wife, Valerie, in a tiny hamlet on the North Norfolk coast of England.